THE WORLD WAS THEIR STAGE

H. BEDFORD-JONES

THE WORLD WAS THEIR STAGE

H. BEDFORD-JONES

ILLUSTRATIONS BY

GEORGE AVISON
MERRITT BERGER
PEDAR CAVANAGH
JOHN RICHARD FLANAGAN
PETER KUHLHOFF
J. CLINTON SHEPHERD
RAYMOND SISLEY

ALTUS PRESS • 2019

© 2019 Altus Press • First Edition—2019

PUBLISHING HISTORY

Originally appeared in the April 1940–October 1941 issues of *Blue Book* magazine (Vol. 168, No. 5).

"About the Author" originally appeared in November 16, 1929 issue of *Argosy* magazine (Vol. 208, No. 1). Copyright 1929 by The Frank A. Munsey Company. Copyright renewed in 1957 and assigned to Steeger Properties, LLC. All rights reserved.

THANKS TO

Everard P. Digges LaTouche, Gerd Pircher and Janice Roberts

TABLE OF CONTENTS

SHYSTER HERO

INSANITY, IN its milder forms, bespeaks either an addled pate or a sublime genius. In the case of my friend Peder Cavanagh, the decision is difficult to reach. Being an artist, he relies on the artistic temperament, which is a peculiar quantity.

That he has a hypnotic effect upon people, even upon the editors who buy his sketches, is undeniable. When Cavanagh really turns on his big, bluff, blue-eyed Norse-Irish personality, he is irresistible; if this happens in his own studio, surrounded by ship-models and sea paintings and sketches, he is supreme. He could persuade anyone of anything. The devil of it is, that he is usually right.

When I walked in and saw him finishing the sketch of a nude, I was astonished.

"Hello!" I said. "This is something new for you. Where's your model?"

"Dead." He switched the easel around toward the light, and left it. "Take another look, while I wash up."

I studied the sketch, fascinated; it had the damnable charm of Cavanagh himself—an indefinable, appealing quality.

"I'm going in for theatrical stuff," he said, coming back and standing beside me, as he wiped his hands. He was pleased by my expression of interest. "This, for example," he amplified, "takes one back to the very origins of the theater in dim antiquity."

"Garden of Eden?" I asked.

*"Citizens, judges,
I demand that you
sentence this woman
to death, if—"*

"No levity; I'm serious. One of the immortal stories of art and history, Harry, that has so modern an angle it might have happened yesterday. In fact, it happens every day. Blood and romance, tears and the shadow of death, beauty and—"

"Omit the flowers, my dear fellow," I broke in upon his rhapsody. "You've got something in this sketch; no sales-talk is necessary."

"Not for sale, dammit," he retorted. "This is beyond price—"

"Did you say the model is dead?" I interrupted again.

"Yes. I've been trying to recapture something: a dream of classical beauty, Athens in its ancient pristine loveliness. The air-effects; that's no joke, you know. They say that the air of ancient Athens was responsible for its beauty and mental vigor—some vague electric quality in the air. Today, we'd call it violet rays, and send sinus-sufferers there. Here's a finished sketch, to go with that nude. A bit of water-color work."

He began to fumble among his sketches stacked on the floor, and got one out.

"Never mind it," I said. "You know very well I don't like water-colors."

"This is different, though. Ever hear of Eleusis?"

"Of course. A town fourteen miles from Athens. The famous Mysteries of Demeter were celebrated there—the Eleusinian

Mysteries. But see here, Peder—I thought you said this had some connection with the theater?"

"So it has." He hoisted his picture to the easel; then, in front of it, he suddenly clapped another sketch—this time showing the same figure and face, but clothed in a flowing robe.

"Look at this, now," he said. "Same girl. You need the color in this gown, or *peplos,* as it was called. The ancient mysteries, like that of Eleusis, were the oldest of all theatrical performances, and of course strictly limited to men as actors and audience."

"Never mind about that," I said, looking at the sketch. "By thunder, Peder, you really have something here! Don't tell me you didn't use a model. There's an exquisite grace in this figure, in the features—"

He silenced me with his outburst of fluency. He was off full speed.

"Listen! I want you to get this right: You've got to see the girl's background in a literal sense. She wasn't precisely what we'd call a model of propriety today; but in Athens, remember, customs and morals were very different from our standards. Now,"—and he jerked away his sketches,—"here's the water-color."

"Ah!" An exclamation broke from me. I leaned forward, entranced by the color and balance and glowing beauty of the scene.

"This was her house," said Peder Cavanagh, and pointed. "Look! Here's the glitter of blue sea in the distance; the silver-green olive groves, the white buildings of the city, all a frame for the subject. And in the foreground, against a house-wall lifting to the right, her terraced garden—"

H I S   V O I C E   rambled on, but I forgot it. He had somehow captured that light and intoxicating air of Athens, unique in its balmy quality. It carried the scent of a thousand blossoms, for spring was everywhere. Flowers hedged the garden paths, and fruits were in full bloom.

Against the house-wall was a fountain surrounded by cushioned marble seats. An awning of bright-hued Anatolian weave was stretched to keep off the sun. On every side were exquisite bits of art—marble statuettes, figurines of wood and ivory and gold. The wall was faced with magnificent Persian tiles, plundered from some Eastern temple or palace, showing very curious details of Oriental worship. Against this blaze of color sat a young man, reading aloud the immortal lines of an Iliad written on bleached parchment from Pergamos.

The voice of his auditor broke in upon his reading.

"Ah, Skopas! You read well, but not well enough. As in everything else, you're admirable but not supreme."

He broke off, frowning, to bend half-angry eyes on the woman to whom this house and garden belonged. He was handsome, well-built, and in his eyes burned the fire of desire and a desolate longing.

"Phryne! Will you never yield, will you never love me?" he burst forth. "I'm ready to pour riches at your feet; with them my faith and loyalty and service—my whole self! To win your love, I'd gladly die tomorrow. Yet you always say the same thing. What can I do to show myself supreme, as you demand?"

"Prove that you're not ordinary, my dear Skopas. For example, look at me! I'm supreme, the most beautiful woman in Athens. Perdiccas the sculptor has said so, and he knows. Why should I bother with ordinary men?"

Her voice blended with the humming of the bees and stole like music upon the fragrant air; its soft, husky vibrance was indescribable. So was she herself, as she reclined upon the cushions. No woman, but girl, aflame with mischievous, dancing vitality. She wore a long, gossamer-thin peplos of blue, upon which disported tiny silver doves, the bird of Venus.

"True," Skopas said thoughtfully. He gazed at her lovely hair of raw gold, her eyes like sapphire, her face that in repose was the face of a goddess, and in animation was like a flashing, sun-glimmering ocean wave.

"Yes, that's true," he went on. "You're not like other girls, Phryne. You have extraordinary fancies, impulses, curiosities. You do daring things. You predicted that the frieze of the Parthenon would come to life; and then you danced, veiled, on the steps so that people thought the miracle had happened. You refuse to show your face abroad, except here in the garden or when you serve in the temple of Venus. You are unpredictable, and beyond understanding!"

"And supreme!" She laughed softly, luxuriously, as she stretched herself. "Suppose I became an actress and went upon the stage?"

"You'd be glorious!" he cried quickly. "You'd be the most wonderful Antigone, the most charming Kassandra, ever seen!"

SHE GRIMACED slightly. "Nonsense, Skopas. I don't mean to worship the Muses in the theater itself. I mean the older stage, from which our theater came. I mean the stage which existed back and back into the dim past before there was any history; the ancient and primeval stage, which constituted a worship of the olden gods, with masks and characters and ritual."

He started slightly. "Not the Mysteries, Phryne? You know that no woman can take part in the Mysteries. It is forbidden. No one has ever spoken of those secret things; no writer or poet,

no sculptor or artist, has ever alluded to what passes behind the dread seal of the Mysteries!"

She regarded him, half-smiling. "True. I forgot that, Skopas. By the way, the Mysteries at Eleusis are to be celebrated next week—the spring festival. Aren't you one of the officials?"

"Yes," he said, not without pride. "I have charge of the characters in the chief parts; I cast them, costume them, coach them. There's a rehearsal at Eleusis tomorrow."

"Well, here's luck to you!" She lifted a silver goblet and sipped the cool wine, and seemed to change the subject altogether. "Do you know, Skopas, I rather like you! If you'd do one thing for me—just one thing—I'll give you anything you ask."

He stiffened. For a moment he stared at her, his eyes eager and impetuous.

"Name it!" he said curtly, color rising in his face. "By the gods, I'll do it!"

"Agreed, then," she said. "An oath, remember, by all the gods! I understand that in the Mysteries next week, in the worship

*"It would mean certain
death!" he said.*

of Demeter the earth-mother, the characters of Proserpine and other women are played by men. Well, assign one of those parts to me. That's all."

Terror seized him. His eyes dilated, the color ebbed from his face. All in a moment, he became quiet as cold cinders.

"That's impossible," he said in a low voice. "I have sworn an oath, by Demeter herself!"

"You just now swore by *all* the gods," said she, smiling. "In either case, you must become a breaker of oaths, a man forsworn! Therefore, choose the better way; break an oath, and win me, have my love! For it shall be yours—I swear it!"

Sweat started on his forehead.

"Your accursed curiosity!" he broke out. "You want to do what no woman has ever done. I might have guessed it. Why, you'll be torn in pieces! The Athenians will never endure to have a woman profane the Mysteries! It would mean certain death."

"Not at all," she said coolly. "You forget that I'm in the service of Venus, my friend." And she touched the blue robe significantly. "A servant of the gods cannot be adjudged to death."

"But you'd be banished or sold into slavery, at the best," he said hoarsely.

"Silly!" Her eyes warmed upon him. "Who would know?"

"The gods would know," he muttered.

Swift anger shook her. "Get out of here!" she cried, with a flash of fury. "I'm sick of such talk. Be a god, instead of a man, for once! In that case, come back at twilight, and if your lips burn for mine, I'll give you a trifle of advance payment. Otherwise, stay away forever! Now leave, before I forget my oath and change my mind altogether, you craven! I offer you what other men would be glad to have, and you prate of the gods! Go! And don't take that Iliad with you, either. It belonged to the great Euripides, and I value it as an association copy."

Skopas departed, in mingled anger and dismay; which, as she well knew, would presently kindle into desperate desire.

F I V E Y E A R S before, she had come out of Bœotia, an awkward little farm girl, to peddle cloves in the city. Now her awkward country name was gone, and all her past was gone with it; as Phryne, fairest of the fair, she had won to the very summit of fame. Wealth had been showered upon her; all Athens raved of her beauty; and her name was extolled throughout Greece and the isles. Sculptors and artists vied for her services as a model, and the great painter Apelles had immortalized her features.

A little love, a little kiss—there was far more to it than that, and her profession was a proud one in Athens. Intellectual companionship, a sharing of joy and sorrow and problems, was the great thing; had not Aspasia been the inspiration of Pericles?

Left alone in the garden, Phryne caught up the scroll of the Iliad, and mouthed the golden lines; they were intoxicating as the air itself, and she rendered them with a passionate delight, a feeling, an elegance which was marvelous to hear. As the liquid music of her voice came to a pause, another voice broke in:

"Bravo! Never before have I heard poetry declaimed with such loveliness, upon such lovely lips!"

Phryne glanced up, in startled surprise and anger.

"Hello!" she exclaimed, with a touch of rough Bœotian slang. "Who left the door open?"

Hyperides laughed, as he came forward and saluted her.

"I bribed your servants to let me enter unannounced. Forgive them, and forgive me; I craved a sight of beauty unaware, dear Phryne. The fault was wholly mine."

Her face cleared. She looked up at him with a sunny smile.

"You're irresistible, and you know it! Hyperides, where the devil did you get your magic? You're not handsome; you have a glib tongue, but that's not rare in Athens; and yet, somehow, with all your drawbacks, you do contrive to say the right thing at the right time!"

He was a dark, shrewd man, famed for his knowledge of language and speech; The Rhetorician, they called him in the city. Wealthy and unscrupulous, a born lawyer, he knew every twist and turn of legal phraseology. And behind this was a certain magic, as she said—a deep knowledge of men's hearts and minds, and the innate character which gave him an ability to play upon them as upon a lyre.

"And yet, Phryne," he said, almost sadly, "not all my wit nor wealth nor clever speech can make you love me!"

"That's true," she rejoined. "And the reason, Hyperides, I think, is that you provoke an instinct of combat in me. Instead of flinging my arms about your neck, I want to fight you off, match my wit against yours, pit myself against you!"

"It's a pity," he said with a sigh. "You and I together could do great things; I need your invigorating energy, your daring, your courage, to back me up in various matters. I've just returned from Chios, where I've been handling that involved old tangle of Demetrios vs. the Chian Wine Corporation, that goes back to the time of the Persian wars, and I think it's all straightened out. I'm practically sure of the decision."

"You would be," she commented. "Also, of your fee."

He laughed lightly. "Of course! I tried to find you at the

Temple of Venus last night after my boat got in; I was hungry
for a sight of you. But you were not there."

"No; I don't go on duty till next month," she rejoined.

"Good! I'm going to lay siege to your heart, I warn you! I've
brought you back some lovely doves, and a cask of the finest
wine in Chios."

PHRYNE SHRUGGED, with a return of her irritation.

"My dear Hyperides, can't you make love with something
better than presents?"

"How?"

"I don't know. If I were ever on my knees to you in an agony
of fear—if you could do something no other man on earth could
do—oh, I don't know!" She flung out her arms in futile despair.
"That's just it; I don't know! I'm sick of these petty, ordinary men
who are all alike; I feel that I can only love a man who stands
out from the mob, a man who has the courage to carve out some
new course, to do something different, whether right or wrong!
Skopas could do it, but he lacks the backbone. You could do it,
and you're too wary, too sure of every step. I want a man who
can gamble magnificently!"

"I see you're in poetical mood," said Hyperides dryly, with a
gesture toward the Iliad. "The heroes are all dead, my dear. We're
living in a practical age. You're like all the younger generation.
You want to live dangerously; you seek thrills and new experi-
ences. You'll take any kind of a chance, if you can only do something no one has done before, or shock the world and thereby
get a tremendous kick out of it!"

She bent a lazy, half-affectionate smile upon him.

"Hyperides, you must be a mind-reader! Decidedly, you fall
in with my mood. But you don't seem very upset by it all."

"I'm not," said the lawyer cheerfully. "I can wait. There comes
a time when your type of girl falls, and falls hard. As you just
now said—when you're on your knees to me in an agony of fear,
then you'll realize my true worth."

Phryne, returning to her party, amazed them
all by the triumphant exultation of her dancing,
while the Cretan sage clashed at the cymbals.

"On my knees to you? Zeus forbid!" she exclaimed scorn-fully. Then she melted. "But I do like you, really. And I'll prove it by letting you walk with me as far as the Temple of Poseidon."

"Why on earth are you going there?" demanded Hyperides in surprise. She laughed gayly.

"Because when there was a storm the other day, I vowed a

sacrifice to the sea-god if a friend of mine came safely home from sea; and I must go and pay for it."

"A friend? At sea?" He stared at her, half-comprehending. "You can't mean—"

"You, stupid! Of course!" With a burst of laughter, she rose, slipped on her sandals, and flecked a corner of the blue transparent robe over her head. "Come on."

"Then you do care a little!" Hyperides cried joyfully.

"Nonsense! I thought I might need a lawyer one of these days," she retorted. "Ready?"

SO, TOGETHER, they left the hillside house and walked to the sea-god's temple, where Phryne handed over clinking gold to pay for the sacrifice of a white bull—no small amount, either. Hyperides, rather moved, knelt in a prayer of thanksgiving for his safe return. When he came to his feet, she was gone, and only the lingering echo of silver laughter sounded from the busy street when he rushed out in search of her.

She tripped lightly home, her face covered as usual. Her name flew along the streets as she passed; men turned to look after her, eagerly; shops were emptied for a glimpse of her, whose face was seldom seen of men in general. "Phryne is going by! Phryne the divine is passing! Phryne, the Toad!"

That was the meaning of her name. They had given her the nickname years ago, when the poet Memnon, at some banquet, had compared her mobile, animated face to a sun-flashing wave of the sea.

"Ha!" shouted somebody. "A green wave! She must be green in the face like a toad!"

The name had stuck; and Phryne, proudly swearing it would become the most beloved name in Athens, had made it an emblem of conquest and achievement.

THAT NIGHT a dozen scholars, poets and philosophers reclined in the banquet-room of Phryne's house; they ate and drank, and as the heady wine took effect, waxed eloquent. This was no wild orgy, but a feast of the intellect. It was only thirty years since Alexander had conquered the world, and these men could speak at first hand of Plato, of Socrates, of Euripides and a dozen more, as the wine was passed around.

But Phryne, fleeing her guests, sat by the fountain in the garden, and there in the starlight talked with the tormented man who had sought her out.

Skopas gulped down the wine she thrust at him, and took heart. At first he had scarcely been able to speak, for his tumult of soul, but her warm fragrant presence rallied him, and the wine gave him tongue.

"May the gods forgive me! I'll do it, Phryne; if you still demand it, I'll do it for love of you. Yet I beg you to give up the wild idea!"

"Of course I demand it. Come, dear friend, be calm," she said, and put her cool slim hand on his. "Why, your pulse is racing like mad! Take it calmly, Skopas. Tell me, first, how it will be arranged."

"Simply enough, after all," he said in a wretched voice. "Young Heracles, the cobbler's son, is a la-de-da sort of chap, as you may know; rather effeminate. He was to take the rôle of the Muse, Clio, who brings a message from the gods in—in a certain part of the work. He's badly in debt. Well, I've squared him, that's all, on a pretext that somebody else wants his part. He's going to a farm in Bœotia on Monday, for a drinking-party with some friends. Nobody else will know he's not taking the part assigned him. You'll meet me late Monday afternoon. I'll reserve a room at the Temple Tavern in Eleusis. I'll have the costume and mask, and will coach you in your part. You can go directly from the tavern, masked and costumed, to the temple with me."

Phryne caught her breath, and clapped her hands softly.

"Splendid!" she cried with enthusiasm. "Splendid! Why, Skopas, you're wonderful!"

"I don't feel that way," he retorted bitterly. "It means betrayal, treachery—"

"Nonsense! It means just this!" she exclaimed, and in an ecstasy of delight flung back her robe. She drew his hand to her, placed it on her heart, and her arms twined about his neck. "This, Skopas—my lips, myself, my love! I promised you as much; I keep my word. Kiss me, Skopas, and think only that the gods are kind, and approve what you've done! For if they did not approve of your devotion, they would certainly interfere and prevent the matter!"

The argument was rather good, to the mind of Skopas; and much better was the proof of it. When Phryne was in generous mood, she gave with all her heart and soul; and if her generosity toward Skopas was merely an impetuous, momentary giving, provoked by elation, it was none the less effective.

When they separated, in the cool starlight, Skopas had forgotten all remorse, all his wretched self-accusations; he was in for it now, with a swagger and a wild brave laugh, and so rapt in his love as to be blind to all else.

But Phryne, returning to her party of poets and philosophers, amazed them all by the brilliance of her wit, by the blazing eloquence of her tongue, and by the triumphant exultation of her dancing. She danced for them as never before had she danced, while old Statiros the Stoic wheezed a drunken melody on the pipes, and the Cretan sage Idomeneos cocked a wreath askew on his ruffled gray locks and clashed away at the cymbals. It was a wild, delirious, ecstatic dance; and Cleon the poet wrote a rhapsodic poem about it which may be read to this day in the Bacchic Anthology.

B U T   O N the Monday afternoon, in an upstairs room of the Temple Tavern at Eleusis, a different scene took place.

The fourteen-mile highway out from Athens had been crowded most of the day. There were the officers and participants in the Mysteries, several hundred in all. There were the young men, who were about to be initiated into the first degree that evening, some boisterous, some half fearful; for all agreed, solemnly, that this initiation was a dread and terrible experience that touched more upon death than on life. Then there were the masses of men who formed the main body of the mystic brotherhood, most of them in hilarious mood, so that every wineshop in Eleusis was crammed to the doors, and the rollicking old soldier song about the red-haired girl from Babylon was roared forth on all sides, with the unpublished verses Alexander's army had brought back from Persia.

IN THE upper room at the Tavern, the excited and eager Phryne listened to all that her tutor told her, learned her part perfectly, listened intently to his grave coaching. Skopas, beneath his outward desperate calm, was in a state of nervous panic. The Mysteries would continue for two more nights, and the prospect appalled him.

"Whatever happens, keep your head!" he cautioned the girl. "Tonight occurs the crime, the murder; tomorrow night, the tomb scenes, the appeal to the gods; and on the final night, the story of resurrection—the fertility symbolism. For two thousand years and more, this drama has been played out on this very spot, and kept secret. Remember, it's death for both of us if you're suspected!"

Phryne smiled. "You should worry, my dear. You were willing to die for me, you know."

"But not in too unpleasant a fashion," replied Skopas gloomily. "That rascal Hyperides would love to see me out of his way. I met him today, and he smiled in a way I don't half like, and flung out a dark hint that Athens might not be too healthy a place for some people he knew.... Well, well, now go over the pass-signs once more!"

She did so, and he nodded in satisfaction. Then she bared her bosom, and he bound her breasts tightly with cloths. Her golden hair was cut and trimmed, and darkened with a wash of color. When she was dressed in the robe of a Master of the Mysteries, Skopas gave her the cloak that represented her costume, and over her sweet face placed the simpering mask of the Muse, Clio, binding it firmly in place. She walked across the room and back, imitating the walk of a man, and he nodded.

"Perfect! Come, then."

They went together, and were lost in the scurrying throngs passing into the temple enclosure.

T H E   S T A G E fronted the huge courtyard. Torches and cressets smoked into the night sky, lighting the serried masses of faces, thousands upon thousands jamming every nook and cranny. Off stage, watching, waiting, Phryne had no fear whatever. The imposture was easy beyond belief. Compliments were showered on her by the other actors, who vowed that for once young Heracles had a rôle that suited him admirably. Soon she would pass on the stage, give her single speech, and take her place opposite the chorus.

Her cue was approaching. As she awaited it tensely, there was a commotion behind her. A sudden voice uprose:

"There he is, yonder. In the part of *Clio*."

A panting, straining-eyed man was shoved forward to the side of Phryne.

"Master Heracles! I've run all the way—your old father has had a stroke. He begs you to come to his side as soon as— By the immortals, this is not my master!" The man broke off, staring around. "This is not Heracles, I tell you! Look at his hands!"

Others came crowding around. Phryne heard her cue from the stage. She made a hasty effort to break through the circle and escape to the stage. Half a dozen hands caught hold of her. With an angry cry, she sought to break clear; and then, so swiftly that she scarcely realized it, disaster engulfed her. Someone jerked at her robe, disclosing her white thigh. Another hand wrenched at her mask, and laid bare her face.

"Profaned! The Mysteries are profaned! A woman, a woman!"

The wild, shrill yell halted everything; and then, voice upon wolfish voice, rose the infernal howl of the pack for blood—her blood.

She chilled to it. An awful, insuperable terror struck into her, as the whole place shook with the yells for vengeance. No one, as yet, knew who she was. The robe was pulled half away, confirming the cheat.

"Make her the victim of the ritual!" went up the pealing yells. "Tear her to pieces! Rip the flesh from her!"

Luckily, the crowd could not get at her, here in the wings; the maddened thousands threatened to tear the very stones of the theater apart. The temple guards closed around her, and the priests of Demeter. Someone reached her with one fearful blow across the face, that brought blood from her mouth and nostrils; then she was hustled away into a rear room of the temple, safe and under guard, but sobbing hysterically, smeared with blood, shaking with stark terror as the ravening shouts mounted higher and higher.

What happened out there? She did not know, could never be certain. Into those thundering voices, however, came a sudden yelping satisfaction, a blood-excitement, as dogs yelp with heart-hurried tongues when the kill takes place. After that, the noise somewhat died down.

The room in which she lay was filled with figures, staring at her. Priests of the temple, and with them masked actors, the chief players in the Mysteries. In her frantic terror, she shrieked to them for mercy, for pity. They talked of taking her forth, stripping her, and handing her over to the mob.

Suddenly a new voice was heard, a new figure pushed forward. It was Hyperides, who stood looking coldly at her for a moment, then turned and addressed the others.

"Brethren," he said in his compelling tones, "wait one moment! Our brother Skopas has paid for his folly and weakness; that is just and fitting. But it is not fitting that a woman should be slain in this holy place. Do you know this woman, whom Skopas introduced? No; but I do. She has committed an offense against the gods, against the whole city! Better let her be taken to Athens and brought before the tribunal of the

Heliasts; we have avenged the broken oaths of Skopas; let the courts avenge the affront to the laws!"

"Who is she, Hyperides?" came the beating questions.

"Phryne, the Hetaira."

NOW THERE was fresh tumult of incredulity and amazement, as this news spread. Vaguely, Phryne realized that Skopas had been caught and killed, somehow; it did not matter. Amid the clatter of tongues, she cried out to Hyperides not to desert her. He looked down and spoke, so that no one else heard.

"Quiet, you little fool! Don't wipe your face; leave it all bloody."

She relaxed, as she had been flung by the guards, and lay quiet.

For three days she remained in the cell, alone, uncared-for, like a wild beast.

Her quick wits began to recover from the paralyzing spasm of terror. Hyperides had come to the rescue, then! She heard his voice, through the confused uproar in the room. Bad enough, he said, to have shed her blood at all on this holy ground. The priests agreed; she, as she lay, deftly smeared the drops from her nostrils across her face, so that she seemed badly enough hurt.

The arguments of Hyperides won over inflamed passions. When he pointed out that Phryne was in the service of Venus, the priests instantly demanded that the secular authority take her in charge.

Bound and beaten, she was sneaked out of the temple by a side passage, and there forced into a closed litter. Soldiers guarding her closely, they took the road to Athens.

ALREADY ATHENS was in tumult, for rumors had spread that a woman had profaned the Mysteries. Once more the ravening mob-voices rose, demanding blood; and Phryne, who had revived to the point of demanding luxuries and comforts in her prison, was only too thankful when she was flung headlong into a cell and left with bread and water—but safe from the wild throngs who sought to tear her into bits.

And there, for three days, she remained in the cell, alone, uncared-for, like a wild beast. Crowds came thronging to look upon her, flinging mud at her through the bars; the guards saw to it that no actual harm was done her. To her wild demands for comfort, assistance, an advocate, deaf ears were turned.

Now, for the first time, her audacious spirit failed her. Gone was all the glamour of life; she crouched in a corner, unable to escape the mud that spattered her, the curses that rained upon her. And in her heart dwelt fear, deeper and deeper, as the throngs outside her cell door voiced savage demands for her life-blood.

ON THE third evening, when there was no one else by, a guard thrust a stool into her cell, gave her the evening ration of bread and water, and announced a visitor.

Hyperides entered, seated himself on the stool, and greeted her with a low chuckle.

"Well, my dear, things seem to be going excellently!"

"You too?" she retorted. "I thought you were a friend. 'Excellently!' Then you too are against me."

She burst into tears, sobs shaking her mud-spattered body.

"Nonsense!" said the lawyer calmly. "I've been appointed to defend you. Tomorrow at sunrise, you come before the tribunal of the Heliasts for sentence."

She quivered. "Tomorrow!"

"Precisely. Of course, as you're well aware, no human being can save you."

In a paroxysm of terror, she flung herself at his feet, begging for help—a knife, a vial of poison, anything to save her from the torture.

"Suppose," asked Hyperides, "I do what no other man on earth can do? I trust you recall our conversation on the subject."

IN THE dim light from the torch that burned outside the door, she stared at him. He remained inscrutable, calm, a trifle quizzical.

"Do you really mean it?" she asked in a low voice.

He reached out and touched her head, with caressing fingers.

"My dear, I've never ceased to love you. As you, in your heart, love me. Come, confess it!"

"Yes, Hyperides," she said humbly. "It is true. I can tell you now; if you can save me from my own mad folly, I am yours, and yours only. But it's so hopeless! You can't do it."

"Let's see about that," he returned. "You've done something that'll go down in history; luckily for yourself, you learned so little about the actual Mysteries that there's no particular reason to shut your mouth with a gravestone. For three days you've lain here while the people have worn out their rage. By tomorrow they'll be ready to swing around, given the proper publicity and stimulus. I have fifty men ready to go about town tonight and start the campaign in your favor. The pendulum of public opinion—you remember the stories about Aristides, of course."

"Public opinion! Who cares about that?" she demanded wildly.

"I do; I don't want to see you banished," he rejoined. "It would be inconvenient if I had to go into exile with you. The publicity I'll get from winning this case will bring me all the paying law business in Athens, my dear."

"By winning it?" she repeated. "You mean—you can save me?"

"Of course. Up to this point, I've handled matters adroitly," he said complacently, "if I do say it myself. Now, in the morning, I want you to look your best."

"Look my best!" A bitter laugh escaped her. "All Athens has stared at me for three days in this pigsty. I haven't even a clean peplos; how can I look my best?"

"That's my business," said Hyperides. "I'll have your slaves here before daybreak, with whatever clothes you direct; they'll bathe you, arrange your hair, perfume you, see that you're at your best and loveliest. There's no mark from the blow on your face?"

"I think not," she replied. "My nose is still sore, but the swelling's gone down."

"It was a great stroke of luck that I was able to wangle the sunrise session of court," he said thoughtfully. "You see, the judges are nearly all elderly fellows. They'll be up early; they'll come to court with the memory of their wives all too clear-cut in mind; frowsy, sleepy women, mussed and disheveled, fit to give any man the horrors. Then they see you, fresh and lovely as rosy-fingered Aurora herself—"

"Oh, stop it," broke in Phryne impatiently. "You can't win this case with a pretty face, Hyperides. It's too serious."

"I know it. That's why I intend to demand the death-penalty."

"You— *What?*" Her voice broke. "By the gods, are you crazy?"

"Crazy like a fox, my dear," he said, chuckling softly. "You'll see!"

"Well, what's the defense to be?" she demanded. "I can't lie out of it. You can't pull any sob-story about a dying mother and the innocent virtue of a young girl, the way you did in the Simonides affair; I'm too well known. What line are you going to work on?"

"That, my dear, is my business," he replied coolly. "My entire plea will consist of five words, and they'll win the case. What are they? No, by the gods! I'd not breathe them into the ear of Apollo himself! They stay locked in my own brain, until they're uttered." He rose. "Now get all the sleep you can, and trust to me, my dear."

He stooped, touched his lips to her forehead, and strode out.

Somehow he inspired confidence; his vivid personality had an appeal, an overpowering influence like magic itself. For the first time Phryne dropped off to a slumber that was undisturbed by nightmares of blood and vengeance and horror. She slept, and slept soundly.

WITH EARLIEST dawn, terror returned as she was roused by guards; but it was only her two tiring-slaves, who greeted her with tears of joy. They had brought everything, and they fell to work with soap and water and cosmetics and perfumes, shampooing her hair into golden luster, going over every inch of her glorious body, and rubbing her into a tingle and a glow of color.

Just as the guards came to take her before the tribunal in the rising sun, they were done. Her gossamer blue robe with the silver doves was drawn over her head as usual, and between the steel-clad guards, she set out on her fateful journey.

Her guards were silent; the streets and housetops were silent, although jammed with people. She had shrunk from the thought of this procession, past the Pompeion to the Eleusinian Gate, outside which the tribunal sat. She had anticipated new curses, new yells for vengeance. Instead, there came only silence, and low whispers. Once or twice a shrill voice was lifted against her, but it died quickly.

She perceived that Hyperides had been right. Public opinion

She danced for them as never before she danced,
while old Statiros the Stoic wheezed a drunken
melody on the pipes, and Idomenos cocked a
wreath askew on his ruffled gray locks.

had swung around—helped, no doubt, by the fifty men working hard the previous night with suggestion and clever words.

NOW THE huge court of the Pompeion was past; here was the city gate. Outside, the high marble tribunal was shut off from the crowds by armed guards. At sight of it, Phryne's steps faltered for a moment; then she recovered and went on.

The judges were waiting; the prosecutor and Hyperides were waiting. A bailiff led her to her position in front of the judges, grave and elderly citizens, for the most part. The sun had just mounted the eastern sky, and the flood of level golden light pierced through that veiled and humble figure, lightly revealing the tender lines below the blue transparent robe. The judges stirred a little, leaned forward. Court was opened.

Hyperides came forward, greeted Phryne, and spoke under his breath.

"All's going well. Now, for the love of the gods, don't open your mouth! No matter what I say or do, keep quiet!"

"Agreed," she said in a low voice.

He turned, and went to the prosecutor, and spoke rapidly. The dour, harsh-eyed prosecutor stared at him in amazement, then frowned.

"Very well, Hyperides. But if this is one of your damned shyster tricks, look out!"

"It is not. I swear by Apollo,"—and Hyperides lifted his hand toward the sun, speaking earnestly,—"to do exactly as I say."

The other grunted assent. Together they approached the judges, and the prosecutor spoke out.

"Your honors, if it please you, we've agreed to waive prosecution. Counsel for the defense stipulates that there is no defense, that his client pleads guilty, and that he himself will demand the death-penalty. Under these circumstances, I am content to save the time of the court by permitting him to speak—reserving, however," he added with dour suspicion, "the right to object."

"You shall have no cause to object, upon my honor!" said Hyperides.

The judges conferred, and promptly agreed in the matter. The clerk of court then read the accusation. It set forth—and it made undeniably ghastly hearing for Phryne—the crimes of the accused against gods and men, by her deliberate profanation of the sublime Mysteries. No words were spared in describing her offense against the state and its institutions, and against the gods and against religion.

The chief justice turned to Hyperides.

"Does your client plead guilty or not guilty?"

"My lord," said Hyperides, "it was established in the case of Epaminondas vs. Glauco, in the fourth year of the Macedonian régime, that in any case involving sacrilege, counsel is not allowed to plead for his client. The prisoner must plead in person."

The chief justice nodded and turned to Phryne. "Prisoner, you have heard the accusations. Do you plead guilty or not guilty?"

PHRYNE LOOKED up, startled and confused and bewildered. The urbane smile of Hyperides became almost a grin, as she threw back the corner of the robe, baring her lovely face.

"Why—why—yes, I'm guilty, of course," floated the soft music of her voice, more beautiful than ever in its agitation. "I'm sorry, with all my heart. The fault was—"

"That will do," said the chief justice. "The plea is guilty. Counsel will proceed. We shall have no need for the assembled witnesses, I take it?"

"There is no evasion, no excuse, no denial," said Hyperides; and the prosecutor nodded agreement. Then, with a glance at the faces of the judges, Hyperides stepped to the side of Phryne and turned, ignoring her pleading, terrified eyes, her pallid features.

"Citizens of Athens," he said abruptly, his voice ringing in the tense silence, "I shall attempt no oratory to confuse the issue. Here, it is clear-cut. Indeed, as a pious and devout servant of the gods, I have no choice. I believe that you are with me, and that every citizen of Athens is with me, in feeling that this woman should suffer death."

He paused. Phryne swayed slightly, half opened her mouth as though to protest, then remembered his admonition and remained silent. But from the serried throng outside the line of armed guards arose a swift tumult of cries—and Hyperides gave them full time to register on the judges.

"No, *no!* She is in the service of Venus! She's too beautiful to die! No! We're not with you. No, *no!*"

Urbanely disdainful, Hyperides went on with his marvelous smooth eloquence:

"Athenians, there is no argument, no evasion. Banishment or exile cannot be the sentence in a case of sacrilege. One penalty, and one penalty alone, can be imposed: that of death. As citizens and judges, you may of course acquit this woman; but if you find her guilty, you must decree her to death. And," he added impressively, "I demand it! I demand nothing less—"

As though the words were a signal, the crowded masses broke into catcalls and boos. These grew, from scattered voices into wildly vociferous yells of dissent. Hyperides seemed not at all astonished by this evidence of popular indignation; perhaps he had even expected it. When the tumult was silenced, he went on:

"Citizens, judges, there is no more to say. I demand that you sentence this woman to death; I demand that you decree her to be given the cup of hemlock, that her body may become black and bloated and misshapen. I demand that you decree her to be pierced by the sword. I demand,"—and his voice became stentorian,—"I demand that you sentence her to death, if—"

He reached out suddenly, caught hold of Phryne's blue robe, and with one movement jerked it clear of her body.

"If you have the heart!" he concluded, and stepped away.

S O   U N E X P E C T E D was his action, that it was absolutely stupefying. Phryne, left nude except for her golden sandals, uttered a low, bewildered cry. She stood in utmost confusion for a moment, the level rays of the morning sun transfusing all the exquisite lines of her body into golden glory.

No actress could have assumed this posture of affrighted modesty; it rendered her a thousandfold more beautiful, more lovely. She reached out her arms with an imploring word, a gesture of appeal, but Hyperides snatched the robe away from her reaching hands. The touch of pantomime was so genuine, so graceful, so obviously unstaged, that one surging breath of awe and delight burst from all the crowded citizens, and swelled into a roar of acclaim and applause, a roar that swept up and was sustained.

Hyperides, with one glance at the faces of the judges, handed back the blue robe, and Phryne donned it in haste. The judges were hastily conferring. Hyperides turned away, and was met by the prosecutor, who came close to him and spoke in a low, intense voice.

"You dirty chiseler! Some day I'll get you for this!"

Hyperides bowed slightly, mockingly.

"My dear counselor," he said with his cynic smile, "you should praise the gods daily, because they bestow upon you the inestimable gift of hope! Listen—there's the verdict!"

His words were drowned in a roar of applause and delight from the crowd.

THE ROAR died; silence fell. Here was the garden once more, the picture on the easel, the studio all around; I was back in the present, staring at Peder Cavanagh. He had actually bewitched me, or I had bewitched myself under the magic of his voice and personality.

"Like it?" he asked, smiling.

I drew a deep breath. "You're a genius, confound you! Why, you really brought that slick lawyer to life; you made him a flesh-and-blood person; you created a shyster and made me like him!"

Cavanagh grinned.

"A shyster lawyer is human, like you or me; what's to prevent liking him? As a rule, he's quite a popular fellow, except among the pompous stuffed shirts who hide their own dirty work behind legal technicalities. Boy, when it comes to a choice between a hypocrite and a confessed trickster, give me the trickster every time!"

Even when Peder Cavanagh is ethically wrong, you have to agree with him.

DAUGHTER OF CLEOPATRA

HERE UNDER the marble walls of the theater, the empty street was bathed in brilliant North African moonlight—empty except for an uncertain approaching figure. An old retired veteran, by his semi-uniform, and drunk by his walk. Lentulus, strolling aimlessly along, paused and awaited the old fellow, who came to a halt and saluted.

"Ha! Roman—senatorial rank—look like a soldier. Greeting!"

"Greeting," said Lentulus, smiling. "Drunk or sober, you have a good eye, my man. The Twelfth was my corps. And yours?"

"Centurion of the Twentieth, sir." The old fellow drew himself up. "There's a colony of us veterans settled here, up the valley. Stranger in Cæsarea, sir?"

"Just landed today, Centurion," rejoined Lentulus. "A beautiful city you have here."

"Isn't a patch on Rome, sir," hiccuped the veteran. "Not a patch. Have you seen the Queen yet?"

"Not yet. Nor the King."

"Ha! King Juba—he's an old drone who writes books. Roman puppet. Selene was married to him and shipped off here to Africa—saved her life. Old Octavian would have her murdered in a minute if she showed any political ambitions! Selene, named for the moon goddess. Daughter of Cleopatra and Mark Antony—ha! There was a man for you! My old commander, sir: Antony. Wonderful man, wonderful! Well, well, I must be

28

getting along. My wife will be waiting. She's a terror, sir. 'Night to you!"

"Good night," said Lentulus gravely, and the veteran meandered away down the street.

The young Roman drew the balmy air deeply into his lungs, and gazed about. He could appreciate the loveliness of this city, the capital of Numidia; he knew, too, that the veteran had voiced something of the truth regarding the queen of this land.

Selene, Daughter of the Moon, was also daughter of Antony and Cleopatra. She had been shunted off here by the evil old Octavian, to get her out of the way; it was true that Octavian would have her murdered in short order if he suspected her of ambition.

"That's why he sent me to make a report on her," murmured Lentulus, gathering up his toga. "But what a city she's built here! Ruler and goddess alike, transplanting here all the Greek culture she so dearly loves.... Ah, it's beautiful tonight!"

Beautiful, indeed, this city modeled on Selene's beloved Alexandria. Here were the same wide streets, the same two harbors, similar buildings, in some cases built with actual stones and columns brought from Alexandria. And here was the most beautiful theater in the world, a Greek theater. Lentulus turned to it, and strolled into the building.

ALL DESERTED in the moonlight were the marble walls, the lower boxes for people of quality, the stage dominated by its triple row of pillars with Corinthian capitals. Beyond and below, down the hillsides of the city, the forum and royal palace, the baths and public buildings, stretched to the sea. But here was regal beauty, empty and lovely in the staring silver moonlight.... Not empty, either! A voice sounded from the stage, a voice like a sigh. Nothing moved there. The voice came from the wings, a voice gentle as the very moonbeams, restrained and silvery.

"What a night it would be to give the Agamemnon, the immortal drama of Æschylus! Moonlight, and a flaming torch, and the tragedy of a hero! What a performance it would be, here above the moonlit sea—how much better than a daytime performance in sun and heat!"

"Oh, Æschylus is too highbrow, too hard to understand," drifted another voice, also that of a woman. "Euripides is far better. More action in his dramas! Take the Hippolytus, for instance—"

"Very well, then take it!" broke in the first voice, with a tinkle of laughter. "Let's see, now; what's that chorus we like so much? It goes like this—"

The voice lifted in the rolling Greek lines, soft-cadenced and lilting. Lentulus stepped forward a little, entranced by that voice. He knew those words very well:

> *Could I take me to some cavern for mine hiding*

Lentulus set her down with an oath of dismay and anger. Blood was seeping over her wrist.

In the hilltops where the sun scarce hath trod,
Or a cloud make the home of mine abiding
As a bird among the bird-droves of god—

The voice failed, then sounded in mild irritation.

"There! I've forgotten the next verse!" From Lentulus broke a soft laugh.

At the corner of the stage, he could now detect a small, exquisite figure in the moonlight. He turned, lifting his voice against
the resounding marble wall behind him, and continuing the
quotation in superbly cadenced Greek:

> *To the strand of the Daughters of the Sunset,*
> *The apple-tree, the singing and the gold;*
> *Where the mariner must stay him from his onset*
> *And the red wave is tranquil as of old!*

He stepped forward. The shape of the woman moved, her
bared head and massed hair enveloped in misty radiance. She
made direct inquiry, in that voice of lingering music.

"You are no actor! A Roman—and by your toga, of senatorial
rank! Who are you, friend?"

The young man smiled up at her.

"Charming nymph of the moonlight, names no longer count
in Rome, where any tradesman can buy adoption into an old
family! Mine is Lentulus. And yours?"

"Oh! You are Lentulus!" she exclaimed. "Well, I am Olympia.
Wait a moment."

She slipped away into the shadows. Lentulus caught a
murmur of voices, both liquid-silver and enchanting. He waited,
amused by this adventure on his first evening in Cæsarea. Presently Olympia returned, small, dainty, flower-perfect.

"You speak beautiful Greek, Lentulus! Are you a stranger in
town?"

"I arrived today from Ostia and Rome."

She peered at him curiously, a smile on her lips, and then
nodded.

"I REMEMBER, a report came to the palace. Lentulus, of
patrician family. Until three years ago, an officer with the Syrian
legions; military attaché to the court of King Herod of Judea;
then back to Rome, and now in the service of the emperor. A
simple traveler in Numidia—in reality, here to report on political matters to Augustus."

"Daughter of Cleopatra and Marc Antony—ha! There was a man for you! My old commander, sir, Antony."

The young man stood transfixed and chilled by these words. At his chagrin, his disconcerted air, Olympia broke into a gay trill of laughter.

"Oh, we're in constant touch with Rome, my friend! I'm one of the queen's ladies. We shall treat you as a guest, not as a spy—one who speaks such perfect Greek deserves our hospitality! Come, I shall take you in charge myself, and you shall give me all the gossip from Rome. I have a villa in the west end that I'm not using. Will you let me place it at your disposal, and my friendship with it?"

For a moment the Roman was staggered by this offer. He perceived instantly that he was dealing with no palace servant, but with some great lady of the land. It flashed upon him that the intelligence service of Queen Selene must be nearly as good as that of Augustus, and was infinitely more charming. His decision was immediate.

"With all my heart, if you're in earnest!" he said cheerfully. "I've heard of African hospitality—"

"Even to a spy," she broke in, with a brusque gesture. He recoiled from the word, and she broke into a laugh again. "Come! Can't you take your part, your rôle, in good grace? We're in the theater, friend—be an actor! Well, then, suppose we leave the stage. Escort us back to the palace."

"Gladly," said he.

"And after that, the night's young. I'll go with you and see you safely established in the Villa Olympia. Don't expect litters and slaves and Syrian or Roman luxury. Here in the land of Berbers, we stand on our own feet, and ceremony be hanged. Come!"

HIS ASTONISHMENT deepened, as he obeyed. Olympia and her companion preceded him from the place; he followed in surmise. The second figure was draped, her voice low, her face hidden. Evidently women of rank. Mystery, however, enveloped that second woman; when they reached the palace gates, the guards saluted and stood away. The second figure passed in; Olympia turned to Lentulus.

"Shall we go to my villa and talk, while slaves fetch your luggage? Spy of Cæsar and spy of Selene—eh?"

"Your frankness," he rejoined dryly, "captivates me. By all means!"

As they went on past the palace and turned westward, he marveled at this royal dwelling, for Rome herself had nothing like it. The moonlight softened and enriched its lovely marbles; diorite columns, serpentined Italian marble, porphyry from Egypt, dazzling white Greek and Carrara marbles, all brought to enrich this royal palace in Cæsarea, the new Alexandria.

Passing to the west of the Circus, where games and gladiatorial combats like those of Rome were coming into great vogue, the two reached the fashionable residential part of town. Lentu-

*"You are no actor!
A Roman—and
by your toga,
of sensational
rank! Who are
you, friend?"*

lus was struck by a sudden thought; who could that mysterious
companion have been, except Selene herself, the Daughter of
the Moon? He recalled the murmur of voices. The Queen had
set her companion to entangle this emissary of the old and dying
Augustus—

His train of thought was abruptly broken off. They had
reached a glorious little villa built of the beautiful yellow and

rose Numidian marble. Slaves greeted them; lights were brought; and Lentulus found himself transported into luxury and beauty that could only have been equaled in the Greek Orient.

There was nothing of the Roman in this charming villa. The rooms were grouped about a central patio, where gay tiles, fountains, mosaics and statues met the eye, and huge water-lilies floated in the ponds as in Alexandria. Here Lentulus sank down on soft rugs beside Olympia, while slaves brought fruits and wine and cakes; a freedman took his signet, in order to get his luggage from the tavern—for he had come to Africa as a simple stranger.

He resolved upon swift and abrupt attack. Even as he was choosing his words, however, awareness of the girl beside him set his senses reeling. He looked at her, and broke into impulsive and unintended speech.

"Strange, strange! You are woman, not a goddess—yet this is like the other time. A sense of strangeness, of mystic influences about me; as though I were in the very presence of the gods! You are only a woman; yet I can feel it—"

He broke off abruptly. She smiled, but watched him intently, and spoke.

"I look like my mistress, so perhaps you take me for a goddess also! But what of the other time? When was that? Are Romans So intimate with the gods?"

Lentulus flushed, but went oh awkwardly: "It's not easy to tell. It was four years ago, just before the death of King Herod. The crazy old despot sent to kill all the children in one of his villages-he had no end of damnable delusions, you know. I was on the highway that night, riding to inspect the summer camp of Herod's legions, when I met a man, a woman and a baby. The woman was in a bad way. Later, I realized they must have been in flight from that village, though at the moment it didn't occur to me. Not that it would have made any difference—"

His voice trailed off. Presently, in the silence, he went on:

"I HELPED them, gave them food and directions for the Egyptian caravan route, and a bit of money. They were only Jews, of course, but they impressed me, and I felt that strange sensation of tingling awe. Perhaps it was the baby; I don't know. I asked where they were going in Egypt. They did not know. The Jew was a carpenter by trade. He said, I remember, that it did not matter whither they went, and used the curious phrase: 'Tomorrow all roads are one!' I've often thought of it since. A certain truth in it. Well, they went their ways; I went mine, and that's all. A lame little story."

"Lame? No," came her rich voice, deeply stirred. "Who knows, Lentulus, when one meets the gods? They come, they speak, they pass—we don't suspect. Tomorrow all roads are one! Yes, a deep meaning in those words, perhaps."

"I didn't mean to bore you with all that," he said, abruptly conscious that he must get to prosaic things. He looked at her again. Selene! A stupefying sense of shock smote him. Selene! No, no, it was impossible. Her name was Olympia. She merely looked like Selene.

"That's not what I meant to say at all," he went on, hesitant, awkward. "It's something important. You could help me get the message delivered, if I dared trust you."

"Trust," she ordered laconically. Lentulus frowned slightly. He felt helpless before her. Trust? It meant putting his life in her hands. Trust her, indeed? This woman seemed a girl, but she was woman—thirty, perhaps. One could never be sure of age; she was one of those rare women whom life and love and childbirth and suffering touch lightly and leave eternally youthful. She was small, exquisitely made so far as one could tell for her modest, snowy robes; and she was not beautiful; yet she was marvelous in sheer beauty. In animation, in speech, in laughter, she changed and fairly radiated a magnetic charm.

"All right." Abruptly he produced a coin, a silver denarius of Queen Selene. He pointed to her silver head, and to the disk and plumes of Isis. "Here's your Selene," he said, almost roughly:

"born on the feast of Isis, Daughter of the Moon, hailed with prophecies. Do you know the prophecy made at her birth?"

"Do you?" asked Olympia.

"Yes; that in her the East and West should be united, the empire of Rome and Egypt be made one—in other words, that she would destroy Rome, as Anthony and Cleopatra almost did. Augustus gave her this kingdom, with a complaisant, scholarly husband. They've made it a great and wealthy empire. They can call up a hundred thousand fighting Berbers. Their navy is powerful. Theirs? Hers alone. She, Selene, is the real ruler here."

"True, perhaps," she commented, and nibbled at the luscious grapes.

"What's the situation in Rome? She has enemies there, bitter enemies; at last they've won the ear of the old, doddering, dying Augustus. Livia, the Empress, the mistress of poison and assassination, hates Selene and fears her. Augustus sent me here to make a report on Selene, on this province of the empire, her kingdom; if I report that she's a menace to Rome, he'll not hesitate to destroy her."

Olympia's face paled a little. Her eyes, searching him, rebelled with inner fires.

"Did anyone else send you?" she asked.

"You seem well served with spies here yourself," he retorted. "What do you fear?"

"I don't fear; I hope," she said softly.

HE DREW a deep breath and smiled.

"One man in Rome is the friend of Selene, has been her friend since boyhood," he made slow answer. "Some say he loves her; I don't know. He told me to deliver a message to her, secretly, as soon as possible. Can you get me an audience with her?"

"I can," she rejoined. "What's the message?"

"That's none of your business."

"So? Does it come, by any chance, from Tiberius?"

"Life's everywhere; just enjoy it, you and
I! Now there's the time for freedom, for
wine and flowers and dancing!"

He started. "Yes! Tiberius, who'll be the next Imperator when
Augustus dies."

"I thought as much. The message is important?"

"More; it's urgent," he replied curtly. Then, as she measured
him with thoughtful gaze, he made an impulsive, irritated
gesture and flung caution to the winds.

"Hell take all pretense and sparring! Look at the face on that coin, and at your own; you're Selene herself, as I thought. I must give you the message, for it means life or death. Beware, said Tiberius, of the Greek physician Loxias; he pretends to come from Alexandria, but he was sent from Rome. There you have it."

SHE BETRAYED no astonishment, but her eyes widened a trifle.

"Indeed! The physician Loxias arrived last week from Alexandria; the Queen was ill, but he has cured her. I'll see that your warning reaches her at once. You'll see her at the Festival of Isis, day after tomorrow. The moon will be at the full two nights from now."

She paused, twisting the ring on her finger.

"Don't deceive yourself," she went on. "I'm not the Queen; I'm Lady Olympia. It's my task to learn your secrets, to inspire you with the proper report for Cæsar's ears. But I do carry the Queen's signet." She removed the ring and handed it to him. "It is her dearest possession. The head upon it, like the head upon the coin, does look like me."

Lentulus examined the crystal intaglio. "Exquisitely done. It's the Queen?"

"Not at all; it's her mother, Cleopatra. This ring belonged to Cleopatra; it's the only thing of Cleopatra's that Selene possesses, and she treasures it for that reason."

Watching her replace the ring on her left hand, Lentulus felt the contrast of her quiet poise with his own tumultuous confusion. Not the Queen, after all! He had been hasty, impetuous, boyish in voicing his thoughts. She looked at him and smiled.

"You're not like most Romans," she observed slowly. "Rarely are they generous, noble and impulsive of heart; they're like Cæsar himself, shrewd and crafty and subtle. But you are different, Lentulus. With you I can talk freely, even if you're a spy. Strange words, those you quoted! I can't forget them. 'Tomorrow, all roads are one!'"

Lentulus leaned forward. The moon had risen higher, and

The Greek recoiled with one
wild shriek—a shriek of
horror and comprehension.

a drift of silver struck down into the patio, touching her with misty radiance. It was March, and spring; the balmy African air was sweet with flowers. Everything combined to stir the heart in the young Roman.

"Very well," said he. "Whether you're Queen, slave-girl or courtesan, matters nothing; in my eyes you are yourself, the most beautiful of women! There need be no secrets between us. Remain here in your own villa. Stay with me; as you've been ordered to do, learn all I say and do and think—I ask no better. Tomorrow the festival of Isis begins. They tell me people are already crowding into the city. Be my companion for the festival!"

A smile touched her lips, faint and mysterious; her eyes were amused.

"You flatter me! Certainly you don't lose any time—"

"Don't be obvious," he broke in, a little hoarsely. "I'm not

joking; it's as I told you: the second time in my life I've had this
feeling that the gods were close. It's so now. If you're not the
Queen, then you must be even more of a goddess than she is.
I ask nothing of you, Olympia; merely fulfill your duty, be my
companion!"

"Oh! Then you don't know what our festival of Isis means?
What it is?"

"I know nothing about it," he said frankly. "The worship of Isis
is forbidden in Rome. I care nothing about it. All I care about
is to be with you."

She looked at him for a long moment, then rose.

"I believe you." She held out her hand to him and smiled.
"Good night. I grant what you ask; I'll return here in the morning, and until this time tomorrow night we'll be companions.
One day out of life—why not? I never met a man like you. Good
night."

She turned and started away. "Wait! Don't forget!" he
exclaimed sharply. "The warning to the Queen!"

She stopped, still smiling. "I don't know why Cæsar, old and
suspicious and dying, should have trusted you, Lentulus; but I
know why any woman would trust you. Good night."

AND THIS time she was gone, and the night was empty.

He dreamed of her as he slept, thought of her when he waked.
Her profile, like that of the Daughter of the Moon on the silver
denarius; her radiant, shining presence, moon-misted and serene
and aloof. Some breath of the gods was surely in her. He had felt
the same about that Jewish family fleeing the sword of Herod;
a sureness, a serenity, a godlike radiant presence. Four years ago,
that was; yet he remembered it as though it had been yesterday.

He had come to Africa filled with speculation and curiosity respecting Cleopatra's daughter; now it was gone. He could
vision this Olympia as the real power behind Queen Selene,
shrewd, wise, tactful. She resembled the Queen; she probably
steered the policies of the kingdom. That the guards knew her
crystal intaglio ring, was highly significant.

With morning, he questioned the slaves he found attending him. They spoke freely; Lady Olympia was the daughter of a Berber chieftain, now dead; she had traveled afar, was the confidante of the Queen, and had never married. All this confirmed his opinions. He could not better fulfill his mission here than in following his heart's dictates. Scarcely had he breakfasted, when she arrived, alone. Her appearance startled him.

He exclaimed with surprise. "Olympia! But it's not you at all!"

"On the contrary, good sir!" She broke out laughing. "If I'm to guide you about the city, I don't want to be recognized. Are you disappointed? Perhaps you don't want to be seen in the company of a plain Berber girl?"

"In any guise, you're the loveliest woman in the world!" he exclaimed gravely. "I dreamed of you; I think I'll dream of you all my life."

"Then let's be off, and temper dreams with reality," she retorted.

They departed together. She wore a dark Berber gown, hooded, half concealing her face; and her face had been touched with blue lines, imitating the tattoo marks on cheeks and brow and chin worn by the Berber woman. She would pass unnoticed in the throngs.

Throngs such as Lentulus had seldom seen, even in Rome; and he discovered that this festival of Isis corresponded to the Saturnalia of the world's capital, a feast of love and fertility and reproduction when all restrictions were lifted and the balmy African air was one long amorous sigh of unrepressed desire. He realized with a shock why Olympia had been amused by his innocent request. Then he thrilled to memory of her reply: One day out of life—why not?

Berbers by the thousand, shaggy tattooed warriors; veterans from the camps and colonies of Roman legions, old soldiers who had campaigned in Syria and Germany and Britain, men who had served under Pompey and the first Cæsar, Julius the Divine. Nomads from the desert in the south, Greeks from the east, Romans everywhere, Egyptians everywhere, black Sudanese; Armenian and Carthaginian traders.

WHERE TO? They discussed the problem as they headed for the Forum; Lentulus found his companion effervescent, carefree, bubbling with girlish laughter and eager for mad, wild pranks; it was the carnival spirit all around them. The Circus and the games? No, said she with a grimace; too bloody. The theater? No; a stock company of slapstick comedians was performing there for the troops. Too vulgar.

"Suppose we merely circulate?" she suggested. "Life's everywhere; just enjoy it, you and I! A Greek company will give some classical drama next week— Sophocles; but now's the time for freedom, for wine and flowers and dancing!"

"Done with you!" he cried with a rush of boyish enthusiasm. "Come on—don't stop to think—into the procession yonder!"

He caught her hand, forced her into a run, and they broke through the gay crowd.

A procession was passing in the middle of the street— elephants, dancing girls, priests of Isis, carts of flowers being flung broadcast, tipsy legionaires and shrieking *hetairæ* aflame with carnival madness. They broke into it midway. Lentulus leaped to a cart, seized garlands of flowers, caught a shepherd's pipe from the hand of a frenzied dancer—and turned to see Olympia despoiling a scandalized Egyptian priest of his sistrum, a string of bells mounted on a holder. The priest shrieked for help; the crowd roared with laughter; Lentulus hung Olympia with flower-wreaths, and with pipe and sistrum they lost themselves in the throngs, dignity flung to the winds.

Cafés and wineshops were cramped; shops were closed; and everywhere was entertainment. Jugglers, buffoons, peddlers abounded; wherever there was room to make a pitch, a crowd had massed close.

NOW AND again Lentulus noted a Greek, a thin dark limping man, who stayed well away from them yet was ever recurring on the scene. Someone spying on him? It was possible; he dismissed the matter carelessly.

As the afternoon wore on and wine got in its work, as the fiercely chorused yells of thousands lifted above the city from the Circus and the games there, spirits became more riotous. Music ran higher; madder and more delirious waxed the crowds. Night would soon come, and the glorious moon herself to climax the first day of festival, with temple groves resounding to torchlit dancing and the laughing sighs of lovers.

Sunset flared. Olympia, drunk with laughter and excitement, was dancing with gay abandon amid a throng of shaggy Berbers, men and women; Lentulus looked on, listening to the raucous voices and barbaric tongues. She staggered at last out of the wild uproar and caught his arm.

"Enough, enough!" she gasped with ebbing laughter. "Day is going, and—"

A burst of maudlin yells rocketed up. A party of drunken seamen from the fleet struck into the crowd full tilt and seized on the Berber girls. Knives flashed. Instantly the whole wide street was in a snarl of savage tumult.

Blood flowed fast. Curved Berber knives ripped from waist to gullet; seamen's dirks stabbed home; men died. The scene became wild riot and fury unleashed.

Hands snatched at Olympia. Lentulus put her behind him; he struck out shrewdly and coolly. His shouts brought a pack of Legionaires into the uproar. A staggering rush bore him off his feet. Recovering, he saw Olympia in the arms of three seamen, fighting with them. He leaped in; the Legionaires burst the crowd asunder, and Lentulus picked Olympia up in his arms. He carried her out of the storm-tossed area to comparative quiet, saw that she was senseless, and looked around to see the limping Greek approaching.

"Ah! The lady is hurt!" exclaimed the Greek.

LENTULUS SET her down, with an oath of dismay and anger. Blood was seeping over her left wrist and hand; in her forearm was a jagged rip from a knife-point.

"I can take care of it, master," said the Greek quietly. "I have much skill with hurts; this is nothing serious, but must be bandaged. Give me a strip from your toga." He produced a wallet and got out a little vial of unguent. "Here's a salve that will cure the hurt and cause it to heal without a scar."

The fellow took charge, with deft dexterity. Lentulus gave him a strip of his toga, and the Greek smeared the salve on it, then bandaged the hurt arm neatly.

"Don't disturb nature," he said warningly. "Let her waken by herself; all's well."

He turned away. Lentulus thanked him, offered him a coin, but with a slow smile he refused any payment, and disappeared in the gathering twilight.

Looking around, Lentulus saw that the theater was close by, apparently deserted. He lifted Olympia in his arms; in two minutes they were away from the crowds and tumult of the street. He felt her arms tighten about his neck, heard her laugh a little, and knew she was awake.

"The theater!" she said softly. "Why not? Tell me, what happened?"

"You fainted; your arm was scratched by a knife, and we're out of that mob."

"Stop here, before we come to the stage—there's running water. I need a drink!"

He halted. Her face was close, to his, and in his arms he held her against him; the perfume of her was in his nostrils. Her slender, fragile, exquisite perfection stirred him. Briefly, hungrily, their lips touched.

After a moment, he set her down beside the fountain. She quite ignored her hurt arm; a splash of water, a laugh, and she was dragging him toward the stage.

"Come! There's no one here. I've always wanted to take the

part of an actor; it's absurd, that they don't allow women on the stage! I'll be an actor, without a mask, just as I am. A rôle—oh! You know Euripides?"

"Every line," said Lentulus, chuckling.

"Every line! Of all his ninety-two plays? You must be a paragon! Do you know the place in the Andromeda, where *Perseus* is hiding behind the rock, and they both speak to the moon?"

"Yes."

"Good! We'll do that. Then we'll go home and bathe and rest and watch the moon come up." She drew him to the stage. With sudden recollection, he interrupted her:

"One moment! I quite forgot to ask you. Did you give the Queen warning about that fellow Loxias, from Alexandria?"

"Oh! Yes, yes! She was startled, anxious, grateful; she dismissed Loxias at once and forbade him the palace. She wants to thank you herself. She'll see you tomorrow evening." With this, Olympia whirled, took actor's pose, made believe to adjust her mask, and spoke softly. "Ready? Make believe there's a rock to hide behind. Pretend the chorus is along the back—leave out the strophe and antistrophe. We'll give the lines to the moon; and perhaps, when she rises later, she'll answer the prayer!"

S H E WA S in an impish, sprightly mood. The vast theater, cloaked in gathering night, was like an empty hollow shell; the stars faintly pricked out their wonted patterns upon the faintly greenish sky. Her voice lifted and took on surety, in those words of sheer romance in which lovers across the ages had echoed the great romantic poet.

' "*Gild the gray stars, and weave upon the night thy robe of lovely silence! Mother Moon, linger awhile upon the steeps of dawn, and grant my heart's desire in mystery!*" '

' "*Aye, mystery!*" ' declaimed Lentulus, picking up the rôle of Perseus. ' "*Against the harsh gaunt day defend, with all thy silvern wizardry, my longings and my love. Aye, gild the stars till every twinkling starry point takes tongue to tell her of my love! Hear me, O Moon! When evening steals the dim day's life away and in thy*

beams the dark world glorieth, hear me and grant my prayer, and
bless my love!" '

' *"Ah, bless my love!"* 'Olympia's voice was very music; in those
words of the hapless *Andromeda*, those words so mystic and
tender; booed off the stage at first hearing, they had gripped
the hearts of lovers in succeeding centuries. She went on, softly:

' *"Ah, bless my love! Whether on land or sea, wafted within some*
billowing high-flung cloud, or lost upon a far heroic quest in some
lone land where no man wandereth——" '

Her voice became faint, and failed. Lentulus, thinking she
had forgot the lines, gave low prompting:

' *"Bear him my love, and bless——"* '

She made no answer. In the gloom, he found her hands
outreaching. He stepped swiftly to her, and she clung to him
with a quick cry.

"No use, no use! My head's swimming, I've lost the mood.
Give me your arm; we'll get back to the villa, and by moonrise
I'll be myself again. I'm tired, and my feet hurt."

At these prosaic words, he broke into a laugh, and they left
the theater together.

When they gained the villa, she had recovered her high spirits. A bath, a change of garments, wine and fruit and delicious
repast—

"And the moon!" added Lentulus. "The day you promised me
isn't over yet, you know!"

"I know only too well," she said softly, and left him to ponder
her meaning.

THE MOON lifted, round and nearly at the full. The little
patio was quiet, peacefully remote from the roaring, careering
city. Lentulus, in grateful relaxation, sipped his well-watered
wine and talked of the East—Alexandria, Judea, Antioch. And
she, nestling among the thick rugs woven by Numidian tribes,
spoke of the Pillars of Hercules in the West, and the islands
afar in the ocean beyond them which King Juba had discovered

and named Canaries, after the wild white dogs roaming upon
them. The moon rose higher; magic filled the night. Presently
they were talking of themselves and of destiny.

"Remember, I'm a spy," he said, smiling. "What shall I tell
Cæsar about your Queen, whom they call the Daughter of the
Moon? Is she ambitious? Does she hope to throw off the yoke
of Rome, the Rome which destroyed her mother, her family?"

"No," she said gravely. "When Selene walked in golden chains
behind the triumphal car of Cæsar, as a girl, her spirit was
broken. Now she has a docile, unloving husband, an enormously
wealthy kingdom; she speaks all tongues, studies philosophy, is
content. Her mother, Cleopatra, loved greatly; but Selene has
never loved, or betrayed love."

"SUCH ARE the externals," said Lentulus. "What's the
reality?"

She turned to him, all shimmering pale and lovely in the
moonlight.

"The reality? An uphappy woman, whom you've saved. Who
sent that Greek? The Empress Livia, the mistress of poison!
You've saved the Queen from him. She'll reward you. Wealth;
a principality in the mountains, power here in Cæsarea. The
Berber tribes worship her; the Roman legionaires, who loved
her father Antony, love her. The Roman *procurator* here is a weak
and greedy fool. Juba, the king, will do as he's told. What do you
see in all this?"

"You," said Lentulus. A sudden sense of shock ran through
his veins, as he perceived the drift of her words. He touched her
bandaged arm, gently. "I'm still surprised that blood came from
this hurt, and not the divine ichor flowing in the veins of the
gods! All the things you mention, fail to dazzle me, Olympia.
I've no great family or position—"

"You have honesty," she broke in.

"Honesty, then," said he. "Betray Rome? In a minute, to win
you. Yet it would not be treachery; I owe Rome nothing. Yet I've
nothing to offer you."

"Everything," she said in a low voice. "Everything! More than I can make you see, my Lentulus. You make the whole world different. Augustus sent you because he trusted you. Tiberius gave you that message, because he could trust you. I've spoken frankly with you, because I could trust you. And yet, Lentulus, I've lied to you in one thing."

He laughed, and stooped his lips to her hurt arm, and kissed it.

"Never mind!" he checked her swiftly. "Tell me tomorrow, if you like, when I come to the palace. Here beneath the moon, I swear myself to you; I transfer all allegiance to you—my life, my heart, my soul!"

"Very well. Tomorrow, then; and tonight—this one day out of life—"

Higher climbed the round silvern disk across the sky. The blissful hymn of the nightingale had sunk to rest. Suddenly a queer, sustained sound began to drift up from the city; it was felt rather than heard, at first. Lentulus lifted his head, listening; something in that sound, some note in it, disturbed him.

Olympia stirred, and sat up. "My hand throbs!" she murmured, and took the crystal intaglio ring from her one hand, transferring it to the other. A startled word escaped her. "That sound—what is it? Listen!"

The sound increased. It took on an accent of fear, of dismay, of terror. Into it crept a deeper voice; the rattle and roll of Berber drums across the night.

"Something's happened!" exclaimed Olympia. "That sound—the wailing of people by the thousand! What is it? What can it be? Ah—by the gods! Look!"

She pointed upward. A gasp broke from her. Lentulus glanced up at the moon; something wrong there! Realization jerked at him. The black segment of a circle was creeping into the edge of that silver disk. An eclipse!

"Be calm, be calm," said Lentulus, feeling the woman beside him clutch at him, sensing her tremor of fear. He drew her gently to him, and kissed her lips. "It will pass. An evil omen, I grant you, but—"

She broke in, almost wildly:

"An omen? No, no! Worse than that—ah, you don't understand! The Queen, Selene, the Daughter of the Moon! This betokens something terrible to her. That's why all the people are in fear. An eclipse, just now, at the very festival of Isis—ah, be careful! You hurt my arm—"

He was startled by the hot touch of her skin; and she had said her hand was burning! But before he could speak, she sprang erect. From the street outside came a mad clatter of hooves, the clang of chariot wheels.

"They have sent for me! I must go to the palace!" she exclaimed. "No; wait here, my dear. Don't stir. I'll go out to them—Quickly! One last kiss!"

He caught her in a swift embrace; she clung to him for one long moment. Then, as voices reverberated on the night, she tore herself away, and with a low sob was gone, running.

Lentulus reached for a goblet of wine, and sipping it, sank back on the soft rugs. He was rather amused by her terror, by her wildly disturbed air. Like the average cultured Roman of his day, he viewed omens and portents with callous skepticism.

So he sat watching while the circle of blackness cut into the moon's silver face, and listened to the faint tumult rising from all the city—the mingled voices, the drums, the chanting. Darkness came and passed again. Gradually, the moon crept clear of the fateful shadow. Lentulus, finishing the flask of wine, laughed at thought of the terrorized Berber hordes. Covering his face from the moon, he stretched out and was asleep instantly.

WHEN HE wakened, a slave was shaking him. He sat up; morning, by the sun, was well advanced. Blinking, he heard that a messenger had come from the palace, one of the Queen's ladies. He hurriedly brushed up, and was aware of a swelling, mournful ululation that came from everywhere and hovered above the entire city, as though uncounted thousands of voices were blended in some wailing chant.

At sight of the palace lady, he halted abruptly. She was a grave and matronly woman, her features so stricken with grief that the Roman was seized by a sense of shock.

"Who are you?" he demanded.

"I have a message from Queen Selene, lord, and I bear a gift for you," she said, extending her hand. Into his palm fell a ring. A crystal intaglio, a glorious thing graven with the profile of Selene and the insignia of Isis. Queen Cleopatra's ring.

"Oh! Lady Olympia's ring? What does this mean?"

"There is no Lady Olympia," she said. "This ring belonged to the Queen of Egypt, and to her daughter Selene. She who sent it to you has passed through the door of death to more radiant life, as those who know the mysteries of Isis are aware—"

Deathly pale, Lentulus caught at her.

"Stop prattling!" he cried hoarsely. "By the gods, say what you have to say!"

"An hour ago, lord, the Queen died. She ordered me to bring you this ring."

"Died! She—the queen? No, no! She can't be dead!" stammered Lentulus.

"A hurt in her arm was poisoned, lord. She bade me give you this ring, and tell you to remember the words of the Jew. What she meant I do not know, for her speech was difficult. It was something about tomorrow, about all roads being one."

Lentulus, convulsed by a spasmodic horror, scarcely heard these last words.

"Poisoned? You say the scratch in her arm—poisoned?"

As the meaning of the words, and their implication, reached his brain, he started back, staring wildly. Then he drew the edge of his toga across his face and stood motionless, frozen by an awful and ghastly realization that stopped his very heartbeat.

Poisoned. His own hand had helped apply that bandage, had

held the wounded arm. He remembered, now, the salve applied to that bandage, and a fearful conjecture wrenched at him. He bared his face and turned his burning eyes to the woman.

"Tell me something. Do you know of a physician named Loxias, who was forbidden the palace?"

"Yes, lord."

"What did he look like? Describe him."

"He was a thin, dark man, and limped slightly as he walked."

A groan burst from Lentulus. He groped for a seat, sank into it, and again covered his face from sight. The ring was grasped in his hand. Now, too late, he understood the lie she had told him; that ring made everything plain. She had been Selene, even as he first suspected. Selene! Dead.

LATER THAT day, amid the wild lamentation and mourning echoing up from all Cæsarea, Lentulus walked into a tavern on the waterfront. He had been seeking, seeking, and now he had found his man. The man was here, booking passage aboard the first ship leaving for Rome, a trireme sailing this very night.

The limping Greek recognized him with a sharp start, and then turned to him with a fawning smile of greeting.

"Ha, lord, is it you again? Well met. Great things have happened, it seems."

"They are still to happen," said Lentulus, and put his hand to his girdle.

The Greek suddenly shrank away from those grim, blazing eyes—recoiled with one wild shriek that rang terribly, a shriek of horror and comprehension and terror, ending in a groan as the steel drove home.

"Give me passage to Ostia in this ship," said Lentulus to the crowding shipmen. "My errand in Africa is ended. Here are my Credentials—on official business of the Emperor!"

His errand, indeed, was ended.

KETTLEMAN TOOK me home with him to see a suppressed film.

One of the great Hollywood directors, Kettleman is a queer genius, experimenting in queer directions. To all the accusations and criticisms hurled at the movies, he has one very true answer: "We make what we must; since ninety per cent of the public ignore intelligent pictures, as they ignore great symphonies, we give 'em what they demand."

"That answer," I told him, "is perfectly true; but it is not the truth at all."

He grinned faintly. "I guess so; it's a good excuse for making damfool pictures that are slipshod, historically incorrect and so forth. The one I'm going to show you is part of an educational program I dreamed of turning out."

"Why was it suppressed? Sex?"

"Heavens, no!" he rejoined. "It was to be a panorama of the theater in technicolor, but that fellow Donald, up in the studio, finally junked the idea. He claims people aren't interested in anything about the theater, that they want blood, romance, action! Funny thing is, this picture has all of these—and something more. It deals with the survival of acting and the stage in the darkest medieval ages. Donald saw only the opening, a vista of hilltops in Normandy, and turned thumbs down without seeing the rest."

"Nothing very dramatic about hilltops," I commented.

"The greatest drama in all history was played on a hilltop outside Jerusalem," he snapped. I told you the man was singular; his mental flashes were always at an angle, somehow.

Kettleman had a private projection-room in his big house. He took me in, supplied a drink and a cigar, and began to fuss with his projector. The room lights flicked off. On the screen facing us appeared a "still" in technicolor, a landscape aglow beneath a round silvern disk which, in another night, would be the fullest of full moons. A landscape, a hilltop interspersed with huge jagged bits of rock; in the distance, a castle tower and the glint of water.

"Hang it! The projector's stuck—have it fixed in a minute," said Kettleman. "A curious fact; the earliest French mystery plays went by the name of *puy*. Why? Because the word signified a hilltop. It was a reminiscence of earlier dramas back in pagan ages. Here you see a hilltop in Brittany, by the sea, in feudal days of blood and fire and universal war, when the drama was preserved in the hearts of common folk as a joyous relief from the horrors of an intolerable existence."

"I didn't know there was any drama then," was my comment.

"The Dance of Life, the most ancient of all pageants, that of fertility, the earth-mother, an old pagan survival! Then, remember, the people were oppressed and ground down and trodden underfoot like weeds, by their lords and masters. The people of the earth were like wild beasts, in that period."

"That same period," I objected, "gave us the most glorious of romances—look at the story of Tristan and Yseult."

"Bah! Look at the story of Jehan and Elaine!" he barked. The machine began to click; the film moved; the scene moved. Needless to say, it was a sound-film.

Yet for a space there was no sound. The figure of a woman, a girl, appeared like a wood-nymph girt with fluttering moon-glints and garlanded with pearls. Her figure grew more clear. She was actually clad in rags and tatters; twined in her flowing

red-gold hair were flowers. She moved with such symmetry, such utter grace, as apparently to mount upon the very moonbeams.

Dancing about those jagged ancient stones, approaching the flat central rock, she came to sudden frightened halt. She stood at gaze, transfixed. The high white moon etched her lissome shape, her masses of flower-starred hair, her profile of purest beauty and nobility. Behind her evident terror was a nervous strength; one sensed in her a singular desperate courage, as though she were faced by some unavoidable terror, and yet fronted it with heart unquailing.

"No, no!" A gasp broke from her. "You are dead—it cannot be you—"

From the central mass of rock, a shadow detached itself, stood out clearly, and came toward her. The girl's fright died.

An incredulous cry of joy broke upon her lips, and her arms lifted eagerly.

"Jehan! Dear Jehan—you're real, alive, flesh and blood!"

"And can prove it, Elaine!" said he, as his arms went about her. They clung together, wordless, lip to lip and heart to heart.

"They said you were dead," she murmured. "All the village thinks you dead. Your poor mother died last month. And I—I have had no heart left."

He was a young man, but shaggily bearded, clad in ragged garments, marked by hard travel and privation. Unlike the average peasant, there was no cringing in his manner; he held his head high, and the harsh lines of his features held a resolute, indomitable expression rarely found among the people of the earth. As they stood together, he turned the girl and pointed to the distant mass of the castle.

"And they think me dead also," he said, a bitter menace in his voice. "The noble Lord of Fécamp, his slender voluptuous ladies, his knights and men-at-arms—aye, they think me dead. Here, little heart, sit down and rest, while I tell you about it."

He drew her down on the great flat rock, where in olden days the Druids had performed their mystic rites. She nestled beside him, tremulous, still incredulous of his reality.

"You know how my sister was taken to the castle yonder, and how she killed herself after the Lord of Fécamp had finished with her and gave her to his soldiers," he said. "You know how I cursed them, how they came and seized me and took me to the castle; there they whipped me and loaded chains on me and made me a beast of burden."

The girl shivered, and touched his cheek with pitying finger. Yet there was nothing unusual in all this; the serfs of chivalry were born to such a destiny.

"AN ENGLISH knight visited the castle two months ago," he went on. "He won me at dice from the Lord of Fécamp, and took me when he left for England. The ship was wrecked on the coast below here, for a storm seized us. Most of those on board were drowned; only a few escaped to tell of it. So I was accounted dead with the rest."

"We heard," murmured Elaine, "They mourned for the English knight."

Jehan laughed harshly. "He did not drown; I killed him, took his money and clothes, and got ashore. Elaine, it's wealth! Money, real money of silver and gold, clothes, arms! All hidden and waiting for us. I came to take you away from this horror, to the country of Eldigonde the sorceress."

The girl lifted herself and drew back, horrified.

"Jehan! Are you mad? Poor Jehan—you have suffered—"

HE BROKE into a swift, joyous laugh, and kissed her strong fingers.

"No, no, I'm quite sane, my dear! Far below here on the Breton coast, is a land of safety for you and me. The country is wild, densely wooded, a tangle of rocks and trees; no feudal lords own it. Instead, it's inhabited by free people of the earth who have fled there. In that wild land they live safely, freely, joyously! And the wise old woman, the sorceress Eldigonde, is the only ruler, for her wisdom is great. All the wealth for which I paid in blood and flesh and tears, is waiting there. I came to take you back with me. A boat is hidden here at the shore, below the castle. You'll go?"

"Yes, yes! It seems like some dream, Jehan—yes, of course I'll go!" she exclaimed in stammering haste. "I can't believe it's real.... But, Jehan! I can't leave until after tomorrow night. It is the festival, you know; the dance of life."

He nodded. "Aye. The dance of life, that we celebrate in secret to the moon! And God help us all if they find out about it, there at the castle. You remember how the Sieur de Courcelles burned eleven of his people alive, three years ago, for celebrating the festival?"

"There's no danger here, Jehan," said the girl. "Everybody at the castle will be drunk tomorrow night; the Lord of Fécamp is to celebrate his birthday, and has invited a crowd of gentry in. Besides, Felipe Brieux will be ready to touch off a signal-flare if there's any riding from the castle. No, it's safe."

"And you, my dear?" Jehan stroked her glossy hair. "Do you still wear the hump on your back and the scar on your face that Nanny Dubois taught you to paint on?"

She shivered slightly. "Yes, of course. Marie Lianceau was married last week to Pierre, and he had to take her to the castle for—the *droit de seigneur*. Oh, Jehan, it was terrible! She was out of her senses for two days afterward. Two of the castle officers were riding by the field where I was working, and saw me, and came over for a closer look; luckily they saw the scar and the humped back, and went away. But I was frightened."

*A kindly soul, with a heart for the maids
who were sport for soldier and noble!*

"May heaven blast all these rulers of earth!" cried out Jehan
passionately. He launched a torrent of curses, in a blaze of shaking wrath. "These lords and seigneurs who oppress and torture
us, who own us body and soul—some day they'll be swept away!
Their castles will be razed, they and their brood drowned in their
own blood—you'll see!"

"Hush, Jehan! They'd hang you for saying such words!"

He laughed bitterly. "I'll say worse before I'm dead. But now,
little heart, I must get away and find hiding over tomorrow; I
dare not let another soul know I'm back. I did hope to see my

old mother; but you say she's dead, so let it pass. She's resting at last, poor soul! I'll meet you here tomorrow night, after the festival. Then we'll go quickly."

"With all my heart, Jehan," she replied. One last embrace, one clinging, eager kiss of rapture, and he was gone, melting into the shadows whence he had come.

And high time. As the girl stood staring after him, a scuffle of *sabots* and the murmur of voices reached her; a dozen other girls of the village and district around had arrived to join her in a rehearsal of the dance.

They greeted her joyously, half fearfully, all in a tumult between terror and excited anticipation; there was one screw-backed old hag from down the shore, who hobbled along importantly. It was her place to see that the ancient ritual was followed, the dances and the songs rightly given, for thus they had been handed down from forgotten days.

So, laying off the wooden *sabots*, the girls circled and sang, postured and tripped among the rocks that the forgotten Druids had left behind. All was done blindly, in passive obedience to the croaked directions of the old hag; she herself did not know the meaning of the words uttered, for to her they were only sounds, just as the gestures and actions were meaningless things, relics of the dim past.

But luck followed upon the festival. When it was neglected, pestilence and bad crops came, and war. The old gods were forgot, their very names blown nowhere with the dust of centuries, their fanes all crumbled and their memories grown black beneath the stars; but racial instinct still preserved the rites of ancient days. To these poor folk, crushed under such oppression as the world has seldom seen, this yearly festival was a symbol of hope and beauty, an escape from the horrors of daily life, a prayer, half-realized, to the primal earth-gods and the forces of nature.

None the less, it constituted a fearful risk. In the eyes of chivalry, they had no right to happiness; woe betide them if they were caught at it! Then would rise the cry of "Sorcery!" with

*"I—I am only a peasant,
Messire Pierre," she said.
"I am no lovely lady."*

tortures and burnings and mutilation to follow. The Black Death
and other fearful plagues had not yet come to sweep away nine-
tenths of all people, rich and poor alike, and make human chat-
tels valuable; the land was crowded; serfs were thick in field and
village, to be mauled or killed or hunted down like wild beasts
in drunken riot.

LATE UNDER the moon, Elaine stole home a to the
thatched cottage, still in a fervent riot of thought, and tucked
herself away. Weary as she was, sleep came hard. Jehan alive,
here, within reach and touch! This in itself was a miracle; but
what lay beyond seemed utterly incredible. That there should be
any place beyond the reach of tyranny and cruelty was to her a
fantastic vision, beyond the power of the brain to comprehend;
yet Jehan had come to take her there!

If, indeed, it were all real and not a dream…. She awakened
in the morning, suddenly to clasp hands to bursting heart. True
or real? She could not credit it, until she found on her finger

*"You're no peasant lass,
not any sorceress neither!"*

the circlet of gold Jehan had put there at parting. A gold ring! She stared at it, then hurriedly tore it off and hid it from sight. There was no such treasure as that anywhere in the district; only a knight might hope to possess a gold ring, or one of the pretty beauties at the castle.

"UP, SLUT, up!" came the voice of her bent and twisted father, roaring angrily. "Our lord's overseer has commanded that the entire upper field be finished today—up and out!"

Elaine had scant love for her father, who viewed her innate delicacy with sneering derision. He was a brute like most of his kind, warped by hard labor and torments. Perhaps there was truth in the story that she sprang not from him, but from that night when her mother, a bride, was handed over to the lord of Fécamp. This "right" had instilled new blood in many a peasant family; and amid the cringing, tortured serfs was to be seen many a, head held proudly, such as that of Elaine or of her lover Jehan.

She dressed swiftly. Her father looked on with an evil grin while she donned the false hump she had invented for safety's sake, tying the straps over her shoulders and below the budding round of her breasts. Over this, her ragged robe. Then, while he taunted her about the good price he should get for betrayal of her ruse, she swiftly applied the magical paint Nanny Dubois had given her, making a red ugly scar that drew her cheek and lips askew. A kindly soul, old Nanny, with a heart in her shriveled deathly corpse for the poor maids who were sport for soldier and noble!

A swallow of thick soup, a rush for the field, and the work was forward, with clump of wooden shoe and drip of sweat, and many a groan for aching back and loins.

Today, however, aches and pains were forgotten, in the glorious vista that spelled an end to barbarous oppression. Freedom and safety! It seemed too good to be true, in this nightmare of a life.

Afternoon brought guttural cries of warning flitting across the fields, from hovel to hovel. Armed men were riding from the castle! They came—the Seigneur himself, a band of visiting knights and lords, ladies on their palfreys, men-at-arms in helm and chain-coat, pennons flashing and gay laughter ringing as the dun deer fled before, and the horns sounded high. A stag broke from covert and fled across the field of springing grain; with shout and horn, the riders plunged after, hounds baying wildly. It was the natal day of the Lord of Fécamp, with a stag of ten hurtling to the kill!

ELAINE RAN with the others, all scurrying like frightened quail as the rout headed for them. She saw her father trip and fall. The dogs went over him in a rush, but one of them turned to spring at him; struggling up, he fought the beast frantically. With a torrent of oaths the Seigneur himself rode down the panic-stricken man, lashed him with a whip, and sent the men-at-arms to finish him. A lance went through him, and another. The twisted body relaxed, and the laughing ladies kneaded it into the mud as they galloped over the poor clay.

Two of the castle riders wheeled their horses as Elaine ran, screaming, to the side of the dead man. They reined in, laughing, but as they sighted her scarred face and the hump between her shoulders, they put in spurs and went on at a gallop, with a coarse exchange of jests. The other folk crept out from hiding and bore the spattered corpse home.

"Lucky they didn't take a notion to ride all of us down!" said somebody.

Grief? Elaine felt none, pretended none. This father of hers had been her chief potential enemy, in fact. Now she was alone, but not for long; tonight would end all of that, forever. So her father was laid under the earth. Before the grave was filled, the castle overseer arrived and gave orders that she was to marry a widower of the district, on the morrow. Hump or no hump, she could breed new serfs to labor in the fields.

"And," he added with a laugh, as he departed, "when the ceremony's done, you'll go up to the castle for the usual entertainment. You're no proper quarry for the Seigneur, my lass, but the men-at-arms are not over-particular."

Elaine assented humbly, and repressed a shudder. What if Jehan had not come back last night? Fate would have been hard at her heels.

THE LONG afternoon dwindled into sunset, and she ate a lone supper and thought of Jehan, hiding somewhere along the rocky shore. Her father's death would make no difference to the celebration of the festival; the dance of life was something that rose above mortality and human chance.

With darkness, there was a hush and a stir over the whole countryside. From near and far, shadowy figures were stealing along the winding roads and across the fields, toward the hilltop where the ancient rocks thrust up toward the stars.

In the vague starlight, they wended toward their goal, slipping from bosque and covert to converge on the one point, silently enough, like animals. Only, now and again, a clucking of tongues sounded as crones and wise women from scattered points came together; old outcast hags like Nanny Dubois, who practiced wizardry of nights, and brewed herbs to make the sick well, and afforded the poor folk shrewd but subtle advice in all problems of their wretched lives.

On the hilltop, along the hill flanks, dim serried ranks of half-seen figures gathered. They waited tense, expectant; they had stolen away for this one night of freedom and joyous celebration in secret. Grouped beside one of the great rocks, Elaine and her companions bided motionless the moment of their appearance, for other things came first.

The first orange light of the rising moon trembled up the eastern sky. From all that assemblage came a murmurous gasp of greeting, a breath that passed along the hillside and died into silence. Shapes appeared in the dim, slowly growing glow, capering amid the high rocks; grotesque shapes, clad in the guise of wild beasts.

The Dance of Life had begun.

It was an eerie, uncanny thing; for as yet the golden round of the moon was not up. Monstrous shapes disported themselves, masques of wicker and fur which had been long weeks preparing in hidden places. All was done in silence, save for hoarse breaths and pantings of effort. Closer to the great central stone worked the rhythmic movement until, as the circle of the moon lifted gradually, all that wild company stood revealed for one moment, full-etched in horn and hoof and claw and bestial ecstasy.

The shrill note of a reed pipe sounded. Suddenly and completely, the strange figures separated, leaped away, and scurried into cover. They vanished, and in among the rocks came men clad in skins, to the thin tremulous music of many reed pipes, dancing and weaving in upon the fiat central stone.

They carried burdens, images of animals; in olden days, no doubt, these had been real animals for sacrifice, but now the creatures of earth and sea were too hard to come by, too utterly valuable, for such offering. Upon the flat rock were laid the simulated fish and beasts, while the dancers went through the olden ritual of oblation and festival. It was a strangely wild and vivacious thing to see, and mightily stirred the hearts of the watchers, so that ejaculations and eager voices began to rise on all sides.

EVERYWHERE THE grain was springing in the sown fields, life was stirring anew in leaf and beast; and here beneath the moon was the festival of fertile earth and joy. The men drew back; the thin pipings changed to a different air. Elaine sped a quick word at her companions, and the tattered gowns were flung aside. She leaped forth, and they after her, clad in little besides the flowing disarray of floating hair and twisted ropes of flowers.

What a dance this was, beneath the flooding golden light of the risen moon! The slim figures swept among the old monoliths in steps of wild abandon; murmurs of amazement sounded as Elaine was recognized, now without hump or scar, slender and perfect and lovely. "A miracle, a miracle!" swept the murmured words, but she heard them not, nor cared. For, somewhere in the outer darkness, she knew that Jehan watched, hidden, and she flung herself into the jocund exhilaration of the piping music and the floating steps.

The steps quickened; the music quickened, as the dancers neared the central stone, their lissome shapes transfigured by the moonlight and lifted afar from everyday semblance. Never had those drear-eyed watchers beheld such grace and beauty, except at this annual festival; as the reedy pipings struck into swifter rhythm, as the voices of the dancing girls took up the ritual of strange unknown words, the men dancers joined in.

AND SUDDENLY all was a wild ecstatic rapture, the dancers bursting into evasion and pursuit among the jutting rocks, the watching throngs swept by a contagious frenzy into hoarse cries and panting exclamations—until, without warning, a fearful frozen silence struck them all.

One wild and terrible scream, from the moonlit spaces beyond the hilltop, wailed across the night, and was followed by the blare of a hunting horn.

The awful realization smote one and all, as a rushing clatter of hooves sounded. The watcher had failed, the castle folk had surprised the festival! Shrill and despairing shrieks flared up, to be drowned in a roar of shouts and clarion cries. The phantom watching figures melted like mist, as knights and men-at-arms came charging, with glint of mail and flutter of pennon and thrust of red-tipped lance.

"Kill!" rose the shout. "Kill! Sorcery—kill!"

There was killing enough, without mercy, amid frantic fleeing and mad pursuit. Old Nanny Dubois was plucked up bodily by a spear and hurled atop one of the jagged rocks, to shriek away her life. Swords glinted; horses trampled.

But the little group of girls, shimmering golden in the moonlight, could not flee, for the circle of armed men had ringed in the hilltop and came plunging at them, with wild fierce laughter and eager hands. Hither and yon they drove in terrified flight, to be run down or pulled down by knight or squire among the Druidic stones.

Elaine, crouching in blank panic, was aware of a wild ringing voice above her, a man stooping from the saddle, his arm circling her body. She was lifted, scooped up, held in an iron grip despite all struggles; while the rider, with a voice triumphant, thrust in his spurs and sent the powerful destrier plunging down the hillside and away, through the silvery blood-smeared moonlit night.

The stark cries lessened; the roaring laughter died away upon distance; the great steed slowed his pace and halted. The rider, holding, her in his arms, leaned forward and kissed her, and looked laughingly into her face, and then looked again, his hot mirth dying out.

And she, staring up helplessly, saw that he was a stranger, a young knight handsome as a god, no doubt one of the Seigneur's

*"Thus," he cried, sweeping the strings, "and thus! A
salute to life! A salute to life and love and ecstasy!"*

guests. There was no cruelty in his face, no barbaric fury. Instead,
he seemed gentle and bright with youth.

"What!" he exclaimed. "Here's a prize if ever was one, but not
what I thought. You're no peasant lass, nor any sorceress neither!
That is, unless I'm bewitched myself."

"Have mercy, have mercy!" Her voice fluttered at him wildly.
"I've done no wrong—let me go, I pray!"

He caught sight of the golden ring which she had put on her finger. The soft moonlight concealed her work-hardened hands and feet; she lay in his arms, her flower-starred hair flowing about him, her heart palpitating against his own, her warm fresh loveliness all real and glowing.

"Maiden, who are you?" he demanded curiously. "Some sweet naiad from the land of, Prester John? Some nymph crept out of the sea to dazzle men with her beauty? Perhaps the Lady Morgana herself, come from the morning star to find a lover among men? Quick! Your name!"

"Elaine," she gasped out, her eyes wide upon his smiling features and glorious youth. She had never dreamed a man could be so nobly handsome.

"Elaine! A name of poesy, of old romance!" he said, and suddenly gripped her hard, and kissed her lips. They were not brutal kisses, but most sweet and lingering, so that the terrified heart within her melted, and a silver fire like moonlight coursed through her veins. Then his head lifted.

"COME, SWEET lady, your promise!" he said, breathing hard as he looked into her eyes. "I am Pierre de Louhac, your very humble servitor and liege knight; for my sins, I am a poet, with a lute at my saddle-bow where a helm should ride. Promise me that you'll not fly away upon the moonbeams, or glide into the water, or vanish in the thicket—swear it, by the True Cross! Then I'll set you down, and if we kiss again, it shall be of your own free will."

"I swear it, I swear it!" she panted desperately.

He gently let her slide to earth, and dismounting, took the cloak from his shoulders and fastened it about her throat, so that it enfolded her slim body. And he sighed a little as he stooped and kissed her hand.

"Now for my lute, and you shall tell me whence you came, Lady Elaine. For I wot well you are no mortal creature, but some lovely lady come from the bounds of fairyland. Even though you be some fair sorceress—but that cannot be, since you swore by the Cross. Therefore you must be all gentle and lovely as you look, since it is impossible that so rare an ornament of heaven itself could have sprung from earthly stock."

She stood trembling, knowing too well, alas, that she was no fine lady at all, but a poor humble peasant girl with a fate worse than death awaiting her in the Seigneur's castle.

They were in a craggy desolate spot above the shore, a lonely place with the world shut out and only the silvern meadows of the sea sparkling away below. She watched with eyes of wonder as Pierre de Louhac loosed a lute from his saddle bow, and the great horse arched its heavy neck and muzzled him lovingly. She did not know that man and beast could feel love and friendship; she had not known that any belted knight, born to oppress and rule and kill, could be so gentle as this man before her.

"Be seated, sweet lady!" he exclaimed, smiling at her as he strummed upon the lute. "How beautiful you are, with flowers in your hair, and your eyes like two stars! Come, sit on this high rock looking toward the sea!"

She complied, not certain whether he were a bit insane, or playing some cruel jest, or just what he seemed. Soon, however, she perceived that there was no guile in him, and no cruelty at all.

"I HAVE come from the south, Lady Elaine," he said, "where the wine and the heart is sunny, where people of the earth are not slaves but free. I rode with the Lord of Fécamp tonight to the hunt, little dreaming that the hunting was of poor folk making merry! No blood is on my hands this night; but when I saw you, destiny came upon me; and I knew that I, Pierre de Louhac, had been fated to capture some sweet queen from the land of the fays, and so I took you."

She comprehended his compassion, his youthful fervent ardor, his imagination; and she held forth her hands to him, smiling faintly. The music of his voice was wondrous to hear, and there was naught to fear from him.

"I—I am only a peasant, Messire Pierre," she said; "I am no lovely lady."

He laughed aloud.

"N O N S E N S E ! W H E N did a peasant lass wear a golden ring? When did ever a peasant have such beauty beyond the world as yours?" He swung a hand toward the far-glinting sea. "Look out yonder, Lady Elaine, and tell me whence you came! From some far land of Lyonesse, it may be, or from a palace glorious, on some far mountain crest; or did the dancing moonbeams bring you from heaven itself to delight the hearts of men?"

Under his glowing words, something of the rapt ecstasy of that hilltop dance, so terribly checked, crept back into her heart. She laughed, and shook back her hair; when a flower fell, he caught it up and crushed it against his lips.

"A song for a flower, then; and perchance another kiss, to make you mortal maid!" said he gayly, and fingering the lute, struck into song.

What he sang, she knew not, for the words were strange; but she nestled in the warm cloak and gave herself up to enchantment and dream as his voice rose in golden glory.

Dream? Enchantment? She knew it could not last, and abandoned herself to the moment with a surge of venture audacious. The frightful vision of Nanny Dubois writhing and dying upon the high rock died away. To her lips came all the old stories of elves and sprites, of mermaids from the sea and the gently-caressing nymphs in forest depths; as she murmured of these things, Pierre de Louhac listened, entranced.

"It is like the tale of Tristan, who died so happily for fair Yseult!" he exclaimed. "You came to me tonight, sweet Elaine, like a benison to heal inward hurts. All this land is adrift with evil and dark cruel things, and the only sure kind touch from any hand is that of Death. Look: tonight I was in sorrow and wonder that such things could be, and you have made all life bright for me! What was the dance we interrupted?"

"The dance of life," she said. "I know not what it means, for it has come down from olden times, but that is the name given to it. The dance of joyous life and hope and springing leaves and fertile fields."

"Kiss me," he said, looking up at her, a glow in his face. "Kiss me, and then dance for me alone—just a step or two! Throw aside the cloak, and dance."

She leaned forward. Her white arms found him, and her lips. Again that wondrous singing fire coursed through her veins; and springing suddenly upright, she let fall the cloak and danced with a burst of heedless happy rejoicing. She danced as never before, in glorious abandon—and suddenly caught up the cloak, laughing, and whirled it around her body.

"Ah, to die upon such loveliness!" sighed Pierre de Louhac, with the look of one rapt in dream. "You are my captive, fair Elaine, but I am yours a thousandfold! Will you ride with me?"

"Ride with you?" She stood staring, brought back to earth. "Whither?"

"Across the world!" Laughing, he flung out a hand. "Mount and ride! You shall be my lady fair, clothed in silks and satins and jewels; I will ever be your true and loyal knight, singing your praises under every roof we reach! We'll go to the Lord of Fécamp's castle here and now, and I'll uphold you as queen of beauty!"

"No, no!" She shrank; that name abruptly broke the charm, the thought of that castled keep of terror and doom. "Oh, you are mad! And I'm mad to let you bewitch me!"

She crumpled, in a flood of tears.

H E, N O T knowing all that lay in her heart, was bewildered and all astray. He could not know that she was in tears for her friends and companions, the girls who had danced, now taken to the castle. And Jehan, far-wandering in the night, lost and desolate, or perchance dead!

Perplexed, he touched his lute, and sang a plaintive, tender little song that went straight into her heart. Her sobs quieted; presently her head lifted, and she spoke to the youth, very sweetly and sadly.

"Dear Messire Pierre, I must tell you the whole truth: I am no lovely lady from sea or moonbeam land; I am just Elaine, a serf of the Lord of Fécamp, a laborer in his fields, a chattel of his hand. Tonight was the festival, and we who danced were his serfs. You saved me from those wolves, and I am grateful; but now mount your horse and ride away. You know the truth. It is a sad and sordid truth, and all your dreams are nothing. I am a peasant, and you are a knight, and the little play is ended. Ride away, and scorn me."

Pierre de Louhac stood up, and smote his lute joyously.

"Not so, by the loving wounds of God!" he said, with earnest impetuous words. "Gentle lady, that man is lonely and desolate and old, who looks upon life with bitter disillusioned eyes, and sees things at their worst. May the blessed saints preserve me from being such! Your loveliness is the most rare and beautiful thing I have found in this life of evil. You are Elaine from across the sea, and I shall hold you so until I die."

"Will you not listen to reason?" she exclaimed. "I can never be one of your fine ladies—"

"No, for you are above them all!" he broke in hotly. "Reason? It's the curse of all mankind. As you danced tonight the dance of life, so we two shall go through the world, joyous and triumphant, not looking with gloomy dark eyes upon things as they are, but touching them with poesy, lifting them into what they should be! When you touch my cheek with your hand, it is an angel from heaven who comes down to inspire me to song; when you ride behind me, it is all the beauty and mirth of the world perched at my shoulder."

"But you are a poet, dear Pierre," she said, smiling.

"And you shall be one too, if you love me a little," he replied.

"You are like a dream," she answered. "You are not like other men I have seen."

He fell to laughing. "Why, that's love, no less! Ho! Sweet Elaine, you've hit upon the very truth of life and youth and love! A kiss upon it!"

She leaned to him, and he caught her in his arms, his finger-tips caressing her fair body as his lips caressed hers. She clung to him, yielding and abandoning all reason, in this embrace that blotted out the whole world.

But the great horse, forgotten, whinnied shrilly in the moonlight, and shook himself with a clank of gear. Pierre de Louhac leaped up, and caught at his lute, laughing.

"Thus," he cried, sweeping the strings, "and thus! A salute to life! A salute to life and love and ecstasy! There shall be no grief and evil in the world; the sunlight shall shimmer upon every heart. You and I, fair Elaine, shall go down to the golden ways of romance hand in hand. Hark, how good gray Ramon summons us!"

Indeed, hearing his name, the powerful destrier shook himself again, and turned his head, looking upon his master. Elaine came to her feet, and drawing the cloak more closely about her, shivered. From afar came a riotous blast of horns, a shrill distant sound of savage voices. A harsh, clanging bell rang thinly.

"Something has happened!" she exclaimed in quick alarm. "Listen! It's the tocsin from the castle—something has happened!"

PIERRE DE LOUHAC laughed aloud. "Aye, this has happened; you and I have met!" he cried, while his fingers touched the lute at his breast. "All the world shall ring wild peals, but they have naught to do with us. Ours is the dance of life, sweet Elaine; let the whole dreary earth reëcho to the dance of death, and we shall behold it not. For ours is the springing tender blade of green, the song in the morn, the smile of the sun on the budding earth, love in the heart and a brave salute, a salute to life—"

His words ended upon a jerk, that shook his whole body.

The lute was riven asunder with a splintering, rending crack. Out of the dark dusky wood close by, came the ringing twang of a bowstring. Pierre de Louhac spun around, and clutched once at the feathered shaft which stood out of his heart, and out of the riven lute; he looked at Elaine, and tried to speak, but no words came. Then he fell, and she stood in palsied, stricken horror.

From the dark covert sprang a swift lithe figure.

"So you're safe, Elaine!" It was Jehan, strong and resolute, in his hand a long English bow of yew, longer than himself. "I've had the devil's own time tracking you here. I put a shaft into that hound of hell—aye, through the Lord of Fécamp himself! Hear the tocsin and the horns? They're riding and killing this night, to make up for it."

The girl's lips were loosened. She broke in upon him with a long and wailing shriek that was echoed from the rocks and smothered by the trees and the moonlight.

"You've killed him! Jehan, Jehan, you've killed him! And he was so kind, so gentle— Oh, it can't be true. Not you, Jehan, not you!"

"FAITH, YOU seem sorry to see me!" said he, with his quick, harsh laugh.

From her lips came another cry, wild and incoherent. She collapsed, all of a sudden, and lay quiet in the moonlight; her bare arm protruded from the cloak, and her hand touched the dead hand of Pierre de Louhac as he smiled at the moonlight.

"Now, here's a queer business for you!"

And wagging his shaggy unshorn head, Jehan came forward, unstrung his bow, and stood looking down at the silent, senseless girl. Gradually his face softened.

"Poor child!" he murmured. "Poor frighted, hunted lass! It's just as well, and saves a power of trouble. The boat's close by, and ere dawn we'll be far down the Breton coast. Poor lass! The devil's paid out; and this fine noble lord is another heartless tyrant gone to hell—two in one night. Lucky I came along just in time to save her from him!"

With which, he went to Pierre de Louhac and took everything of value from the body. Then, shouldering the senseless figure of Elaine with scarcely an effort, he strode across to the shadows and plunged out of sight. For a little, the crashing of brush could be heard as he made descent to the shore and his hidden boat; then silence.

Across the silvern moonlit stage a slow figure moved. It was the massive shape of the horse, coming to the man who lay on his back in the streaming light, a feathered shaft pinning the broken lute to his breast. Upon this stage the moving figure ceased. The horse stood with head drooping, its questing muzzle nudging the white still hand that would finger the lute no more.

T H E   F I L M   had run to its end. A snap, and the room lights whipped on. Kettleman turned to me.

"Like it?"

"Of course. But where does it link up with the theater?"

He waved his hands excitedly.

"Confound it, everywhere! This pageant or instinct from pagan days, was essentially theater. It kept the stage alive; upon this pantomime, mimicry and ancient ritual was based the sense of drama that later flowered into being. From a naked hilltop came a naked stage, which in course of time evolved painted scenery!"

"But why make a tragedy of it and kill off the poet and dreamer?"

"They're always killed in real life," he said testily. "You dullard, couldn't you see any symbolism in the thing?"

"Well, all I could see was that the girl lost her vision and was carried off to fulfill a barbarous destiny of motherhood to a lot of starveling brats."

"Isn't that the fate of every woman?" he cried triumphantly. "And like every woman, she retained the most precious, the rarest, the most beautiful thing in life—a secret memory!"

"Hm! Well, maybe," I admitted. "All the same, perhaps it's just as well that the picture was never released. Ideas, they say, are dangerous unless explained fully."

Kettleman has not spoken to me since that day.

OUTLAWED!

MAY IN Deptford village, and the moon at full above the gray spire of St. Nicholas. Her silver light floated down, warmly caressing many a corpse-face rolling past in the wide river. Roses were in the air, for June lay upon the morrow, but upstream over London rested the quivering horror of the plague. Here in the tavern garden a long board was set with cloth and glass, candles unflickering under the rose-arbor, the wide Thames glinting radiant beyond. A motley throng sat at this table, with a fair, genial man at one end; he had a laughing face, a jovial face, but reckless. Indeed, a reckless and godless man was Kit Marlowe, and worse.

At the other end of the board sat the lone woman of the party, a radiant lass in a neat but common gown, broken shoes, and a necklace of flowers about her throat. In her features lay a forced folly, a desperate laughter; under the lurking fright was a piercing sweetness and tenderness. Even in the moonlight her fresh-washed wealth of hair was like massy gold.

Marlowe, who had begun to drink heavily, lifted his goblet.

"Tomorrow brings June and more roses for Deptford," he cried blithely. "Therefore—more wine for me, and a toast to the blessed damsel who queens our board!"

A burst of voices rang applause. "How be she named?" bawled someone.

Marlowe's gaze swept the company with a touch of scorn.

"A pretty face needs no name and brooks no questions. We

be merchants, clerks, gentry and God knows what, gathered here in hasty flight from London town. If Queen Bess be fled from court, here's Queen Cicely to seek our homage! Cicely, royal salutations!"

Laughter rose, and coarse jests. Rascal or gentleman, lackey or soldier, all these had fled from the terror that stalked through London. Under shadow of the plague, a rogue with money was good as any lord, and could drink as deep. One man, however, spoke out at Marlowe; he was a man in black, a furtive, snarling figure with angry, brooding eyes.

"So you're Master Marlowe, the poet, the agnostic, the man who denies God and heaven!"

"Or hell," added Marlowe, with a roaring laugh.

"I've heard of you, and no good neither."

"That's more than I can say of you, who sit at my board and revile me! What's your name, if you were bequeathed one by any lawful sire?"

"Richard Bame, clerk of Cheapside, am I, and no godless runagate."

Marlowe, a spark in his eyes, was about to reply when the server came and whispered at his ear. Instantly he forgot Bame, and his fist crashed on the board.

"Hola, hola! Rivo Castiliano! Bring him here quickly and set a place! Look you, friends—here's Dick Tarleton of My Lord Chamberlain's company come to seek me! Drollest of all players, most perfect of all fools, the rarest thing in the whole wide world, a loyal heart!"

Marlowe leaped up, hands outstretched as Tarleton approached.

"Come to our hearts, you divine rogue!" he went on gustily. "Not a man here ever heard o' players or poets. To the lot of 'em, fame's but a jade stamped in gold or siller; but here's a lass to raise an ache in your heart! Cicely, fair queen, this be Dick Tarleton of the sober brain and the true spirit!"

TARLETON CAME to the table. He was a quiet young fellow with a rugged, mobile face that could screw into fantastic shapes; but it was grave enough now. He flung off his riding-cloak and swept the lady an exaggerated reverence.

Straightening, he gave her a second and sharper glance, and bowed to the boisterous greetings of the company. He looked once again at Cicely, before he turned and caught the arm of the poet.

"Kit, come aside for a moment or two!" he said. The server

was setting a place and bringing a chair. "I've private word for you. Art drunk?"

"Impossible!" Marlowe, arm in arm with him, swung away down the shell-edged garden path. "Should know me better than to suspect such a thing, Dick."

"Who the devil are these people?"

"How the devil should I know? They straggled in during the day, fugitives from London. But the lass—ah, Dick, the lass is a jewel, a gem o' Samarkand, a very pearl of Araby! She was trudging at a cart-tail. I had her bathed and dressed. Who? Bah! The only name I know is Cicely. I bade 'em all to dine with me, and here we be."

"Then they're not friends of yours?"

Marlowe laughed. "Under this terror, Dick, names and friends are all forgot. Man wants only liquor, and somewhither to flee. Escape for mind and body, that's the cry! I find it rare good fun. These prating cowards, clerks and gentry and merchants— faugh! One but plays with them!"

"You've fallen into your satanic mood, have you?" said Tarleton. "Years ago Ben Jonson called you the kindest heart alive; and that was years ago. When you were young and the royalest of friends—"

"Pox take you, Dick! A sermon?" burst in Marlowe fleeringly.

"No, an errand. I've money for you to squander on that feck-less trull—"

"Careful, lad!" Marlowe halted, and his voice bore warning. "I said the lass is a jewel, and so she is, and hath within her some-thing rarely noble, some quality delicate and fragile that leaps to one's soul. You'll see. Within the hour you'll be her slave. Well, well, no more of this. You bring news?"

"Aye, from Ned Alleyn. He's off with a company o' players to Bristol and the west country. He left a purse with me, saying it was a debt he owed you. I've had no chance to bring it, until now."

Tarleton produced a purse. The poet took it and pocketed it.

"Rare Ned Alleyn! Wilt ever forget him in my Tamburlaine? The lordliest presence of them all! What news from your own company? Is Ben Jonson i' the city?"

"He's gone. Everyone's gone, scattered in mad flight," said Tarleton. "Will Shakespeare and his brother are gone—"

"They would be gone," Marlowe broke in sourly. "I never liked that fellow, Dick. Is it true that you and the other players swore an oath, after that first play was writ for him by another man, never to reveal the secret?"

"Kit, Kit, would you trick me?" Tarleton asked reproachfully.

"If I admitted any such oath, you'd know all. You're not a player, but a writer. I can't let you into what is, after all, a secret of the profession."

"That's answer enough," laughed Marlowe, and he clapped Tarleton on the shoulder. "Old friend, it's a sorry business when the clink o' siller enters into the making of plays. When oaths are sworn. When a rogue is exalted into a great man, upon pretense. When a cheap and petty brain hangs upon the repute of a great and noble brain—"

"Kit, forget all this; you've been drinking," cut in Tarleton abruptly. "And I must be off. I'm riding on, to look up my married sister in Gravesend and stop with her."

"Nonsense, lad! You'll bide here with me."

"Only for a bite and a sup. Art doing a new play?"

"I was, but am no longer." Marlowe looked back at the candles and the company. His fair, eager face was curiously twisted in the moonlight. The gentle kindness of it stood out strangely and strikingly. So did the dark and terrible evil of it, as he went on:

"She's been here two hours, Dick, and the world's different. I know nothing of her, yet I know everything. She's the most rare and delicate creature alive. I've no more than brushed her lips with my fingers—"

"Good God, man, are you serious?" exclaimed the other. "You, the foremost poet in England, the genius of us all, greater than Jonson himself—struck mad by a Bankside wench? I know her face, at least; can't remember where I saw her. Some light-o'-love."

Marlowe put an arm about Tarleton's shoulders and shook his head, smiling gently.

"Lad, I'm close to thirty, and in my time have looked up more than one lane. What counts most is not what has been, but what is! Reality takes a different aspect under the wings o' death, Dick. You don't know her—"

HE BROKE off abruptly, looking back at the table. The boisterous mirth had fallen silent. Forms were stealing off into

*"So you're Master
Marlowe, the poet,
the agnostic, the man
who denies heaven!"*

the darkness. The company, one by one, were leaving the half-eaten feast.

"They fear you, Dick," said Marlowe soberly. "You're just from London, and the terror of the plague is on them."

"Then I'll go—"

"Silent! You'll not. I'm glad your coming has rid me of them. After all, the quicker the devil takes the lot, the better! Look you, lad; I've a new argument in regard to that book which they call the Bible—"

"For shame, Kit!" Tarleton swung upon him with abrupt anger. "Now I know you're drunk and the devil in you. Sober, you're a poet, a dear fellow loved by all the world. Liquor makes you a rascal, a sorry blackguard, a blaspheming, loutish, crafty fiend planning evil to all around… Oh, Kit, Kit!" The comedian's voice broke with sudden agonized appeal. "Will you not see the truth ere it's too late? The noblest heart alive, when sober; and in liquor a foul beast plotting harm to everyone!"

Marlowe broke into a laugh. "Come, lad! Every man has two men in him."

"You have a devil for one o' them," said Tarleton bluntly. "That's why you wanted to know about the oath, with all your fine ranting talk about the clink o' siller and so forth! You're drunk and blaspheming and plotting evil! It's no secret. You, who might be so high, are another man when drunk, and the foul fiend himself is in you!"

Marlowe, still laughing, caught his arm. "Come, Dick; back to the board! As for what ye say, this wanton talk plagues me not. I've heard it often, and it's not true. If I deny God and man, it's from conviction, not from drunken folly. Besides, I'll drink no more this night. Upon my honor. Nor, perhaps, tomorrow neither—tomorrow and tomorrow! Honor bound."

"Good, if ye mean it. No more wine tonight, upon your honor!"

THEY CAME back to the table and the candles. Of the entire company, only Cicely remained, and two men. One was

Richard Bame of the angry eyes; the other sat at Cicely's right hand. He was over-dressed, with a fur-trimmed tabard, green silk doublet, rich lace at throat and wrist, and a profusion of gold chains and jewels. His features were smooth and strong, but his eyes were deep, smoldering, dangerous.

"So fear hath spoiled the supper, for all save us—" began Marlowe. The scowling man, Bame, came to his feet.

"And your blasphemies have spoiled it for me," said he dourly. "Good night."

He went striding away. Dick Tarleton took the place prepared for him and began the meal, hungrily.

Marlowe stood looking at the man beside Cicely.

"Well, good stranger? Neither fear nor blasphemy can spoil your meat?"

The other shook his head. "I've supped wi' the devil before this."

"You're flattering," Marlowe said dryly. "How shall we name you?"

"Francis," replied the other. "A simple country gentleman, my lord."

"Lord me not, ye fool!" snapped Marlowe. A snarl showed in him. All at once, the fine gentleness was gone from his face. For a moment it showed the stamp of a diabolic, sneering fury; then this passed, and Marlowe shrugged and smiled again.

"To me, every poet is a lord," said Francis calmly. He gave Cicely a sidelong glance. If there were no fear in his eyes, there was suddenly no lack of it in hers. "Having paid a full two shillings for upper stalls to enjoy more than one of your plays, may I not worship here free and gladly at your shrine?"

Marlowe looked at him. "A fulsome rogue, and I think a lying one," said he calmly, then pulled out his chair and sat down and fell to meat.

Francis showed no offense, but smiled and spoke under his breath with Cicely. Dick Tarleton glanced from one to another

*Once a hand shot out of the water
as though pointing at them.*

His ranting words stopped at nothing.... In the
midst of it, Sir Francis did what he had come to do.

and ate, and spared no wine. Marlowe, not touching his cup,
looked up as Francis addressed him.

"Master Marlowe, will ye drink a health with me?"

"I will not," said Kit Marlowe curtly. "I'm drinking no more
wine this night. Dick, wilt go out on the water with me and
Cicely, later? Full moon, the river, and a boat to be had—you
shall prick a lute, Dick."

"Not I," said Tarleton. "When my horse is baited, I'm for

Gravesend. Hm! Master Francis and good Mistress Cicely, we've met before this. The Francis tongue hath a touch of Yorkshire that rings familiar."

"Not to my knowledge," said Francis lightly, and Tarleton knew it for a lie. But when he glanced at Cicely, she smiled and nodded to him, a twinkle in her eye.

"I've seen you often, at the theater. You and Kemp, the tragedian, were with Master Burbage the day I spoke with him."

"Ha! By the saints, I remember now!" Tarleton laid down his knife and stared. It came to him how fair she was; another sweet caught in the devilish net of Kit Marlowe—a net apparently all tenderness and nobility, but with Satan grinning at the drawstrings.

"AYE, I remember now," went on Tarleton. "You wanted to play a part. Kit, that's the truth—she wanted to play a woman's part! I swear it! Who has ever heard the like?"

"It's no such nonsense as you seem to think," protested Cicely quickly. "Why shouldn't women be players, too? Why should women's parts always be played by boys? That's the real nonsense!"

Marlowe leaned forward, his eyes warm. The liquor was dying out of him now, as Tarleton could see.

"So you want to play on the stage!" he said to Cicely. "I think it'd be marvelous. All the better that it's never been done. And you came to Diccon and he hemmed and hawed and put you off—good old Burbage! Gad, I can just see him! Must have outraged him to the soul—the very idea of a woman on the stage!"

He slapped his thigh and roared. Tarleton laughed, Cicely smiled; but Francis sat with his gray eyes on Marlowe, giving no sign of any emotion.

"I should like to try it," said Cicely, and sighed a little. "I know I could do it."

She was fair and slim, a slender girl but well budded, her hair like spun silk, her face wide and lovely to see, for all the look

that sat in the blue eyes. Tarleton regarded her with open interest, now, and his heart leaped to the meeting of eyes, for she was
gazing straight at him.

"You shall have the chance," spoke up Marlowe. "I swear it,
lass! Tarleton, lad, why not do a bit with her? A snatch of my
Edward Second—see how it might run on her tongue!"

Cicely looked at Dick Tarleton, and his heart scurried again.

"We—we could not, here i' the garden," said he. "Too many
folk about; it would cause great scandal, were it known."

"Scandal enough without it," spoke up Francis, a certain
unctuous pleasure in his colorless voice. "Master Bame hath
gone to lay complaint of blasphemy against poor Kit Marlowe.
Says he, that a man should so talk against God is sheer lawless
rascality, and the talker an outlaw or should be."

Tarleton looked again at the man, and could make nothing of
him, except some vaguely familiar hint. A queer impassive man,
young enough, but something grim in his eyes of agate-gray.

"Why, we'll take to the water!" said Marlowe. "A barge, with
rowers; a lute for you, Dick, and for me as well. Queen Cicely
to sit enthroned as we float—and you, Sir Fop, with your gold
chains and talk of outlawry, will you accompany us?"

"Thanks, I'll to bed," said Francis. "But not *my* talk of outlawry,
mind you; that was Bame's doing. Outlaw you may be, Master
Kit, in godly eyes, in all decent eyes—outlaw, and a foul beastly
thing in shape of man. However, that's naught of my affair, and
I'll wager all my golden chains against your belt and dagger, that
I can drink you under the table in an hour's time."

"Done," cried Marlowe, evidently between laughter and fury.
This smooth way of hurling insults in his teeth and smiling them
away, baffled him. "Stay! Not now, though; I've sworn to touch
no more wine tonight. Tomorrow noon, let's say!"

"Aye, tomorrow noon." Francis rose, and bent over the hand
of Cicely, with a bow of Castilian grace. "Fair queen, make the
most of your poet by this silver moon, for he'll be too drunk to
see it tomorrow night!"

He swaggered away into the darkness and was gone, toward the tavern. Marlowe turned to Dick Tarleton and besought him to stay the night. The player, looking past Marlowe's cheek, met the gaze of Cicely.

"Stay!" said her eyes, and her face confirmed the word.

"Why, then," said Tarleton, "I'll stay, Kit. Since you're drinking no wine for love o'me, the least I can do is to play up to you!"

MARLOWE SHOUTED for the landlord, got a bed put in his room for Tarleton, arranged about the player's horse, and secured a barge and oarsmen. He flung away toward the tavern in search of his own lute. Dick Tarleton found himself alone with Cicely.

"Quickly!" he said to her, his eyes urgent. "What's he to you?"

Whether it were the candles or the moonlight, color rose in her cheeks.

"Nothing," she said bitterly, "but how can I help it? If he wants me, he must have me. I've no choice. All my world was wiped out by the sickness. I can't earn my bread by singing madrigals and playing the lute."

"You don't know him," Tarleton said hotly. "See him in liquor, before you decide. The poet then becomes a ravening beast— crafty, elemental, brutish! Those who loved him have turned from him. His friends warn others against him, as I warn you."

"Perhaps he needs me," said she.

"No. I need you," Tarleton rejoined, and looked into her eyes.

"AND YOU call yourself his friend?" Her voice held a hint of scorn.

"God forbid! I'd save him if I could; no one can," said Tarleton. "The nobler part in Kit recognizes your worth and loveliness; the devil in him will debase and kill you. He has done this to others. There was a lass only a year ago—a certain Mistress Anne—who died because she thought he was an angel, and found otherwise. Indeed, it is no secret how liquor makes this frightful change in him, as it has changed his whole life. But I'm staying until the morrow, because of what I read in your face, and because of what my heart tells me."

She laughed in faint derision.

"A play-actor who misses no chance at a light-o'-love, eh?"

"Shame to you for those words," said Tarleton quietly. A flicker of the candles brought out the grave, earnest lines of his face. She leaned forward, suddenly contrite.

"I'm sorry, indeed I am! But who am I? Nothing. A toy for men. I must fight all you men—him, and you, and that one who was here last—"

"You don't have to fight," broke in Tarleton. "Instead, trust. Fight the others; trust me. Keep that thought in your mind. Who was that fellow last here? That Francis? A liar, by the feel of him. You know him?"

"No," she said. "But he frightened me. There was some terrible thing in him—a deadly hatred, perhaps. I could feel it; just as I feel faith and kindliness in you."

Tarleton grunted. "And what feel you in Kit?"

"Fascination and—and fear," she said. "Something wonderful yet terrible."

"Keep your feelings to yourself, unless you want to burn for a witch," he said quickly. "Above all, trust not Kit with such words. A stoup of wine or two, and he'd scheme to see you burned. Here he comes. Tomorrow, say the word and I'll face him down, and take you away to my sister in Gravesend; and I'll ask naught in return."

Kit Marlowe came with a laugh and a gleeful shout. He swept them up in his impetuous way and all three hastened down the paths to the river, where a barge with four rowers was now waiting at the landing.

Cicely took the lute from Marlowe and pricked it deftly. Never was Kit more charming, more merrily debonair; he sang his own songs, and Cicely sang, and Dick Tarleton did a bit or two in character until his clowning set them in a gale of laughter. Then the boatmen were roused to song likewise, what with brown ale and Marlowe's urging, and took up the old Saxon drinking catch, with its silly rhymes:

Take a deep deep draft, and think of how we laughed
When the tankard fell adown on the fat old abbot's crown....
So drink your fill of the beery rill
And then go down in motley.

Thus all made merry on the silvery radiant tide, wherein every now and again flashed a white and horrible face rolling down in deathly wise to the sea. Once a hand shot out of the water as though pointing at them; this made Cicely cry out and cover her eyes, but Kit Marlowe only hummed another catch.

He who devils this devil around
The fitter the saint will be!

"Not a half bad philosophy, whether applied to a bottle or a loose habit!" exclaimed Tarleton, laughing. "I'll apply it to the Virginia tobacco and never smoke another pipe, Kit, provided you'll do the same with the bottle. Eh?"

"Avaunt, tempter!" Marlowe clapped him jovially on the shoulder. "I'll do nothing of the sort. What, abandon good liquor? Never while I live, lad—never!"

Later, when the lass had drifted off to sleep and the rowers were heading back to the Deptford landing, Tarleton touched the poet's arm and spoke very softly.

"Ye saw the corpse-hand pointing, Kit? Look, now; maybe to you it was pointing, in warning. Try none of your tricks with Cicely."

Marlowe stared at him in the high moonlight.

"*My* tricks? You dare to speak thus?"

"Think of Anne Shipley, Kit. With her death, ye lost your last friends. I've hung on longer than most, but now it's ended. I'll take this lass from you if I can, so there's fair warning."

The poet took a deep breath, and laughed a little.

"Why, Dick, I could love ye for those words, loved I not this fine fellow Tarleton already! So, you're taken with her? I am also. I'll not let ye catch her away from me; and there's fair warning back at you. But you and I are friends, can win and lose like friends, and no need o' swordplay."

He put out his hand, and Tarleton gripped it.

"Well said, Kit, and truly meant," he answered sadly, "but God save us if you start drinking again tomorrow! Then I'll to sword if I must, for her sake."

"And you, who this same evening called her a feckless trull!" chuckled Marlowe.

"True; my eyes hadn't been opened," Tarleton admitted simply. "Something in her has gone straight to my soul, as it has to yours. Ah, Kit! I'd give her up gladly, could you but have faith and all the high nobility of your genius—"

"Stop whining like an old woman," broke in the poet roughly. "I believe in nothing beyond what I see and hear and feel; that's plenty, too. Genius? Tommy-rot, lad! Away with all that nonsense. Had I not desired to keep my oath to you, I'd be roaring merry this moment, instead of going home with a sad heart and evil presages."

"Evil presages on such a night? Heaven forbid!" exclaimed Tarleton comfortably. "I've seen none and felt none, unless it were that hand rising from the water and pointing. By the way, who is that man with the queer eyes—that fellow Francis?"

"Who knows or cares?" retorted Marlowe. "Dick, you've given me straight, true words; I thank you for 'em. Now wake the lass and ask her choice. If she'll have you, take her and begone, with my blessing."

"Not so," Tarleton objected. "Sleep on it, Kit. If I'm o' the same mind regarding her in the morning, I'll take you at your word."

S O   T H E Y came back to the tavern and stumbled up to bed. Marlowe was snoring in no time, but Dick Tarleton lay staring upon the moonlit window, sleep evading him.

He was under no illusions about the splendid brawny Marlowe, the genius whose young thunderous voice had rung through England. The poet was not yet thirty, but for the past two or three years had been more and more silent as the frightful change crept upon his life. That generous, noble spirit had been gradually gnawed away until now the mere breath of alcohol wakened a malignant flame in the man....

Wakening, Tarleton found himself alone in the room. He dressed and went down to the inn-yard pump, discovering that Marlowe had gone to the river with some townsfolk in order to see some great ship newly anchored there. His ablutions made, Tarleton went into the ordinary for his morning draught, and was sitting there over a long pipe when Cicely made her appearance. He rose, and they laughed together in joyous greeting.

"You look like a spring primrose!" said he presently, when she was quaffing her draught of milk. "Tell me, Cicely, have ye no relatives?"

"I have nothing," she said with a terrible simplicity.

"That's not the right sort o' talk for a June morning! June is in today, lass!" he exclaimed. "Nothing? You have everything! All I can give you, from name to the silver groat in my pocket. I'm no roaring gallant of nimble tongue, nor one of the gay careless crew who have made the stage and all plays a mess of vileness, to the disgust of sober folk. I'll take ye as ye take me, at face value and the bid o' the heart, if you say the word!"

She smiled as she watched him; it was a tender, wise smile.

"Master Tarleton, I do not love you, nor you me; but I might, I might! Wilt give me time to think?"

"Not under this roof," Tarleton replied bluntly. "Kit said to ask you; if ye prefer me, we go with his blessing. Need not stare, lass! I'm no liar."

"I know that," she replied. "Dick Tarleton, will you help me to play stage parts?"

"No wife o' mine shall set foot on the stage," he said firmly. "Lass, it's a bawdy place. Bacon and Barclay and their ilk will ha' none of it for that reason. Nor shall you."

"Some day," she said, looking out at the blue sky and the river, "some day woman's parts will be played by women, and the stage will discover what it's missed all these years."

"Will ye go home with me to my sister in Gravesend?" asked Tarleton steadily. "Or stay here with Kit?"

Her eyes came back to him and dwelt upon his face for a long moment.

"You know the answer well," she replied at last. "But I'll not sneak out while his back is turned."

TARLETON BEAMED, and reached for her hand, and gripped it warmly.

"We be of a kind, lass, you and I! Go and pack. I'll wait here."

"Pack? I have nothing." She looked down at her dress. "He got me this, yesterday."

"Then we'll get my horse saddled, and another for you, and be ready to go when he comes back, if that suits you. Don't remain long enough for drink to get into him."

"It suits me," she assented gravely.

He gave the orders, hiring a horse for Cicely. They were talking together when one came from the upstairs and joined them with a cheery greeting; it was Francis, his eyes gray and chill as ever. They exchanged a few words, and as he went out to put his head under the pump, Cicely looked after him.

"I know now—I remember!" she exclaimed. "I knew I'd seen him somewhere. He was with the Earl of Montgomery's following; a gentleman of his. Someone pointed him out to me, for he and the Earl were arm in arm and most handsomely dressed. This was at the Revels last Twelfth Night."

"Aye?" queried Tarleton, in amazement. "This agate-eye a great gentleman? And his name?"

She shook her head. "I can't mind it now, but I vow he's the same man. Ah! There he comes—look!"

BUT SHE spoke not of Francis now, but of Marlowe, who came swinging and swaggering in from the open, to stand blinking at the dark room and then cross to where they sat.

He greeted Cicely as though she were Queen Bess in person, then met the eye of Tarleton, and came erect under that steady, unflinching regard.

"What, Dick?" said he. "Ye look at me mortal hard. What's to do?"

"This, Kit," Tarleton said quietly. "Cicely desires to go with me. The horses are ready; we waited to face you with it."

Marlowe's features changed, twisted, became suffused with blood, then paled again. His eyes gripped Cicely with an expression of dismay. He found fumbling words.

"Why, little lass, would ye leave me?"

"It was only yesterday I came, Kit," she said gently.

"But I can't lose you like this!" he cried out. "It's impossible! You must stay!"

"I will stay for a while, on one condition," she told him. "Provided you touch no drop of any liquor, Kit."

"Absurd! That I should let you injure me, condition this and that, prove your unfaith by promises of faith as to a child!" Marlowe said, with a burst of anger. Almost at once it passed, and he drew a deep breath like a sigh. "Well, I found a precious thing and it slipped from my hand," he said slowly. "Go with her, Dick; art a loyal man. How rarely lucky are they that have not spirit to plunge into the lusts of life! My blessing follow after you, Cicely."

With this queer speech, he turned from them, strode out into the courtyard, and when the two followed, he was standing in hearty greeting with the man Francis. They mounted, and Marlowe waved heartily to them, and Francis bowed with the grace of one trained in courts.

They rode out of the inn yard and out of Deptford, taking the downstream road for Gravesend. High twelve came, and passed again; they stopped to eat bread and cheese under the shadow of a hawthorn hedge, and there spoke of Kit for the first time.

"It was nobly done of him," said Tarleton gravely.

She nodded.

"Yes. He might have said many things; I expected him to upbraid me. And if he had begged me, Dick, I must have stayed a while, for very decency toward him!"

"Art sorry now?" queried Tarleton.

"Nay! All's well with the June world!" she said brightly. "Better here than there, with the cold gray eyes of Sir Ralph eating into me like worms!"

"Who?" demanded Tarleton.

She laughed at his gawking face.

"Oh, Sir Ralph Shipley! I just remembered his name, as we were riding. You know… the man who calls himself Francis."

Tarleton sat frozen, until an incoherent cry escaped him. He came to his feet abruptly and his hands were shaking.

"Shipley, Shipley!" he exclaimed, plunging to catch his horse. "God of furies—Anne Shipley's brother! Wait for me here, lass—wait for me here—"

He mounted and spurred; behind him lifted the dust of a madman's riding.

IN THE tavern at Deptford, Kit Marlowe sat with Francis, the two of them drinking with many a jest and racy story. By little and little, Marlowe fell to cursing and blaspheming. True, he had never been a man for monkery; yet in the old days when his star rose so brightly, there had been no venom in his words.

Now it was different, as the heady wine took hold of him. It was strange, almost incredible, how the temper of the man changed. His ranting words stopped at nothing, and what had been a noble mind became a pool of vileness.

In the midst of this, Francis did what he had come to do, then mounted his horse and rode away….

A little later, Tarleton's foam-lathered steed came to halt in the inn yard. Almost at once he found he was too late. The host came running to him with news Marlowe was stabbed, but not yet dead.

"Oh, sir, if ye be a surgeon, look to him quickly!" pleaded

the innkeeper. "There be none roundabout, and he'll not let us touch him—"

TARLETON CAME to where the dying man lay. Sober now—dreadfully sober—Marlowe smiled up at him.

"Dick, lad! Nay, leave my wound alone; I've but a moment or two left."

"I came to warn ye!" babbled Tarleton, kneeling and holding the chill hand. "It was her brother! I just learned—"

"Aye, so he told me. Careful, lad! Speak not the name!" Marlowe's fingers clenched hard on his. "Let him be known as Francis, nothing more. Swear it to me, swear it! Let him go unpursued, unknown—after all, I was to blame for her death—swear it!"

Dick Tarleton swore the oath. Marlowe sighed and relaxed, and smiled again.

"Well done, well done. Dick, he was a curious man!" he said faintly. "He would not strike last night, as he meant, for I stopped drinking then. He had to make me drunk, d'ye mind? And why, think you? He told me before he left. So he could send me to hell in the midst o' blasphemies... he believes all that stuff... he wanted to make sure of landing me in—in hell."

Kit Marlowe died upon the word....

Tarleton did what might be done, which was little enough. With the plague in London and the terror of it everywhere, no one cared whether poet or great lord or street-beggar lay dead in a corner. Lucky was a man to get burial at all, with the Thames so close!

However, Dick Tarleton arranged the burial, securing a niche under the gray walls of St. Nicholas. Keeping his oath to say no word regarding Francis, he set out at last, his face toward the waiting Cicely and Gravesend.

As he rode, he wondered within himself because Kit Marlowe had died smiling, the cold relaxed face very gentle and sweet to look upon. Thus wondering, he rode on, a loyal, genuine fellow who happily suffered not from the tortures and temptings of genius!

And in Deptford town lay the poet of "Tamburlaine" and "Faustus," a voice of gold forever outlawed and silent.

HELL'S MOUTH

IT WAS sheer fatality that when Hilary rode into London, a group of court gentlemen were talking at the gate. Chief among them was Sir John Dymoke, king's champion and commander of the guards. A cousin of the powerful Derbyshire Dymokes, Sir John was a great man at Henry Tudor's court, and ever loved to push himself forward.

Hilary was a merry heart, had a lean face with laughing eyes, a long arm, and a sword that slapped his nag's barrel. His old and mended boots bore polished golden spurs that went ill with his shabby costume, so obviously of foreign cut. He bestrode a sorry barebones nag he had picked up when he landed at Calais, but the old lean-shanks was gayly decked out with green leaves and garlands of primroses; April was in by this time.

The golden spurs caught the eye of Sir John Dymoke, who beckoned guards and stepped forth to halt Hilary.

"Sirrah foreigner," he exclaimed, "how dare a rascal like you wear a knight's spurs?"

The cheerful Hilary drew rein, and produced a number of ragged parchments.

"Foreigner, my lord? Faith, I was born in England, though I'm just from abroad," said he. "Here's my passport, issued by Count Baldwin of Flanders. Another bearing the seal of Prince Jehan of Orange, who dubbed me knight. Another from the lord of Augsberg in Germany, certifying Hilary of Derby to be a free student of the university there; another from the University of Milan—"

Dymoke, who could read, scanned the parchments and the seals, handed them back, and grudgingly waved Hilary on. Learning who this lord was, Hilary spurred the old nag hastily ahead and cursed the mischance that brought his name to this man's attention. No help for it, however; the damage had been done. He could only hope that Dymoke would forget the whole thing.

After eight years on the Continent, Sir Hilary in this year of our Lord 1498 brought back to England a surname he dared not use, a crowbait horse, the shabby clothes on his back, and parchments attesting his scholarship and knighthood as Hilary of Derby. If he carried a fat purse hidden away, he said nothing of it, but hastened into the broil of London town. There he lost himself in the immense throngs of merchants, Flemish and Dutch and French and Hanseatic, who swarmed on the hither

edge of Cheapside. He sold his old barebones nag for a trifle, and took lodgings at the sign of the Saracen's Head.

Before noon he was shaven and shorn, and had paid with broad Flemish silver for a new surcoat of Lincoln green, clean linen and new cordovan boots. Thus changed, he began inquiries for one Jehan Bodel, prying into every nook and corner. The name was known but not the man, and he had no luck until evening drew on.

Knight and Devil were at it, when from somewhere lifted a frantic scream. Then Hell's Mouth exploded.

THEN; AS Hilary was slaking his thirst in a Thames-side tavern, a huge hand clapped him on the shoulder, and a sonorous voice boomed out in Latin:

"Hilarius, the eighth wonder of the world! Hilarius himself, or his ghost afoot!"

Hilary turned. Beside him was a tall, swarthy, monstrous lean man with dancing black eyes and long black mustaches. Hilarius embraced him, incredulous and joyous.

"The Devil himself! Master Satan, well met, well met! I didn't know you were in England. Why, I haven't seen you since we parted at Beauvais a year ago and more!"

Master Satan grinned widely. "I came over two months ago, Hilarius, to take a place with my lord of Somerset's company. *Diavolo!* I speak no English; they speak no Italian. What, say they, a devil who speaks Italian only? We compromise on Latin, but Lord Somerset likes it not and seeks to oust me from the company."

"I'm seeking Jehan Bodel. Do you know where I can find him?"

"Ha! The Devil knows everything!" said Master Satan complacently. "He is to meet me here, and is due at any moment. Poor Jehan has had ill luck. He put on his big miracle-play in some accursed town called Nottingham, and when Hell's Mouth was opened, the booths all around caught fire, the shopmen pursued him at law, and he was ruined. He needs luck, I can tell you! Look—I think I see him at the door now!"

"Careful, Sathanas!" Hilary caught his arm. "We'll have some fun. Introduce me as a mummer just arrived from Italy—say, Petruccio, of Milan."

As he spoke, Hilary changed. He hunched one shoulder, became stooped and round-backed, and drew up the hood of his surcoat over head and face. Even his voice altered and was a whining Italian. Master Satan exploded in laughter, and then sent a bellow of greeting at the man who was pushing through the crowd around the door.

Jehan Bodel was a powerful but gloomy man with saturnine eye and scarred features, a famous writer and player, and producer of miracles and mysteries—that is, he was famed in other lands, but here in England it was different. Here he was buffeted by rude insular ignorance; here a player or mummer was classed with grooms and barber-surgeons and lackeys, by the folk at large. So racked and torn and bloodied was all England by the wars of Lancaster and York that now, in the slow years of recovery under Henry Tudor, a juggler or acrobat won more renown than the cleverest writer or mummer of miracle-plays and pageantry.

HILARY, IN his assumed whine, acknowledged the introduction.

"Bodel, Bodel?" said he, shaking his head. "I never heard of you."

"Never heard of Jehan Bodel?" The Frenchman stiffened. "Never heard of my great miracle of St. Nicholas, which comprises everything from tavern revels and the Crusades to the story of the good saint himself?"

"Never," said Hilary. "And you speak abominable Italian, Messer Bodel. Come! I'm hungry, and have money to buy food and drink for us all. Let's to a table."

They settled down in a corner, Hilary keeping his hooded features out of the light, the lank Satan grinning and chortling, and Jehan Bodel a picture of offended dignity. Meat pies and wine were brought. Hilary flung down a gold-piece, to the amazement of the entire tavern; enough groats could scarcely be found in the place to make change. The crowd eyed these three, two of whom spoke a chattering foreign tongue, with eyes of dislike and suspicion.

"Come, Messer Bodel," said Hilary. "I've just landed in England, and have been for some years a slave to the Egyptian mamelukes. Formerly I was a player and writer of miracles and passions, but now I know little of how the profession goes. In this country, for example—"

*"Foreigner, my lord?
Faith, I was born in
England," said Hilary.
"Here's my passport."*

"It goes sadly, sadly, in the whole world!" Bodel shook his head mournfully. "Alas, that we could not have lived in the glorious days of old! Here in England, chivalry perished with the Black Prince; the Tudor king is upbuilding a land swept by war and pestilence. The Black Death has depopulated the whole realm of earth. The troubadours of the south are only a memory, and Provence is a desert of gray stone. Everywhere war and pestilence and famine, with the profession fallen upon evil days.

We're living in an age of depression, of debased money, of art reduced to a commercial level; moneylenders and swordsmen are become princes, and artists like ourselves are no better than swineherds, lucky to feast on the husks!"

"But Satan still finds work to do?" Hilary cast a twinkling eye at the lean Italian, who chuckled:

"Jehan tells the truth, comrade. Faith, poor Satan hasn't had a square meal for a week, till he sat down to this mutton pasty! Your health, lord, your health!"

Hilary took the hint and ordered more wine.

"Did you ever hear," he asked, "of an English writer and player named Hilary of Derby? By all accounts an arrant rogue, a rascal who would cut a throat or—"

"Stop!" burst out Jehan Bodel. He fingered his dagger. "Stop! He is no such thing; speak ill of him, and I'll have your ears! I knew him well, in France. A man of marvelous parts, of infinite ingenuity, with the voice of an angel! I remember, at Beauvais, he made an arrangement of the Festa Asinaria, the New Year's Eve farce that we presented before the cathedral doors—"

"Ha! I've heard of it!" Hilary caught up his pewter spoon and began to clink it against his winecup. "I remember a refrain. It went like this."

His voice rose, a full, ringing baritone:

"Say Amen, most reverend Ass,
Now your belly's full of grass,
Say Amen again and pray
Like a chorister at play!
Hey va! Hey va! Hey va! Hey!
Open your lovely mouth and bray!
A fistful of hay and the Devil to pay,
And oats aplenty for you today!"

A roar of delight and approbation and laughter came from the throng in the tavern. Jehan Bodel leaned back and crossed himself, and stared affrightedly.

"The very words! The very voice of Hilarius himself!" he gasped.

WITH A shout of laughter, Hilary straightened up, flung back his hood, and embraced the big Frenchman. Master Satan held his sides with mirth. Bodel was pouring out a volley of questions, but Hilary silenced them.

"Careful, comrade! There are reasons for not talking here. Have you a safe place?"

Bodel grimaced. "Only the van, and little Tumbler the dwarf. Six months ago the company was rolling in money; now I've nothing left except Tumbler and the van—bad luck, evil times! It used to be that all Englishmen spoke French. Now they don't, and few of us speak this barbarous language well, so there y'are. The old families, the great lords, were ruined by the wars and a new crop has risen; everyone out for loot, and plague take the rascals of players! If you want privacy, we can find it at the van."

Hilary nodded. "Good! Satan, here's money—buy food and wine to take along. Never mind staring and questioning, man! Either fortune's waiting for us all, or our necks will hang askew on a gallows, and that very soon! Where's your wagon, Jehan?"

"In the fields behind the Temple and Lincoln's Inn."

Laden with flagons and parcels, the three sallied forth, talking in an excited medley of French, Italian and Latin—a tongue known to all players, who still used it in the majority of their performances. Blazing stars and a high white moon lit the narrow streets. Two of the three, at least, were what they seemed.

Hilary, the wandering scholar-player-writer, known everywhere on the continent. Master Satan, famed if not fat by reason of his marvelous portrayal of the foul fiend in all miracles and mysteries; and the great, if momentarily "resting" Jehan Bodel, author and player and producer of many a storied spectacle. Great names, these, from Italy to the German marches, but in England unknown and unsung.

Not that players were unpopular; far from it. The land had been soaked in the agony of merciless civil war these many years.

Now, recovering under Henry Tudor, men turned eagerly to spectacles, to miracles and farces, to anything that would divert and entertain; but they were not critical in the matter. To them, the profession was one of wastrels, loose women, looser men, on a level with thieving vagabonds. The Tower and Temple Gate still dripped with the blood from severed heads, and life was too grisly a scramble for any appreciation of art.

THE THREE strode along. Houses were scarcer now, and in the fields they came upon homeless folk encamped. Presently loomed an enormous covered wagon with horses grazing near by. Beside red embers was a queer little figure who leaped up eagerly to greet them. This was Tumbler, the shrewd dwarf, who stored in his tiny body the devotion and kindliness of an angel.

"Here's meat and drink, Tumbler!" cried Jehan Bodel, unburdening himself. "And look who's here! The great Hilarius—remember how he played with us in Beauvais?"

Tumbler seized Hilary's hand and kissed it, with shrill joyous chatterings. All four now settled about the tiny fire. Bodel and Master Satan waited in somewhat anxious perplexity. Hilary could comprehend this; the life of a player might be silks and satins today, and scourging and chains tomorrow.

"Friends, here's a bid for great fortune at one blow," he said quietly. "As you must know, the King's gone from London, visiting in the north and the midlands. I hear he's to be in Nottingham and Derby soon. Well, if we can get away and catch Henry Tudor's eyes, this company of strollers is made for life! We're the best, the very top of the profession; I've money and will venture the last groat. What say you, Jehan?"

JEHAN BODEL caught his breath. "Glorious—if true! I can't believe it."

"Have faith, you rascal! However, there's much to settle." Hilary lost his gay air and spoke on gravely. "First, Jehan, what would be the best vehicle to carry us a-traveling? I've been eight years out of England, remember. A farce, perhaps? Or the good old morality?"

"Miracles are always safe, but are out of fashion," rejoined Bodel. "Moralities are on the make, somewhat, in the form of guild pageants; but only at certain seasons. Just now, masques are greatly favored. Masques in the Italian manner, a mixture of morality and farce, with juggling and mummers on the side and a bit of swordplay to catch a soldier's eye. We'd need two vans and a dozen players; most of them would have to double in music."

"You shall have them." Hilary produced a purse, clinked it, and handed it over. "My fortune, or most of it, gambled on destiny! Sign up Master Satan, here, for he's a master hand with sword and dagger. He and I can answer for your swordplay."

"Are you an angel from heaven?" exclaimed the amazed Bodel.

"More likely from the other place," Hilary laughed curtly. "You've not heard all. When can we take the road for the center of England?"

"In three days. Broken remnants of the profession are all around London; I'll get another van and the proper troupe in no time. But we must have a license."

"I can get a license from Milor Somerset," put in Master Satan. "His steward would give one only too gladly, to get rid of me. Count it done. We go on the road, then?"

"To Derby, and a day's travel beyond," Hilary rejoined, "where the venture awaits me. If I win, I win greatly. If I lose, then it may mean the gallows for us all."

The others remained silent. They divined something more than play-acting ahead, and Hilary sensed the unuttered question. In all fairness, he must answer it with plain words. He could trust these three absolutely.

"If I were recognized, which is unlikely, or if my true name were to become known," he said then quietly, "I'd be hanged, drawn and quartered. My whole family came to that end eight years ago. I escaped, a stripling, and got to France and safety, hiding under the guise in which you now see me."

*"The sharp-witted little rascal brought ill news: The
city's being combed for one Sir Hilary de Grenville."*

"I always felt you were no common man," said Jehan Bodel
in a low voice. "Treason?"

"So charged, at least. Another family wanted what mine
had—and got it. There's the whole thing in a nutshell." With a
change of manner, he turned to the Frenchman. "Sathanas tells
me you had bad luck in Nottingham."

"Terrible," said Bodel.

"Then we'll avoid that place and go direct to Derby, giving
our first performance there and picking up news of the King.
On our way to meet him, we'll play at Edgekill Castle, just

north of Derby. It's now held by the Dymoke family, which is none of mine."

"Oh! And there?" queried Jehan Bodel thoughtfully.

"There I pick up what belongs to me. It's safely hidden, and has awaited me eight years. That's all. Do you risk the venture, Jehan? Your silence argues hesitation."

"Bah! I was wondering how we might help you more greatly," said Jehan, and Master Satan grunted assent.

Hilary laughed lightly.

"That's help enough. I'd best keep my name secret, even from you; not for lack of trust, but you'd be that much safer should ill luck hit us. Now, what about writing the masque?"

"Oh, simply done!" grunted Bodel. "I'll adapt my St. Nicholas pageant. A noble knight's part for you, eh? No armor, just surcoat and sword. Right?"

"Right." Hilary rose. "I'm off; must buy a good horse tomorrow. Send me word when you're ready to take the road."

All went well, except that, at the last moment, the dwarf fell ill and must be left behind, to follow on horseback. He could spend two or three days under a leech's care and still pick up the slow-moving van without trouble, long ere Derby was reached. A gentle fellow was this Tumbler, very merry and stout of heart, with the agile brains of his ilk.

Six-score miles from London lay the craggy hills of Derbyshire, and the Derwent beyond, in England's very center. It was slow progress for the two enormous vans, double-deckers; below were the living-quarters and dressing-rooms, up above was a stage-platform. They creaked along at snail's pace.

O N   T H E   way north, Hilary worked on the script of the piece with Bodel, getting it fashioned to suit his purpose and the persons of the company. These were a dozen in all, chiefly French or Italians. If the three females included were not precisely blessed damozels, at least they could play a full dozen rôles and be thrust into Hell's Mouth at the end of the show with loud repentant cries, to a good conscience. The great feature of Jehan

Bodel's production was this Hell's Mouth, an old bit of stage property which he had elaborated into a wonderful affair.

"English Hilary and his company out of Italy—there's our title," said Hilary. "An Englishman at the head of it; that will raise curiosity and down all prejudice against foreigners! Better make it a two-hour show at Derby, Jehan, cutting out all the *St. John Baptist* incidents. At Edgekill, we'll make it full three hours; the extra hour while I'm offstage will give me the time I need."

Finally, Hilary rode on ahead of the company and came into Derby to make the advance arrangements; he kept to his hunched figure and unnatural voice. He had no trouble with the burgesses, who regarded foreigners askance but met an English player with right good will. They granted him the marketplace before St. Alkmund's church for the performance, and everything was planned for the following evening. The wagons would arrive next day.

WITH EARLY morning, however, Hilary found himself shaken awake. Jehan Bodel was standing over him, spattered with mud from hard riding.

"I came on to join you here with warning," said the Frenchman, looking anxious. "Tumbler caught up with us last night; the sharp-witted little rascal brought ill news, I fear. There's a hue and cry in London. The whole city's being combed for one Sir Hilary de Greville, an exile under attainder. He has recently come from abroad to foment a plot against the King's life. Rewards are offered for him. Couriers have gone to the sheriffs of the shires ordering that he be seized or killed on sight. He's said to be a young man."

Hilary shook the hair out of his eyes and stared up.

"Well? What's that got to do with me? The name's a common one."

"*Diable!* Tumbler made sure it was you!" said the other blankly. "They have a description. The golden spurs, passports from Orange and Flanders—"

"Come, listen to me." Hilary drew Bodel down beside him

on the bed. "I've no more need of those passports. All this is the doing of the Dymoke family. I met Sir John Dymoke when I entered London. He's put two and two together. Now the whole tribe are out like dogs on a boar. If they get me out of the way, ye see, no one could ever contest their ownership of Edgekill Castle. Bah! Let 'em seek Hilary de Greville and be damned! They'll not find their man in English Hilary the mummer!"

"Then it is you?"

"Aye."

"And the plot? This plot against the King's life?"

"A lie, upon my honor! My only plot is to get what belongs to me; gold, the family papers, the bills of exchange that are hidden away in that castle. Upon my honor, Jehan!"

Bodel nodded, and drew a long breath. "Then all's well. Now, we'll help you to get away from here—"

"Get away?" Hilary burst into a laugh. "Don't you see, I'm safely hidden already? No better could be asked. So no more of it. Now, I've great news for you, Jehan! We're to play before the King himself."

"The King! Henry Tudor here?"

"No. He's spending a fortnight hunting and amusing himself—where, think you? Why, at Edgekill Castle, of all places, with his friend Sir Hugo Dymoke! Think of it, think how luck plays into our hands! Tonight we give the show here tomorrow night, at Edgekill. I've sent word there to let 'em know. They'll seize such a chance to divert the King, never fear!"

Jehan Bodel shook his head gravely.

"My friend, think of the risk for you! According to Tumbler's news, the King is determined to root you out; you're supposed to be plotting his death—"

"The King knows nothing about it," broke in Hilary. "Besides, Henry Tudor doesn't cherish old grudges, from what I hear of him. It's the Dymoke family who want to root me out and end the house of Greville once and for all! Even if the Dymoke who saw me at London gate were to be here in Edgekill, he could

*"What I chiefly want," said Hilary, "are
the bills of exchange. There's gold too;
take what you can, and so will I."*

look at me and never recognize me in Hilary the mummer. It
was those accursed passports, with their mention of Hilary of
Derby, which started all this hue and cry. Well, when do the
vans arrive?"

"In three hours, or less."

"Then let's get the day started, and I'll show you around."

Since Hilary, here in Derby town, was a limping, hunched,
humble rascal with lines of age etched in his lean face, Jehan
Bodel was soon convinced there was little or no danger. By the

time the vans creaked into town, he was in high spirits; and when afternoon brought a courier from Edgekill with word that the company would be highly welcome there and would be expected next day, the mercurial Frenchman was soaring.

As for the dwarf Tumbler, he grinned and kept his tongue between his teeth.

THUS, THAT same evening, the first performance of the masque went off uproariously; it was part miracle, part masque, part juggling show. *Satan* and the *Knight*, behind vizors, did their sword-play. *Satan* was finally driven into the fiery mouth of the huge paper dragonhead that represented Hell, and the poor lost ladies were shoved in by lesser devils for whom the jugglers doubled. With Virtue thus triumphant, a rich harvest was reaped from the town and country folk and the burgesses and the clerics, who highly complimented English Hilary upon the moral tone of his Italian company.

Long before dawn, the vans were off, creaking northward toward Edgekill. Hilary jogged along with Master Satan and Bodel, on horseback.

"No wonder you had bad luck in Nottingham," said Hilary, "if you handled your sulphur and gunpowder and brimstone with reckless hand like you did last night, Jehan!"

"Eh? It was necessary, man! Hell's Mouth must look the part!"

"But we're not due for hell yet, I trust!" Hilary retorted with a chuckle. "Last night I removed some of your tarred tow and shavings. As it was, that paper dragon near went up in flames."

"Ha! So it was you! I thought the effect fell rather flat." Jehan Bodel laughed and shrugged. "Very well, my friend, I'll have a care. But remember, for the King himself, Hell's Mouth must look better than a child's bonfire!"

In midmorning, a company of horsemen overtook the vans, and drew rein. Here were a pair of knights with attendant squires, a dozen men-at-arms, and as many archers. In one of the knights, Hilary recognized that same Sir John Dymoke who had admitted him to London town. But Sir John did not give him so much as a second glance.

Learning that the mummers were bound for Edgekill, as were they, the two knights rode on again in high good humor, after a trifle of jesting with the Italian damozels and the shrill-voiced, impudent dwarf.

Tumbler's shrewd little eyes missed nothing. Later, asking for a ride behind Hilary's saddle, Tumbler spoke softly.

"Good Brother Hilarius, you looked very hard at those knights! Danger?"

"None," said Hilary, smiling, "provided you keep your mouth shut."

"Oh, trust me! But never trust the plaguey jade called Fate!"

"After eight years, Fate's on my side this day."

"On your side, aye, and ready to drive a knife into your armpit! That's her way; so have a care!"

Hilary shrugged, but kept the warning in mind. It was well meant....

Toward noon they came to Edgekill and found the castle nearly empty, everyone being off at the hunt. The bailiff welcomed them and placed everything at their disposal. Their coming was a distinct event, and the King was eagerly looking forward to the night's diversion, so they could do whatever they desired.

DURING THE troubles following the Wars of the Roses, Edgekill had suffered great damage, the outer walls being breached and ruined. This served to enlarge the courtyard, very happily, and Jehan Bodel took charge of the preparations. Hilary remained inconspicuous in the extreme. He had not even advertised the name of English Hilary here, and the company were, presumably, all Italians.

The huge dragon-head which served as Hell's Mouth was erected and covered from sight. It connected with the lower part of one van. The second van was across the courtyard, with various other stage settings between. The choicest part of the whole show, it was reckoned, came when Satan and his hapless dupes were sent to their doom amid fire and brimstone. Therefore, two country wagons were obtained and set up beside the dragon-head, with a platform built upon them to hold the seats of honor.

Late in the afternoon came Henry, with him was Sir Hugo Dymoke, and all the royal suite—not too many, since the King was no lover of show and fancy trappings. A few of the local gentry had assembled, so the castle was well crowded; archers and servants were everywhere, cooks and servers scurried about, and the place was a bedlam.

The performance was to begin late, after everyone had supped, so that all the world would be free to look on.

The sun was sinking when Hilary drew Master Satan apart and fell into low-voiced discussion. The lean, powerful Italian was to be his helper this night, in his private business, and Hilary had figured every detail accurately.

"When the *John Baptist* episodes begin and we're offstage," said he, "follow my lead. Every soul will be crammed in and about the courtyard. There'll be no one inside the castle, and we'll have the best part of an hour to work."

"But how to get in without being seen?" queried Sathanas.

"Go in openly by the side door yonder. It's to be kept clear all evening. They'll take us for part of the show, good devil!"

So the sun sank down, and Jehan Bodel made ready his fire and brimstone, and men fell to work at the trenchers and broached the ale-casks. The time was drawing close, since King Henry was no hand to sit over the winecups.

Lamps were lit in the vans and the dressing-rooms were readied. In the courtyard, torches and flambeaux were ablaze, with fresh fuel piled on all sides. The ranks of onlookers began to swell, crowding into every nook and corner, even perching on the ruined walls.

AT LENGTH Sir Hugo, and his cousin Sir John from London, came forth with their guests, and the crowding ranks cheered the King lustily. Henry, with those of highest degree, took station on the platform over the wagons, beside and above Hell's Mouth; although for the moment this remained shrouded and dark. A great clacking of tongues arose, trumpets sounded, Sir Hugo gave the word, and the show was on.

Jehan Bodel read his prologue in Latin, his exquisitely modulated voice charming all those who could understand, while Tumbler the dwarf echoed the words in squeaking English for the benefit of those below the salt. Then the first episodes of this gayly jumbled miracle-masque went forward.

Hilary made a marvelous *St. Nicholas; Master Satan* roared and ranted at his best, decked out in flaming red hood with horns, his tail shaking like a monstrous viper, and one boot shaped like a cloven hoof. Bodel became first a merry jongleur, later a turbaned Saracen. Time and place were entirely abolished, so that *St. Nicholas* and the Saracen sultan were cheek by jowl when necessary, and everything was very merry.

The fair Italians played their part and doubled in other parts. Amid frantic applause the first portion came to an end. While the dwarf tumbled about the courtyard like a mad thing and the jugglers drew gasps from the watchers, Jehan Bodel made haste to change into the simple garb of *John Baptist*.

Hilary emerged from the van in his knightly surcoat of flamboyant satin, gold spurs agleam, the peak of his long cap falling athwart his face. He touched the arm of *Master Satan* and headed for the side entrance, where the archers in leather cap and jerkin were massed about an ale-cask. Thinking it all part of the show, the archers made way with laugh and jest. The two figures passed into the castle, and were lost to sight.

Along the corridors strode Hilary, who had not seen these rooms since he was a young fellow of eighteen. He came at last into a long, empty hall where torches spluttered along the walls, and glanced around as he went toward the wide fireplace, where no fires blazed in this warm spring weather.

Formerly, the stones above the great hearth had been carven

into the cross of the Grevilles, the square scarlet cross with its five golden bosses. Now that was gone, broken away with hammers, and only the scar remained. Hilary went to one side of the fireplace and put his weight upon a stone there, and the stone swung. A narrow but high opening was disclosed.

"A torch, Sathanas!"

Satan snatched a torch from the wall and followed into the opening. The stone swung shut again. Here was a high and narrow passage through which wide shoulders could scarcely scrape, and at the end a little room piled with musty hampers and boxes.

"All the Greville goods and gear piled here, in the hour of peril," said Hilary, looking around. "Clothes, goods of all sorts— let 'em go! The two chests are what we want. They're not locked. Locks were of no avail if the Dymokes had found the secret of this chamber!"

There were two small chests of iron-bound oak, thick with dust like everything in the place. Under the torchlight, they got the lids thrown back, to lay bare parcels of all sizes and shapes, some heavy, some light.

"Here's a jumble—garments, jewels, everything!" said Hilary. "What I chiefly want are the parchments and the bills of exchange on Antwerp and Ghent merchants, still waiting to be presented and honored. There's gold, too; that will be in the heavier packets. Take what you can, and so will I. —Ha! My father's shirt of fine Milan steel links! That's not to be passed up. It fits my rôle, too."

THE FINELY woven mesh slithered through his hands. Laying surcoat aside, he donned the light steel shirt, then slipped the surcoat on again, over it. In his haste, in the semi-darkness, he could not observe that when the shirt was spread across his chest, over the wide front of it blazed the scarlet cross with its five bosses, the cross of the Grevilles. His surcoat covered it from sight at once.

Little packets of jewels, wads of vellum, rouleaux of gold—

these vanished into pockets and were stuffed under belts until both men were strangely swollen figures. In the musty room, sweat gathered upon them. The torch was flickering its last when Hilary turned once more to the secret entrance.

"Go first," said Hilary, laughing. "If we meet anyone, you'll draw a scream from them! At the courtyard, I'll chase you over to the van with my sword whirling. Ready?"

They came out into the great empty room, still empty. Upon Hilary fell relief as the stone swung shut. Relief, and a vast, triumphant exultation. Here was the best of his patrimony regained, wealth eight years hidden away and lost, now his own, to hold all the future assured.

When they sighted the courtyard, one glance showed there was not a moment to lose. *John Baptist* was beheaded, the crowd was roaring applause, and it would soon be time for both *Knight* and Satan to take the scene.

THEY TOOK it now, in the midst of the tumult—*Satan* roaring and galloping along, the *Knight* after him with sword glittering. Yells of delight went up, and the two of them disappeared in the farther van. Here, hastily, they tumbled the loot from their persons, while Jehan Bodel took charge of it all and stowed it safely away.

"Quick!" he panted at them. "Out and to work, while I get Hell's Mouth ablaze!"

Donning their visors, they hurried out, *Satan* capering through his lines and the *Knight* following. A proper knight he looked, from head to golden spurs, being no longer a hunched and whining figure. When he seized a lute from one of the damsels, and his lilting baritone lifted joyously in the ballad Jehan had written, stark silence fell upon the entire courtyard. For this was the ballad of the Tudor Rose, in honor of the King, and it was deftly done and royally sung.

The song ended, and the *Knight* saluted. Grave Henry rose from his seat in impulsive delight. Down at the masked figure he tossed his gloves, fine embroidered gauntlets sewn with seed-pearls.

"My thanks, sir knight!" he said, and sat back again while applause roared.

Hilary donned the gauntlets. *Master Satan* spoke his cue line about the mouth of hell. Abruptly, Hell's Mouth came into view as the fusees were fired. On all sides arose murmurs of awe and amazement. That enormous dragon's head, into which a man could vanish at one leap, was suddenly ablaze inside and out, with scarlet fire and brimstone at the bottom, and the painted paper outlines of the dragon hideously distinct.

Steel clashed. Knight and Devil were at it now, slap-dash, in a display of swordsmanship that fetched rolling tributes of wild applause from archers and men-at-arms. But, in the midst, from somewhere lifted a strange scream—one frantic scream of terror.

Then Hell's Mouth exploded.

It was appalling, soul-wrenching. On the instant, a tremendous flash of flame was everywhere; flame that clung to garments and wagons and blazed up luridly. At the same time, a huge biblowing cloud of smoke rolled everything into murky chaos. Men shouted, women shrieked like mad things. The platform crashed under simultaneous movement of its heavy load. Fire was streaming up from the wagons, bedded with old straw.

Hilary, aghast, dropped his sword. He hesitated, swung around, and went into the blazing hell with one leap, hurling himself up to the wagons, straight into the midmost terror. He stumbled over frantic figures, over up-ended planks from the platform. The thick smoke was lurid with leaping flame on all sides.

Choking, Hilary found what he sought—the King's tall shape in its furred gown, blazing spots of scattered tar and brimstone licking at the garments, the obscure shapes around in panic flight or all asprawl. He got his arms about that tall figure and slapped at the tongues of flame with desperate effort, beating them out and out.

"Steady, Your Majesty!" he coughed. "Hold tight, now!"

A SUDDEN burst from the straw below leaped up all around them. His thin surcoat was afire, the furred mantle was ablaze. Hilary slapped and fought the flames away; through it all, the King remained cool, unhurried, alert. Hilary guided him to the looming van, to the ground, and around behind the van to cool night air.

"Safe, Sire, safe!" he gasped, and frantically rid himself of the burning surcoat. The gay satin shredded away at last. "There! All's well, and no great harm done, I trust."

"Well enough," echoed the King, with a cough. "Ah, water! It's high time."

Water was being flung. Steam hissed, and choking fumes rolled afresh as the fire died. Through it, Hilary guided the King into the open, and into a new hubbub. Men were rushing about, torches were dancing, and at sight of the King a quick yell pealed up. He was surrounded and borne away amid cheers.

HILARY TURNED aside, led by the voice of Jehan Bodel. He came upon the Frenchman, frantically cursing and lamenting the frightful thing. Something had gone amiss, a twist of burning straw had fallen into a tub of gunpowder and tarred cloth. Others of the company gathered around, with a ding-dong of frantic voices.

And then came the men-at-arms, trampling and seizing, with furious storming oaths. Jehan was knocked over, Master Satan was dragged to the stones and bound. Hilary's mask was stripped off and his arms were twisted together with cords. The Italian women fled shrieking to the nearer van. The others of the company were haled out into midmost courtyard and lumped together. Fury quivered and shook in the air. No one had died, but the fury rose louder and more vehement. A plot, a plot!

The fire was all gone now, the smoke vanished, and the cressets blazed brightly. New yells went up. Hands pointed. Sir Hugo Dymoke came hastily; his cousin Sir John vented torrential oaths.

Upon Hilary's bared mail-shirt stood out the scarlet cross of the Grevilles!

Furious voices shook the air. Knights and squires, all the King's suite, came pouring around with flash of weapons and excited shouts. Here was the man, the man himself, Hilary de Greville! A plot, a conspiracy to kill the King! Hang every one of these scurvy knaves, and first of all this rascal under attainder!

"You have the right of justice here!" Sir John turned vehemently to his cousin. "Hang him with short shrift, Hugo, or none at all!"

"With all my heart, and the quicker the better," said Sir Hugo, and beckoned forth a brace of men-at-arms.

They came, and he ordered Hilary hanged at the castle gate, instantly. Against that roaring tide of fury, Hilary could do nothing, say nothing. Tumbler the dwarf flew at the two men, scratching and screaming. They kicked him aside, and were dragging Hilary off when a calm, steady voice made itself heard. Every move stopped. The voices died. The King came striding forward. Cheers for him arose, and hearty plaudits, and these died likewise.

"Why punishment, Hugo?" said he.

Sir Hugo broke forth hotly:

"Look, my lord King! This rascal is no other than Hilary de Greville, of whom my cousin John has brought news from London. Here's proof of the whole affair—this damnable business was a conspiracy to murder you! Here's Greville himself, a traitorous dog like all his family, plotting this treason! By God, I'll hang him at the gate yonder!"

"But," said the King quietly, "no one was hurt. A few people trampled, a leg or two broken—no more. True, the fire was all around me, but one man slapped down the flames and saved me from injury. So, my good gentles, why a hanging?"

A dozen voices broke forth, wild imaginings became sworn facts. Hilary had been caught sword in hand, his treason proven, traitorous murder in the very act! A dozen had seen him prowling in the smoke, a dozen had heard him shouting death to the King!

But Henry stepped forward and the voices died away once more, as he looked Hilary in the face, and reached out to the bound arms. He pointed to the royal gauntlets, now wrinkled and shriveled, the embroidery gone, the seed-pearls now only brown burnt dots.

"There's the answer; here's the man who brought me out of the fire," he said in his calm way. "Sir Hilary de Greville, I thank you for having saved me this night. Go your way in peace; you shall be eased of your attainder as quickly as my word can reach London."

UPON THE sudden dismayed silence rose the shrill voice of Tumbler the dwarf, who flung himself blubbering with joy upon Hilary and Jehan, while Master Satan, when he understood, fell upon his knees before the King.

And this, as Henry was wont to affirm made the merriest miracle-play of all—that Master Satan went on his knees to a Tudor, before the very mouth of hell!

THE BISHOP'S PAWN

ANDREINI RAN down the narrow street, gasping for breath; sighting a tavern's lights, he checked his pace. Shouts and oaths resounded in his wake. He clapped his sword into scabbard and swung into the tavern's big room. A glance showed him that the place was empty except for one man sitting at a table by the fire.

Swiftly, Andreini hurled himself at another table, uncleared, where men had eaten and drunk. He sprawled into a chair, dropped hat and cloak beside him, wiped a smear of blood from his hand. Not his blood; two men had died, back there.

He leaned forward across the table. With adroit mobility, the dark, vigorous features became vacuous, maudlin. His strong, unafraid eyes grew bleary. As the landlord came and took his order, he was the very picture of a nodding, wine-sodden rogue all but under the table.

Now, controlling his heaving lungs, he waited. Would that one man at the other table give him away? A young man, handsome, cloaked and sworded, a gem on his finger; another of these damned French nobles! They were all arrogant and treacherous, thought Andreini, and he was not far wrong. In 1613 Paris was a place of intrigue, assassination, death. The young Louis XIII was a boy; his mother, Marie of the Medici line, ruled France with her own favorites....

"Nevers! Nevers! Ho! Where's the damned rogue who insulted the Duke de Nevers?"

A burst of voices, a stamp of feet, as half a dozen men with steel out came crowding into the tavern. Andreini lifted one of the pewter cups on the table, drunkenly.

"God save the noble Duke de Nevers!" he hiccuped. "Greatest man in France!"

They crowded out again with impatient oaths and were gone roaring on down the twisting street. The man at the next table-Andreini judged him as twenty-seven or eight—broke into a laugh.

"Well done, monsieur!" he exclaimed. "Lucky they didn't see your left cuff-it's badly blood-stained. Will you do me the honor of joining me, since I have some time to wait here? I am no friend of Nevers, by the way, but am a stranger in Paris."

The speaker was thinly affable, imperious of eye and voice.

Andreini, flinging off his pose, broke into a laugh and rose. He was only twenty-two, and quick at friendship.

"With all my heart!" he responded. He went to the other table and bowed, his sharp eye catching closer view of the man's ring. An episcopal ring, the amethyst of a bishop? Ridiculous!

"I too am a stranger here," he said. "Permit me: Jean Baptiste Andreini, from Italy, and going back there empty-handed and empty of purse."

The other laughed heartily. "That's the strangest thing I've heard since I came to Paris! I'm Armand du Plessis, at your service. Sit, be comfortable, the night's young. Landlord! Wine! And a fowl from the spit for each of us! Well, my friend, devil take me if you didn't play a deft trick yonder! You should be a mummer, a strolling actor!"

"S O I am," said Andreini. He saw the quick incredulity in Plessis' eye, and smiled. "Oh, not one of your French mummers who help quacks sell their medicines on the Pont Neuf! In Italy an actor is held in high esteem as an artist. I had hoped that I might get commissioned by the queen to bring a company of players here. My parents were well known in France; years ago, the queen signally honored my mother. But I've failed. It's impossible to get any entry to the court. My latest try was with the Duke de Nevers—and you witnessed the result. I think I accounted for two of his bravos, however."

"Nevers," said Plessis slowly, "will end in a bad way, I fear."

Andreini laughed. "Why did it seem so strange that I've had no luck in Paris?"

"Faith, because you're from Italy! The court, the city, half France, is in the hands of Italian adventurers like Concini, now Marshal d'Ancre, the queen's favorite. Any Italian should make his fortune here in a year, if he's unscrupulous enough."

"Perhaps, then, I'm not unscrupulous enough." Andreini's vigorous features became whimsical. "Yet, in another sense, I also find it very strange that Paris has no place for me."

The other lifted his eyebrows.

"Why?"

The younger man explained, in his warmly winning manner: Here in Paris people were too busy killing one another to take

any interest in the stage; the only theater here was the Hotel de Bourgogne, most of the time unused.

And yet, in Italy, the stage was the favorite pastime of courts and princes. In Spain, the renowned Lope de Vega was producing famous plays. In England, creative activity was at its peak with Shakespeare, Marlowe and others. With all this, added Andreini, the time was fast ripening for Paris to vie with other capitals as a theatrical center.

"The time's coming, and I'd like to be the man to bring the stage into fashion here," he concluded. "All I need is the chance; the queen has favored Italian companies of players who come and go. I want to come and stay. The time's ripe for France to have a theater of its own, I'd stake my life on it!"

"Then, my friend, you shall have the chance to stake your

life," said Plessis, a spark kindling in his sharp eyes, the eyes of a cynic. "There's a game afoot; if it's won, you shall win greatly. If lost—you take your chance. You'll fit into it admirably. Will you make good your word, and gamble?"

CALMLY ANDREINI met that imperious gaze; but his pulses leaped. He knew well this was some intrigue, probably of the court. His chance!

"Yes, monsieur," he replied. "But I've told you that I have scruples."

"You need have no more than I, who am a bishop."

A bishop! Andreini laughed heartily. "Very well, very well! In that case, monsieur, I'll take the gamble."

"Good. My friend, even if we lose, you still have a chance to win. I'm interested in theatrical matters, I'm doing a bit of play-writing myself; if your neck isn't lost, you shall go back with me to my diocese and teach me more about the art of writing plays."

ANDREINI SOBERED suddenly, at a flash of that amethyst ring.

"Monsieur," he said gravely, "were you jesting in your claim to be a bishop?"

"Devil a bit!" And, with his reply, Plessis chuckled. "In France, my friend, such places are all in the appointment of the crown. Thus, at twenty-one, I was made Bishop of Lucon—the filthiest, poorest, and most wretched bishopric in France. Six years later, I am no better off; but things will change. The most important factor is the ability to grasp the chance when it comes."

"That's why I've accepted your offer," Andreini said shrewdly.

Plessis laughed.

"Well said! You fit into this niche admirably; the queen honored your mother, you said? Well, tonight you shall help save the queen's party and the queen herself, from these over-proud nobles who would depose her as regent. Do you know where to find the Rue des Mauvaises Paroles?"

"No."

"You'll find it close to the Bureau des Postes. Go there now, at once; await me. I have a house there where I live while on my infrequent Paris visits." As he spoke, Plessis twisted the ring from his finger and extended it. "Take this. My servant is named Cadillac; he'll take care of you. Get some sleep; we have the rest of the night for action. I'll be along in an hour or so with everything you may need."

"Tonight, you say?" said Andreini, as he took the ring. He was astonished.

"Yes. There's to be a ball at the Louvre. It will last till daylight."

The Louvre! The court! The queen-regent! Dazedly, Andreini gathered up hat and cloak and was at the door when several men entered; he stood aside to let them pass. They were all masked, but he caught a glint of jewels, and one furred mantle was embroidered with the insignia of the Sant' Esprit; the wearer, then, must be one of the greatest nobles in the realm!

For these men, the Bishop of Lucon had been waiting. Assured of this, Andreini plunged off into the chill night.

Winter was not far distant, and darkness had come at an early hour. He found the little street. He found the house, an abode of poverty. The servant took him to a cold room; doffing only boots and sword, Andreini stretched out on a bed, drew a tattered blanket over himself, and was asleep at once. Youth had rebounded swiftly; he dreamed of fame and fortune as he slept, and when they awakened him he leaped up with new eagerness—only to stare blankly at what greeted him.

Candles lit the room. Two men had aroused him; they were clad all in black, and bowed to him with the greatest respect. One spoke in Italian.

"Eminence, we are here to assist you. It is time to dress."

Upon a chair near by, Andreini beheld the scarlet biretta and robes of a cardinal.

Before he could speak for astonishment, they were at work upon him. He fell in with their task, since they refused to answer questions. His merry humor returned; no doubt he was to play the part of a cardinal, a prince of the church, in some masque or pageant at the court this night!

They dressed him carefully. The white linen collar was spotless; and under the folds of this, they drew the ribbon of an order; the jeweled decoration glittered on his chest. A scarlet skullcap, the biretta clapped on above it. A huge sapphire ring. And, under the robes, a long and very business-like Milanese stiletto, almost as good as a sword.

"Come, Eminence," said one of the two attendants. The other flung open a door; Andreini, passing through, heard his voice: "His Eminence, Cardinal Ferrari!"

Andreini stopped short. He was in the largest room of the tumbledown little house; before him sat the black-clad Bishop of Lucon and two other gentlemen whom he knew must be great nobles. One of them wore that furred mantle bearing the insignia of the Sant' Esprit.

They eyed him keenly and silently. He drew himself up, and his voice rapped out upon the silence of the room with biting acerbity.

"So, messieurs, this is the greeting you give a prince of the church?"

"A thousand pardons!" Plessis was on his feet instantly, bowing low; Andreini extended his hand, and Plessis kissed the sapphire ring, then looked up with laughing delight in his long-nosed, narrow features. "Permit me, Your Eminence! My brother, the Marquis de Richelieu; and Marshal de Bassompierre, the first soldier of France."

THEY GREETED him with mock respect; Richelieu in silence, an intent, handsome, unsmiling man, and Bassompierre, he of the furred mantle, rolling out a jest and a roaring burst of laughter.

"He's good, Armand, he's good!" he cried. "Here, Richelieu— wine for the Cardinal! A toast with you, honest churchman; health to us all, this night, and the Bastille for the Comte de Marillac!"

Armand du Plessis

Wine was on the table. Andreini, ignorant to what it was all about, took the glass handed him, clinked it with the others, drank, and sank on a stool. Instantly, the room became still and grave with tension, as Plessis took up the word.

"My friend, I'll be brief. This evening the Papal nuncio, Cardinal Ferrari, was to have arrived in Paris. On the road from Orleans today, his coach was attacked by armed men—by Marillac and other gentlemen belonging to the Duke de Nevers; they were masked, but we know their identity well enough. Their purpose was to kill the Cardinal and seize his dispatches. They killed his secretary and thought him killed, but left him only wounded; he is badly hurt, however. They missed the most important letters and dispatches, getting away with others that do not matter. So far, clear?"

Andreini nodded and sipped his wine, wasting no words. He knew suddenly that his head was damnably loose on his shoulders!

"Nevers is leading, under cover of his man Marillac, a conspiracy against the queen and the Italians at court," went on the young bishop, caressing his goatee placidly. "The Cardinal was bringing letters vital to the queen—assurances of money and support from Italy and Savoy. Nevers is announcing at the Louvre this evening that Cardinal Ferrari was killed by assassins hired by the queen and Concini; he's playing for quick, hot action, with Marillac primed to assassinate Concini. What then? Nevers will probably seize the queen, the regent, and the boy king, before morning. You understand?"

Andreini nodded again. After all, it did not matter particularly who was who, in his mind. He could not hope to understand the ins and outs of this business. But here Bassompierre spoke up, in his hearty soldierly manner.

"Almost too bad to stop the game, Armand! That damned Concini disgraces the office of a marshal of France!"

Plessis darted him a glance and a thin smile. "Agreed; but let us save him so that he can be killed by the right people, at the right time. Now, my friend from Italy, we plan to introduce you to the, queen's presence in an hour from now. Satisfied?"

Andreini shook his head. "First, there may be someone who knows Ferrari. Second, I look too young for the part."

Plessis shrugged exasperatedly.

"There'll be no one there who knows him. And cannot you, an actor, make yourself look older?"

"Certainly. But—"

"Then, attention!" rasped the bishop. "You're not to be introduced to the whole court; merely in private, to the queen—which means to her council as well, and the great lords with her. Nevers will be there. So will Bassompierre. You'll hand her your letters; we'll provide you with an imitation secretary and servants. Then withdraw, the coach will bring you here—and the Cardinal vanishes. Nevers is blocked, the plot is checked, and the truth will become known tomorrow. They'll wonder, but never know! The Cardinal, of course, will later say that he sent someone to represent him. Satisfied?"

Andreini reflected upon the question; his head really felt very loose indeed. He was too proud to back out, however; and this singular ecclesiastic inspired a certain confidence, far more than did the gorgeous, massive Bassompierre—who had been born Betstein—or the dour Henri de Richelieu. Some inner fire burned in this young prelate that communicated itself to him and sparked in his soul.

"Why should I not be satisfied? Why should I?" he replied, and shrugged. "I am no one. The question is, are you satisfied? A few lines in my face, powder on my hair and my eyebrows, a pair of spectacles to my eyes, a little dark stain to my face—"

He assumed the thick lisping accent of an Italian, blinked at them, drew down his jaw, and put on ten years in an instant. There was nothing to threaten his identity; it was an age when cardinals or bishops or princes might be boys in years, when a nuncio of Rome might be a prelate or a soldier or an influential relative. The impossible was a part of everyday life—some princely whim might land a gypsy in a royal palace.

This was precisely what Andreini encountered, a little over an hour later.

WITH COACH and servants, and a silent little man who posed as his secretary, Andreini drove into the pile of masonry that was more like a fortress than a palace. Bloody was the Louvre, every foot of it drenched in blood by duels, assassinations or dark deeds like that of St. Bartholemew's Eve.

Bassompierre and Richelieu had gone on ahead to attend to his reception. Armand du Plessis, who had no post at court, accompanied Andreini to give him some final coaching, and was going to remain in the carriage. In the courtyard, however, everything was wild turmoil; nobles and lackeys, coaches and sedan-chairs, torch-boys, officers, guards and palace officials. Here, too, was a crowd of young nobles who had fetched a gypsy crone into the courtyard and were surrounding each coach as it arrived and stood waiting, with the crone telling brief fortunes, racy as she dared.

Andreini found them at his coach door, found a torch thrust close to give light, found the crone gabbling—and then she fell silent. At sight of the Cardinal's robes, the whole pack fell silent, abashed. The gypsy woman, unable to draw back, flashed

Andreini presented the packets of letters to the queen. "I shall hope for the honor of a private audience, within the next few days," he said.

her eyes at the three men inside and her voice lifted in a hoarse cackle.

"Red shall be still redder ere the red dawn comes! Here's the wrong man in the red robe—there'll be an end to laughter when the other gets his hat!"

She was dragged away, still screeching, by the pack of young nobles, one of whom had the grace to apologize.

Plessis, in his corner, laughed softly.

"You heard?" He jogged Andreini with his elbow. "The wrong man, ha! My friend, if ever I wear that biretta of yours, there'll be less laughter and more common sense in Paris! Well, here we are. Luck attend you!"

Andreini and the secretary alighted. The guards saluted. A chamberlain bowed low; he had been sent to bring His Eminence to the private apartment of the queen. Marie de Medici was not gracing the ball tonight with her presence, by reasons of health, but was receiving a chosen company in her own quarters.

And now, as he followed into those torch-lit corridors, Andreini began to realize for the first time just how loose his head really was, beneath the red skullcap and biretta. For he was playing at being a prince, in the house of kings; and the rapiers of those around him were not for show but for use. All eyes were turned upon him, with curiosity or astonishment, and his heart nearly failed him when, after stairs and passages and guards, he was led into a great antechamber filled with brilliantly clad women and still more gorgeous men.

They fell silent, staring at him, openly amazed by his appearance. It was hard to face them, to walk through them, to smile amiably and make a movement of the hand that might be taken for benediction. But the chamberlain kept on, came to a door beyond, and the door was opened. "His Eminence Cardinal Ferrari!" So Andreini came into the presence of the queen—Marie de Medici, stout and middle-aged, swathed enormously in her rich robes, and so reeking with perfumes that the senses reeled.

S O M E H O W H E remembered all Plessis had told him; he got through the ceremonious greetings without a blunder. All the while, he was conscious of the faces around; faces astonished, furious, threatening, bewildered. Nevers, tall and darkly handsome; the weak and cowardly adventurer who had become Marshal d'Ancre; Epernon, Bassompierre, Vendome, Conde and others of the great lords; the ladies of honor, and a few Italian faces, women and men, more powerful in France than the great princes themselves. Most of those faces were amazed and hostile, as Andreini realized; therefore, this plot to seize and depose the queen must be widespread!

A seat was placed beside Marie; Andreini took it, pleading fatigue and nearsightedness, and sheltered his eyes from the glare of the candles. The queen, having finished with formality, greeted him in the Italian that everyone here spoke, and all the vigor of her volcanic nature leaped forth.

"Your Eminence, I have heard the most shameful stories this evening! In fact, your arrival is so amazing to everyone that we cannot understand it. Why, we were told that your carriage had been attacked, that you were hurt—or dead! Only a few moments ago one of our gentlemen brought definite information that these stories were true!"

"Oh!" said Andreini, glancing up and meeting the gaze of the Duke de Nevers. "No doubt it was a mistake; I've met only one French gentleman all the way from Orleans here, and he was very pleasant. Marillac, I think the name was. Eh, Orlando?"

The little secretary bowed. "The Comte de Marillac, Your Eminence."

Nevers changed countenance. The queen plunged into questions. Andreini through his secretary presented the packets of letters to her.

"Your Majesty may have every confidence," he said, "in the help and backing of Savoy and Tuscany and Rome; as regent and guardian of King Louis, you represent France. I shall hope for the honor of a private audience, within the next few days, when Your Majesty may be somewhat recovered in health."

"And then, perhaps," intervened Marshal d'Ancre smoothly, "you may wish to make some complaints regarding annoyances on your journey here? It will give us great pleasure, Your Eminence, to sweep away any unpleasant memories that may have occurred."

Andreini met the weary, crafty eyes of the Italian, and wondered.

"Oh, there were none!" he rejoined cheerfully. This Concini, he perceived, was no fool, had not been tricked at all—ah, of course! He must be in on the scheme of imposture. The queen was not. She met Conde, Nevers and the others with a mocking defiance; in fact, she made it very plain to everyone that now she was more than able to cope with whatever arose. And so she was. These letters from the south and east would redouble her strength. Everyone would flock to fawn upon her, now that money and support were assured her.

Andreini was pumped for news of Italy. With some effort he kept to his rôle; none the less, his eager youth peered forth, and his winning personality broke through the words, until the man himself became the center of interest for all. The dull and stodgy room, so filled with jealousies and suspicious hatred that men feared to speak their minds, became transfigured. Wit and laughter leaped forth, dignity was lessened, stories began to breed, none too decorously either.

AMID A burst of laughter, Andreini caught the name of Richelieu. Someone had just come from the ballrooms, bringing the story; it seemed that the marquis had encountered the gypsy crone, who told him no pleasant fortune. He would be slain in a duel and another man would make his name famous—so she said. Richelieu had flown into a fury. It was all a bright joke; such was the measure of humor at this court. But, to Andreini, it occurred that if Richelieu were to die, his younger brother Armand du Plessis would bear the name. This young bishop from the country, Andreini realized, might yet become a great man.

Theaters? A question from the queen, and now Andreini struck into what he really knew. He had fulfilled his mission here, and caught slight gestures from Bassompierre telling him to be off; he disregarded them. Marie de Medici had a vivid interest in the subject, and he determined swiftly to make the most of the occasion. After all, he was gambling with his head, and here was his chance to win something.

HIS FLUENCY, his knowledge, his vehemence, delighted the queen. She asked advice, and he gave it freely.

"You should have an established company of players here, Your Majesty. There's one theater well suited to such a company, the Hotel de Bourgogne. Why not bring Italian actors here, add French to them, and gradually build up a French school? I know the very man for your purpose—young Andreini, son of the famous name."

"Oh, of course!" The queen clapped her hands. "I remember—Isabel, that glorious woman who had been given degrees by universities because of her learning—you say there is a son?"

"Yes, Jean Baptiste Andreini, Your Majesty. I feel sure that a letter from you, a commission to bring his own company here, would prove the ambition of his life! He is at Florence, or at least his company is there—"

"I shall write him at once, tomorrow!" exclaimed the queen eagerly. "A splendid idea, Your Eminence, splendid! I thank you for it. Yes, I remember his mother well, poor woman! When she died, they refused her Christian burial because she was an actress; and the whole city of Lyons turned out to do her honor, to atone for the disgrace! What became of her husband, the poet and actor, who wrote so many plays?"

They were speaking in Italian, rapid and low-voiced, but not in any confidential manner. Andreini, as though casually, traced a circle on his knee with one finger, then other circles. He knew that this sharp-eyed woman would recognize the Medici crest, and at the sign would watch his words carefully.

"After her death, Your Majesty, he never appeared on the stage again. He used to say that with more care, her death might have been avoided; it was a most unfortunate accident. He devoted himself to instructing his son in the whole art of the theater. In the words of the nimble Harlequin: Knowledge never comes amiss, and is more potent than gold, more faithful than friends or guards!"

"A wise saying. The son should be just the man for us; I'll write him with my own hand. Better arrange for money too, I suppose." With an abrupt break in the conversation, she turned; Andreini had not judged amiss her Italian subtlety of mind. "M. de Bassompierre!"

The noble approached with a low bow. "What guards are on duty?" she demanded.

"The guards on duty tonight are, I believe, the company of M. de Marillac."

"Indeed!" The queen darted a glance at the Duke de Nevers. "You will have the goodness to replace them now, instantly, with the company commanded by the Baron de Pont-Courlay, who will remain on duty until further notice."

"At once, Your Majesty." Bassompierre bowed again, so far as his marvelous starched lace collar would permit, and with a shadowy smile on his bluff countenance, departed.

The Marshal d'Ancre suavely intervened. This adventurer, whose name of Concini was the most hated name in Paris, suggested that the Cardinal must be weary, and offered to take him to some refreshment. The queen at once dismissed Andreini in the most gracious manner, giving him her hand and assuring him of a private audience whenever he so desired.

Andreini had to admire the neat way in which he was shuffled out. Concini took his arm and led him through the apartments, talking earnestly of nothing, while the secretary followed. Once a door closed behind them, the Italian abandoned all pretense and clapped Andreini on the shoulder.

"Excellent! Well done, indeed!" he exclaimed. "Bassompierre could only give me a hint or two, and very luckily too, because I've met the real Cardinal Ferrari. What's this about the guards? It was a plot?"

"Yes," said Andreini. "The marshal knows, and so does the Marquis de Richelieu."

Andreini

"Good. I'll see him immediately, then. Bassompierre told me to get you to your coach; I'll send my lackey with you by the private stairs."

THE LACKEY was summoned. Concini, in token of his admiring gratitude, pressed a ring upon Andreini's finger, and hastily departed. Under guidance of the lackey, Andreini and his secretary by a devious way gained the cold courtyard where the coach was waiting. The guards, surprised at their appearance, summoned the coach. Andreini perceived that squads of men were coming and going; Bassompierre was putting the palace in charge of more secure guardians.

Into the coach, now, while the horses pawed the cobblestones and from the enormous building came the sound of viols and flutes and gay voices at revelry. The coach door slammed, the wheels rumbled.

"All well?" came the voice of Armand du Plessis. "Why is the guard being changed?"

"By Bassompierre, at the Queen's orders. Yes, all's well. Concini's on the alert. He gave me a diamond ring that must be worth a thousand livres by the look of it."

"You'll probably find the stone full of flaws," said the bishop dryly.

"Is this masquerade finished?"

"Thank heaven, yes!"

"Then give me a hand," said Andreini, "and I'll get out of these damned clothes. As a costume they're lovely, but I'm wrapped like a mummy."

Plessis lent a hand; the secretary lent a hand; and as the carriage swayed and rumbled, Andreini got out of his luxurious but muffling robes. The imitation secretary folded and laid them carefully aside; they belonged to the real Cardinal. This secretary was in actual fact Cadillac, the lackey of Plessis, and a shrewd and able fellow. He gave his own greatcoat to Andreini, now stripped to shirt and drawers.

"Hello!" exclaimed the bishop. "This doesn't look like the shortest way home—what the devil is in those rascals?" He tugged at the window on his side, got it open, and sent an angry shout at the driver and groom on the box. In reply came a burst of laughter, and a whipcrack so close to his face that Plessis jerked away from the window with an oath.

"Those are not our men, monsieur!" exclaimed Cadillac in alarm.

"So I perceive. And horsemen behind us; neatly trapped, by my faith!" The young bishop turned to Andreini. His voice was cold and calm. "Sorry, my friend; I made a bad mistake by waiting in this coach! They replaced our men, and I knew it not. Now we're caught."

"Why?" demanded Andreini. "What can they do with us?"

"Kill us, you fool. Cadillac! There's a chance they may pay more attention to us than to you. If you can get away, do so. My brother, Richelieu, promised to return to my house and meet us there; you'll find him quick to aid us. Andreini, get into the Cardinal's cassock again—throw it around your shoulders, anything to keep their attention on you and me. Quickly, now! It may give Cadillac a chance to get away."

Andreini obeyed, and barely in time. The coach slowed. The clatter of horsemen behind swept up close. They turned in at a courtyard which was bright with the ruddy flare of torches. Plessis reached for the door-handle, and clapped Andreini on the knee.

"You to the other one!" he said swiftly. "Now!"

Not waiting for the coach to stop, he flung open the door and leaped out. Andreini did the same on his side, hampered by the scarlet robe and letting it fall as he struck the cobblestones.

The following horsemen swept around the two men. Guards from the gates hurried to join them; laughter and oaths resounded. The glitter of steel warned Andreini against any attempt to fight. He made none. Laughter redoubled at sight of his costume, the cassock being now gone.

"Here's your Cardinal!" shouted someone. "And the other, who's he?"

"The little Bishop of Lucon!" came reply, amid more laughter. "Where's Marillac?"

"Inside. Fetch the cassock along. Better close those gates, there!"

Just when Cadillac had gone, how he had managed it, Andreini had no idea. A torch was thrust close to the coach, it was seen to be empty; there was no sign of the lackey anywhere in the courtyard. So much laughter was going on, so loud were the oaths and high talk, that he might well have made his escape unobserved; and certainly no one missed him.

GATES CLANGED shut; a house in Paris was built to stand seige, and frequently did. Arms gripped by a man on either side, Andreini was hustled along after Plessis into the house. It was a handsome place; they stood in a long hall where lamp-light touched upon old armor and tapestries and portraits. At one end of the hall, a stairway rose sharply to a landing, then twisted around and out of sight. By the foot of these stairs was a huge litter of straw, where servants were packing some hampers and casks.

"That straw, those stairs!" said Plessis in low, swift Italian, and gave Andreini's ankle a kick. "Not now. Be ready for anything. Use your wits or die!"

They were dragged away from each other. Their weapons had already been taken; now there seemed to be a wait. A number of gentlemen appeared, tramping through into one of the rooms off the hall. Bravos and soldiers clustered at the doors. Suddenly there was a stir. Into the hall came three men, breathing oaths.

One loosed a shout at the servants:

"Cease the work, you dolts! Unpack everything. We're remaining here."

"Yes," said Plessis, with dry irony. "The Louvre remains occupied, Marillac."

The other paused briefly—a man with hot eyes of fury, and a reckless, headstrong air. His two companions wore the sash of guard officers; members of his own company, no doubt. He looked at the two prisoners, and gestured.

"Bring them in."

He and his companions strode on. Andreini and Plessis were shoved after. They came into a fairly large room with painted walls and ceiling. A dozen gentlemen were grouped about a table where wine and silver flagons and salvers of food were set out. They greeted Marillac with acclaim. Andreini comprehended that this must be Marillac's house.

"Where are all the ladies, Marillac?" demanded someone gayly.

"I sent them out of Paris." The Count seized on a flagon of wine, quaffed, and wiped his mustache. "Ah! Well, my friends, we've lost, thanks to these two rogues yonder. Nevers and Conde will be here in an hour or so. What we most need now, is information."

Andreini scanned the faces and figures before him, and found no luck in them. Hot arrogant features, cruel eyes, men stamped with the lowest forms of vice; yet, because of high birth and place, flaunting in the world's face their depravity and disregard of any law human or divine. Honest men there were at court, and brave, but not in this circle of dissolute nobles.

Eager tongues broke forth in all sorts of rumors and statements regarding the Cardinal, the bishop, the queen regent, Bassompierre—while Marillac quaffed his wine and Plessis stood cool and disdainful, and Andreini eyed the men around him warily. Then the Count set down his goblet, demanded silence, and stepped up to Armand du Plessis.

"You may be a good bishop, monsieur, but you're a damned unlucky conspirator," he said harshly. "I hope you realize it?"

"At least I'm good at something," Plessis smiled icily.

"You impudent little provincial!" snarled Marillac furiously. "Because your brother is a court favorite, you take on the airs of a great noble! Well, who's this rascal masquerading as a cardinal? And who's behind all this tasty bit of intrigue? Speak up, unless you want to be put to the torture and made to speak!"

IT WAS no idle threat, as the faces around bore witness. Hands were at poniards; let the explosion start, and murder would be let loose in an orgy of blood. Greater men than this little country bishop had been stabbed to death and flung out in the gutter, to be picked up by the watch.

Abruptly, the voice of Andreini quavered upon the room.

"Monsieur! No torture! Spare me, spare me of your grace, and I'll tell all!" he cried out. Terror filled his eyes, distorted his face. Fear shrilled in his voice. He pointed at Plessis. "Take him away, and I'll tell you everything! Don't leave him here to curse me! I can't tell you the truth if he's looking at me!"

ARMAND DU PLESSIS lost his calm. He swung around with a bursting oath.

"A pox on you, you damned Italian rogue! Be a man and—"

"Take him outside," broke in Marillac, gesturing the guards. They surrounded Plessis and dragged him out of the room. The

two holding Andreini released him, at another gesture, and
followed.

"I'm not a noble, your excellency," whined Andreini, clasp-
ing his hands in entreaty. An ecstasy of fright shook him. His
eyes rolled, his voice pleaded at them: "I can't stand the torture;
I was tortured once, and I cannot stand it! I'll tell you everything, all the names, what the queen said, everything! Give me
a crucifix—I'll swear it!"

Small chance of any sacred symbol being found among these
gentlemen!

They looked upon him with contempt, but also with swift

*The poniard plunged to the hilt in Marillac's body—
and the sword came free as Marillac staggered.*

interest. In his passionate plea, Andreini came to one knee, lifting his clasped hands to Marillac, with such desperate cowardice in his manner that the Count snarled a disgusted oath.

"Not a bad idea, Marillac!" exclaimed someone. "Here, give the fellow a draft of wine, then swear him on your sword-hilt and we'll get the truth out of him!"

Others applauded. A flagon was filled and thrust at Andreini; he gulped down the wine, spilling it over his chin and shirt, coughing, wiping his lips. Marillac, poniard at girdle, hitched around his baldric so that the cross-hilt of his sword protruded.

"Lay hand on that, and swear!" he commanded.

Andreini, still on one knee, gripped the hilt with his right hand. He lost balance; he tottered, flailed at the air with his left hand, pitched forward—and that left hand gripped the poniard.

Then, swift as trained muscles could flash into action, he was up and on his feet. The sword stuck in the scabbard, as he had feared. The poniard did not. It came free, it plunged to the hilt in Marillac's body—and the sword came clear as Marillac staggered. A weapon in each hand, Andreini was darting for the door before anyone fully realized just what had happened; before Marillac's death-cry rang upon the room, even.

The door flew open. In the hall was Plessis, a group of men about him. Andreini was upon them like an angel of vengeance, bloody poniard flashing, rapier darting at them. He thrust one man through; the others broke and scattered.

"Quick! To the stairs!" he cried.

The bishop stooped, caught up the sword of the hurt man, and ran for the stairs. None of the guards were in this direction. As he joined Andreini, he said:

"Apologies, my friend! You even fooled me—here, you rogues! Out of the way!"

The servants, now at their unpacking, scattered hastily. Behind, shouts and oaths and armed men were erupting. Andreini leaped to the stairs, and swung around. He saw Plessis pausing at a lamp-stand below the stair-post; with one blow of his sword the bishop knocked away glass and shade, and held the flame to the straw at his feet. It caught. A leap, and he was on the stairs with Andreini, laughing wildly, excitedly.

"A good bishop should make hellfire serve him well!" he cried in a gay voice. "That's a line for one of your plays, Italian—up a little farther—right! You take the wall; I'll take the rail—"

The flames had caught the masses of straw, with a thick smoke and a crackling roar, mounting to tapestries and woodwork. The servants were screaming and bawling; down the hall came a rush of nobles and soldiers yelling vengeance and curses. The foremost came leaping through the smoke, to meet the rapiers awaiting for them.

Andreini felt a shocked sense of admiration at sight of this bishop's swordplay. It was swift and beautiful to see; Plessis had his point in and out like a flame. And, being above those who came, he thrust only for the face. Then Andreini was in the game also.

IT LASTED only a moment; but it was like a scene from some half-imagined hell. The first men through the veil of smoke, nearly all smitten through face or throat, rolled in agony and screamed and coughed. The others plunged full upon them, trod on the bodies, slipped in the blood, yelled in blind panic as the smoke hid everything—and Plessis, descending a step or two, deliberately thrust one man through, then another.

"There's an episcopal bishop's blessing for the rascals!" he panted. "Now, friend—back! Back and up, before they realize we're gone!"

The attack had ceased, for the moment. The smoke had thickened, as water was flung upon the flames; Andreini was choked and gasping now, feeling his way up to the landing and then on in clearer air and darkness.

"Don't waste time!" exclaimed Plessis. "Here, stick to me. Make for the back. The front windows will be shuttered. The back, and the garden!"

Closed rooms, a strange house, and pitch blackness; how they managed it, Andreini never knew. Fumbling through dark rooms, and at last to a window, while behind them the house rang with yells and streamed with smoke, and shook to the pounding of men's feet.

Plessis leaned far out, and pulled himself back, cursing.

"A hazy sky, no stars, but it seems like a roof beneath. The kitchens, perhaps. I'll chance it! You hang out and grip my hand."

He let himself out. Andreini got a handgrip on him, lowered him, and caught a joyous word. He let go, and himself took the greater chance of hanging and dropping. All went well, however, and a moment later they dropped to the ground below, and slipped off into the gardens, and so to the rear wall.

TEN MINUTES later Andreini, heedless of his unconventional costume, was watching a singular scene, at the front of Marillac's house. The street was bright with torches. In the entry stood the Duke de Nevers, one of the greatest nobles of the realm, passionately denouncing the Bishop of Lucon to the King's Lieutenant, whose party of fifty archers of the watch surrounded the entrance. They were actually armed with pikes or muskets, but still bore the name of archers, in sympathy with the past.

Nevers denounced the country bishop with fiery heat; Lucon had killed M. de Marillac of the guards, with two other gentlemen, and had hurt or wounded many. On the other hand stood Cadillac, lackey of the bishop, crying to heaven for vengeance on Marillac and others who had kidnaped the good prelate and were holding him prisoner even now.

"May Satan fly away with me, if I know what to believe!" cried the perplexed and angry officer. "A bishop, you say? A bishop to kill gentlemen of the guards? Then the guards had better take to theology!"

"Precisely my opinion, monsieur," intervened a new voice, a voice calm and poised and unhurried. From Cadillac broke a cry of joy, as the Bishop of Lucon pressed through the guards and came into the full torchlight. He bowed composedly to the officer, and to the Duke, who stared slack-jawed.

"SEEMINGLY THERE is some curious mistake, gentlemen," he went on affably. "I am the Bishop of Lucon, true; but it is obvious that, having just arrived, I could not very well be killing gentlemen inside the house yonder. Nor, being afoot, and safe, have I been kidnaped and put to danger—plain, is it not? Therefore, M. de Nevers, your friends and gentlemen have evidently made a mistake in someone's identity; and this rascally servant of mine has been drinking and imagining things. You rogue! Go home instantly; and as penance, give your breeches to the beggar at the corner yonder, who has none. Quick about it! You shall have a dozen lashes tomorrow, for your punishment.

M. de Nevers, my profound apologies. And M. the Lieutenant of the King, my thanks for your good-will and my regrets for having disturbed you! Good evening, gentlemen."

And with another bow the Bishop of Lucon went his way. As he later observed to his guest, it was the shortest and most profitable sermon he had ever preached; and might well have closed with an admonition on how much even the best-educated person can learn from the theater.

"I only trust, my friend," he added amiably, "that you will also find the evening profitable, aside from that ring upon your finger."

Andreini smiled. "I shall, you may be sure, if the queen does not forget her promise to commission me and my company of players!"

The other nodded at him sagely.

"There are two really regal attributes of Marie de Medici," he observed. "First, she knows the very slight importance of the truth. Second, she knows the tremendous importance of a promise! If she promised to write you with her own hand, she will do so."

And she did, the letter even today attesting what a profound cynic was the Bishop of Lucon, and what an excellent actor was Jean Baptiste Andreini.

FIRST WOMAN

KILGORE TOSSED the sheaf of papers to the table. "There's the new play; I'll have no share in it. The thing's vile, Mordaunt. You may be Master of the King's Players and friend of half the court gallants, but you'll come a cropper unless you call a halt on this obscenity."

Sir James Mordaunt chuckled. "Hal, the people will love it! Art become a Roundhead Puritan, eh? You've changed queerly, lad, since we came down from Oxford together."

Mordaunt had been an actor and a good one, before he inherited a title and went into the business end of the theater, with a lease on the Globe. The two men were sitting now in the greenroom of the Globe, beneath the boxes; a fire was blazing in the hearth, for it was a cold February afternoon of 1629.

A handsome man was Mordaunt, talented, witty, with a superb arrogance of air and feature that became him well. Only Kilgore was aware of the shadow behind those bold eyes, of something awry in the man's nature, like a stratum of rotten rock in a hillside.

"I've not changed, James," replied Kilgore. "I think you have. Five years ago, that play would have horrified you. Today you laugh at it. I'll have none of it; that's flat!"

Mordaunt sipped his mulled ale and stretched his toes nearer the fire.

"Bad policy, Hal, to quarrel with your bread and butter."

"My bread? God forbid!" said Kilgore angrily. "Do you ever

give the grand plays of Marlowe, of Shakespeare, of the others? No! Instead, you put on hastily written things stolen from some Spanish farce, depending upon obscene jests to carry them across!"

"An excellent Roundhead sermon, by gad!" Mordaunt's tone was light, but his eyes darkened ominously. "Here, take some of the good Virginia weed, and think upon Sunday night, when Ma'mselle Rachel startles the world—the first woman ever to play upon our English stage! There'll be triumphs for us all, and greater ones to come. Too bad if your refusal to take part in the next play should force the breaking of your contract—after the Sunday night's performance."

A startling threat here, but Kilgore gave no sign he heard it.

He took his big pewter tankard from before the fire, quaffed the warmed ale and filled his long-stemmed pipe. It was not without an inward sigh that he cast a glance at the other man— handsome, successful, beloved of the women and a friend of gallants. There was all he himself might have been, and was not.

Smallpox had marred his face, ending his dream of fame and fortune as an actor. A man could not hide his skin under paint and powder, as did the boys who played female rôles. He had flung himself into comic parts, and had great skill in arranging and altering plays; thus he was useful in the King's Company, but could easily be replaced.

The French war, last year, had wiped out his entire fortune. Love too had been frightened off, by that scarred cheek of his. Most of his friends in the profession had taken umbrage at his opinions. Small wonder, then, that his grave, strong features held a deep bitterness, as Mordaunt went on:

"For your harsh words, Hal, the day's past when the people are content with bear-baiting outside the theater and tragic ranting inside. We give 'em what they want; shrewd wit, a bit o' spice, none of your heavy soberside stuff. Leave that to the damned Puritans! If ladies of pleasure frequent the pit, that's none of our business."

Kilgore checked his impulsive words. He was no Puritan; but the headlong dive that the theater had taken since King Charles came to the throne, was only too clear to him. The traditions of restraint of an older generation were swept away; depravity and vice ran rampant in plays and pit alike. Mademoiselle Rachel, discovering the nature of these plays, and the meaning of some of her lines, had protested indignantly; but she had too bitter need of the money to throw up the job that had brought her to London. A grand young woman, this Rachel, and Kilgore's

"Bear with me. Until tomorrow, let us be friends."

heart warmed to the thought of her—in which sentiment he was not alone.

"I'll not argue the matter, James," he rejoined. "Nor will I act in that new play."

"We've drifted far apart of late," the other said darkly.

"Far apart," repeated Kilgore, uncompromising. He puffed at his pipe. "Break my contract, eh? I suppose you need me the first night with Rachel; then you can throw Jem Alleyne into my part."

"Confound you!" Mordaunt's eyes glittered at him angrily. "Leave me in the lurch, and you'll never again tread a stage in London town, Hal Kilgore!"

AT THIS way of putting it, Kilgore broke into a laugh.

"Saddle me with the blame and threaten me to boot, eh? Nonsense, James! You've no threat that has teeth. I'm sick unto death of this stage and its obscenity. Besides, all the theater, as a whole, is sinking lower every day and will soon be done for. A higher type of dramatic form is rising."

"What? Puritan sermons?" sneered the other.

"No; masques. You know how they're in favor abroad, and

they have a great future here. Decent people can attend them without having to hear language no courtesan can stomach. They'll survive, when the stage itself is abolished."

"Fat chance of that!" said Mordaunt, laughing. "Wait till we've set the new fashion with Rachel and you see how people crowd to hear the pretty creatures rant and rave! Real women, instead of painted boys! And the more spicy their language, the more delighted will the audience be."

Kilgore choked down his anger. Mademoiselle Rachel had come from Paris to show how women's parts might be better played by women than by boys; she was rehearsing with them now for the first appearance of any woman on the English stage. The scandal of it was shaking half London, with street preachers invoking hell-fire and brimstone on all sides; and, it must be admitted, with some excuse. The other half of London, which at the moment was the more important half, was thrilled and expectant and eager to see the novelty.

Rachel, who knew little or no English, was meanwhile being taught her rôle, parrot-fashion.

"And while I think of it," went on Mordaunt, with a chuckle, "we'll touch up Rachel's part a bit. She'll not need to know that the words mean; faith, that'll make it all the more fetching!"

THIS WAS the spark. Kilgore's face changed, and his voice leaped.

"Mordaunt, she's a good woman, a fine woman. You'd not play so dirty a trick? Surely, not even you could be sunk so low as that!"

How those words bit! Into the dark, lean features of Sir James Mordaunt crept a flush of quick anger.

"So there lies the land, eh?" he sneered. "Well, put her out of your mind; she's mine, or will be when the time's ripe. She's for no prating Roundhead."

"She's not for you, and mayhap not for your theater either," rapped out Kilgore, with a flash of temper that he regretted instantly.

Mordaunt half rose. "What d'ye mean by that, damn you?"

"That she's too good, of course." Deftly, Kilgore saved himself from revealing too much. "She's too good for you, and for this pit of obscenity you control."

"Oh!" Mordaunt relaxed, finished his ale, and rose. He looked down at Kilgore with coldly biting eyes. "Well, until Sunday night our roads still run together; keep to your own side. We'll part friends, at least on the surface-provided you take my advice. Leave Rachel alone. Better still," he added, "give her the full advantage of your handsome countenance; then she'll not be tempted."

He swung out of the dressing-room.

Those last words had been cruelly arrogant beyond belief, deliberately lashing Kilgore on the raw; well did Mordaunt know how sensitive he was on the subject of his scarred face. Yet, deeply as they pierced, Kilgore was far too strong of soul to let himself be flung off balance. He quivered to the hurt, but he gave no reply. After all, he was making his own plans for a stroke that would be more devastating than any words.

He knew Mordaunt's threats were not idle ones. Between these two men the olden friendship had ripened and rotted, to burst like a mildewed fruit upon the rock of occasion, when Rachel came to London.

"And now he means to fatten her rôle with more obscenity and lie to her about it!" Kilgore thought angrily. "Well, thank heaven our paths divide! Today's Friday; on Sunday night it's ended. And I'm ended as well—unless Arlington has the right answer tonight!"

FINISHING HIS ale at leisure, he enjoyed another pipe, and his nerves were calm again when the players began to arrive for rehearsal. Mordaunt returned, escorting Rachel; her radiant presence, her broken English, and her youthful charm made the dingy greenroom seem a different place.

For the sake of warmth, the rehearsal was held here. In her rôle of French lass in London, a rôle and play slapped together overnight to take advantage of her poor English, Rachel was bewitching. Even the company could scarce keep a straight face as she mouthed the bawdy allusions which she herself did not understand; but Kilgore went through his lines grimly. As they stood together for a moment, he had the chance he sought.

"Tonight?" he said under his breath. He spoke French well.

"At nine," she rejoined, and it was understood.

She was divinely feminine; a graceful, sloe-eyed creature radiating magnetism and personality. To Kilgore, she was something far more. He had learned her depths of warm friendliness, her shrewd wit, her mental acuity; he knew, too, how rare and delicately precious a spirit abided here.

From her first arrival in London she had trusted him, as indeed did most people. Hal Kilgore held many an unguessed secret in his keeping. He knew she was no haphazard wench, and the old Frenchwoman who posed as her mother was actually a servant. More than this, his knowledge was vague. She had not even told her actual name.

Of her shadowy background, he knew that her father had forfeited his life and his estates because of some plot against Richelieu—one of many. Left a beggar, the daughter took the name of Rachel, joined a company of players, and had made her way. She was no great lady, but came, he thought, from some good provincial family. And this was the sum of his knowledge.

Rehearsal ended, Kilgore hastily departed. He went to his lodgings, obtained a hurried supper, changed his careless garb for richer attire, buckled on his sword-belt, and was off again, footing it across London to the house of Lord Arlington.

Upon this hour hung destiny. All his plans and hopes were coming now to fruition or to complete ruin. His great dream was coming true, or it was not; within a moment, upon a word! For he had shared this dream with Arlington; and Lord Arlington had in his younger days written a masque; consequently, the seed fell upon fruitful ground.

Not that Arlington was any exponent of the virtues. Kilgore's father had known him before the day of ruin and poverty; hence Kilgore appealed to him, for at least he could see the practical side of this vision. Since the death of King James, four years back, Arlington had been out of favor, aloof from London and the court, spending most of the time at his noble Tudor estate of Carlin Hall in Sussex. His last employment, at the French court, had ended very badly—indeed, it was said that Richelieu had demanded his recall. Despite this, Arlington was too subtle and unscrupulous a man

Upon this hour hung destiny; his hopes were coming now to fruition—or to complete ruin.

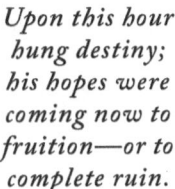

to remain forever in disgrace, and Kilgore was confident the upswing would carry himself and his dreams with it. If he did not admire Arlington's methods, at least he could admire the man.

HE FOUND Arlington alone before a warm fire, a decanter of wine on the table with glorious tall glasses of Venetian make, and tobacco. The two shook hands, and Arlington turned quickly to the table, filling the glasses. He extended one.

"Success, Kilgore!" he exclaimed, smiling warmly. "A health to my masque, and to your future! The masque will be played for the King. You will play it. Success!"

The glasses clinked. Mordaunt scarcely tasted the wine; with those words, he knew that everything was won. So it was, both for himself and for Lord Arlington.

This nobleman was neither handsome nor impulsive, but he had a warm, winning air and the ability to gain men's trust. Deep eyes in a chunky face whose heavy lines were belied by a sparkle of humor—physically he was an awkward man, but mentally alert and flashing of spirit. Those who trusted him too much came away second-best, it was said; but Hal Kilgore had everything to win and nothing to lose.

"King Charles will visit us at Carlin Hall after Easter," he said, and in those words Kilgore realized that the upswing had started. Arlington, after Easter, would be one of England's rulers once more. "And the masque—why, Kilgore, 'twas a noble inspiration! The masque will go straight to his heart! The changes you made in the manuscript are splendid."

"I'm glad you approve them," said Kilgore.

"I'll turn Carlin Hall over to you. Lady Arlington will remain there; I'll stop in London a bit and settle a few things; you shall go there as soon as you're ready and take full charge of the production. Success!"

Another health was drunk. Kilgore understood that his production of this masque must win the King's heart; he had no worries here. Now he was thinking beyond, of his own dream.

"And have you considered the other matter?" he asked.

"Oh! Egad, Kilgore, it's a great idea!" Arlington fairly beamed. "I've discussed it with one or two friends. Granted the King's favor, of which I think we're assured, the scheme's a magnificent one—a bid for Puritan favor too, mind you. There's one doubtful point, and that's this French actress Rachel."

Kilgore's brows lifted. "Doubtful?"

"Aye. Thus far we've taken your word regarding her. We'll see her at the play, of course—"

"You'll see her in half an hour," broke in Kilgore, smiling. "She receives us."

"Excellent! And she's not bound to Mordaunt and the Globe?"

"No. He wanted to see if the experiment succeeds; he was not too sure how the people would like a woman on the stage. So he made no contract. Now I've warned her, and both of us will leave the Globe after the one performance on Sunday night. Mordaunt can get some other girl to replace her overnight—I happen to know of two or three women he had in mind, before he resolved to bring Rachel from Paris."

"Then all promises well." Arlington leaned back, his eyes twinkling, and filled a pipe for himself. "If she makes a success in the one performance, and leaves, the public will tumble over themselves to see her once your new house opens."

"Eh? My house?" repeated Kilgore.

The other laughed.

"Just so. The plan is that you're to be placed in full charge; none of us will appear in the venture. There's no question about the money end of it. We'll subscribe ten thousand pounds if need be. Meantime, I'll advance what's necessary. You know what it means?"

KILGORE TOOK fire. For himself, here was fame and fortune; but greater than this was the fulfillment of the dream

that was more to him than ambition, and the fact that others had realized his vision and found it good.

"It means the greatest thing that's ever happened to dramatic art!" he exclaimed. "It means the end of the old theater, the rise of the new! No more of these bawdy plays. Instead, a house where only masques and such things are given, where wit replaces vice, where nimble flights of fancy and poetry may appeal to the nobler side of our audiences!"

"And also something more practical," Arlington added, suddenly grave. "It's the practical side that interests me and the others, Kilgore. This Rachel isn't the first woman to act on the English stage."

"What? But she is!" replied Kilgore, astonished.

*Arlington sensed
the threat too late;
swift as light, the
man lunged.*

Arlington shook his head.

"No. In 1593 a performance of 'The Jew of Malta' was given before Queen Elizabeth. A Manchester lass was on the stage that night, for the first time. Her name was Jenny, and she was no lady but a prostitute. She made trouble; the Queen was furious; that ended females on the stage. Now, when your Rachel appears, there will be a tremendous Puritan reaction—in fact, it's already begun, as you must know. Add to this, the present situation that threatens bloodletting on all sides; d'ye see the point?"

Kilgore hesitated. It was true that dissension and hatred were rising to terrific heights, these days. At this moment King Charles was in a senseless and stubborn battle with Parliament, stopping little short of actual force. Headstrong nobles fought one another, and Puritans fought the wastrels of fortune.

"No," said Kilgore slowly, "I'm afraid I don't see what you're driving at."

"Let the theater continue as it is and you have a tremendous irritant. Well, I propose to abolish it altogether! We'll take the part of virtue; away with this Satanic abscess! Away with this theater that debases fair womanhood! Away with those foul rogues who dare to employ women in public representations of virtue unrewarded!"

He affected a nasal whine, and a thin, ironic smile played about his lips.

"Now d'ye get it, Kilgore? Abolish the theater, by gad! At one stroke, we make a bold play for Roundhead approval, and do it in the King's name! Then we make use of your one playhouse that remains—where masques, not plays, are given—to affect popular opinion. We make use of it, deliberately, cleverly; here's an instrument that can be of enormous value to us! Why, damme if we won't have the Puritans themselves writing masques!"

"I should have known," said Kilgore thoughtfully, "that you'd serve your own interest somehow."

Arlington, far from taking umbrage at the words, laughed in cynic amusement.

"Right; and here my interest lies in avoiding ruin. Charles is alienating London; and no King can endure in England if the City is against him. With Wentworth, Newcastle and one or two others, I propose to change all this and avoid a civil war; the theater and the printed word will be our greatest aids."

Kilgore nodded, and his face cleared. "Why not? A good cause; count me in, with all my heart! May I offer my congratulations upon what is evidently a return to power?"

"AYE; AND mine, upon your ability to see the future!" Arlington rose and clapped him heartily on the shoulder. "Lad, I've all the strings of ambition in my hand. When the King visits Carlin Hall, Arlington becomes another Buckingham—

and of greater value to England than was George Villiers, God rest him! There are abuses to be corrected and hot hearts to be assuaged; and I'll not lose by the doing, either. Yet no one else can see what I see ahead," he added with deepening gravity. "Bad going to worse, the King and the people at loggerheads-stubborn ruler, and people cherishing their liberties! That's the thing to avoid; conflict, ruin, bloodshed! And with your help and that of the stage, I propose to do it. All ready? Come along, let's be on our way."

Thus abruptly, he showed Kilgore his heart, and then closed the matter to discussion. But the brief revelation held the player spellbound.

Arlington could write a masque, and a good one; as envoy to France he had tried wits against Richelieu and failed; as one of the ministry, he had botched things and fallen before the more brilliant Buckingham. But now Kilgore saw a new and different phase of him. The cynic, self-seeking nobleman had become attuned to vision. He, and he alone, grasped what might come of England's internal dissension; he, and he alone, could swing Newcastle, Wentworth and the other great lords to act with him. Even, perhaps, the King.

And as sounding-board and agent and assistant, Hal Kilgore and the new theater of the masque and pageant! The evil of the old theater swept away, and with it, for the nonce, all plays and drama; these would return, of course, but in cleansed form.

"One thing," said Kilgore, as they neared the lodging-house where Rachel and her supposed mother lived. "I would say to do away with the taint of the old theater by never letting it get started in the new. Masques are no new thing, but we'll give them new strength and meaning. Therefore, I'd say to keep them clean from the start."

"Agreed," Arlington replied. "My sister and wife will take parts in the masque at Carlin Hall. The Queen, accustomed to masques at the French court, will set the fashion at Whitehall; I have her word for it. Therefore, rule your new domain with an iron hand! And if it would please you to be Sir Harry Kilgore, you can earn the title by Easter."

So he had the Queen's backing! Kilgore perceived how deeply Arlington had already builded, and how sure were the foundations. This heartened him, even more than the hint of a knighthood; past any doubt, Arlington was the man of coming power in England!

W H E N   T H E I R destination was reached, Kilgore was walking on air.

Rachel received them in the sitting-room of her lodgings.

Afterward, he remembered her pallor, her confusion, when Arlington stooped over her hand with his polished French phrases; at the moment, however, Kilgore noticed nothing, so exhilarated was he by the glorious vista ahead.

He could not contain himself for the sheer joy of it, but poured out before her all that it would mean to her as well as to him—performance before the King, the favor of the Queen, a theater in London, where only the finest type of spectacles would be given. More than this he said not, for Arlington had cautioned him regarding the need of secrecy; but this was enough to gild all the future for them both. It brought a sparkle of laughter to her eyes, and Arlington was obviously captivated by her charm; he expanded; he threw off his years; he set free all the merry vivacity which in other days had made his name famous. The man was transformed, and Kilgore marveled at what he saw. There was no doubt that Rachel had set herself to bewitch him, and had succeeded.

"O N   S U N D A Y night, I shall prove my devotion," said he, laughing. "I'll have one of the boxes above the greenroom, and shall have the honor of acclaiming the first actress in England! And after the performance, you and the entire company shall then dine with me. Agreed?"

"Sir James Mordaunt has already bade me to supper," she replied, with a pretty blush. "How can I offend him, milord?"

"Nonsense! How not?" broke in Kilgore, laughing. "We quit the Globe company, you and I, after the performance! Therefore, no halfway measures—as your new manager and producer, I command you!"

She swept him a mock-humble curtsy, and turned to Arlington.

"You see, milord, I am helpless! Let it be as you desire."

So it was settled.

Afterward, as the two of them walked along the cold street, Arlington, with a touch of fantasy, blew a kiss to the stars.

"Kilgore, she's all you proclaimed her, and more! The world of the theater has changed forever; I'll wager anything that after Sunday evening there'll be never a play produced without at least one actress! When do you plan to take her to Carlin Hall?"

"If possible, on the Monday."

"Wise man! My coach shall be at your disposal. Every gallant in London will be sighing his heart out for her; get her away at once into Lady Arlington's care. Faith," he added, laughing, "were I ten years younger and less pleasantly married, I might be among the gallants myself! But she's a rare woman, Kilgore; rarely beautiful and rarely virtuous, if I'm any judge, and must come of a fine family. She's not here all alone?"

"No; an old woman who poses as her mother, and whom I take to be a family servant. And, I believe, a lackey of some kind. I've not set eyes on him, "but Mordaunt mentioned him once or twice. Hm! Mordaunt won't be a joyous man on Monday; I'd like to hear him rave!"

"Your Mordaunt, be damned to him, had best not rave too loud," said Arlington, in his carelessly arrogant way. "His day is done; yours begins; and since siller talks better than any tongue, as the Scots say, here's a hundred pounds to bind our bargain. No, thank me not! We'll go far together, Kilgore, and England shall forgive us much that we've left undone, for what we do from this time forward."

Kilgore pocketed the purse, parted at Arlington's door with

a warm clasp of the hand, and went back to his own lodgings a new man.

He slept that night upon fitful dreams; he could scarce believe what had happened. At the darkest point, the door to life and fortune was opening before him, and if he had met the slings of fortune valiantly in the past, he must now greet the future with shrewd care. Gone was bitterness; when he wakened in the morning and got out soap and razor, he looked into the mirror with a smile.

"Thou rascal face!" he exclaimed to the pock-scarred countenance that greeted him and smiled back. "No longer a symbol of defeat, exchange that sullen indignity for a brave and confident token of the future!"

He laughed as he began to shave. Life was once more good. And he owed it all to one man, the only man in England who could see his vision—and who could see a farther vision as well.

He could look around him now with new eyes. The riots in London, the fury against the King, the struggle with Parliament, the bitter-voiced Puritans—all this would pass, for one man had a vision of what was needed. One man, who had learned from sad experience and from failure how to create aright and how to succeed in greater things. Arlington, seeking no longer the road of personal ambition, but guided by a truer and nobler aim!

"That way has changed the destiny of nations and men," reflected Kilgore. "Without this vision of his, this virtue of having learned from bitter experience, England might well go to wrack and ruin and even to civil war. Instead, it comes to adjustment. Just as I myself, but for this man, would have lost future and hope and my own vision—whereas I now see clearly, and have work to do that shall erect a dream into glorious things!"

He was busy at the Globe this day; there were some new decorations, a simple set to erect, for the platform-stage. He was already full of ideas about the new theater, with a proscenium arch and a stage no longer surrounded by the audience, in the Italian fashion.

Further, his were certain details to manage regarding costumes for the morrow, and for the dress rehearsal this afternoon. They marveled at him, one and all; even Mordaunt, who showed up with dour mien, warmed a bit.

"Hast changed heart, Hal?" said he, speaking privately. "Gad, you look ten years younger! You'll stay with us?"

"Not I," Kilgore rejoined, with a smile. "It's the prospect of shaking from my feet the dust of this stage that's made life gay!"

Mordaunt's face darkened. "Then, by heaven, you'll never set foot on another stage in London town!" he snapped, and turned away.

Kilgore could well afford to laugh at threats this day, but there was no further jar; having vented his spleen, Mordaunt gave his attention to business.

The dress rehearsal, again held in the green-room to avoid the expense of heating the outer space, went off to a nicety. Rachel arrived, escorted today by her lackey—a tall gaunt square-shouldered Frenchman who swaggered like a bravo and wore his sword slung in a baldric, French-fashion. He was a man of forty-odd, Kilgore estimated, and spoke no English at all.

As for Rachel, at first Kilgore fancied that she avoided him; but when he secured a word with her apart, she smiled and putting her hand in his, said gently:

"My friend, bear with me; until tomorrow night, let us still be friends."

"What do you mean by that?" he demanded quickly, searching her face. "You don't seem yourself today."

"I'm not myself," she said, and her eyes met his with a sudden hard light. "I must do you hurt, and myself as well; there's no way out, so face it and make the best of it. Can you carry on your program without me?"

"If necessary, yes," he rejoined, startled. "But why? What has happened to change you? For, by heaven, you're changed!"

That queer coldness in her eyes, that hardness, was past understanding. It wakened him to a storm of dismayed emotion.

From a friend, a confidant, an intimate, she had abruptly become distant, another person indeed. From dismay, however, he passed to angry readjustment.

"My program—you mean by that word all the dream, the vision of which you know?" he went on. "Yes, it can proceed without you or without me; it's greater than either of us. But why should it? Why are you changed? Why, only last night everything was agreed!"

"That was last night," she said coldly.

"What's all this mystery about?" demanded the exasperated Kilgore. "Come, let's have it out and reach an explanation! Has something happened that I don't know?"

"Yes," she replied. "Let it wait till tomorrow night; then you'll understand everything. Upon my honor!"

KILGORE'S FACE cleared.

"Agreed, then! And you'll sup with Arlington?"

"No, I will not," she said bluntly. "Ask no more now, I pray you!"

Kilgore whistled softly to himself, thinking that he understood. Perhaps Lord Arlington had not been so platonic after all; something had happened, evidently, to set Rachel against him. Well, it might be overcome or mended.

If not—then what? Kilgore did not mistake her nature; she was headstrong, for all her gentleness, and had a steely something within her eyes that might hint at trouble. He had set his heart upon having her, and had builded upon her acquiescence in his dream; but that dream could go its way without her, if need were. The loss would be great, the disappointment grievous, but she was not an essential.

"The one essential is Arlington," Kilgore reflected. "If she wants to back out of it, well and good. Perhaps Mordaunt has made her some glittering offer, and she's inclined to take it; that's her affair. I've done my best for her."

He was, indeed, more than a little inclined to resent her

attitude, for his interest in her was vivid and personal; he had fancied that she was even able to overlook his scarred face, that in her eyes he could read the things he had sought and never found. Not so? Then best discover the truth now, he told himself, and not live in self-deception. Ahead was a future too great and glowing, too filled with action, too pregnant with destiny, for any assaults to be allowed to shake it at this stage of the game. Find the truth, accept it, make the best of it!

"Even if I must flatter Arlington and play the sycophant, it'll be in a grand cause," Kilgore told himself that night, as he thought upon the matter. "He's the keystone of all, and on him I must build for our mutual advantage. Damn the women! Who can understand 'em?"

MEANTIME, HE had the hundred pounds for assurance.

Sunday wore its anxious length at last, a Sunday wherein half London was whipped up to screaming pitch by strident Puritans. A woman on the stage! The point was magnified out of all proportion until it rasped the nerves like a raw wound; one might well believe that Satan himself was appearing at the Globe this night.

In consequence, the place was jam-packed that night by opposition crowds. Court gallants, Roundhead-hating city men, gentry great and small, ladies of the only sort who might appear at such public interludes—boxes and pit were crammed. Link-boys flitted their torches in the streets. Heads were bloodied here and there. It was a bawling, riotous, lustily forthright crowd, anxious to applaud Satan and all his works.

And applaud they did, while the walls shook. Rachel scintillated until even the actors of the company were astonished; never had she seemed so radiant, so filled with abundant life and energy and laughter. The platform-stage, almost surrounded by the audience, was directly under the boxes built above the green-room; in one of these boxes sat Arlington and some friends, aiding the thunderous applause. Gifts and coins came rattling upon the boards; it was a harvest for all hands this night.

In the final act Kilgore was on at the opening, then off for good. At his exit, he glanced up at the boxes, and to his surprise saw that Arlington now seemed to be alone; he thought little of it, however. He made haste to shift into his street-clothes, and as he was doing so, an attendant brought him a hasty word.

"My Lord Arlington's compliments, Mr. Kilgore, and he asks if you'll join him in his box, since his company have departed."

Kilgore nodded assent. Just what the program was for the evening, he had still to learn; probably Arlington wanted him to talk to Rachel, he thought. No one else was in the green-room, at the moment, except the queer French lackey who had accompanied his mistress, and who sat guarding her clothes and playing absently with his grizzled chin-tuft.

His dressing finished, Kilgore hastened to the box overhead. In the most recent rebuilding and overhaul of the Globe, these boxes had been given some comfort as well as privacy from the boxes to right and left. When Kilgore stepped in, Arlington gave him a smiling glance and a gesture; Rachel was on the stage below. Silent, Kilgore took a stool and listened. That smiling greeting was enough to assure him that all was well.

And now, in what followed—where lay chance, where lay careful design? Kilgore never learned. But surely it was not by chance, that Lord Arlington sat here thus alone!

FOR SUDDENLY the curtain at the back was lifted, and into the box stepped the stalwart grizzled lackey. He spoke in French, swiftly, imperatively:

"Milord! You do not remember me?"

Arlington looked around. "Eh? Who the devil are you?"

"Milord, you should know me. I was the servant and lackey and friend of the Comte de Caulain, whom you knew some years ago in Paris."

"Eh?" Arlington came to his feet, and at the name his face changed. "Upon my word, so you are! What are you doing here?"

Kilgore, astonished, saw the lackey bow respectfully. The

man's grave manner gave him no disquiet; nor did Arlington appear alarmed.

"Milord, M. le Comte was beheaded, you may recall, because he trusted you," came the words. "You betrayed him to Richelieu. Because of you, the damned Cardinal murdered him and left his daughter a beggar."

Arlington frowned abruptly. "I had nothing to do with the matter. Be off, fellow! I didn't even know your master had a daughter."

"But she, monsieur, knew that her father had a murderer," said the lackey, still with that grave, intent manner. "She is down there, on this stage; Rachel, they call her. She wanted me to tell you this."

"Gad!" Arlington started. "You can't mean—upon my word—Here, you damned rogue—"

It all happened in an instant. Kilgore caught the motion and leaped to intervene; he was too late. Arlington sensed the threat, too late. For swift as light, the man whipped out his sword and lunged, and lunged again.

Kilgore was upon him, only to meet a stunning blow between the eyes from the pommel of that sword. It dropped him senseless.

When he was brought to himself, the box was jammed. The curtains had been dropped, shutting out the roaring crowd; he found Arlington asking for him, and stumbled to his knees beside the dying man. Arlington's fingers closed on his.

"Too bad, lad!" came the faint voice. "It's bitter irony—that she should destroy the dreams—that dreams—that dreams must perish like the sunlight! Good man, Kilgore; we might have gone far together—"

A cry burst from Kilgore, as the words failed, as the fingers within his relaxed. A cry of grief, of shock, of despair; and not for himself nor for his own hopes either, but for this man whose hopes and ambitions had been so much greater than his own, embracing all England—and now forever gone.

The lackey? He was never seen again; indeed, it was whispered that the Foul Fiend had taken the shape of that man in order to come and claim his own. Kilgore knew better, for if the lackey was gone, so was the mistress, and gone forever.

O F T E N A N D often, in days to follow, Arlington's words recurred to him. That dreams must perish like the sunlight—strange words! Everything was gone now; there was no other man in England with Arlington's vision, or the power to transmute it to reality. He and his future were gone too.

Yet from the bitterness of these lost things Kilgore had a richer and truer reward than comes to most dreamers. For during two whole days he had seen all his hopes and ambitions coming true, and their reality attested, and their worth recognized… even if they must perish like the sunlight.

Like the sunlight, indeed? But even for a dying man—does sunlight perish?

TWO SWORDSMEN OF GASCONY

"NOT A shot has been fired, not a man has been killed, for three days!" said the young man who was furbishing his sword. "And they call this war!"

"When it rains in Flanders, it rains," exclaimed one of the others, with a rousing Gascon oath. "Ha, comrades! Our youngster pines for the bloody fray! Your first campaign, M. d'Artaignan? Take is easy, *mon ami,* take it easy and be thankful!"

Artaignan, an angry flash in his eye, regarded the speaker, met only a wide, jovial grin, and dismissed his choler. It was no time to be angry or start quarrels; the damned rain, he told himself, took the heart out of anger as it took the heart out of war.

He reached for his wide hat and cloak, drew up his boot-tops and buckled them around his legs, and stepped out of the miserable cowshed in which he and his companions were quartered. To right and left were other sheds, tents, wagons in pairs with canvas stretched between—anything and everything that would protect the troops from the weather.

Gloomily, Artaignan stamped along. He was not tall, but was lithe and admirably well-knit. A tiny mustache and Vandyke attempted vainly to age his unlined and youthful features; he had the eager zest of a boy, the impulsive explosiveness of a true Gascon.

Here all France had come to war—and it rained! The lines of artillery were silent. Through the drizzle appeared the walls and spires of Arras. Completely invested and cut off from relief

"*A mountebank's daughter?*"
*murmured
Bergerac. "God
forbid! Rather,
a princess!*"

though they were, the Spanish, German and Flemish troops
that held Arras for the Hapsburgs fought stubbornly on; it was
the summer of 1640.

Artaignan eyed the gray walls, eyed his own front lines. These
were occupied by the flower of the French army—the regiment

"Not at all, comrade," declared Artaignan. "An angel fresh from the heavenly choir."

of Conti and the various companies of the Guards, the volunteer nobles who had no discipline whatever, hot pride of birth, and the ability to fight like demons. Certain of these companies were composed exclusively of Gascon gentlemen.

Suddenly Artaignan halted, turned; his nostrils quivered like

the nose of a dog scenting game. A sound had reached his ear.
It came again. It was the slithering clash of sword upon sword,
accompanied by low oaths and gusty words. He glanced around,
questioningly.

Now occupied by the headquarters staff, a straggling hamlet
had nestled here under the city walls. The ears of the young
Gascon led him between two cabins to an enclosure at the rear,
bounded by a cattle-shed and a manure pile; here he came upon
a dozen men standing and watching two of their number at
sword-play. Artaignan's face fell when he saw it was no duel.
He was about to turn away, when an amazing thing caught his
attention.

The two men were fencing with naked blades. One of the
two was a grizzled, masterly man; the other, activated by an
incredible energy and a dazzling skill, was much younger, with
scarred features, an enormous hooked nose, and dark liquid eyes
that fairly flashed fire. What took Artaignan's eye was that this
younger man was talking as he fenced—talking, jesting, laughing, and yet maintaining a display of swordsmanship that was
positively miraculous. He could have killed his opponent easily,
had he wished.

"Pardieu!" The older man sprang back. "God save me from
ever facing you in earnest, Bergerac! I've had enough exercise
for the day."

Bergerac turned, laughing. He caught the gaping, admiring
gaze of Artaignan; for a moment the two looked at each other.
Then a hand clapped Artaignan on the shoulder. It was Captain
Duret de Montchenin, of the regiment of Conti, whom he had
met recently.

"*Holà*, comrades!" cried the officer. "Allow me to present a true
Gascon from the company of M. des Essarts.... M. d'Artaignan,
making his first campaign with us!"

Flushed and eager, Artaignan was presented, was welcomed;
Gascon voices rose high; the rich Gascon accent beat upon the
air. Highest and richest was the voice of the swordsman, ringing

out his own high-sounding titles—Hercule Savinien de Cyrano de Bergerac—embracing Artaignan with garlicky gusto, hurling oaths to the sky, and fancy Gascon jests at those around.

THE RAIN had died to a faint drizzle. Bergerac donned his plumed hat, adjusted the scarf that was the only uniform of the Guards, and passed his arm through that of Artaignan.

"Come along—a drink to friendship and destiny! Until this cursed weather clears up, we can't expect any exchange of arms with those Germans; it's weather for wine, and I know where to find wine. How old are you, my friend?"

"Twenty-one," said Artaignan, who was actually just eighteen.

"Precisely my own age! Admirable! Au revoir, gentlemen! We go to seek adventure!"

The two swung off together, arm in arm, Artaignan charmed by this attention from so notable a swordsman. They talked as only Gascons can; rather, Bergerac did the talking, for his tongue ran madly. He talked, naturally, of himself, and Artaignan learned all about him.

Bergerac mourned only one thing: he had never been the principal in a duel, although he had frequently served as second—hence, his scars. He was in the company of M. de Carbon Casteljaloux, every man of which was a redoubtable Gascon; he had received a bullet through the body at the siege of Mouzon; he had attended the College of Beauvais; he bragged of love and fight; he was a poet, but he intended to write more serious things and had even started a fantastic romance about a visit to the moon.

SWAGGERING INTO a canteen, they roared for wine. Both were in funds. Bottle after bottle was emptied; Artaignan, who drank with caution, was amazed at the capacity of Bergerac. He had little to tell of himself, being newly come to Paris from the south, and nothing at all to brag about; but he had an imagination.

The little chateau of the Batz family at Lupiac—nowhere near

Artaignan of the Montesquiou family—grew and grew until Bergerac, who had never seen the town of Bergerac, stared with his large eyes bulging. The silver a-clink in Artaignan's pocket became thick *louis d'or* in endless quantity. Bergerac swallowed hard and changed the subject.

"What tragedy is this siege! That is, for a poet. Did I tell you I was a poet?"

"Yes," said Artaignan. "Why is this siege tragic? I think it's

*Bergerac turned,
laughing. He caught
the admiring gaze
of Artaignan.*

superb! All the great regiments, the great soldiers, the great men,
of France are gathered here—"

"And not one of them will be remembered for it." Bergerac
wagged a long finger before his hooked nose. "Comrade, look at
the two of us: a great man like you, destined to become a marshal
of France, a soldier with an eye of steel—and me."

"The greatest swordsman in the army, I think," said Artaignan
with simple naïveté.

Bergerac flushed with pleasure at the compliment, but shook his head.

"No, comrade; I am a poet, a writer, a satirist. I shall write books. They shall make me famous. I shall be remembered in France, you will be remembered, as having been here at the siege of Arras! The others, great men today, will be forgotten by posterity. I know a great man when I see one. You shall become famous, I tell you!"

Artaignan was astonished. "You, a superb swordsman, intend to become a writer?"

"Aye." Bergerac emptied his bottle and called for another. "I'll impart you a secret. I swagger; I second others in duels; I have no quarrels of my own—why? Regard this nose, my friend. I'm a sensitive man; a look, a word, wounds me to the quick. So I force myself to become an incomparable swordsman. I kill poor devils to build up a reputation. I am first in every assault on the walls yonder…. Do I hate those Spaniards and Germans? Not I. Why, I detest fighting! But you see, I am doomed to it. Later, I shall leave the army and write books, and be happy. And we, you and I, shall be the only men remembered by France as having taken part in the siege of Arras!"

"Your pardon, monsieur," spoke up a quiet voice. "What you say is quite true; but a third name will, I am positive, be mentioned with yours."

The two turned. Artaignan started to speak, checked himself. The young man who had entered unobserved, and who stood close to them, was both remarkable and impressive, to his quick eye.

Not, perhaps, to an older eye; it is an odd fact that youth often perceives in youth all the promise of the future. In this bronzed and hearty young fellow an older man might have seen only a queerly attired, fantastic youngster. Artaignan, with quick prescience, beheld a youth of eighteen who had the manners and knowledge and presence of a man of thirty; the brown, mobile face, the deep and penetrating eyes, startled him.

"Ha!" exclaimed Bergerac. "Who can rank with a poet and a soldier, fellow?"

The young man smiled. He wore a black suit tricked out with gold lace, a black coat, a black hat with black plume.

"I have two personalities, gentlemen," he said, his voice richly mellow. "I am the grand equerry, at the moment, of the great and inimitable Doctor Sarasin, a renowned physician and student of the Grand Magic, who will cure the ills of your body and tell you the past, present and future. He, with his daughter and his equipage, is now outside."

"The devil!" ejaculated Bergerac. "Is this your path to fame?"

"No. Having guided the eminent Doctor here, I now leave him and return to my own affairs at Amiens." The visitor bowed, half mockingly. "I am, gentlemen, neither a Gascon nor a noble. I am a strolling player, at your service; an actor, a capable actor, but one who also can write a comedy, a tragedy, a bit of farce, what you like! And when next you hear of me, Messieurs of the Guards, I shall have a great play performed at Paris itself. I shall be a writer of comedies at which the whole world shall laugh!"

"You seem to know the future yourself," said Bergerac.

The other bowed again.

"Thank you. I do. At least, I know my own future!"

"I believe you!" exclaimed Artaignan with energy. He spoke impulsively; something in those mobile features moved and spurred him. "Monsieur, join us in a bottle of wine now, and share our future! A marshal of France, a poet and writer of books, a writer of plays to shake the world's belly with laughter—excellent!"

"Thank you, but I must leave you and be off." The other turned to the door.

Bergerac halted him with a sudden bellow.

"Stop! Who the devil are you? What name shall be linked with ours in fame?"

The young man, pausing in the doorway, flung them a laughing look.

"The name of Molière, comrades. Adieu!" With this reply, he was gone.

Bergerac, laughing, quaffed his wine. "A droll fellow, that!"

"Rather, a man who may well fulfill his boast," asserted Artaignan gravely. "Come, let's step out and have a look at this remarkable Doctor Sarasin. Not to mention his daughter."

"*Pardieu!* Let us see the daughter, by all means!" cried Bergerac.

Together they stepped to the doorway, just in time to see young Molière, astride a saddled horse, go spurring away with a slap-dash of mud and water. Across from the canteen, beside the ruins of a burned cabin, the equipage of the Doctor was drawn up, and the great man himself was unhitching two horses from a caravan or wagon that was like a small house on wheels, with steps and a door at the rear and windows at the sides.

The two exchanged a glance, caught up their hats to fend off the drizzle, and were out on the instant. Not because of the eminent physician, but because of the charming face and figure descending the steps to help with the horses.

"A mountebank's daughter?" murmured Bergerac. "God forbid! Rather, a princess!"

"Not at all, comrade," declared Artaignan, loudly enough to be overheard. "Rather, an angel freshly come from the heavenly choir!"

The young woman turned, smiling, a light in her eye that set Bergerac to twisting his mustache, and Artaignan to controlling a racing pulse. She was adorable. Bergerac became poetical, even rhapsodic; but Artaignan, who was of a somewhat calculating nature, tempered his adoration with a slight—very slight—critical leaven. She was almost too perfect, he reflected; it was hard to believe she was true.

DR. SARASIN joined them, invited them into the dry warmth of the caravan, which was cramped but neat and clean, and procured wine from the canteen.

The eminent physician, who followed the example of the

great Nostradamus in combining with his healing abilities a certain degree of astrology and magic, was an expansive fellow who talked without urging. So did Bergerac, preening himself splendidly. Artaignan and Henriette, as the young woman was named, said very little; but by means of looks alone, Artaignan flattered himself that they had reached a perfect understanding before the visit ended.

Sarasin, a strapping, handsome man of extremely impressive demeanor, intended to have no clients about the caravan, and said so frankly. He purposed going about the camp with his satchel of vials and phylacteries, while Henriette remained here. This position within the purlieus of headquarters offered her any needed protection; but she was, as Sarasin seemed confident, entirely able to take care of herself.

Before leaving, Bergerac expressed a desire to become acquainted with the Doctor's wizardry.

Sarasin laughed and shook his head.

"Messieurs, to be quite frank about it, that is my daughter's share in the business. I tell you this as friends, confidentially. To others, to the world in general, I am of course the great Sarasin, and I can prate learnedly of all the dark masters; but I depend on her to do the work in this respect. She has a natural gift which is marvelous! Will you tell these gentlemen something of their future, Henriette?"

"Not now, Father. I'm tired," said the girl, with a shake of the head. "Shall we say tomorrow, or tomorrow evening?"

"As you prefer, mademoiselle," Bergerac rejoined. "Tomorrow evening, by all means!"

"Come, then, at ten o'clock, when the world is quiet," she said, with so ravishing a smile that Bergerac was overjoyed.

Sarasin questioned them about the disposition of the headquarters staff. He intended to spend this evening, and every evening, presenting his letters of introduction and seeking out nobles and captains; as he said, between eight and midnight a man could better establish himself in the confidence of great

men, than in a dozen working-days. During the afternoons he
would visit the wounded with his sovereign healing balms.

Artaignan reflected—strictly within himself—that to any
enterprising young man this general arrangement should prove
providential. In leaving, he did not imitate the bows and flour-
ishes and oratory of Bergerac; instead, he stooped to kiss the
hand of Henriette and murmured two words under his breath:

"Nine tonight."

STEADILY THE rain fell; Sarasin had predicted that it
would continue for the next day or two. As the two young men

splashed back toward their billets, Bergerac was in ecstasies. He was already rhyming a sonnet to Henriette.

"When we see her tomorrow night, it will be finished," he declared. "Comrade, is she not a living marvel? Saw you ever such wise and witching eyes, such wit and beauty?"

"Frequently," replied Artaignan. "She's pretty enough, in a way; but I don't find her interesting. The father is probably some mountebank from the Pont Neuf, working the provinces; and the girl is a trifle too wise."

"Mordious!" Bergerac mouthed, rolling Gascon oaths. "You're inhuman, an anchorite, a cold, sparkless, flabby caricature of manhood. How can you look upon her, and not fly into raptures! I'll work on the sonnet this evening, polish it tomorrow, and you'll see its effect tomorrow night."

"The name of Molière, comrades, shall be linked with yours in fame."

"Not I." Artaignan affected to stifle a yawn. "You'll keep the appointment; I have more important things to do."

Bergerac rolled his eyes, twisted his mustache and swore anew; he was delighted at this attitude on the part of his new friend.

At nine that night the rain was pitching down steadily once more. Sarasin was gone. The caravan was dark, but to Artaignan's cautious tap the door opened, to show candlelight. He entered; the door closed behind him; and he was speechless with astonishment.

HENRIETTE, YES—BUT what a Henriette! No laughing bourgeois girl; but a fine lady, garbed in the most magnificent silks, sparkling with jewels. He was not sure that the gems were real, but the effect was the same.

"Here, as at our chateau near Strasbourg, I can be myself in the evenings," she said. "My father was ennobled, you know, by the Elector. It pleases him to travel in this manner; it pleases me to pretend, during the daytime, that I'm a simple peasant girl. But I am not."

The only immediate effect this had upon Artaignan was to redouble his ardor; and when his calculation yielded to ardor, Artaignan was irresistible. At the moment, he believed all she said; nor was she averse to proving her regard for him.

When Artaignan recollected the young actor Molière, with a stab of jealousy, she laughed lightly and told of meeting the actor in Amiens, where a company of strolling players were engaged. Molière had undertaken to guide her and her father here, being well acquainted with Arras; that was all. Entirely all, as she avowed, and sealed the avowal with a lingering kiss that ended upon an abrupt and startled separation.

Sloshing steps outside, a hand rattling the lock. Then Dr. Sarasin entered. He seemed to find nothing singular in the situation, but rid himself of his wet cloak and hat, and with great satisfaction recounted how headquarters had made him welcome. Artaignan took his leave; and as he pressed the hand of Henriette, inquired when he might see her again.

"Your friend comes at ten tomorrow evening," she said, smiling. "You come at nine; if you like, I'll tell your fortune, Monsieur."

The look that accompanied these words sent him away walking on air, despite all the sloshing mud and the wet weather.

Morning, and guard-duty in the rain, rather sobered his ardent reflections. There must be, he felt, something strangely amiss with this father and daughter; however, why worry over the kindness of destiny? She was beautiful; she was kind; she hungered for him as he did for her, and nothing else mattered.

Bergerac came seeking him, in the afternoon, and recited his sonnet with gusto as he raved about Henriette. He uttered a thousand extravagances in his boisterous jovialty, then proposed a bout at fencing. Artaignan, nothing loath, accompanied him to shelter of the nearest shed; the floor was cleared, and they fell to with rapiers.

Artaignan, on the previous day, had noted that in attack Bergerac was superb beyond compare, gifted with a fiery élan before which nothing could stand; he himself, therefore, took the offensive at the start, and kept it. Each time Bergerac began an attack, he broke it up and forced the other to the defensive again. In vain Bergerac raged; this young guardsman, who certainly lacked science, had a wrist of sheer steel and an uncanny ability to divine an opponent's weakness. And never once was Bergerac permitted to sweep into his magnificent offense; his ferocity was discounted before it began.

TIME AND again the gathered guardsmen broke into applause. Artaignan himself was amazed by his own efforts. Just as it seemed that one or the other must fall victim to these super-human exertions, a sharp voice sounded. The two separated. Artaignan, wiping the sweat from his eyes, saw M. des Essarts.

"Messieurs!" exclaimed the Captain. "Orders, if you please: An hour before dawn, you will take over the advanced trenches.

Provided the rain has ceased, as is foretold, the cannon will begin to talk at dawn; an hour later we shall have the honor of leading an assault, which may take the enemy by surprise."

Cheers greeted this announcement. Artaignan and Bergerac saluted and embraced, congratulating each other warmly. Bergerac, finding that his own guard company was not included in next morning's operations, obtained permission from M. des Essarts to fight beside Artaignan. Then Artaignan took him aside.

"Comrade, this means a short night's rest. I advise you to let the young woman of the caravan alone this evening; postpone your appointment."

"The devil! Tomorrow night I may be dead!" Bergerac burst into laughter. "Postpone? Not I! But you should come with me tonight, Artaignan, hear me read her the sonnet, and watch her eyes fill with tears!"

"Thanks; I might become envious. And remember, she tells your fortune! It might be embarrassing if witnesses were present—eh?"

He winked significantly. Bergerac roared again, thumped him on the back, and they went off in search of wine.

That evening, the rain ceased and the stars began to show. The artillery fell to work removing tarpaulins and cleaning guns; the powder was broken out of its dry storage. The whole French camp became animated and expectant.

BUT ARTAIGNAN, at nine of the clock was admitted into the narrow quarters of the caravan, and again surprise shook him.

Henriette was alone as before; her greeting was warm, her lips were inviting—but no longer was she the great lady. Flanders poppies were braided into her dark hair; a necklace of gold coins clinked over her bosom; she wore fluttering gay-hued silks; gold rings danced in her ears; jewels flashed on her fingers. At Artaignan's expression, a laugh chimed on her lips and her eyes flashed with impish merriment.

Little by little he overtook the caravan,
swaying and careening down the road.

"Who but a gypsy could tell the fortunes of warriors, my hero?" she cried. "I make a very good gypsy, they all tell me."

"My word, you're marvelous!" broke out Artaignan. "You've never been so beautiful, never! Henriette, I adore you!" Then he remembered the three lanterns outside, like a triangle, above the entrance. "Why burn three lanterns, by the way? It's a waste."

"My father's orders," she said with a shrug. "How should I know? Look at our pretty things; we had a number of nobles from headquarters here this afternoon."

Artaignan looked around. Wine, and silver goblets, a huge silver holder for the candles; across one end of the space, behind the seats of the driver that let down to serve as couches, was stretched a tapestry. He turned from all this to the girl.

She liked him; she was sincere; her lips told him there was no falseness in her heart.. But presently she drew away from him, seized an immense kerchief of red-and-yellow silk, and knotted it about her head.

"Let me tell your fortune now, while I am in the mood, before your kisses make me forget all my cunning!" she exclaimed.

Artaignan laughed. "I'd sooner hear your own fortune, lovely one! There's mystery about you, about your father, about your presence here—mystery! What does it mean?"

"But I've told you!" She drew up a stool and seated herself at his feet. "Come, your hand! You know all about us; now let me discover about you…. Ah! Ah! This is terrible—you are inconstant and fickle!"

SHE LOOKED up, met his eyes, and broke into gay laughter. Then, grave again, she searched his hand. Her lovely eyes widened.

"Danger! I see danger to you, tomorrow, an hour after dawn!" came her voice. "You will be in peril; be careful, be careful! Ah, what a career I see for you—destiny like an arrow—wars and intrigues—and women. Great people around you, princes and kings—"

"Come closer to the mark," broke in Artaignan, half mockingly. "What is my age?"

"Your age? Eighteen; can that be true? You seem so much older."

She glanced up. Artaignan bit his lip with youthful mortification, and nodded mutely.

"And your name?" She searched his palm anew. "Strange! It is not Artaignan at all. It is Batz. Charles de Batz."

Artaignan jerked his hand away angrily. What the devil! This girl must indeed have some uncanny power! Then, before he could speak, came interruption—a fist at the door, the voice of Bergerac outside.

"Name of the devil!" Artaignan leaped up. "He came ahead of his time!"

Henriette laughed softly. "He'll not stay long, I promise! Here, quickly!"

She was holding aside a corner of the tapestry at the end of the room. Artaignan, with a joyous burst of relief, caught up hat and cloak and slid into the space behind the tapestry; it fell before him.

He was there a long while. He began to suspect that she was deliberately prolonging the scene.

Bergerac, he of the great nose, was in magnificent form. He declaimed; he bragged; he swaggered; he became a poet of melting voice and real charm. When he read over the sonnet he had composed, even the listening Artaignan was amazed by the beauty of the imagery and sentiment.

"But I must tell your fortune!" broke in Henriette. "Sit here, my hero; let me sit at your knee—no, your other hand! That's right."

Bergerac uttered some jest, which she cut short.

"This is strange—strange!" Her voice, to Artaignan, was startled. "Why, you have never seen Gascony in your life, my friend! Your very name—ah! It's not Bergerac at all! I see the name of Cyrano, Savinien de Cyrano—a fish-market in Paris—"

An outraged bellow from Bergerac, then insistence from
Henriette, left Artaignan convulsed with wild mirth. Gascon?
The swordsman was no more a noble Gascon than he was a
Dutchman! All his swaggering and loud accent were pretense; a
fish-market in Paris, forsooth! But how the devil did Henriette
know this, except by witchcraft?

SUDDENLY A dead silence fell. Artaignan, listening,
heard nothing; until, abruptly, close by Bergerac's voice and
step sounded.

"Odd, very odd indeed! One sees odd things here in Flanders—but never before have I seen tapestry with feet, booted
feet!"

In swift horror Artaignan glanced down—but too late! The
tapestry was stripped aside; he was face to face with Bergerac.
Even in this instant of crisis, he was mystified; he could have
sworn that his feet were well behind the tapestry.

What followed was, on Artaignan's part, extremely fast thinking; never had his cool calculation served him better. Bergerac,
his face suffused with passion, quite lost his head; but Henriette, despite her assumption of terror, did not. Nor did Artaignan, who saw that one wrong word would drive the mortified
Bergerac to extremes. And he had no desire to face the rapier
of an enraged Cyrano, now or later.

"My dear Bergerac!" he exclaimed with his charming boyish
smile, as soon as he could get in a word. "I confess I hid myself in
here in order to have the gratification of hearing your admirable
sonnet delivered as only you could deliver it. Upon my word, it
was most sublime!"

Bergerac stared and gulped. Artaignan, with a wave of the
hand, continued:

"As to all that nonsense our pretty friend told you, forget it!
Absurd! Am I not a Gascon myself? Have I not been in the
town of Bergerac a score of times? Why, she even tried to tell
me that my name was not Artaignan.... Yes, upon my honor!"

Bergerac's jaw fell. His injured vanity was appeased; then Henriette struck in:

"Gentlemen, gentlemen! Pardon my ill-advised nonsense, I beg of you. M. de Bergerac, will you permit me to make amends?"

Bergerac, utterly at a loss, his ready tongue for once silenced, did not know what to think. Artaignan, catching one look from her, held his peace and waited. She caught up Bergerac's wide plumed hat, took the big gaudy silk kerchief from her head, and knotted it about the crown and plume of the hat.

"There!" she exclaimed, eying it with satisfaction and turning to Bergerac. "My gage for my most noble knight! Before the attack begins tomorrow, leave the lines and go toward the city gate, with a friend or two, They will send out an equal number to meet you; it has been done every day. Fight them, vanquish them-and come back to me! Will you do this? Will you pledge your bravery, your sword, your skill, for your lady?"

Bergerac's eyes flew wide. He took fire instantly; all the romantic attributes of his nature were kindled. It was true that such challenges from one side were usually met from the other side.

"I will proclaim Henriette the most beautiful demoiselle in all the world!" he cried, kissing the fingers of the girl. "I'll plant your gage on the walls of Arras; I'll sing of it in the estates and empires of the moon, in the castles of the sun—"

"But don't approach the city gates alone, or you might get shot," broke in Artaignan. "Have a companion, one at least. May I offer myself for that honor, Monsieur de Bergerac?"

BERGERAC TURNED to him, embraced him in delight, and vowed eternal brotherhood.

"I see you're a very lucky man in love," went on Artaignan, catching the eye of Henriette and winking at her. "You'd better get to rest, comrade; I'll join you presently. Most unfortunately, I'm compelled to await the return of good Dr. Sarasin, having a message for him from M. des Essarts."

Henriette took Bergerac's hand and turned him to the doorway.

"Come, monsieur, help me take down two of those lanterns," she said. "Besides, I have a last word for your ear alone."

Blushing adorably, she led him outside and closed the door.

Artaignan eyed Henriette critically as she reëntered, bearing two of the lanterns, extinguished. Once again he wondered, why those three lanterns?

She turned to him, radiant. "So, he's gone. I told you he'd not stay long!"

"Apparently you made him happy," said Artaignan. She came close to him, her lovely face suddenly earnest.

"Why not? Yes, I sent him away happy, that you might remain. And you reproach me for it! You, for whose sake I have done so much!"

"Reproach you? Heaven forbid!" cried Artaignan, and caught her hand. Everything fled out of his mind except her loveliness, her closeness, her waiting lips and their slow inviting smile.

IN THE chill grayness of dawn the wet earth was beginning to steam. The advanced trenches were astir; stoups of wine and loaves of bread were passed about; weapons were readied; cannon, to right and left, began to vomit smoke and thunder. Supporting troops were gathered for the assault.

"Time!" exclaimed Bergerac, and leaped to the breastworks and beyond. Artaignan was after him instantly. They ignored the exclamations, the angry orders from the rear; discipline scarcely existed for the Guards companies.

"Beautiful sunlight!" exclaimed Bergerac, cocking his hat over one ear. Artaignan glanced at the kerchief's bright splotch of color.

"I'm glad I'm not wearing that gage of love," he said dryly. "It'll make you a superb target if some muskets open on us!"

"Nonsense! We're the heroes of the army this minute,"

bragged the other, strutting like a lord. He glanced around. "Ha! Look, comrade! One can see the caravan from here!"

His unuttered thought, reflected Artaignan, probably was that Henriette could see them. He turned, his eye sweeping along the lines behind. Yes, there were the headquarters tents and cabins, on slightly higher ground. The caravan was in plain sight.

"Hello!" Artaignan halted suddenly. A startling supposition shot into his mind; he began to think fast. "Bergerac! How did she know last night there was to be an attack this morning?"

"You no doubt told her. And it was no secret."

"I told her nothing! And it was strange how you discovered me, behind that tapestry."

"I, discover you?" Bergerac began to laugh heartily. A musket-shot, and another, from the walls ahead, and the whine of bullets, failed to check his laughter. "Comrade, I'll be honest; she pointed out your boot to me."

"The devil!" Alarm beat at Artaignan's brain. "She wanted you to find me, eh? She had that damned kerchief all ready—why? She had planned this excursion of ours—eh? I tell you, Bergerac, there's something very singular about all this!"

"Plague take it! Listen!" Bergerac swore heartily. The trill of bugles reached them; drums began to roll; shout upon shout pealed from the lines. "The attack! Ahead of time! We've no chance now to issue any challenge.... Look! Here they come behind us—quickly, comrade! At least, we'll lead the assault."

Musketry banged out; cannon thundered; powder-smoke drifted in a thick mist. But Artaignan recollected those three lanterns.... A signal to the city? And the Sarasins were from Strasbourg, she had said, therefore were German by origin. What was behind it all?

HIS BRAIN ceased to ask questions, as the yelling men caught up, and he struck into a run to keep in the lead, beside Bergerac. The attack was on, well ahead of the time set.... It was on, it was surging at the walls and gate.... It was smashed and shivered and broken to pieces. Instead of being surprised, the enemy were in readiness. A frightful hail of cannonballs, of musketry, of every imaginable sort of missile, was poured into the assailants.

The gay kerchief guided Artaignan to the fallen figure. His first thought was that Bergerac was dead; blood was gushing from his throat, torn by a bullet. Kneeling, Artaignan saw that the jugular was not cut. There was a chance. While balls whistled and screamed around, he improvised a hasty bandage, called other men to his aid, and they carried Bergerac back to the lines, his hat and the gay kerchief still jammed on his head.

Once there, Artaignan got hold of a surgeon; Bergerac had been laid beside one of the cooking-fires. The surgeon examined him and shrugged.

"He may live; a near thing. I'll do what I can for him. Ha— look out for his hat, there. It's almost afire!"

Artaignan seized the hat, which was close to the blaze. His eyes fell on the kerchief; for an instant he froze in every nerve. That kerchief! Upon the gay silk, he saw written words appearing; then they faded and were gone. The truth flashed upon him; secret writing, made visible by the heat! He held the kerchief above the fire again, read something of that writing, enough to show that his worst suspicions were true. Then, cramming the kerchief under his jacket, he was gone at a wild run.

He came charging up to the burned cabin, and halted, staring. The caravan was gone, completely gone! Before the canteen was a soldier holding two saddled horses. Artaignan turned to him.

"That van—where is it? When did it go?"

"Oh, the caravan!" The soldier laughed. "A few minutes ago, monsieur; the driver was in haste. I directed him on the Amiens road—"

With one leap, Artaignan was in the saddle of the nearer horse. The animal plunged, the soldier was knocked aside; next minute, the young man was dashing through the camp like a madman.

O U T   O F   the camp at last, loud shouts and trouble behind, and ahead a lurching object on the road. Little by little he overtook it—the caravan, swaying and careening wildly, its two horses at gallop. Artaignan gained, came abreast of it. He caught sight of Doctor Sarasin, with white contorted face, at the reins. Sarasin lifted a pistol and the weapon exploded. Artaignan's hat went with the bullet; but that instant of distraction had terrible consequences. The reins were loosened, the horses plunged frantically at the pistol-shot; as they veered, the ungainly equipage careened; smashed sideways into the poplars alongside the road, and piled up in wreckage.

Screams came from the interior of the caravan. Artaignan, dismounting, flung himself at the splintered ruins. A hand showed, a face, a head…. It was Henriette. He caught hold of her, helped extricate her, dragged her out. Trembling, unhurt but overcome by terror, she looked him in the face and, with a low cry, pitched forward in a dead faint.

He left her and turned to Sarasin. The eminent doctor, pitched from the wagon seat and trampled by the frantic horses, was a mass of mud and blood. He opened his eyes, as Artaignan wiped his face clear; he was dying.

"So, you scoundrel!" exclaimed Artaignan, in mingled pity and anger. "A spy for the enemy, eh? You and your daughter, both spies!"

"Not my daughter," Sarasin said faintly, between convulsive gasps. Death was in his throat, in his eyes. "Actress—great talent—both of us from Strasbourg—doing our best—our best to help—"

He groaned, and his voice died. A snarl escaped Artaignan.

"Strolling players, by heaven! Like that fellow what's-his-name—Molière! He was one of your fine gang too, was he?"

"No, no." Sarasin's voice weakened. "He knew nothing—no one else knew…. Ah!"

He whimpered, and the life escaped him, and he lay limp.

ARTAIGNAN STOOD up. He saw everything; it was damnably clear. That kerchief, with information of vast import to the enemy in Arras—clever, this Henriette! Devilish clever! He went to her, stared down at her unconscious white lovely features; and the anger died from his eyes. An actress, a strolling vagabond—and a spy!

His face softened. Last night was last night; today was today. He pulled the silk kerchief from under his jacket, stooped, and tied it about her dark hair. She still wore the gypsy costume. How well she had played, both gypsy and great lady!

He came to one knee, touched his lips to her forehead, and rose. How the devil had she known the truth about him, about Charles de Batz? And the truth about that swaggering Gascon, really bred in a Paris fish-market? Spies, and the knowledge of spies, no doubt.

"Adieu," he said softly. "Adieu! And henceforth, for Charles d'Artaignan, may the foul fiend fly away with all actors and actresses alike!"

He turned to his horse, swung up into the saddle, and rode away to learn whether Bergerac lived or died. He need not have worried. After all, it is only because of the gashed throat which turned Cyrano de Bergerac from soldiering to literature, that the siege of Arras is remembered by posterity.

THE WICKEDEST WOMAN

O N T H I S dark and chilly evening the narrow London street was filled with traffic of all kinds and all conditions. Link-boys escorted sedan chairs or cried their services; coaches rumbled along with drivers bawling; barrow-men and hawkers crowded along anywhere. In the thickest of the jam, as it came to a momentary halt, was a plain dark closed carriage.

The driver turned to his fare, a girl well under twenty, handsomely attired in peach satin, an Indian shawl flung about her head and bosom.

"I be main sorry, mistress," he quavered. "It baint my fault—"

She broke in, laughing: "Then there's naught for sorrow, and Drury Lane must wait!" Her voice was fresh, eager, and cheery, but her tongue obviously had no education. "Ha! Look there, look there! Oh, the beasts!" she cried suddenly, leaning out at the window.

Two link-boys were chivvying a frightened dog, a lost, bewildered, worthless cur that had dashed into the street just as the traffic started up again. Their flickering torches lit him as he stopped short, terrorized.

An angry shout pealed up. A young man darted forward and scooped up the hapless cur in his arms.... He was too slow. A coach was upon him, its driver shouting him aside, and lash flicking at him; he was struck by the pole and knocked sprawling, senseless.

With a most unmaidenly oath the girl whipped open her

*Men leaped to her
aid; the unconscious
man was lifted into
her carriage.*

carriage door and sprang out into the street. The torches struck
upon her figure as she darted to the side of the senseless man; the
dog had wriggled away and was gone. She faced the horses fear-
lessly, waving her hands at them, sending them into a frenzied
rearing. Her voice rang out in a torrent of furious objurgation,
threats and, it must be confessed, most fluent curses. London
in 1668 had few niceties of language.

Coaches banged and traffic snarled. Shouts, oaths, wild

cheers, drowned her words. A name was heard; it was caught up instantly; it swelled into a roar of recognition and admiration.

"Nell Gwinn, lads! Mistress Nell, God bless her! Back, back! Make way for Nelly!"

Men leaped to her aid. The unconscious young man was lifted into her carriage. She climbed in and supported his head against her shoulder. Amid more hearty cheers, the traffic moved on once more. She called sharply to her driver:

"Turn aside! Get out o' this whirlpool; we must take him home."

"But mistress, you're late now!" replied the driver. "Drury Lane is waiting—"

"A pox on Drury Lane, and you too!" she stormed. "A man who could risk himself for a dog is worth all the cursed theaters in the world. Do as I tell you!"

Capricious, headstrong, utterly regardless of anything except her own whims, Nelly Gwinn was to be obeyed. She was the idol of the stage, of the King, of half London; the other half execrated her very name as a symbol of shameless vice.

The young man stirred a little. He was not good-looking, and he wore sober Quaker gray. But there was blood on his cheek, and she quieted him with tender deft voice and hands.

"Calm 'ee, now.... Quiet, lad, quiet! You're safe. Rest 'ee gentle-like. Whither bound?"

"Artillery Walk in Bunhill," he murmured. "Important… Mr. Milton's house—" He went limp, drifting again into unconsciousness.

"All right, coach!" said Nelly briskly. "Artillery Walk, Bunhill. Find Mr. Milton's house, wherever that is."

"It be a dreary way to Bunhill Fields, mistress! Let me take you first to—"

Mistress Nell's furious gust of language staggered even the coachman.

"Besides," she concluded with more practical assurance, "I'm late now, and if I get there in time to speak the epilogue, naught else matters. And Mr. Dryden won't be there this night.... Drive, drive!"

The carriage creaked on, endlessly, through the evening.

AFTER A time the young man came to his senses, but only dazedly. Finding himself in the arms of a charming sweet-scented young woman who sopped his wound with her kerchief and babied him, he was dumfounded and awkwardly shy.

However, he came to himself in time to direct the driver to the house of Mr. Milton. Nelly now found that his leg was hurt as well as his head; she sprang out and insisted that he lean upon her. He did so, and they walked up the garden path together. Nelly pounded at the house door. It was opened by a woman, who uttered a cry at sight of the young man.

"Why, 'tis Tom Ellwood!"

"Whoever he is, he's hurt," spoke up Nelly tartly. "He gave this address—"

To her intense disgust, a hullabaloo arose; three girls of varying ages, whom she mentally designated at one glance as slovenly minxes, and two rather doltish young men of Puritan aspect who stared round-eyed at her, helped Mrs. Milton take care of the young man, who yielded to their ministrations with a groan.

The young men might well stare. Nelly had tied her bloodstained kerchief around the hurt head; and although she now made shift to pull the shawl about her bosom, she hated the fools for staring. And she meant to have the kerchief back again, for it was valuable.

"WHO IS it? Who's arrived? What's the noise about?" drifted a voice from another room. Nelly walked in and saw a man sitting before a cheerful fire, a long clay pipe in his hand, and on the table beside him a cup, a liquor-flask and a bowl of herbs.

"A fine sloppy tarradiddle of a house!" she flung at him. "I bring home a hurt man, and they all fall upon him like clucking fowls! What kind of women have ye here, anyway?"

"One kindly soul that full deserves the name," said the man, lifting his head, "and three prattling, useless vixens who despise their own father and are not worth their salt. Ha! A new voice in this dull world, a voice of youth and energy and fine splendid bravery! Come hither, voice, that I may judge thy face."

Nelly shut the door behind her, to close out the noise, and came forward. She saw that the man was blind; a fair, rugged, aged face. With impulsive contrition, she dropped on her knees before him, caught his outstretched hand and pressed it against her lips.

"I'm a silly prating wench! I'd not have hurt you for the world, master. You talk like a play-actor."

"A compliment of which I am not worthy." His words rang with such scathing sarcasm that Nelly was startled, then remembered. A Puritan household, a nest of sanctimonious Roundheads, no doubt! She knelt motionless. His fingers, gnarled and stiff with gout, touched her wealth of hair, slid down her face to shawl and dress. "Why, voice, you have youth and beauty and fine raiment!"

"Never mind me. This is Mr. Milton's house, so I suppose you're him," she broke in. "Look 'ee, the lad has a golden heart! That damned cur—"

She told of what had happened; and her uncouth tongue told more than she knew, no doubt, for he smiled a little as he listened.

"Voice, what's your name?" he asked whimsically, when she finished her tale.

She plucked at the first name to mind.

"Dryden—Ellen Dryden."

"What!" he cried out. "Not a kinswoman of my friend Dryden the poet?"

"La, no!" Her dismay was real enough now. "I never heard of him. My father—at court! He's none of your fine gentry and poets—"

"Oh, at court!" His face darkened. "The vilest court on the face of this earth!"

"That's true. They're all thieves and rascals," she said happily. "A pack of dogs that deserve the gallows, and betray their master daily. Foul-witted dogs, fawning upon him and snarling against each other; treacherous—"

Her impulsive words, incongruous upon such a tongue, made him smile again and lift the long clay pipe to his lips. She, checking herself, rejoiced that she had concealed her real name. It would be ill liked in any godly Roundhead household such as this.

"So ye fetched Tom Ellwood! An honest Quaker lad, and doing a sad errand for my sake—but let that pass," ruminated the blind man. "He has a golden heart indeed; but you, sweet Ellen, have one decked with pearls of price! You'll stop and sup with us.... No protest! I'll have your carriage sent away. I heard the wheels in the lane. We'll get you another. Why, child, you're a very shaft of sunlight sent to lighten a dark hour in this house! Or are you a child?"

"No, thank God! I'm nigh eighteen. If it would please you, indeed, I'll stay and gladly. But," she added doubtfully, "I'll say you fair: I'm none of your Puritan breed, so I mistrust my welcome."

Milton broke into a laugh.

"Dear Ellen, you'd be thrice welcome, even were you that scarlet Nell Gwinn in person! I'm still master under my own roof. I can feel your presence like sunlight. You bring a rare breath of honesty and bravery and beauty into the room; it delights my heart. Now, lass, put herbs from the bowl into this cup, and water, and liquor. Not too full, since temperance becometh all men. Dost know what this drink is?"

"Why, yes!" Nelly obeyed his command, and sneaked a round gulp of the heady liquor for herself. "Lord Buckhurst hath a fancy for it—though not with temperance! Julep is the name."

"Aye. From the Arabic *gulab*, or perfumed water. Many thanks." He sniffed at the cup she put into his hand, and tasted approvingly. "Excellently mixed. This joy, to life so friendly and so cool to thirst! Child, can you see this cordial julep, that flames and dances in his crystal bounds? Is't not warming to the eye?"

"Nay; this cup isn't crystal," she said in her practical way. "You—you spoke of Nelly Gwinn. Do you know her?"

"God forbid! The wickedest woman in London!"

"Well, I saw her once. She didn't look wicked at all."

"Sweet child, Satan never looks his part! That poor aban-

*"I'm a silly prating wench! I'd not
hurt you for the world, master."*

doned creature who shares the vicious life of a vicious Stuart is
the unhappiest wight alive."

"Well, she didn't look unhappy, either," Nelly said tartly. "You
know nothing about the King, master, so speak no ill of him.
And if you know her not, what right have you to judge her? I
think you have a good ear for gossip, and a tongue too devilish
ready to enlarge upon it!"

The blind man chuckled. "I stand rebuked, and most worthily.
I have a sarcastic, infernal tongue, 'tis true. And you a loose one,
far too apt at oaths for seventeen! Where did you pick up these
words and phrases, that sound so ill upon the tongue of modest
youth?"

She evaded this question merrily. The man charmed her; he used words beyond her comprehension, and yet in his blinded presence she felt a sense of awe and veneration—why, she knew not.

"La! Would it please you, master, if I played the prim innocent godly child of modesty? I can do that most admirably, and whine a psalm through my nose as good as Praise-God Barebones himself."

With a catch of the breath, she broke off: "Oh, forgive me, forgive my cursed damnable vixen temper! I meant not to make a mock of you or of your beliefs—honestly, I did not!"

HE PATTED her cheek with his stiff fingers.

"Mock all you please, and I'll echo your mockery. My beliefs? I have none; all are fled and gone and scattered like dry leaves." He had a way of pronouncing his *r's* hard, which lent harsh bitterness to his words.

"I mind something the great Galileo said, when I saw him in Florence long ago," he went on, as though talking more to himself than to her. "He was an old man then. 'The sere leaf that hath lost its stem of faith,' said he, 'is but a sorry thing.' And now I'm an old man too; all I've lived by is swept away, and faith's an empty parody. Aye, mock all you will, and I'll cry you havoc and let loose the dogs of skeptic mirth!"

She looked up into his rugged face. "Why, master, that sounds like Shakespeare!"

"So it does; the noblest of poets, laughed to scorn these evil days!" He uttered a curt laugh. "Even honest Dryden, who makes a god of tinkling rhyme, says Shakespeare is done for and forgotten, because he was no rhymer. Where on earth did you hear of him? Who reads Shakespeare in these rotting times?"

"Read? Oh, la! I've never learned reading," she said carelessly. "But I can trace letters, master; that is, my initials. It's a useful art sometimes."

He seemed not to hear, and was lost in his own thoughts.

"Shakespeare! Aye; he wrote four words I envy him, and

would that they were mine. '*The multitudinous seas encarnadine.*'
What a glow they hold! And he too knew the emptiness of fame.
What a play he would have made of Samson, had he writ it! Yet
I may make a fair poem there, since my own days are like those
of blind Samson, and as futile."

He broke off, fumbled for his pipe, and then voiced rounded
lines:

> "*Though fallen on evil days,*
> *On evil days though fallen, and evil tongues,*
> *In darkness, and with dangers compassed round.*
> *And solitude—*"

Nelly stared, while he puffed the pipe alight and then continued:

"Dangers! Think of it, after these years, the hounds are giving
cry once more! I publish a poem, a book, and they suddenly
remember me, to yap of treason and prison!"

"Oh! Then you're a poet!" broke out Nelly, and clapped her
hands. "Why, that explains it! I mean, the reason I like you,
master. There are too many sour people; that's what makes wars.
I like poets, because they're gay and kind. The same as you are, if
you'd just watch your tongue. I have to watch mine too."

"Ah, child, you're a delicious morsel!" The blind man lost his
bitter mood, pinched her ear, and smiled in affectionate amusement. "Yes, a brave honest breath of sunlight, a joy to the heart
as you must be to the eye! No guile, no deceit…. I can feel a
dishonest heart as though it flaunted banners. Yours is open as
the day. Ah! I hear my good wife's step—"

All in a flash, Nelly pulled up a chair and was seated demurely,
hands in lap.

THE DOOR opened, and Mrs. Milton came to them, her
face anxious.

"John, I have sore news for you," she said. "Tom's not greatly
hurt; I've put him to bed. But he brought an evil word. I must
speak with you alone."

"Nay, speak out, speak freely!" exclaimed Milton. "Good wife, this is Mistress Ellen Dryden. A maid with somewhat Bœotian tongue but purest Attic heart; a sunbeam for blinded eyes. She stays to supper. And now let's know the worst."

Nelly guessed that his phrases conveyed meanings beyond her grasp, but it did not matter in the least. Her heart had gone out to this blind man. His personality, his character, had encompassed her like a tremendous force. A poet, a blind man, and in danger!

Yet she was a primly modest lass, making Mistress Milton a deep curtsy and taking the edge of her chair again.

"You've welcome, my dear; we owe you much for your kindness to Tom Ellwood," said the good woman, and turned. "John! He saw Sir Thomas Agnew. There's naught can be done. Annesley is helpless, as he wrote you today. The charges are to be pressed hard. That rascal Morely hath the ear of the Council, and his venomous envy has poisoned their hearts—"

Milton waved his hand. "Enough, enough! Ye said it all in five words: There's naught can be done! Let that end it. The pinpricks of envy are too little things—"

"But John! The Tower's no little thing! And treason!"

Milton smiled. "My dear," he said quietly, "when one thinks of all the great and noble men whose heads have fallen to that false cry of treason, doesn't it make the heart leap and quicken? What a goodly company to welcome one poor blind rascal across the threshold! The very concept brings a benison of grace!"

Like a force loosed upon the room, his presence filled it, compelled the two women motionless. His words rang and lifted sonorously; his face was alight with grave majesty that held them in awe.

"The more the flame, the more the law has found to burn in man. So said poor Bacon, in his last days; true words! The mind hath grown too great for the enduring of lesser minds, and is cut away. The greater the mind, the less can the world endure it, in these evil days. *There's naught can be done;* splendid words! I'd not lift a finger to stay this compliment of envy. I'd not lift my voice to rebut the perjury and hatred—"

Nelly, in sudden comprehension, was on her feet. Her indignant fury blazed up.

"No, no! Ye can't mean it!" she cried hotly. "A good man, a noble man like you? It's a lie! Ye've no treason in you! A cursed rascally lie!" She faced Mrs. Milton, her blue eyes twin coruscating pools of wild wrath. "They can't do such a thing, and they sha'n't! He's a poet, and he's a good man, a good man!"

Milton smiled. "Child, before I was a poet alone, I was a meddler in affairs of state. Now, like many a better man, I'm a blind beast of burden, a scapegoat. Let it be. Vex not yourself with my affairs. Wife, is she not a sweet precious thing? A brave heart, a lovely child!"

"Brave indeed; dear lass, for your words I love you." Warm-eyed Mrs. Milton drew Nelly to her in a swift embrace. "Fret not about these matters."

"Fret not? Why, devil take me, I'll do something about it! Damme if I don't speak—"The shocked expression of the good woman brought Nelly to herself; she checked her outburst. "I'll speak to my father. He's got a post at court—" She broke off, lamely.

"Nay, now, think no more of it." Mrs. Milton, still startled, patted her hand. "Dryden, is that the name? Perchance a relative of our good friend the poet? But he'll be here presently himself. Tom Ellwood saw him too, and he'll bring us better news, I trust."

Panic seized Nelly. She could not stay to sup with them; she invented excuses, stammered truthfully that she was no relative of Dryden's, did her best to get away at once. No use; the blind man insisted that her promise be kept. For his sake! And in the midst, one of his three daughters came, a bit sullenly, to announce supper ready.

NELLY GAVE up, and resigned herself to fate. None the less, emotion seethed within her; every time she looked into

Nelly's indignant fury blazed up. "No,
no!" she cried. "Ye've no treason in
you! They can't do such a thing!"

that rugged yet gentle blinded face, her heart swelled for the
evil of the world, evil which she knew full well. Indeed, she
knew little else.

They sat about a candle-lit board, not bountiful but well
provided; a little old silver, a little rare crystal, fine bleached
hollands linen: The three daughters, slatterns who winced under
the blind man's biting tongue. The young men had departed;
Tom Ellwood was asleep in another room.

Nelly noted that her hostess murmured grace, but Milton,

with a sarcastic scowl, ignored it. When one of the girls made
some mention of religion, he lashed out cold words that checked
the mention instantly. Nelly shrewdly held her peace and offered
no mockery; she sensed that Milton, despite his words to her,
would welcome no levity in this respect.

MIDWAY OF the meal, the knocker sounded. The eldest
daughter answered, and called back to them:

"It's Mr. Dryden, Father."

Nelly braced herself; then, as Dryden appeared, desperately
held a napkin to her face. He came into the room, tall, smiling,
elegant: a man of forty or thereabouts, handsome, resplendent,
with the sardonic wit which had made him famous. He bowed
to Mrs. Milton, touched his lips to her hand, exchanged a warm
clasp with the blind man.

"I've an engagement to sup later, thanks," he said, "but I'll
sit and smoke a pipe with you. This news is frightful—" Nelly
lowered her napkin. He looked at her, saw her for the first time,
and froze. Into his staring gaze came amazement and incredulity.

"Good God!" he said under breath.

"Ellen, my dear, allow me to present my friend John Dryden,"
said the blind man. "A child who bears your own name, Dryden,
but claims no relationship. A sweet child, a dear lovely lass,
unspoiled and primrose-fresh."

"Oh, la!" exclaimed Nelly, staring round-eyed at the man she
knew so well, who had written for her his wittiest and wickedest
comedies. "Not the great Mr. Dryden, surely? The poet who is
said to have written an entire epilogue of twenty lines rhyming
with the word *door?* Oh, sir! I am truly overcome!"

Dryden swallowed hard. The word was not *door*, but no one
else here knew of it. She smiled and extended her hand, and
her eyes challenged him. He came to her and gallantly bowed
over her hand.

"Stop it, you she-devil," he breathed.

She laughed happily. He could not take his eyes off her. He

lit a pipe and listened to all the story about Tom Ellwood, and ever his gaze came back to her.

"Zounds, Mistress Ellen!" he said, when the tale was done. "You should go upon the stage! I'll warrant that you'd become the toast of London."

"Oh, Master Dryden! A poor wench like I?" she exclaimed. "The stage is a wicked place, they say; full of temptations and such-like."

"But you remind me somewhat of Nelly Gwinn," said he. "You have the same—"

"Dryden!" broke in Milton with quiet force. "I'll have no such talk at this table! Make no comparison between this sweet unspoiled child and that accursed vile creature who flaunts her vice openly in the face of God and man, and holds this sorry Stuart king of ours in her chains! An orange-seller, poor wicked lass!"

Nelly put her tongue in her cheek. Dryden choked, colored, and apologized with a stammer. But turning to the blind man, Nelly spoke abruptly:

"Oh, master, be not so harsh in judgment, I pray you! My father says the King is kind to all; and those closest to him best know his fine qualities."

"Aye," put in John Dryden wickedly. "Those closest to him should know!"

She ignored the thrust. "And as for the orange girls," she went on, "they're not all bad. They mew and tweet a lot, but they live and die no man's friend and all women's haters—"

She checked herself. Milton laughed.

"Child, hast no hard words for anyone?"

"Aye, for those who would cry treason upon you!" said she.

THEIR LAUGHTER died, and faces lengthened, as she thus brought to the fore what lay so anxious in every heart.

Dryden leaned forward. "I've heard about it, and I can't fathom it," he said. "What charge can stand, in God's name?

After the Restoration and your first troubles, the Indemnity Bill secured you against future charges. You can't be touched now for anything that happened."

"Apparently that isn't the question," said Milton dryly. "The poem I published last year is the thing that's raising the torch now. Treason, they whisper; a veiled allegory in which our honest Charles Stuart is typified as Satan."

Dryden swore in hearty astonishment, apologized quickly to the ladies, and brought his fist down on the table till the dishes rattled.

"Absurd! Oh, foul ignorant absurdity!" he cried indignantly.

"Nothing is too absurd to be made a candle for envy's flame," observed Milton calmly. "No, friend; absurd it may be, but the fact remains. I had a note this afternoon from Annesley. The Council meets tomorrow; he says arrest is certain."

"Annesley!" echoed Dryden in blank dismay. "If the Earl of Anglesea can't protect you against these rascals— Why can't he see the King?"

"He talked with Charles Stuart this morning and was told that one pestilent poet more or less mattered nothing in the world." Milton's lips twisted with appreciation of the sarcastic utterance. "Annesley protected me before, but he has no power now."

DRYDEN EXPLODED in a burst of tempestuous fury that minced no words. Mrs. Milton gave her daughters a glance; they rose and left, and signaled Nelly to come with them. But Nelly had no such intention.

" 'Paradise Lost'—the greatest work of poetry that's appeared since Marlowe died, to be thus libeled and made into a tool to serve envy!" Dryden was in a passion. "It's past all belief! You, the greatest poet in England, to be thus treated! It makes the blood boil!"

"Cool it with tobacco, good friend." Milton smiled and put out a hand for his pipe. Nelly seized it, filled it, lit it over a candle and handed it to him, while Mrs. Milton watched in shocked astonishment.

"Does Mr. Dryden think you a better poet than Shakespeare?" asked Nelly innocently.

"I fear not." Milton drew at his pipe. "Neither of us are good rhymers, in his opinion, and there's no poetry possible without rhyme—eh, Dryden?"

"He should know," murmured Nelly sweetly. "Just think! Twenty rhymes to the word *door*, and all beautiful poetry too!"

Dryden flung her one look of white-hot fury, choked down his wrath with an effort, and turned to the blind man.

"You're the greatest poet in England, in the world!" he said gravely. "Yet I do think that if your 'Paradise Lost' were in rhyme, it would be still greater. And I'd love to prove it by taking your own magnificent lines, putting them into a play, rhyming them—"

"Why not?" said Milton indulgently, puffing at his pipe. "By all means! Tag my verses if you please! Your cunning artistry would honor me."

"I thank you," said Dryden, pleased. "Now, back to more pressing business. Somehow, somewhere, this vile affair must be nipped before it comes up in Council! But who can do it? Whom can we reach? Rochester's at Bath, taking the cure. Buckingham's in disgrace. Ha! There's Buckhurst, Earl of Dorset to be!" he exclaimed, and drove a maliciously sardonic glance at Nelly. "The Gwinn woman was his mistress…. Now he's playing like a moth with the King's latest flame, the Frenchwoman Louise."

"Oh, I saw her the other day!" spoke up Nelly. "She was long in the flank like a sway-back horse, and had a neck like a swan!"

Dryden could not repress a grin.

"Well, I'll get to work tonight, now! Somehow, the King must be reached. He'll be supping with one of his mistresses. He must be made to stop this nonsense; he can do it with a word. Luckily, I'm in funds. These venal creatures who surround Charles—"

"Wait!"

WITH THE word, everything seemed to stop; the world itself. The blind man laid down his pipe. His voice broke upon the room like an organ-tone, so deep and great was his emotion and his grave majesty.

"My friend, you mean well; you're a true man, a loyal friend," he said slowly. "But I forbid you to carry out your intent. Venal creatures indeed! Bribery!" He appeared to choke upon the thought, then continued:

"All I have left are my pride, my sacred honor and my self-esteem; I'll not have them sullied and brought to naught at this late day. It is to my pride that evil rogues seek my life. It is to mine honor that the rulers of the land would do me away by perjury and hatred, because they fear my writings. And my self-esteem brooks not that I should grovel before such men. Much less would I have you or anyone else seek the influence of public prostitutes.... Good God, that this English realm should sink to such a level!

"No, John Dryden! I charge you, upon your immortal soul, permit no such action! Smirch not my name by putting it into the hand of vileness, seek not the wiles of vicious women. Why, it's an insult that leaves the soul affronted and appalled! No man can harm me, do what they may, and I refuse to harm myself. I would writhe in agony to know that this vile body's salvation was wrought by the foul touch of Cleveland or Gwinn or any such— No, no! You have my mind, Dryden. Obey it."

DRYDEN BOWED his head, as though before a nobility that left him overwhelmed.

"Greatness," he said slowly, "has walked among us like a ghost, this night."

That he was deeply moved, was evident. He glanced at Nelly; she sat very white and quiet. But now, upon the silence, she stirred and put forth her hand, and laid her fingers upon those of Milton.

"Are you afraid?" he said, half sneeringly.
"Yes, but not for myself," she replied.

"But I shall go to the King, Mr. Milton," she said in a low voice. "I shall go to him and tell him that you be a main good man, and the best poet in England or the world, and that he must not permit this crime. May I do it?"

Milton's rugged face softened, and he lifted her fingers to his lips.

"Dear child of sunshine, dear child of brave heart, you speak the impossible; you cannot reach Charles Stuart, nor speak with him."

"But if I can, have I your permission to tell him what a good man you are?"

"Why, of course!" he said, lightly smiling. "Tell me, Mistress Ellen, when shall I see you again? For we must meet; you must come here often. We have music of the evenings—" He checked himself; one could read the thought in his face. Perhaps he would not be here of evenings, but in the Tower, or worse.

"I'm sorry," she said. Her eyes flitted to Dryden; he was sitting watching her, in disgust and cold anger. "Not for a long time, perchance; you see, we all be going north in a day or so, north to the Humber for a long visit."

"You have a coach, Dryden? Will you take the child home? Do, I pray you."

"Why, yes, because you ask it," said Dryden. Again his look was cold. In his face Nelly read a chill resolve. "Tell me, mistress, do you spell your name with a *y* or with an *i*? In our family it may be writ either way. So may that of the most charming actress and the wickedest woman in London, Nell Gwinn."

She knew that he was playing with her in his cruel way, that he meant to reveal her true name, that he was infuriated because she had won Milton's consent by tricking him.

Quietly, she went up to Dryden and looked into his eyes; her back was turned to Mrs. Milton. Under Dryden's hard gaze, her face became a piteous pleading thing.

"I've heard it said that Nelly Gwinn herself spells her name with an *i*, Mr. Dryden," she said. Two tears gathered at her lashes and fell on her cheeks. "But I've never learned spelling, or such things. It will be mortal kind of you to take me home; the kindest action in the world."

Her words were nothing; her face, her eyes were everything. They held her whole soul, in pleading, agonized beseeching. Dryden was shaken; he was still more shaken when she put out her hands to his, and he found her fingers cold and trembling.

"Are you afraid?" he said, half sneering. Still her great eyes held their grip on his own.

"Yes; but not for myself," she replied.

With an effort, he brushed her aside, broke into a laugh, and loosed the tension.

"Why, 'tis a pleasant child and full of strange fancies!" he exclaimed cheerily. "Yes, we must off at once. John Milton," he said, going to the blind man with a hearty hand-grip, "you shall have your way; I obey your desires. But I shall see Annesley tonight if possible. I shall do what I can, as you would have me do it; that's a measure of my tribute to you."

FIVE MINUTES later, farewells said, he was handing Nelly Gwinn into his coach, a fine handsome coach. But as he got in, he paused and spoke to the man on the box.

"Drive down the lane. At the corner, stop and wait till I give you orders."

He slammed the door; the horses started; the coach creaked and swayed down the narrow way, and presently came to full stop. Then, in the darkness, Dryden broke the silence.

"Nelly, you damned vixen, I gave in to your pleading!" he said in a hot passionate voice. "I could not shame you before them. But I'm going back and tell 'em the truth. You tricked him basely; by the Lord, I'll not have it! There's the noblest man in England, and I'll not stand by and see him toyed with in his blindness by a wench—"

"You may say too much; better stop," said Nelly. "What will happen when you tell him? Shame me? No, you can't do that. But you can betray him, poison him, hurt him to the very quick—you and your devilish misdirected friendship! La, what a prattle-tongued fool you would be, worse than any old gutter harridan shrieking bad words at the wind!"

"What do you mean?" he demanded quickly. "Hurt him, betray him? Not for the world!"

"Perhaps he guessed Nelly Gwinn's heart better than you could," she said. "He thinks Mistress Ellen is a pleasant child of sunshine.... Why, John, he has a kind memory of me! To find he had blasted Nelly Gwinn to her face would make him writhe; he's a gentleman, more so than any gentry of the court."

"And you think he'd accept his life at your hands?" said Dryden scornfully.

"Not at the hands of Nelly Gwinn. No. But at the hands of

Ellen the child, yes; he said so himself. Still, he'll never know; not a soul will ever know, John. I'm supping with my friend at midnight."

It was thus she spoke, aye, and thought, of the King.

"Before he sups with me this night," she went on, "Charles will write a letter and send it to the president of the Council. You know that I never meddle in anything; this time, I'm meddling. And you must never tell Mr. Milton or anyone else." She laid her hand on his arm, and suddenly her voice broke: "John, John, this is my greatest part—the greatest rôle I'll ever play.... For God's sake don't spoil it!"

At last he vouchsafed grudging words.

"He's become the greatest poet in England. Men of wisdom and renown seek him out daily. His fame has returned. The whole country would cry out in horror if he were beheaded.... And should I let him be saved in a way he has himself refused?"

"You fool, would you rather see him beheaded?" she cried out impatiently. Anger consumed her, all in a moment. "Very well—choose, then! Choose, and a pox take you! Choose, you damned virtuous high-minded gentleman, with the filthiest wit in London! Let his death or life be your decision—yours, whose pretty lines make the very painted statues blush to hear 'em spoken!"

She paused, then went on, scathingly:

"You, whose greatest boast is that you amuse the gallants of the court—what with? Vile words you'd not dare speak in his house, foul jests and conceits that would shame you to have uttered at his table, or brought before his mind. And you, you— on such a man as you, on such a devil's poet as you, hangs the life or death of this man! Not on you, but on your imitation flashy nobility—"

"For God's love, have done, Nelly!" he broke in, and his voice twisted upon the darkness like a groan. He reached out and took her hand in both his own. "Upon my soul, you have the noblest heart in the world! Let it be as you say. I'll not spoil your rôle, upon my honor; I did not understand, Nelly. But I do now. And I honor you, sweet child of sunshine; Mistress Ellen, to me also you shall ever be as you were this night. There shall be this secret between us. I pledge you my word."

He brought her fingers to his lips.

"Oh!" she exclaimed, sitting erect. "What you said a moment ago about the whole country crying out—why, that's the very thing! That will spell sense to Charles.... Good! Hurry, John!"

DRYDEN OPENED the window, gave the coachman directions, and the coach jounced away.

"One thing more," she said. "I hated you, when you sat there eying me in cold anger; and I admired you too. Never mind my shrewish tongue. There's great loyalty in you, John Dryden, and there's great loyalty in me, and there's damned few people in London who know what the word means. So we'd best stick together and be friends."

"Egad, wench! An admirable notion, a most excellent notion!" he said, in his old light voice of gayety. "You and I and the Theater Royal against the world! What will Charles Stuart say to it, I wonder?"

Her ringing laugh joined in his, and put emotion to flight.

"If I'm any judge, he'll say that you'd make a devilish good poet-laureate of England—sink me if he won't!" Then her laugh died suddenly. "But I'm sorry—oh, John! I'm sorry with all my heart for one thing that must happen."

"What?" he demanded.

She was silent a space, and sighed, and answered sadly: "That the child Ellen has played out her part, and can never again meet the noblest man in all the world."

"Amen," said Dryden, after a moment.

THE SWAN OF USK

HENRY VAUGHN was riding toward Brecon town from his gabled manor-house of Newton (known to the Welsh folk hereabout as Trenewydd) and his road wound along the river Usk.

His sorry wheezing nag, so poor a beast as to be not worth the stealing, was all he had left. He himself was decked out in his bravest—frayed, patched, faded garments, but the best he had to his name. Under his hat with its frayed plume, his face was like a cold, heavily chiseled cameo, the numbed and lifeless face of a man who has seen too much. He was riding, as he thought, to speak the words that would bring home a bride to Newton's poverty; he did not dream that fate lay in waiting for him ere he came into Brecon, and that destiny bestrode with him the sorry nag.

His gaze dwelt upon the brawling Usk, the river he so loved; his gray eyes warmed, and his aquiline features, now sharpened by past wounds and fever, softened and became touched with a wistful tenderness.

"I did not know there was such beauty left to see," he murmured.

This was Wales; but in these latter days Wales shared England's bitter lot. And the whole of England was one hideous reek of death and ruin; the ideals and faith and culture accumulated through past ages were swept away upon the tide of war;

and men said that civilization itself was set back a thousand years, if not destroyed utterly.

Vaughn's first presage of strange things to come—though he did not recognize it as such—arrived when he saw Granny Blodwen waving her stick at him from the roadside. He slowed the all too willing nag. The old beldame, reputed to be a witch, reached up to him a little bundle of herbs and simples she had gathered for him, and spoke in Welsh.

"Here are celandine and clary and others, all gathered when the sun was out, young master," she gabbled. "It is strange that you, who have killed so many men and have more to kill, should now be a physician and a healer of men."

Vaughn regarded her with somber gaze. "I'm a soldier no more, Granny, and I have no more men to kill, either," he said rather sharply.

She blinked up at him and shook her head. "All the same, master, there is blood upon your hand."

"Stop your ill-omened prating, Granny Blodwen!" he exclaimed angrily. "I am riding to talk of love with a lady, and would sooner have blessings than curses."

"You have known Blodwen all your life, master, and never had curses from her," retorted the crone. "I tell you that a king has been seeking for you; and that you will not talk of love with the lady who is in your mind, but with another. And that is a blessing too."

"It is bosh," said Vaughn. "The only king in England is a fugitive, somewhere in the north; and though I fought for him, he never heard of me."

HE TOUCHED spurs to the nag and rode on; but an uneasy fear lingered with him. Old Granny Blodwen had second sight, men said. Still, Vaughn knew she wished him no ill, and she had called her alleged information a blessing. Strange!

And her gift of herbs pleased him. He could trust her not to gather them by night, when plucked herbs do not keep as well. She often brought him such things, always with some sly jest about his having turned from killing to curing. It was the truth; soldier though he was, Vaughn had a gift and a knowledge both of healing and of surgery which had grown upon him through the wars, and now had become his vocation.

The town was ahead; he came to the seven-arched stone bridge, and slowly walked his nag across. With the alert eye of an old campaigner, Vaughn noted a crippled wreck of a man at

the town end of the bridge, but paid him no heed. Such war-wreckage was all too common now.

He looked at Brecon, ahead. The old town, on its rise surrounded by the bowl of the Welsh mountains, was dirty and shabby with the neglect of years. The castle, and the priory buildings up above, were half crumbled. Everywhere some gaunt ruin sat, like a hag of evil personified. Vaughn knew the town might be dangerous for him, because Parliament men were here, and he was known to have ridden for the lost cause of the King; however, they had sore need of physicians and would probably leave him alone....

"Lieutenant Vaughn! Harry Vaughn! D'ye remember Beeston Castle, and how ye cut off the arm of King Harry of Monmouth?" said a voice beside him.

VAUGHN HALTED the nag, looked down at the crippled man, whose face was swathed in rags, and astonishment flooded into his brain. The long agony of Beeston's siege, which had so

"You will not talk of love with the lady who is in your mind, but with another."

nearly left him perished or a crippled wreck for life, welled up anew—wounds, fighting, incredible starvation, the shrieks and groaning of hurt men, and he himself moving like a healing shadow among the sick and dying.

"I remember Beeston as one remembers an unending hell," he said slowly. "All this past winter I have been very ill and close to death because of it."

"But mind ye the actor who called himself King Harry of Monmouth?" said the wreck bitterly. "His arm was hurt and swollen, and ye carved it off for him, and the stump healed. I was the one held the hot pitch to clap on the stump."

"Memory is a painful thing." Vaughn heard his own words as from far away, faintly. "Your voice is vaguely familiar, friend, but I do not remember your face."

"It was familiar to many on the London stage," came the retort. "Smallpox altered it, and changed the face that you knew in Beeston Castle. I was the knight Fluellen, Master Vaughn. Have ye forgot how we used to recite the play about King Harry and French Kate? And how you told us of Sir Roger Vaughn, your own ancestor, who was knighted on the field of Agincourt? And the lass Dionys, who held her father's arm when ye cut it off? Brave Dionys, ye called her—"

The lass Dionys! Henry Vaughn closed his eyes; his pale cheeks became white as death. His hands clenched on his saddle-bow. He had tried to forget all those terrors, and with them the vision of fled, lost beauty. It was only last autumn that Beeston had fallen, but he felt that the year 1645 would remain throughout his life as a turning-point and a memory of unmiti-gated horror. Not even this warm summer sun of 1646 could remove the chill of Beeston from his soul; not even the sweet, gentle face of the refugee girl up yonder at the old Priory, where she was sheltered by Lady Price, could drive from his memory the tawny regal eyes of the lass Dionys. Vaughn opened his eyes again and shook his head.

"Leave be, leave be," he said, stifling a groan. "She is dead, with all the world. I've turned from soldiering to doctoring. I can do naught for you, Fluellen; we're lucky at Newton if we have food for our own bellies."

They were always after him, old soldiers, maimed veterans of his own cavalry troop: he could do nothing for them, and the blunt words hurt.

He picked up his reins and lifted his face, looking at the ruinous Priory far above near the castle. Catherine waited there, a pleasant girl, a sweet refugee. She too had lost everything, and her brother had fallen beside him at Rowton Heath. She loved him a little, and he loved her placidly; he had come up from Newton today to talk about a wedding.

"But she is not dead," a voice was saying. "She is not dead; she has need of you. I was tramping to Newton to find you. We heard you were now a leech—"

Vaughn drew rein. He looked down, his gray eyes staring and dilated.

"Are you mad?" he asked hoarsely. "She died after the siege. A man told me."

The wreck jerked his thumb toward the hills.

"She's there, with Harry o' Monmouth and a few more," he said.

Vaughn caught his breath. "There's an ale-house beyond the bridge end. Meet me inside. Too dangerous to stand here talking. Damned Puritans everywhere."

He urged his sorry old nag onward. The words rang and rang through his brain: *She is not dead! She is not dead—and she has need of you....*

In a corner of the ale-house, feet scraping the rush-strewn floor, they sat over bread and cheese and ale. Henry Vaughn said little or nothing. Fluellen, as he called himself, talked as he quenched famished cravings. And under the talk, Vaughn's brain reechoed those ringing words: *She is alive, alive!*

Strange that she should be alive, that these others should be alive! Her father, who termed himself "King Harry," with such

bitter irony, or this Fluellen, or any of them! Once, before the
world turned upside down, they had been players in London,
warm and fed and laughing, honored by king and nobles, courted
by the gentry, no strangers to damask and jewels and broad gold-
pieces, dancing to lilting lute and viol.

And now all was gone down to ruin with England herself—
the King a tattered foresworn wanderer, nobles and gentry dead,
scattered, forgotten, their homes burned or plundered, their
estates sold, their sorry fragments ground down and robbed to
the last loaf. Not they alone, but ordinary farming folk ruined
and wasted, townfolk looted, churches devastated, colleges
laid waste, all learning and culture destroyed. The whole face
of England swarmed with veterans of disbanded armies, who
murdered for a crust. Even in the walled towns no man's life
was safe....

The lass Dionys! Vaughn choked on his ale. Half a dozen of
them yonder in the hills, a few miles away; a backwash of wreckage, of players who had clustered together. They had found an
iron-workings and had taken shelter there, out of the world,
far from anywhere; her father, King Harry of Monmouth, was
Welsh-born, and the scattered Welsh folk let them stay and
aided them, said Fluellen. But now the lass Dionys was ill and
had sore need of help.

"DO YOU know Scethrog?" Vaughn asked suddenly. "Down
the valley, near my stead of Newton. Close by is the Cwm Pooka,
the fairy valley. Thence came Puck, for Shakespeare heard of him
from my people, as he did about the other Welsh matters....
Well, well, meet me there tomorrow, early in the afternoon. I'll
go with you."

"She needs help now," said the ragged Fluellen.

"She shall have it." Vaughn got out his pouch. He carefully
shared the vial of white powder. It was frightfully hard to come
by at any time, this stuff called Jesuits' bark, but he had bought
some from the loot of Bristol; it was the only thing that would

*"She is not dead; she
has need of you."*

cure his own fever. The wise Harvey had taught him the use of
it in London.

"Give this to her," he said, with proper directions. "By tomorrow she should be in good shape, and I'll bring what else I have
that may help her."

"God bless you, master!" said Fluellen.

Vaughn smiled. A rare thing, to smile. "Blessings on my gray hairs? Avaunt thee, villain! We'll meet tomorrow."

True, his brown hair was streaked with gray over the temples. These past years he had starved and bled, had ridden by stricken field and flood all over the west country. He had sat beside his old teacher, Harvey the king's physician, who had discovered how man's bloodstream circulates, the two of them wrapped in a ragged cloak under a hedge. He had himself learned surgery, with sword or dagger for tools, where men lay screaming after battle. His face was marked by privations, lined by old sufferings, his hair turning gray, though he was barely twenty-four....

Leaving the tavern, he rode on up to the Priory, where Lady Price and a few women lived amid the wreckage of former wealth and greatness. He talked with Catherine; he talked with the others; but his mind was far away. Complaining that the fever was upon him, he mounted and went riding home again sooner than he had intended. And as Blodwen had prophesied, without talk of love.

Five miles home—down the winding, brawling Usk to the little gabled manor-house of Newton, now stripped to the bone of all comfort, kine and prosperity.

If ever the wars ended, he had been thinking that here he could make repairs to life. Here, with the placid Catherine, he might settle down as a physician, build up the little estate once more, and perhaps watch England come back from ruin— though this did seem an impossibility. And yet, time after time, England had been swept by savage slaughter and by brutal destruction of civilized ideals, only to recuperate and bloom once more; as though in the race and in the very land were some immortal spirit beyond any power to crush completely.

THAT NIGHT, Henry Vaughn sat by a flickering candle in an upper room opening on the summer stars—quill and ink-pot at hand. Now and again he had written scraps of poetry; tonight he tried to calm himself with this pursuit, but a fiercer ecstasy was upon him. The lass Dionys—alive! He no longer felt himself an old, outworn man whose youth was dead. Settle down here, a country physician lost in the depths of Brecknockshire? Devil take such a future! Tonight there were new things quivering in the air.

An odd mixture of old and young, this man sitting wide-eyed by the window, a queer mingling in him of death and life. What he had tried to write down, he could not. Now came to him words he had not sought.

He tried to put them away. This little band of wretched players, he told himself, were not his kind; they were miserable folk, rendered abnormal by horrors and sufferings. He would find the lass Dionys with her beauty gone, her appeal lost. She must be eighteen now.... And Catherine was eighteen.

"Em queer too," he said, biting his lip.

"The whole world's queer these days

We see strange things; we hear strange voices. Like Jeanne d'Arc. No, by God! Like the man I pistoled at Rowton Heath, who sobbed out that he saw all eternity, and then died prating of old Queen Bess.... Like *John Falstaff*, who died babbling of green fields—"

He caught up the quill and wrote, wrote late into the night; and he did not write the pretty little jingling verses that so pleased the placid child Catherine....

Morning came, and noon; and with it two countryfolk needing his help. He talked with them in Welsh, gave them remedies of some simple country herbs, sent them away. Later he mounted the old nag and went to his rendezvous, a bundle before his saddle; it held a few odds and ends that might give Dionys comfort, and an old sweet dress of yellow damask from a box in the loft that had escaped looting. His mother's, perhaps; he did not know or care.

That ragged wreck Fluellen met him in Puck's Valley, and they went on together. The white powder had made a new lass of Dionys, said Fluellen; she had gone all pink and white this morning, at talk of Master Vaughn. There was a Welsh woman

*"The whole world's queer, these days," he
said.... He caught up his quill and wrote.*

lying dead up the hill path, and two dead children with her, he
added; some talk had arisen of disbanded soldiers being about.
God help the ravening rascals if any of the hill-folk caught
them!

Vaughn loosened his sword in the scabbard, and thought of
dead women and children he had seen in the ditch outside Bristol, and the Irish troops lying in heaps where they were massa-
cred. These things gave him a wild, aching hurt to think about,
and he could never get rid of them. Then the thought of Dionys
crowded all else out of his mind, and eagerness swelled his heart.

The two of them went on, not rapidly, striking into the mountains by an old disused path, and from this by a faint track along
a wild hillside to where a great hole gaped, an abandoned working for iron-ore such as the country-folk over Monmouth way
termed a scowle. And at the door of this cavern opening sat

Harry of Monmouth with his one arm; beside him was the lass Dionys, in rags and tatters, but radiant as the dawn.

Vaughn scarcely remembered the greetings, except that Dionys kissed him, and fire ran from his lips through all his veins. King Hal roared for sack and for malmsey, and compromised on water from the spring near by. He was a sad broken man, tall and dark, with deep eyes that had seen all the pits of hell.

"The others? Gone," he replied to Vaughn's question. "Gone to search the hills for bark and herbs and anything that will cook into soup. Fluellen and I must be off too; I've marked a rabbit's warren over the hill, and we'll be back with meat of some sort ere dark. Sit you, rest you, make the lass smile if you can…. Eh, tobacco? Lord love you, man!"

VAUGHN HAD brought tobacco, the only thing he could give old soldiers who had known him; he handed out some to the two men, and caught a breathless mutter from King Hal.

"For God's love, make her cheerful! She's in a bad way."

Then he and Fluellen were off with their cudgels and a rusty sword, first unsaddling the nag. Vaughn came to the girl and held her hand, and looked into her tawny eyes; awkwardness filled him, but her laughter dispelled it.

"Sit here and talk, Harry Vaughn! As we used to talk in Beeston Castle, lad…. Have you found out any more about the Swan of Avon and his friendship with your family?"

Vaughn broke into a laugh, as he settled down beside her.

"My interest has been in staying alive, and not in Shakespeare; he's not much thought of these days, except by occasional players, such as survive. Now tell me about your illness."

This, he concluded, was a quartan ague similar to his own; and aside from the benefit given by the Jesuits' bark, her condition was in no way alarming. Why had King Hal said she was in a bad way? For a long time, he could find no answer to this query.

The old spell of her magic, which had so enchanted him in Beeston, fell upon him once again full force. With her ragged boy's garments and cropped yellow hair, her slim brown body and brown hard features, she might pass well enough for a lad; she had bitter need of the disguise, these days. But to Vaughn those tawny eyes and the husky, throaty voice carried all the blazing spirit of the woman within her, aged far beyond her years by peril and privation.

"In Beeston," she said, smiling, "you used to talk of the fine Hollands sheets, scented with rosemary and lavender, you would sleep in when you got home again. Did you find them?"

"Gone," said Vaughn, "like everything else I dreamed. All is gone."

"But not the dreams," she rejoined softly. "If we lose everything else, the dream remains, Harry Vaughn. I had, and still have, a dream for you. Do you share it still?"

"It's born again this day." His heart went out to her; he kissed her swiftly, eagerly. "I thought you dead; I heard it from what I thought a sure source. I've had a bad time of it myself. The winter was cruel."

"It was cruel to us all, my dear. Father said that you had forgotten us; but I knew better."

SILENCE, BREEDER of words, enfolded them. Thought of Catherine came to him, and he pushed it away; little placid Catherine! He got out the things he had brought, the scraps of herbs and unguents, and the dress. Dionys cried aloud with delight at sight of it, but would only touch it with her fingertips, and eye it with hungry palpitant breath.

"Not now—later, inside there, when it's safer!" she said, glancing at the cavern mouth. "How lovely it is! How strange it will be, to wear woman's gear again! As though no longer were death and ruin everywhere, and one could sing and dance again, and live in quiet homes amid peace and love—" She broke off, and sighed. "Do you remember the pretty words you wrote me about the soul? I have done it often."

VAUGHN SHOOK his head. It was far away and lost. "I have forgotten."

"I haven't." She smiled, and quoted the words. *"Go candidly to the soul, my child, and hearken there to what may be heard at dusk or at any quiet time. Only in these restful moments may you come close to that which is more fleeting than a bright-winged bird and more enduring than a stone! There is strength and power only within you."*

"True; I remember now," he said, nodding. "Why, Dionys, you make the whole world seem different! Yesterday it was a hard thing even to live; today life's precious and full of hope, as though all the evil might yet pass! And last night the stars came close."

"The evil will pass," she said, as he paused. "Remember how you used to quote Bacon's letter written to your father, long ago?"

He nodded again. " *'The gallant soul shall strain and not lose me, saith the Truth; the wrath that rageth shall pass her lightly by. Evil shall fall away, as the dust, quenched by the rain, falls from the stone.'* "

"It is true, it is true!" Like a leaping flame rose her voice. "Just as we have found each other again, so the world shall come right once more; it must! We shall go to London together, Harry Vaughn, in those brave days, and the fame I prophesied for you in Beeston Castle shall come to you."

"Fame, to me?" He smiled. "And to you, perhaps?"

"No." She regarded him gravely, yet with a passionate conviction. "I know what you can do with words, with poems, with letters; and I know that I have the ability to kindle and keep alight this divine fire in you. Call it love or what you like, the result is one. I can do this."

"The mere fact of knowing you alive, did it last night," he said. "Yes, it's true. With you in my mind, with your love and confidence, I can find strange words, mystic powers of speech, thoughts that shimmer with light like very jewels!"

"And as our fathers called Shakespeare the Swan of Avon,"

she went on, "so our children will give you a name—the Swan of Usk."

He smiled. "Isn't there some legend that the swan sings only when about to die? But that's not the point; the swan is the ancient bird of Britain, true."

"That's why the name is given; not for poetry, but for nobility!" she exclaimed. "The Swan of Usk.... I like that name."

"*Olor Iscanus,*" he said, putting the title into Latin. "A quaint conception, surely! I must write a poem to that title."

"You said that last night the stars came close—"

He looked out at the fading afternoon sunlight through the trees.

"Yes. Like the Roundhead I pistoled in the Rowton fight—I saw a vision of all eternity." His voice came softly, his gray eyes were wide. "Like a great ring of pure and endless light in which all the races of men were moving; and there was no death. It came to me that heaven is hope, is energy, and that what death

*King Hal came staggering backward into the
glimmer of the rushlights; after him a grim booted
man who thrust him through. Dionys screamed.*

means is only another life. Differ as they may, at the last all men
are kin, in that they all know something but none knows death;
the sense of something supernal is one bond among them all. No
other link can exist among the races of men except the negative
one: they all know there is a thing they do not know."

He fell silent, then resumed slowly:

"Strange words, strange thoughts! When will man cease to
be a beast of prey and of burden, as we are today? When will
man remember that not only was he created in the image of his
gods—but he himself had created most of them? Our life is a
hurry and scurry between the legs of a row of giant fates, who
are fog if we but knew it. We have a natural right to enjoy the
minutes—the years are only their sum. What niceties of the

grand march from dark to dark are lost, through man's deep ignorance of his own privileges!"

HIS WORDS died away. He drew a deep breath, turned to the intent girl beside him, and smiled.

"You see to what strange fancies you lead me, Dionys! Except for you, I'd draw out of the world; no more soldiering, no more scholarship, merely a quiet humdrum existence blind to everything; in life except the hobbling duties of the day. I had determined to follow this course, be a physician here in a forgotten nook of Wales, marry some placid lass who would perhaps love me a little, and drown out all beyond. But with you, the stars sing and the river whispers strange words, and soaring mystic fancies take fire within me."

She clung to him for a long, breathless moment, and he saw there were tears on her face. Drawing away, she looked him in the eyes.

"Swan of Usk!" Her deep, rich voice flowed into him. "Promise me that whatever happens, you will write the poem to this title, that you will become truly the Swan of Usk."

He broke in, smiling: "I'll do it, yes, whatever happens; but only because you ask it. What you inspire lies beyond this world. We've found each other, and there shall be no more loss, no parting."

WHEN THE blessed daylight was thinning, figures appeared among the trees. Dionys called, and they came in, fearfully; two were women, sunken-eyed skeleton figures, though not old, and three were men—ghastly croaking creatures, cropped of ears and with inhuman faces, yet preserving the remnants of modulated voices used to courtly speech. Former players, these, joined up during the winter; Vaughn knew none of them.

Dionys introduced him; the greetings were joyful, for all had heard of him, and most of them needed his ministrations sorely. They were joyful aside from this, declaring that he had brought them huge luck, for one woman had a bird, not freshly dead but still good for the pot, and the men had a fat trout they had angled from the river, and two dormice—such a feast as they had not known in days.

"But there be signs o' death and raiders about," said one; "and by the river we saw two naked men hanged to a tree, fresh done, their hands cut off and tied about their necks."

"That'll be done by the mountain men," said Vaughn. "They caught two raiders and hanged 'em. The Welsh give these rogues short shrift. Here, let's have a look at your bad eye."

He fell to work, with the instruments and herbs he always carried with him. The women bustled off inside the workings with Dionys, to get supper started.

Vaughn was still laboring by the last daylight, cleansing an infected foot, when King Hal and Fluellen showed up, and amid shouts of jubilation showed their plunder—a brace of rabbits, summer-fat. To Vaughn, the loud ecstasies of these wretched folk were pitiful, although for the matter of that, he himself had not seen a rabbit in the pot for a long while.

His task done, Vaughn went to the spring to wash, and King Hal went with him. He had never known the gaunt man's proper name; he had not asked, and King Hal had ever kept it secret, as though in bitter shame of what was become so tarnished. It occurred to him now to ask, since he had resolved to take Dionys home with him to Newton and there wed her. Before he could do so, however, King Hal spoke darkly:

"Is she smiling again? Aye, she must be; there's an air of cheer about the place."

Vaughn recollected his words. "You did wrong to say she's in a bad way, King Hal; no such thing! She's ill, yes, but in no peril."

"I spoke of grisly ills beyond your knowledge," said the other man gloomily. "She's been prating of death and evil, saying she'd not leave this place alive. God give that your coming has changed all that!"

"Perhaps it has; at all events, she's cheerful enough. Here, take a bit more tobacco, and I'll tether my horse more securely."

"He may betray us, that horse, if any wandering rascals come past—but we'll chance that," said the other. "I've seen no one. By the gods, what a feast is ahead!"

DESPITE HIS campaigning across harried broken England, Vaughn found the place and the crew a strange and weird reality. The iron-workings went into the hillside some thirty feet, widening out at the back, but with a low rock ceiling. Rushlights lit it. A cooking-fire at the entrance was shrouded from sight of any wanderers by rags hung on sticks and by a big shield of wattles. And the lass Dionys wore her gown of yellow damask like a queen.

A queen? Vaughn caught his breath at sight of her; never before had he seen her in any but boy's garments. With a wreath of grasses on her cropped hair, she was become all woman, gloriously so! He dropped to one knee and kissed her hand, and King Hal roared approval.

"You'll play *Catherine of France* with us tonight, wench!" quoth he. "We'll do the play as we did it in Beeston Castle, remember? And you'll be royal *Catherine, Prince Hal's* merry *Kate.*"

Catherine? Why, so it was; the same name. Vaughn had not thought of it before, and he would have stopped the game; too late now, for King Hal was telling the others of it, amid high approbation.

In Beeston Castle there had been a tattered prompt-book; here there was none, but it was not needed, for some of them knew all the lines by heart. The big pot bubbled and steamed until famished bellies could no longer be gainsaid and they pitched in. Still King Hal talked on; he was like a man drunk with joy this night, poor gaunt wastage!

Vaughn had to tell them here, as he had told in Beeston, how Will Shakespeare had hidden out with the Vaughns of Trebarry when Warwickshire was too hot to hold him, for deer-killing. So it came that the playwright had put the Vaughn family into two or three of his plays, and much garbled Welsh lore besides, such as *Puck* and the mythical limping Davy Gam, or Llewellyn, who became Fluellen, and so forth. And the lass Dionys lighted the wretched cave like a daughter of the sun.

The feast drew to a close, though not until the pot was scraped clean. Then clearance was made; the two women carried the pot outside; King Hal and two of the men bore out the shabby dishes and mugs—and suddenly arose a great shriek that chilled the blood, a medley of shouts and oaths and a bellowing discharge of several shots.

KING HAL came staggering into the glimmer of the rush-lights, spouting blood, and after him a grim booted man who thrust him through with savage blade, so that he fell and died as he fell. Dionys screamed once, and the man with the blade laughed aloud.

"To me, comrades!" he shouted. "To me! Here's a young 'un!"

"And something else," cried Vaughn, sword out at last, horror in his heart, the sight of Dionys crouching over her dead father spurring him with agony.

He darted forward; then he halted. The intruder, his blade half raised, drew back. The two men stared.

"Lieutenant Harry Vaughn o' Price's Horse! Sink me if it aint!"

"And you're Langlade of the Guards!" Vaughn choked suddenly on his anger. "Why, ye damned bloody murderers, what d'ye mean by this deviltry?"

Faces and booted figures filled up the opening behind Langlade; the shrieks outside had ceased. Fierce eyes stared. Langlade of the Life Guards—a ragged filthy shape now.

"Out o' the way with 'un, Langlade!" A roar of voices went up. They could all see the girl's figure in the rushlight. "Down with him! String 'em all up and take the lass!"

Langlade tried to quell them by shouting that Vaughn was a king's man and an officer. They only cursed the more and shoved forward.

"Your fellows hanged two of our men today," cried Langlade.

"You lie!" retorted Vaughn. "The Welsh hung them, and good riddance!"

F O R A moment he daunted the lot of them, ordering them out and away; authority spoke in him. Then someone yelped about food and a lass; a storm of wild oaths and shouts went up. A pistol belched smoke, then another. Through the rolling smoke weapons slithered forward, and men pressed in. Langlade cursed and drove in a savage thrust with his blade. Vaughn parried it and gave him the point through the throat.

Another pistol; the fire seared him; the ball pricked at his thigh. He flung himself at them like a madman, thrusting, cutting, battering with the big hilt of his rapier. It was like Edgehill or Rowton Heath again—wild faces through the smoke, savage voices shouting, death everywhere.

They broke; they drew back before him, only to gather and hurl in upon him. He knew this was the end, and fought the more. In the midst of it, a shrill cry went up outside, a blaring shout of warning and alarm, drowned by an outburst of savage Welsh voices screaming for blood.

Now they broke indeed, crowding out again for very life; but not a man of them reached the waiting horses, for the mountain men were upon them, with bill and scythe and knife. Vaughn, panting and coughing from the powder-fumes, found his wound a mere scratch, shouted his name at half a dozen Welshmen making for the entrance, and was recognized and greeted. Then he turned, to care for the lass Dionys.

And in the sudden silence, his heart went cold, to stay cold forever.

She looked up at him in the rushlight, one hand pressed to her breast where the blood welled out over the yellow damask. He fell on his knees beside her, felt for the wound, and knew the worst; one of those bullets had stricken her.

"You said—you said a lovely thing." Her voice came faintly, and a shadowy smile touched her lips. "All that death means is another life—"

He was frozen, incapable of speech or movement.

"The Swan of Usk.... Your promise.... You will remember?"

He stooped and kissed her lips.

"I will... I will remember."

That was all she heard.

He wakened, after a long while, to find Welshmen around him, staring, waiting. The place was filled with the raw scent of blood. Langlade was dead; his men were strung up outside. To the mountain men, Vaughn was known intimately; one of them spoke to him, and he answered in Welsh, almost mechanically.

"She must be buried. And he, her father. He was a king."

He was like a man bemused; they could get no sense out of him, but what he had just said went around. The word passed that this dead man was no other than Gwyn ap Nudd, the king of the little people, and the dead girl was his daughter; awed, the men of the mountains filed out and prepared the graves.

WHEN HENRY VAUGHN rode away toward the brawling river and the road home, the glory of life had come, and gone again. As he rode, chin drooping on chest, letting the sorry nag take its own pace, he saw what the remainder of life must mean to him; a play whose lines would go unsaid, like this play of King Hal and French Kate which had ended ere it began. A dreary round of years wherein he would move like a shadow under the cold stars....

The Swan of Usk.... He looked up at the stars, and tears glittered on his cheeks. What was it she had said? A lovely thing—all that death means is another life! But for him, life had ended back there when the sods fell upon her. The vista that outstretched before him, the long years of emptiness and petty humdrum detail, and the memory of a dream that was dead. He had nothing else left.... Like many another man.

A COACH FOR DOVER

WILL CONGREVE, he of the bright and saucy eye, stood frowningly in the wings of the Drury Lane Theatre. As a privileged character, he had the run of the house; but something was happening there on the stage which assuredly was not on the books.

Mountford, a veteran actor and a prime favorite with the audiences, had the stage; but Mountford was not himself this night. Although it was only the first act of the play, a spirit of dissension was abroad. A figure standing in one of the stage boxes was making interruption, and the crowd was resenting it.

Congreve, who had failed to find Anne Bracegirdle in the greenroom, came up to the prompter with a low query.

"Where's Bracy?" he asked, employing the name by which Anne was known to all London.

The prompter jerked a thumb toward the opposite wings and droned along mechanically, his gaze on the book.

"What's wrong with Mountford?" demanded Congreve.

The old prompter grunted.

"A trull in an actor's mind leaves no room for lines! Besides, there's interference from the box yonder.... Gorum! There he goes again—an exit-cue speech, too!" He shot out the line viciously: *"But mark you this! I can make horns of bones that never grew on stag, nor brushed the leafy bough of oaks!"*

Mountford caught the speech. He ripped it out with furious vehemence, and stamped off-stage toward Congreve. Another catcall and a burst of laughter from the box went up. The audience began to shout its anger at this interruption; the house became a bedlam.

Coming to Congreve and the prompter, Mountford halted in a fuming rage.

"It's that damned rascal Captain Hill!" he cried. "He's been trying to break me up all during the scene.... Ah, listen to that! They'll be tearing up the benches next!"

Young Congreve looked out into the house, his air Unperturbed, even a trifle bored, though he was inwardly excited, for the audience showed its disapproval of Captain Hill in no uncertain terms.

In the opposite wings, Congreve saw old Papa Rich, the manager, frantically pleading with Anne Bracegirdle. She glanced across, sighted Congreve, and waved her fan at him; she was a picture of youth and loveliness in her costume of plum satin. Suddenly Papa Rich, tired of pleading, pushed her out bodily from the wings. With a laugh, she went tripping across the stage to the smoky footlights.

"Ah!" said the prompter in relief. "She'll handle 'em!"

The din swelled up for an instant; then it hushed. She strode straight toward the box in which Captain Hill was standing, a dark, stocky, arrogant figure of a man. She halted, whipped up her fan in the attitude of fence, and stamped three times in prescribed fashion ere she thrust at him. She lunged and parried, and lunged again. In high disdain, she shook imaginary gouts of blood from the fan and sheathed it, with triumphant flourish.

The pantomime evoked howls of delight. The incipient riot was diverted into wild cheers of applause; animosity toward Hill was swamped in admiration for the actress.

"Bracy! Blush for me, like a good girl!" A young dandy, erect in a box, sent up the cry. The crowd caught and lifted it into a roar. "Blush, Bracy! Blush!"

Will Congreve watched her refuse, heard the crowd rave

insistence, saw her at last give assent; but he was not blind to other things.

H E   H A D   shot up like a rocket amid the wittiest, raciest and crudest life in London, that of the stage; but he was very far from the indolent young fop he appeared. He played a part himself, assuming all that he was not. A student lawyer, he believed himself a poet. A green country lad from Ireland, he affected all the hauteur of a great lord—and well enough to get away with it. Poor as a church mouse, he played the rakish profligate, and had not yet been found out.

And now, as he leaned indolently against the edge of a forest set, he was aware of something close at hand—a figure in snowy hat and greatcoat that came sidling up to Mountford. From this figure came a hoarse cockney voice, uplifted above the din from the pit.

"All's done, guv'nor! Coach and four beside Drury 'Ouse at ten o' the clock, and good hosses too. Five guineas for Dover, and no questions asked."

Mountford hurriedly hushed the man, gave him money, bundled him away, shooting swift cautious glances around. A handsome man, Mountford, a man of thirty-odd and a veteran of the theater, able and darkly passionate.

Congreve whistled softly. What the devil was afoot? Usually possessed of perfect *savoir-faire,* Mountford was tonight awkward and distraught, nervous, excited. Some intrigue? Most unlikely. He was married to one of the most capable and beautiful women in the profession, herself a member of the Theatre Royal company.

T H E D E A D hush pulled Congreve's attention back to the stage. Bracy was blushing!

She dropped her head, and from the corner of her eye shyly regarded the young dandy in the box. Catching her full wide lip with even teeth, she turned slightly. A slow pink flush crept over her face. She reached for her fan, and in the greatest of confusion spread it wide; when she dropped it again, her face was a flaming scarlet, her eyes bright with unshed tears of shame.

In the wild enthusiasm that followed, she started to pirouette, faster and faster, until her billowing skirts lifted to a glimpse of flashing legs that spun and twirled her lithe body like a top. She curtsied low; and amid fresh roars of applause ran off the stage and was gone.

Will Congreve swung around. He met the dark gaze of Mountford, read its savage dislike, and nodded amiably. He did not betray how that gaze startled him, what it told him.

"A lovely girl, a girl to love!" he observed. "You've known her long, eh?"

"Twelve years, and loved her all of it," said Mountford. "She was six when she first played; she was the page in 'The Orphan,' and a darling she was!"

"And is."

"And you love her too. Eh, Will?" The tone was challenging.

"Oh, of course! Who does not? All London loves her," Congreve said lightly, affecting to smooth the lace at his wrists. "By the way, you've heard of today's miracle?"

"Miracle?" The somber gaze of Mountford darkened a little. "I don't know what you mean."

Congreve shrugged, finding falsity in the words. "Our London will be talking of it by tomorrow," be said, and went his way, pondering what he had overheard.

A coach for Dover! Passing strange, for a poor devil of an actor. And Mount-ford loved Bracy—aye, and no fatherly love either, if the man's eyes spoke truth! But why the coach? He reflected swiftly, as he sought the dressing-room.

"Mountford, it would seem, dislikes me. And Captain Hill, evidently, detests Mountford; the arrant rogue detests him who would perhaps be rogue himself! And all for love of Bracy! Therefore, Captain Hill, good stupid rogue as he is, no doubt detests me as well. I fear I've uncovered something. And Mountford certainly knows about the eight hundred guineas!"

When he sauntered in, humming a careless tune and pitching his beaver on the table, Anne was in her linen shift, busily plying a needle on a rent in her costume. She surveyed his strapping figure and opened her eyes wide at his new and elegant attire.

"Why, Will! What a rakehelly fop you look! Plum Genoa velvet, egad! And real lace!"

"Ah, but it's for the eye of a lady, my dear," he said, lounging against the wall. "I saw your blush. It was the second miracle of the day: an admirable blush!"

"No fault of yours," she said a bit shortly, but her eyes warmed gloriously upon him. "What are you laughing at?"

"Oh, the first miracle!" he rejoined with a chuckle. "I was there; I saw it happen. Egad, Bracy! You've then no words for me, no tidings of great good fortune?"

"I've had words enough for you, Will, and small good it's done me," she replied with unexpected gravity.

She was very lovely—a delight to the eye and a solace to the heart, and all too well did Will Congreve know it. Too well, indeed! The world was hers; and his love, the love of an unknown scribbler, would be a millstone about her neck.

NOW, MASTER of himself as usual, he refused her challenge to serious talk, and assumed his air of gay banter.

"A guinea for the secret of your blush, Bracy!"

"You haven't a guinea, and you know it," she retorted. "But, for one kiss, I'll tell you the secret."

"Done!" He came to her, put his hands on her shoulders, looked into her eyes. "And how's it done? What's the secret of that marvel?"

Her eyes twinkled. "Why, I just hold my breath!"

He kissed her suddenly, swiftly, repeatedly. "You blessed, blessed thing!" he exclaimed softly, regarding her again. "You're the most beautiful woman in the world, you minx!" The warm color in her cheeks, the tenderness in her eyes, warned him. He checked himself, and broke into a laugh.

"So I haven't a guinea, eh? Wrong, my dear; I've several! And my play, my first play, is sketched out; it's for you; it shall go to you. 'The Old Bachelor,' by Mr. Congreve…. Why, you'll make this unknown Mr. Congreve a famous man! But you've no need of guineas this night, with your eight hundred. A fortune!"

She drew back, shot a glance at the chest in the corner, and looked at him with wide startled eyes.

"Will! How do you know? Who told you?"

"Didn't I tell you I was there when the miracle happened?" He fell again into his smiling, half-sardonic coolness. "It was like a scene in a comedy! They'd been gaming all night and half the day—Ambington, Dorset and Devonshire. They fell to speaking of you, and naturally I listened for lies, but they spoke truth. 'Ha!' says my Lord Dorset. 'She's a good girl, and damned few like her in London!' He swept the gold-pieces across the table. 'Here's two hundred guineas goes to a good girl. Damme, there's plenty gone to the bad ones!' It struck their humor. They made it up to eight hundred, and off went the guineas to the only good girl in London town. And on the heels of it, egad, I won twenty for myself—hence this elegant raiment that struck your eye."

"Oh!" She picked up the nut-brown boy's tunic she had been mending, inspected it critically, and began to get into it.

"Eight hundred guineas!" said Congreve reflectively. He could not even conceive of so much gold at one time; though he had seen it often enough on the gaming-tables, it was unreal as stage money. Ireland had given him a cool head and a bragging tongue, however. No one had guessed his slight acquaintance with coined gold, since he had come to London to study law, and gave himself to poetry and gambling instead.

*Her face scarlet,
her eyes bright
with unshed tears
of shame....*

"And what," he went on idly, "shall you do first with your new wealth, Bracy?"

"Buy a mirror like the one they say the Queen has," she responded promptly. "A long one, in which I can see myself from head to foot."

"Practical wench! Don't use too many of those Spanish papers.... Less rouge, my dear! You're playing a boy's part this act, remember."

"A red-cheeked boy," she retorted. "I know the part better than you."

"No doubt. A fortune, a real fortune! Now you'll be independent of old Rich's whining bargaining contracts; laugh at him and go elsewhere, or double your salary! Now you've a prodigious start in the world. I told you London Would be at your feet, that you could pick and choose the likeliest ducal coronet to adorn your fair brow!"

"A plague on your coronets! My own hair's enough, and heavy enough too."

"True; and more beautiful than any coronet. By the way, I ran into Mountford. He must be moonstruck! He was telling me how he loved you, and damme if his eyes didn't reveal more than his tongue!"

"That's no news," she said curtly, continuing her dressing. "I've known it for years. But he's thirty-odd, and I'm eighteen, so no one else guesses I'd look at him."

Congreve felt vaguely startled. "But Anne! You wouldn't, of course. The fellow seemed to be in earnest."

"Why not?" she returned coolly.

"Why not? Damme, he must be monstrous owly, with a wife who's good and honest and handsome, and playing in this very company! What more could he want?"

"Change," said she, arranging her hair under a boy's cap. Congreve burst into quick laughter, despite his irritation.

"Egad, what a line! I'll work it into my 'Old Bachelor.' Mr. Dryden is reading the first draft of the play now. And I'll work in you and me, and the guineas, and gouty old Ambington's talk when he sent 'em."

Suddenly she turned a flaming tormented face to him.

"A pox on the filthy money! I won't keep it. Help yourself to it, if ye'll have it. I'll throw it into the Thames…. I'll give it away, d'ye hear?"

"Aye, but hearing's not believing, my dear," he rejoined lightly. "You're no such fool. And you're no such fool as to encourage Mountford's villainy."

"Villainy, indeed! He's an old friend of years; so is Mrs.

Mountford. What's more, I'm supping with him tonight, after all's done. At Richmond. And I'll do it whenever I please. So what of it?"

"Why, nothing at all," Congreve replied, with a shrug.

Inwardly, he was disconcerted, utterly perturbed. Richmond? Was she lying? No; he knew her too well. She could not conceive a man so black as Mountford really was, a man she had known so long. She thought she was going to Richmond, indeed. But Mountford knew better. Mountford was for Dover and beyond, with the guineas and the girl, a girl disgraced and robbed and flung into shame for life. For Dover, with a coach and four!

"What's more," she went on heatedly, "Captain Hill hath spoke of marriage, and asked would I leave the stage in such case."

From the corner of her eye, she cast a glance at him. Congreve was aware of it, however, and burst into laughter.

"Captain Hill the bravo, the ruffler, the broken gentleman, the rogue! A fine prospect. Marriage, egad! Well, snap him up on it, Anne!"

She swung full around, furious.

"Will Congreve! When will you give over this eternal mockery and callous jesting? When will you become your old honest self again? You refuse to be serious about anything. You turn whatever I say into a mock. You laugh at me—" Her voice broke a little. "Just now you kissed me; 'twas like your old self, Will! And now you've become all hard and cold once more."

"Why not sup with me tonight, instead of with Mountford?" he broke in.

She started slightly, gave him an eager look; but he had played this chosen rôle so long that the earnest impulse in his words was hidden. She noted only his light smile, his careless lounging mien, his sarcastic eye. She bridled.

"N O ! I cannot break with him; it's important. Besides, you mock me still."

*"Villainy indeed! I'm supping with him
tonight. I'll do it whenever I please."*

"You're a fool, Bracy," he abruptly broke in, and there was no
laughter in his face now. "A fool! To waste your time on rascals
like Hill and Mountford and me, when half the gallants of
London are at your feet, when fame and fortune are yours, when
your whole future life can be made or marred in a moment! Pick
a man of wealth and title; love him, marry him!"

She stared, wide-eyed. "I do believe you mean it!"

"Of course I mean it!" he said brusquely. "Mountford's an
arrogant, desperate ass; wife or not, he's insane about you; he'll
stop at nothing to have you and your fortune in the chest yonder
as well. Captain Hill's a plain utter scoundrel. Shun 'em both, or
you'll be ruined on the verge of your fame and greatness!"

Anger flamed in her face. "And yourself, Will? Once you liked me rarely."

"Oh, I don't count," he said, and shrugged. "A scribbler has nothing to offer in the way of a future. I'll be like old Dryden, sitting about a coffee-house all day and exchanging witty words with dunces. By the way, what of your guineas tonight?"

"Oh, they're safe. The chest is locked. I must take it with me, of course.... Will, do you think Rich might plunder me?" Sudden anxiety sprang in her eyes. "He owes me seven pound ten, and rather than pay it, he might rob me or put me out of the way."

Congreve broke into hearty laughter.

"Anne, you'll write my whole play yet if you don't look out! Old Papa Rich plunder you! Why, it's a rare thought. And you fear a fox, when a wolf's waiting to devour you!"

His laughter brought renewed anger into her face—a hurt, bewildered anger. In the silence they could hear the thumping of the *entr'acte* acrobats, the wailing of the hautboy, the pulsing of the drum. Then the shuffle of the call-boy in the corridors.

"Actus Secundus. Five minutes. Mistress Bracegirdle in men's clothes. On stage, Mistress Bracegirdle and Mr. Mountford. Actus Secundus. Five minutes—" his voice trailed away plaintively.

"WILL, YOU—YOU unspeakable black-guard!" Anne suddenly erupted in passion. "Well you know I'd do anything for your sake. You win my heart, and then trample it. You make a mock of me.... Well, it's ended! Get out of my life; stay out! I've done with you forever; by heavens, I'll prove it to you quick enough, too!" She stamped her foot furiously. "Out, d'ye hear? I'll be played with no more. Ye have no heart, no soul; away with you!"

Behind his mechanical and cynical smile, Congreve felt his heart sink. Alarm pricked at him; she would do something desperate now, and it was his own cursed fault. He was about to speak when he heard a heavy step at the door, a heavy voice, a heavy knock.

"Are you busy, Mistress Bracegirdle? I want a minute with you."

"Captain Hill, egad!" Congreve turned. "Quick, Anne; follow my lead, play up!" He darted to the door, lifting his voice in angry harshness.

"I'll not write another word for you; I'm not writing for my health!" He twisted the knob and let the door swing ajar. "You lazy trollop, you asked for the play, and here it is nearly finished, and you refuse any advance! I'll have my five pounds, or I'll go to the Lord Chamberlain about it!"

Captain Hill was in the doorway, staring; a burly block of a man dressed in full black, except for narrow white ruffles at throat and wrists. A dark, black-browed man with pale blue eyes devoid of expression, who carried with him an aura of suspicion and danger.

"Five pounds?" screamed Anne. "I wouldn't give you five fish-eyes! I wouldn't give five pounds to Dryden, let alone a milk-nosed maggot like you!" She flew at Congreve suddenly and slapped his face with furious palm. "I wouldn't wrap up old chicken guts in the best play you ever tried to write!"

Hill, in his arrogant way, walked in and motioned Congreve to get out. Instantly, Anne turned upon him.

"How dare you come in here and order anyone out? Don't come cock-a-hoop at me, my fine bully, or I'll scratch your eyes out! Away, the lot of you! I'm going on-stage. And you, Mr. Congreve, you needn't come back. I won't have your play."

She pushed past Hill to the door.

"Oh, there are other theaters, and better actresses than you to boot," said Congreve.

She paused to throw back a furious look at him.

"You sniveling pen-nibbler, the play you're writing about your father will never be staged in this theater!"

"Eh?" Congreve looked bewildered. "Play? About my father?"

"Aye. 'The Old Bachelor!'" she retorted, and her ringing laugh died away as she departed.

CAPTAIN HILL burst into mirth; even Congreve smiled ruefully.

"The hellcat!" he said. "She's proud as a goose in a gale! Well, I'm done with her."

"And she with you, by the looks of it," said Captain Hill.

Congreve swung toward him.

"Don't flatter yourself—and with you as well! Mountford's got us all off the stage. Aye, the rascal! Carrying her off tonight, with her guineas, to Dover and Paris."

"What's that?" Captain Hill lost his imperturbable mien, lost his grin, and took Congreve by the arm. "What's that again? What's this owl-eyed rogue of an actor about?"

"You heard me," Congreve said, assuming a sulky air. "A coach waiting behind Drury House at ten o'clock. She goes to sup with him; the blackguard carries her off! I heard the whole thing planned."

A sulphurous oath burst from Captain Hill. Clutching at his sword-hilt, he blasted Mountford in no uncertain terms.

"Amen to that, and more," said Congreve sullenly. "But it'll do no good. He'll stop at nothing; he'll have the life of anyone who interferes. The man's insane."

The soldier was suddenly calm again, but his pale eyes were blazing.

"Insane, is he? Zounds! Steel will slit the throat of a madman as well as any other!" Hill ground out another curse and snarled at Congreve. "And you, you scullery-bard! Be off before I crop your ears and break over your thick head that sword you flaunt!"

He swung around abruptly and went stamping away with a growl of blasphemous profanity.

Congreve whistled softly, closed the door, and swung about. He went to the little brass-bound chest in the corner, that held

Anne's personal effects. It was locked fast. With a nod he sank down and sat on it, glumly.

"Not so heavy but two men could easily sling it into a coach," he muttered. "And now, what've I done? Set two rascals one against t'other; not so clever, perhaps, as it seemed. Poor Anne! She loves me; I cannot break her of it. She tries to rouse my jealousy. Now she's desperate—and only God knows to what lengths a desperate woman will go! Oh, I'm the worst cursed fool in London! When I'd give the whole world to hold her in my arms! Why the devil should I want to build her future on certainty, to see her fame and fortune safely guarded—"

He broke off in gloomy silence. Then he came to his feet.

"Will Congreve, you're a fool, a fool!" he said, with some truth; and leaving the dressing-room went out to the stage door and the cold darkness.

"A fool, and I love her! And for her own sake, must not!" he muttered.

Go to her sensibly, advise her, take her in his arms—why, of course! She would forget all else; by the morrow, they would be married. And the news of it all over London! And her future ruined; an actress married was an actress lost to fame and fortune, in the cynical eye of the period. It was Anne's fresh youth and beauty, her artless ability to cozen all men into loving her, that was winning her already tremendous success. Marriage to a dull dolt of an unfledged lawyer turned poet, would end everything for her.

And now her money: a groan escaped Congreve at thought of the eight hundred guineas. It Was actually a fortune, and blocked him above all else, for he had a fierce youthful pride. It dazzled him into blank despair, and robbed his brain of all sound practical values. A tenth of the sum would have made him, in his own eyes, a rich man.

For he had not a penny, except what he won by gambling. Most of his life spent in Ireland, he had come to London carrying things with a high hand, ruffling it bravely, winning enough

"Oh, ye've opened a way Ye've said
things never to be forgotten!"

at cards to tide him over, risking a debtor's prison daily. On all sides he was thought to be a young man of wealth and family.

He had even deceived shrewd old Dryden, who regarded him as the coming man of letters. Dryden had lost his post as poet laureate when the Stuarts fell; but still, though wearing on toward seventy, was dean of literary England. Dryden, who spent his time sitting in the coffeehouse, scribbling arid discoursing, predicted that Will Congreve would make the world sit up and take notice. Dryden was reading the rough sketch of his play, even now.

A SHIVER took Congreve; the piercing cold was no longer welcome.

He turned back into the theater. Anne had the stage; the pit was roaring with laughter; but he had no heart to watch her. He secured his hat and greatcoat and stalked out, the thought of ten o'clock searing him. It was still two hours away; the best of the evening was ahead; but for him it was ended. He was a fool, and too stubborn to right his folly.

He turned into Russell Street. He wanted to see no one. He turned aside from the parties of gallants or ladies, with link-boys trotting before, their flaring resinous torches blooming like gigantic smoky flowers. He walked on and on in moody gloom.

Without conscious volition, he found himself at the familiar coffee-house, and turned in; a drink, a parry of wit with the gallants, might banish the doldrums. But to his bleak disgust, the place was empty. What with the snow, or perhaps the early hour, no one was here except Dryden, who sat scribbling busily in a corner and cursing his dull quill.

"Will! Will Congreve! To me, stout heart o' gold!"

The lusty call drew him. Old Dryden, pushing back white locks, laid down the quill and leaned back in his chair.

"Why, sir, I'd not disturb you at work," Congreve protested.

"Work be damned! Sit down—have a pipe with me…. Server! Two mugs of mulled ale!"

Congreve dropped dismally into a chair. The keen, shrewd old eyes bit into him.

"Lad, I've read your play—that is, the rough draft of it."

"I regret I let you waste your eyes on such rubbish," Congreve rejoined.

"You're a fool to be writing poetry. Forget such things." Dryden chuckled. "Rubbish? By the gods, Will, stick to comedy! Put the play in shape, write it fair, furbish it!"

"DEVIL TAKE the play! I'm done with the stage and its works." Congreve filled a long pipe from the open tobacco jar, and lit it with a paper twist from the candle.

"Look, lad," said the older man gravely. "I've spent most o' my days with the stage; I know whereof I speak. 'The Old Bachelor' is the finest thing I've read in years; the day after it's produced, you'll be a famous man! Wycherly himself never did a thing half so good."

Despite his gloom, Congreve thrilled to such praise from such a man.

"It's kind of you to say so, Mr. Dryden," he rejoined. He Was stripped now of all his gayety, of all his affected worldliness and boredom; he was just himself, lonely and heartsick. "It's kind of you."

"Damme, what's got into you?" exclaimed Dryden, and seized a mug. "Here, drink up! A health to Will Congreve's first play! Give it to Brace-girdle, lad."

Congreve winced and put down his mug. Dryden frowned at him.

"Art ill?"

"Aye. Ill to the soul, of my own folly."

"A healthy sickness! Splendid! Why, you're all tricked out in Genoa velvet and real lace—better and better! Go lose a hundred guineas at the tables and feel better!"

"A hundred guineas!" Congreve broke into bitter, scornful laughter. "Because I've ruffled it like a gallant, because I've pretended to throw money away, you've all thought I had plenty. I have none, d'ye understand? None! Not a farthing, except what's won at the cards. I'm a cheat, a fraud, a failure, a worthless fool who's tricked himself and lost all that's worth while in life."

His outburst ended. Dryden stared in astonishment and delight.

"Sink me if you're not talking like a real poet, Will! I'll change my advice. Go home this night and write a poem; it should be a brave one."

"This night!" repeated Congreve. "I'm in hell this night."

Dryden's face changed. His eyes warmed; he put out a hand and touched that of Congreve.

"Will, what is it? I love ye, lad, as ye were mine own. I see now it's real trouble; tell it me. Trust me. Empty the sad heart and let a friend give counsel, or whatever else ye may need."

Congreve melted; his proud reserve broke down before this friendliness. All his assumption of rakehell cynicism went to pieces. He blurted out everything; the amazing yet typical story of the eight hundred guineas, his own refusal to spoil Anne's future, the sinister business of Mountford's passion, and what he had done to check this by means of Captain Hill. He laid bare the whole sorry situation, and spared himself nothing in the telling. His touch of Irish speech came back to him in his emotion.

"There y'are; I'm a fool, yet I've done the wise thing," he concluded bitterly. "Or have I? Damme if I know. But Anne's in a mood to do anything, merely to spite me."

"And quite right. You've denied the first principle of love…. Tell the lass!" Dryden said, checking a furtive twitch of his thin lips. "Mountford's a foul rogue; Captain Hill is a plain blackguard. And you've left Anne to their clutches and her own desperation."

CONGREVE GAZED at him from haggard eyes.

"Ye know well I cannot think of love, with not a penny!"

Dryden sipped his ale, puffed his pipe alight, and nodded.

"Will ye let me tell ye three things, and not interrupt?"

"Aye."

"From an old man to a young man, then: First! Bracegirdle's an immense success, and will be a greater success—only while she's young and fresh and clever. She's honest and artless, but she has nothing deep. She'll never marry a lord and make a great lady. Let love uphold her, and she'll go far; let her lose love and follow desperation, and she'll turn into a careless, reckless light-o'-love and end in the gutter. Therefore, let your love uphold her."

Congreve said nothing, but the color rose in his cheeks.

"Second!" went on Dryden. " 'The Old Bachelor,' for a first play, is a masterpiece. It'll be a hit. Your name will be famous when that of Bracegirdle is forgotten; more likely, your fame will carry hers to the skies, for you've put her in this play. You must do others for her. You have a wit, a precision in words, a talent for scenes, that's positively diabolical! Will, I give you my word that inside six months you'll be England's greatest writer of comedies! And this means fame and future and wealth."

He paused, puffing, and a smile stole into his eyes.

"THIRD! I'M no more poet laureate; but the name o'John Dryden carries weight. I have friends and influence. I shall do for you tomorrow what I'd have done long since, had I guessed your financial plight—secure you a State post, which amounts to a pension that'll keep ye from want. And there'll be money provided for all present needs, advanced against the success of 'The Old Bachelor,' which I'll personally guarantee: All this, contingent upon one thing: One simple action on your part, lad."

He paused again. Congreve was alight with a flush of incredulity, of delighted gratitude, of breathless happiness. He gripped Dryden's hand.

"Oh, ye've opened a way! Ye've said things never to be forgotten!" he cried. "I'll do anything you say, anything you ask.... What is it, quickly?"

"Look at the clock, then go undo your boyish folly."

Congreve started. He looked at the clock, which said twenty minutes before ten. With one clutch at hat and coat, he was gone....

The snow had long since ceased to fall; the sky was clearing; the riot was over, and the watch had hustled away the last remnants of it. For a riot there had been, and men hurt; soldiers, said some, had started it, and the mob had stoned Captain Hill, not liking soldiers in any case.

"A clear night with little snow," chanted the sergeant of the watch, as his bobbing lanterns swung off into Russell Street. "Ten o'clock, and all's well!"

Drury Lane was empty and deserted, except for the dark mass of a coach standing outside the courtyard of Drury House. The horses steamed; the coachman stamped up and down the icy cobbles, thumping his arms for circulation.

Starlight was peeping over the chimney-pots; a shadowy group drew into sight, coming from the darkened theater. Two men carried a weight between them, followed by the figure of Mountford, a woman on his arm. They stamped up to the coach.

"Shall we strap it on the boot, master?" asked one of the men.

"No, no! Inside!" directed Mountford, his voice hoarse with excitement. "Inside!"

They swung open the door and deposited the little chest inside, and drew back. Mountford handed the woman in after it, with a bundle she Carried. He drew back to pay the two men, while the coachman mounted to his box.

"There y'are, lads."

"Wot, guv'nor?" one exclaimed loudly. "And wot abaht the other? Doubles it was, says you, if the sojer cap'n got 'is uppance! And 'e bloody well got it, wot wif a stone bashed on 'is 'ead."

"Oh!" said Mountford. "True, true. Wait—there's money in my purse."

A NEW voice sounded, a laughing, ringing voice.

"Never mind, Mountford, I'll pay 'em! Here's for you, lads—a golden guinea apiece!"

Congreve stepped around from the other side of the coach, whose bulking mass had well concealed him. He tossed money; the gold clinked dully on the cobbles; and the two men, with eager cries, dropped to search the coins.

Mountford whirled about as though stung.

"Why, damme!" he exclaimed hoarsely. *"You!"*

"Precisely," said Congreve. "I gather that you managed to rid yourself of the worthy Captain Hill after all!"

"So it was you set the rogue on me!" A burst of hearty oaths escaped Mountford. He clutched at his sword, and steel rasped scabbard. "Away, you damned insolent scribbler, or I'll have your life!"

"And no prompter needed now, eh? Well said, well said!" Congreve's mocking tones stung the actor. "But you've forgot something, Mountford."

"Aye? Be off ere I forget myself, you jay!"

"You've done that already, rascal." The mockery gone now, Congreve drove in bitter words. "Forgot yourself, aye; and your wife, the most honest woman in London! And you'd take the lass to Dover, would you? And then to Paris, safe out of the kingdom. You'd have herself and her guineas."

"You lads!" Mountford motioned the two men with his sword, "At him, lay him out!"

"Not they!" Congreve laughed jeeringly. "Here's gold for you, lads! Let the rogue fight his own quarrel."

Gold clinked again, and the two men dived after it. Mountford, in towering passionate fury, flung himself at Congreve. The latter stepped back, and steel glittered.

"Take it then, you fool!" rasped out Mountford, and let drive.

Steel clashed. A woman's cry echoed from within the coach; the two men found their gold-pieces and stepped away. From one of them broke a sharp cry, as the clashing blades rang loudly.

"The watch be coming back! I see their lights—run for it!" Their heels clattered....

Congreve laughed. "Aye, Mountford, run for it, you rogue! After them, and be safe!"

An oath, a frenzied attack, a flurry of steel. Congreve disengaged suddenly. Swift and high and deadly went his thrust, driven home to its mark. Mountford staggered forward with a mortal cry and a clatter of fallen blade.

CONGREVE SWUNG around, darting to the coach step and the open door. He paused.

"Coach! You shall have your pay, and doubled. Instead of Dover, drive to Richmond—to the Star and Garter. Off, before the watch halts you!"

A joyous eager cry from the coach was cut short by the slam of the door. The long whip lashed and cracked; the horses heaved; their hoofs struck sparks from the stones; the coach rumbled into movement and went clattering away.

Under the cold stars, death in his frozen face, lay the man who had forgotten himself. The actor Mountford, favorite of the Theatre Royal—murdered by some base rival, as was thought by many, or slain in a duel as others believed.... His death remained a mystery unsolved, a riddle unanswered for future years to ponder.

But all that Mr. Dryden predicted came true; Will Congreve's boyish folly was made right forever.

FIRST IN AMERICA

THE WILLIAMSBURG street was dust-thick, and the summer sun was hot; but here in the King's Head was coolness and heady ale and headier company. The House of Assembly was in session, and certain members were more often at the tavern than at the capitol, venting their wordy war with Governor Spottiswood over a mug and a pipe.

Gwynne, walking his shaggy nag through the dust, and aiming for the tavern, drew rein before a new construction bustling with workmen and nearly finished. The city was small, but it was elegant; and this building drew Gwynne's curious stare. He called to one of the workmen, asking its purpose.

"The Governor's new playhouse," came the response. "Going to be opened on Thursday. How's everything in the back woods?"

Gwynne laughed. "Quiet—as far as the mountains, anyhow!"

He rode on, conscious that his appearance was utterly at variance with the elegance of this capital city, but quite careless of the fact. Here in Williamsburg centered wealth and fashion and the best blood of England transplanted to Virginia; not London nor Bath had finer coaches, more gallant beaux and belles, more lordly and aristocratic a social life. And Gwynne was too obviously one of the backwoods wanderers who came down to tidewater from time to time, especially since Governor Spottiswood had come into power. For the braw governor welcomed these vagrants from the back-country, which he himself had explored and opened.

Gwynne was long and lean, clad in weathered buckskin and moccasins, a fur cap perched on his uncut hair. His clean-shaven features were also long and lean, very brown, lined by wind and weather; he was barely thirty yet looked much older. Thin lips, thin nostrils, thin strong chin and gray eyes that could laugh or squint at the sun, and a heavy skin-wrapped pack at his saddle: such was the man who rode into the tavern courtyard and dismounted. He handed his reins to the black slave who ran out.

"Put up the horse," he said. "I may be here two or three days. Bring the pack to my room, as soon as I secure one."

Two men were sprawling on a bench, with long pipes. One clapped the other on the knee and pointed.

"Look at the bumpkin!" he cried eagerly, quite regardless that Gwynne must hear the words. "Egad, Martin, there's our *Americus* to the very life! There's our question answered, our problem solved! Have at him, and hire his costume for yourself!"

Martin, a monstrous thin, shabby fellow, looked up with drink-dulled gaze.

"Aye, belike," he said thickly. "Time enough. He's a harmless rogue from the provinces, and I'll think about it."

Gwynne turned away from them with a catch of his breath. His face tightened and tensed; incredulity flashed in his gaze, to be replaced by a glint of wild, harsh anger. He mastered it and approached the innkeeper, who stood in the doorway regarding him sourly.

"Good day, host," he said in a low voice. "I'll have a private room, if you please."

"You will not, fellow," replied the rubicund host. "With the House in session, and this troupe of players on our hands, we've no room for backwoods vagabonds."

Gwynne smiled. "Come, come! It's a mistake to let the apparel so proclaim the man, my friend. Bestow me in a good room, then send word to the Governor that his friend David Gwynne is here and awaits his commands. And have a barber come to my room, to trim these wild locks. I have some garments in my pack, to be pressed at once. And I want some ale and a bite of food, while the barber's at work."

The rubicund jaw dropped.

"Pardon, your worship!" exclaimed the host, losing his scornful air. "I'll see to it at once. Enter, I pray your worship. The word shall go to His Excellency."

Gwynne walked into the tavern, a thin smile on his thin lips. A harmless rogue, was he? Good God, what a meeting after twelve years! It was now 1718; and it had been 1706 when he had last seen Moonlight Martin in London. Moonlight Martin, and Spark i' the Wind.... Was she here too? No—he remembered with a familiar pang: She was dead.

"A harmless rogue, am I?" he muttered. "To think that this rascal should be here! After these years! And he didn't know me again, praise be."

The landlord bellowed orders at drawers and tap-boys, and himself conducted Gwynne to a room on the upper floor, out of which a slave was hastily moving some personal effects.

"Those rascally players can double up," said the host. "His Excellency has guaranteed their credit or they'd not be here. Is the chamber to your fancy, sir?"

"Quite," replied Gwynne. "How many players are in this troupe?"

"Four, your worship. The two gentry outside on the bench, Mistress Spark, and the sweet Mistress Sylvia. How she ever came in such company, heaven knows!"

Gwynne's heart stopped. "Who, did you say? Mistress Sylvia?"

"A real lady, your worship," babbled the landlord. "I hear 'twas because of her His Excellency hath given them employ; the others are dirt on her ruffles."

Gwynne drew a deep breath. Sylvia! No, not the same; the name was a common one, and the Sylvia he had known was no longer living.

AN HOUR passed; he was a different man now, dressed in sober plum-colored garb, white linen at throat and cuffs, hair trimmed and knotted behind. A slave brought word that His Excellency ordered Mr. Gwynne to await him, for he was coming to the tavern.

Gwynne left his room. He sought the narrow stairs; then, at the turn of the landing, he stood aside to let a lady pass. At least, he thought she was a lady until she came up to the landing and saw him. Gasping, she caught at the balustrade, her eyes wide. Despite her silks and laces and wide hat, her face betrayed her quality. Still young, it was a face of ravaged beauty, but brazen and challenging; and her voice was shrill.

"Dick!" The words burst from her. "Dick Lovell!"

Gwynne bowed slightly. "Your pardon, madam. My name is David Gwynne."

"No, no!" She clutched suddenly at his arm. "You know me, Dick, you must know me! You remember Spark, your little Spark i' the Wind? You mind me well! Ye haven't forgot Drury Lane, Dick!"

"A most regrettable mistake, madam." And Gwynne drew himself away. "Some chance resemblance has tricked you, no doubt."

Leaving her silenced and staring after him, he descended the stairs and turned into the taproom. Here a number of gentlemen were sitting over their wine, pipes alight, voices well roused. They were discussing the Governor with some heat, cursing him for a stubborn domineering tyrant. The landlord called abruptly:

"Careful, gentlemen, careful! His Excellency is coming now, here's his coach!"

Gwynne stepped out into the courtyard, warm with the afternoon sunlight.

The gayly painted, heavily rumbling coach was swinging in from the street. Hostlers and slaves were running; the two men on the bench were straightening up in beery respect. The coach halted, and Spottiswood stepped out—a man of forty, a splendid figure in his gold-laced coat and plumed hat, brawny features stamped with resolution and authority.

An eager laugh on his lips, he clapped Gwynne about the shoulders.

"Welcome, welcome! You rogue, why did ye not come at once to the house and stop With me? I'll take you with me now."

"Thanks, no," said Gwynne, smiling. "I've outgrown the ways of civilized folk, Your Excellency; I'm more at home in a tavern, upon my word!"

"Well, you look damned civilized for a man who's kept company with redskins the past year!" declared Spottiswood. "To your room! I'm wild to talk with you."

He led the way in to the tavern and the taproom, with a nod to the two players who saluted him humbly. From one of these, from Martin, broke a gasp and a wild word. He came rushing after, catching hold of Gwynne, staring at him with wide-eyed recognition.

"Dick! Dick Lovell, for the love of heaven!"

"Be off," said Gwynne curtly. Shaking himself loose, he

David Gwynne

followed the Governor into the taproom, where the drinkers
had come to their feet respectfully. Martin, however, was after
him, seizing him.

"Wait, wait!" cried the man. "You mind me, Dick? It's Martin!
Moonlight Martin, you used to call me…. 'Catch me if you can
and a heel in the moon!'"

"Here, here, what's all this hullabaloo?" demanded Spottiswood.

Gwynne freed himself, and gave the staring Martin a severe
look.

"Faith, that's what I'd like to know, Your Excellency! Who's
this curving shinbone of a fellow? Why, he's a veritable splinter
from a haunted house! He hath the air of a weasel in pain. Look
at those three teeth that jut above a lip of liver, like gravestones
awaiting the companioning death!"

His drawling words were greeted by an outburst of mirth.

*Governor
Spottiswood*

Martin fell back a step, his lean and scrawny features convulsed by helpless fury. Gwynne continued mercilessly:

"And those hands—what hands! Why, stap me if they're not thick, moist hairy pads like sausages a bailiff has long sat upon! I'll warrant they gather airy loot when they scratch among his thatch! Why such long hair, rogue, except to hide cropped ears? And a pillory look to your hangdog visage as well!"

Martin attempted voluble protest, but Spottiswood, who was shaking with laughter, silenced him with one peremptory word and gesture, then turned to the company.

"Rascal, leave your betters alone. Gentlemen! This is my friend and agent Mr. Gwynne, who has been in command of my trading enterprises in the West. I commend him to your kind attention while he's in the city. Now, Gwynne, to your room! Landlord, send us up some of your best Canary, with tobacco and pipes, and permit no one to disturb us."

They turned to the stairs.

SETTLED AT the table in the room above, with tobacco burning and flagons filled, Gwynne made reference to the scene in the taproom.

"Why, the graceless rogue really seemed to think he knew me! Spottiswood, what's all this about a new playhouse and a company of players?"

The Governor stretched out comfortably. "Well, I planned the building to house the trading company, but our fine gentry are slow to back the enterprise; so, for the nonce, I've turned the building into a playhouse. On Thursday, His Majesty's birthday, I'm giving an entertainment at the palace, as they term my house; and we'll go to the play afterward."

Gwynne laughed. "Admirable! But where on earth did the players come from?"

"England. I sent for them. Had to turn off some of them; a varied crew, egad! They were better at pantomime than aught else. With the four remaining, we shall do rather well. One of the company, a Mistress Sylvia, is a most extraordinary person; none of your immoral creatures who infest the theater in England, but a lady, a real lady. She's my guest at the palace now, and brightens the whole place. You must meet her. She's gone on a visit today to the Colepeper plantation—she knew one of that family in England."

"I'm not interested in your players," said Gwynne. "The play's the thing, Spottiswood! Do you realize that this will be the first play ever given in these colonies—that your playhouse marks a new high level in culture and civilization, this side the water? A splendid innovation! And you should make money by it, if you keep it up."

"That's not the point," Spottiswood rejoined. "I want to inculcate ideas—I have money enough already. This playhouse should be invaluable, for that purpose. If we can train a few local persons, we'll be able to put on all the London pieces."

"And what piece are you giving on Thursday? What's its name?"

"A new piece, writ for us after my own wishes. 'Americus: a Phantasy,' is the name. It was provided by Sir Charles Hart, a sprightly gay blade who knows the theater. He's one of my guests, also; came down last month from New York."

GWYNNE CHANGED countenance. His smile waned and died; that name struck into his heart like an evil omen.

"Hart, you say?" he repeated slowly. "Sir Charles Hart?"

"Aye, and with a pretty turn to the lines he writes. But never mind all this; let's to more important business." Spottiswood leaned forward and became animated. "Damme, to think I haven't seen you in a full year and more! Gwynne, things have happened. D'ye recall my talk of iron ore? Well, we've actually located it, on the Rapidan River. Aye, and I'm settling a colony

*"You were ever
an honest lass,
God love you!...
Break it to her
gently—gently!"*

of Germans there to work it. Now I'm laboring hard to get the trading company established, and to force the Assembly and the home government to build forts out to the mountains and the headwaters of the Ohio. It's a hard job."

Hard, indeed; the Governor's schemes were both ambitious and expensive. The burgesses were niggardly, England had no money to waste on these colonies, and the energetic Spottis-wood was rapidly making himself enemies galore.

"But surely," said Gwynne, "I've accomplished enough to make them all see that the fur trade is tremendously rich, if we can grasp it."

"You've done wonders," came the reply. "From a money stand-point, too. Why, man, your share of the enterprise is making you wealthy!"

"I've left the accounts to you."

"They're well kept. But damme if I can make the Assembly see the point! Those fellows wax rich on tobacco. I've forced 'em to see the value in iron mines, but they won't look twice at the fur trade." Spottiswood sighed. "So much the better for ourselves, you might say, but I'm thinking of the whole province, of this whole vast country!"

"I know," assented Gwynne, frowning over his long clay pipe. "But vision's a hard thing to pass on to other men."

"I want your help," said the other bluntly. "This entertainment and play is no idle pastime. Sir Charles did a good job of writing on 'Americus'; it's aimed to present facts to our friends the burgesses. And I want you there. They tell me you came into town today in your buckskins. Eh?"

"Of necessity, yes."

"Then you're the very man to take the part of *Americus*. You can learn the lines 'twixt now and Thursday—"

"I'll not be here on Thursday."

"Eh?" Spottiswood's keen gaze struck through the smoke, and Gwynne nodded.

"I'm returning in the morning. There are reasons. I can leave with you the list of goods we'll need, and you can have a wagon follow me."

"Are you mad? To make this long trip and then return in a few hours?"

"No," said Gwynne. "Not mad at all. Very sane."

Spottiswood eyed him for a space.

"Gwynne, I've known you ten years or more. We're friends. You've never spoken of the past; I've never asked a question. You're a man of education, a gentleman. Why you left England is none of my business. But I'll not let this nonsense come between us. What's happened, to make you leave here in the morning?"

Gwynne's gray eyes darkened. "Your troupe of players, and Sir Charles Hart. If I stay here, there'll be trouble, perhaps bloodshed. Oh, there's no disgrace in my past! But I've carved out a new life, and I'm sticking to it."

"Hm!" said the other. "I might as well argue with a Tuscarora chief, of course, as with you. So that rascally splinter of a man downstairs really had known you?"

Gwynne nodded again. "Twelve years ago I amused myself by taking stage parts under the name of Dick Lovell. I played at Drury Lane in the first performance of 'The Recruiting Officer,' the night Nance Oldfield brought it out. The day after, I was drugged and put aboard a ship for the plantations; I woke up at sea to find my life wrecked, and the person I most loved, dead. That was Charles Hart's doing; he had not inherited a title then. It is just as well that we don't meet now—just as well for his safety, I mean."

"So!" The Governor sipped his Canary. "Say the word, and I'll lay Hart by the heels, even if he is my guest! Wilt lay a charge against him?"

"No. Life's too short to go to law where a sword would serve better."

Spottiswood smiled. "So you'd run away. Well, I'll respect your confidence. The person who died—a woman, I presume?"

"A girl," said Gwynne. "The shipmaster and others aboard had word of it; she died that same night, when a coach overturned. It was after the performance," he went on more freely; after all, the pain had been deadened by long years. "She was a young girl from Norfolk, her people dead; the stage attracted her. She was of good birth and was not the kind to follow the loose life of the average player. She was known to the company as Sylvia Paston. Well—I've spoken to no one else of it. Pardon my inflicting it upon you."

"Why, Gwynne, it's an honor! Sink me if it isn't!"

Spottiswood checked himself, eyeing the lined, bitter features of Gwynne sharply. He remained silent, thoughtful, frowning. At last he spoke, slowly.

"You've put me in a difficult position—a devilish difficult position!"

"I have? How?" demanded Gwynne.

Spottiswood waved a hand.

"Never mind; it is nothing, after all. It's getting late, I must leave. Will you do one thing for me?"

"Of course, if possible," said Gwynne. "What is it?"

"Wait here in this room until I send back a messenger with a note from my house." He rose and put out his hand. "And count me a friend who desires to serve you in all ways possible."

WITH THIS strange request, he stamped out of the chamber, leaving Gwynne staring after him in open astonishment.

Wait here in this room! Well, easily done. Laughing, Gwynne filled his pipe afresh and poured more of the good Canary. It had eased his mind and assuaged the old hurt to impart this confidence to the one man he could trust. He should have told Spottiswood about it long ago, but he had ever shrunk from the subject, keeping it hidden away, himself trying to forget.

This sudden, unexpected meeting in a far corner of the world had shaken the truth out of him, and he felt better for it.

Moonlight Martin! A rascally thief and cutpurse, a hanger-on of the theater, a sly and crafty fellow full of nimble tricks and cheap strategy; so Martin was an actor now! As for his doxy Spark, she had been a pretty lass in past years. No paragon of virtue, this Spark i' the Wind—a fitting companion for Moonlight Martin—yet there was something more in her than mere rascality. She had stuck to Martin, and strangely enough possessed a tender womanly spirit... Gwynne was tempted to term it a sense of decency.

But Sir Charles Hart—ah, there was a very wolf of a man, a rakehelly gallant, a wild spendthrift and black-hearted rascal beneath a veneer of gentility! It was Hart who had caused the drugging and the kidnaping, hating the actor Dick Lovell viciously. As he thought back upon those days, Gwynne smiled a little.

"Why, after all, it was the making of me!" he reflected. "Here in America I've found my place, a new free life, wealth and fortune if I want it! I've a grant of broad acres in the Shenandoah, and if a road is ever built to those parts I can clear the trees and have a regal estate! But what matters?"

Nothing mattered. Ambition had died in him when a girl died....

Sunset was roseate upon the city when Gwynne heard a clatter of feet at the stairs, and a knock came at his door, with voices in the corridor. He opened the door to see one of the Governor's blacks extending a folded and sealed paper. Gwynne handed him a coin and took the missive. Then before he could close the door, came a flutter of skirts and Spark i' the Wind was upon him with eager pleading voice.

"Dick, Dick Lovell! You must give me a word; man, you must hear me!"

"What!" said Gwynne coldly. "Still barking up that tree, lass?"

"I know well enough who you are; you don't fool me. Dick, Dick, give me but a brace o' minutes! It's life and death—not to me, but to you, Dick!"

Gwynne was startled by the wild passionate desperation of her manner. With a light shrug he turned, going to the window.

"Come in, then, and shut the door. As soon as I've read this note, I'll hear you."

She slid in, closed the door and stood against it, panting, her gaze upon him.

He broke the seal and opened the paper. It bore a line of writing in the bold hand of Spottiswood:

> *The name of Mistress Sylvia is Paston. Forgive my telling you in this manner; it seemed best.*

For a moment he actually could not realize what the words meant, until they hammered at him with increasing insistence. Sylvia Paston! Bewilderment engulfed him. Some woman bearing the name of the girl he had known? No, no! He recalled the strange manner of the Governor: this man, faced with telling a friend that all the old story was based upon some error—why, she was alive, alive!

GWYNNE LIFTED his head and found Spark crying out at him. He became aware of her words, that chimed so queenly with this note in his hand, and yet were so dissonant. At first he really thought her insane.

"Why have ye never writ to her?" Spark was saying. "Oh, sir, we thought ye dead in the New World! Word came to us that you had died on the voyage. And ye run off without as much as a by-your-leave, and she crying her eyes out!"

"Why, lass, you're out of your head!" broke forth Gwynne, shaking the paper at her. "Dead? *She* was the one dead. Here's word she's alive, alive—it can mean no less! It was your spindly Martin who drugged me and set me aboard ship; and when I found she had been killed that same night, what mattered?"

She fell back a pace, her eyes like saucers.

"Martin! Drugged!" A storm of blasphemy escaped her; she flew into a frenzy of passionate words, that made little sense, then calmed. "Why, Dick, where's the roguery here? We all thought ye dead; we had sure word of it. She might ha' married Sir Charles and would not. She's kept us with her, because we were your friends. She's trailed us about the provinces these many years, and at last would come to the New World because you, though dead, had started for here."

Gwynne shoved her into a chair, poured wine for her, gulped some himself.

"Let's have the truth of this," he demanded, and between them the truth came.

He was aghast, seeing it all. There had been no accident; Sylvia had not been hurt. They received word that he had suddenly fled with the bailiffs after him for debt, and later came positive news of his death aboard ere the ship reached the Virginia Capes. Who had told it? Who—but Sir Charles Hart?

So it came clear, as twilight settled upon the room. Trickery, lies and gold in the itching palm. It had done no one any good; Sylvia distrusted Sir Charles from the first and would not look twice at him. His hatred of Dick Lovell was appeased, perhaps, and the sly crafty Martin had money in his pouch; that was all. So much done, for so little gained!

"For this, I'll help ye scotch him, Dick!" exclaimed Spark, in a fury. She had been no party to the fraud, as Gwynne clearly perceived. "Look! Martin's naught but a thief, a stealer at the bill. I can tell how he stole a chain from the very windpipe of a keeper of the Tower—aye, and many a pouch besides! We'll have him clapped in jail this very night."

"Hold hard, Spark." Gwynne got a grip on himself. "No word to him of this, no word to any."

"But you'll tell her? You'll see her?" insisted Spark.

HE THOUGHT for a moment. See her? His every pulse was for leaving at a run, gaining the Governor's house, and rushing to her—but, no! Spottiswood had been a wise man. This was nothing to gulp out with hasty speech and hot words.

"Where's Martin now?" he demanded.

"Drinking, with Tom Blood, the other of the troupe," said she. "He swears that you are Dick Lovell or his twin!"

"And he'll be off to tell Sir Charles about it, eh?" Gwynne laughed suddenly. "Why, Spark, I bear 'em no ill will—let it pass! Yes, I must see her."

"It's to be rehearsal in half an hour now," said she. "Before supper. To try the footlights in the new playhouse."

Gwynne caught her arm. "Then keep a close tongue. I'll be there, I'll see her!... Wait, now. Let me think."

He found himself shaken, trembling, all in a fever. Patience, at such a moment, came hard; yet he managed to orient his mind, to conquer his agitation.

He sprang to the table, where writing materials lay. Seizing a quill, he opened the Governor's letter and below the message scrawled a response. He sanded it, folded over the paper again, and put it with a coin into Spark's hand.

"You were ever an honest lass, God love you! Send this to the Governor, now, at once, on the instant; the money will pay a bearer. I'll be at the playhouse. You get a word with Sylvia. Tell her that Dick Lovell is dead, but that David Gwynne is alive; she knows my real name. Break it to her gently, lass—gently! And tell Martin that the Governor hath found another player for the rôle of Americus. Off with you! Half an hour, eh? Get the word to her ear, and I'll bless the name of Spark i' the Wind."

She was gone, staring but compliant.

N O N E E D of candles; in the last of the twilight, Gwynne stripped and got into his old grease-suppled buckskins and moccasins. He slung the long hunting-knife at his belt and clapped the fur cap upon his head. Now for a mask—a strip of the bed-curtains would serve. Rehearsal! He laughed again when at length he opened the door and went quietly down the stairs.

Below, he paused. Voices were riotous in the taproom. Listening, he found that a group of the burgesses were arranging to hold a celebration of their own on the Thursday in the House of Assembly, in order to slight the Governor.

"Why, damme, to drink the King's health in the company of scurvy playactors would be an outrage!" roared somebody. "We'll stay away from the Governor's palace and from the play as well."

Gwynne stepped out into the gathering darkness. A lot the King's health mattered to a man from the Shenandoah country, a man who had found life and hope and ambition after twelve lost years!

The interior of the new playhouse, with the benches not yet emplaced and everything reeking of fresh paint, was of surprising size. So it had to be—for Williamsburg was small but Virginia was large. On the royal birthday, planters would be in from miles around for the assembly at the palace and the general celebration; there would be cock-fighting and throbbing viols; Gloucester Highway would be rolling with coaches, and the first theatrical performance in America would be attended by fine gentlemen with swords at their sides and ladies in silk and satin on their arms.

BUT TONIGHT, the simple scenery was turned to the wall away from paint-splatters. The footlights were all aglow, illumining the stage. Half a dozen slaves held lanterns to light the interior and the entry, when the Governor's coach came trundling up.

Spottiswood alighted, with Sir Charles Hart and Mistress Sylvia bearing him company. They were joined before the door by Mistress Spark and Moonlight Martin and the shabby actor Blood, who followed inside.

There, Martin conducted Sir Charles aside and spoke with him, low-voiced. Spark seized the arm of Sylvia, led her through to the stage; they stood in the wings together, talking, while Spottiswood surveyed the half-finished decorations. He was engaged with the contractor, who had come this evening to display the work, but in the midst of their talk he recollected the business in hand, and swung around.

"Sir Charles! Go ahead with your rehearsal! Are the footlights as they should be, Mistress Sylvia—eh? Where is she? Ah! Splendid, my dear, splendid! They light you perfectly!"

Sylvia appeared, coming down to the footlights. That she was in great agitation was obvious, but she conquered it and swept the Governor a smiling curtsey.

"I understand, Excellency, that you—that you have secured a new player for the part of *Americus*," she called to him. "When does he appear?"

"Eh?" Spottiswood looked around. "Oh, nothing is certain yet. Don't wait for him."

"But what of me?" Martin pushed his lean length forward. "That's my part, Your Excellency; if you've secured a new player, what of me?"

"To the devil with you, rascal," snapped Spottiswood. "Go through your lines and ask no questions. Ready, Sir Charles?"

"Damme if I understand all this, but we're ready," said Hart, advancing to the footlights, and ordering the others to the wings.

He was a slender, handsome man, darkly resolute and attired

in the greatest elegance. Tapping his snuffbox, he announced the prologue, and Sylvia came down center with an elaborate curtsey to the imaginary audience.

"Egad!" exclaimed Spottiswood under his breath. "Her like has never been seen in the province! 'Twill cause a sensation!"

His admiration was deserved; if Sylvia were past her first youth, she had entered upon glorious summer of womanhood. Her beauty held a charm, a radiance, a glowing appeal that Spottiswood had never before glimpsed. Even Sir Charles watched her with a fascinated air.

"Well done, well done, Sylvia!" he applauded as she finished. "Why, you'd put Oldfield and Bracegirdle themselves to shame! Well, come along, *Americus!* Where are you? Martin, you rogue—it's your entrance!"

Martin was hot making an entrance, however. The paper bearing his lines had been torn out of his hands by a man in stained buckskins, Who suddenly appeared and thrust him aside—a figure striding forward toward the lights, Whose face was hidden by a black vizard. From Spottiswood burst a rousing exclamation, cut short by the voice of this *Americus*, voicing his lines with superb intonation.

But, at the first ringing tones of that voice, Sir Charles Hart stood transfixed and staring. He put up his snuffbox; a startled oath escaped him. "You!" he exclaimed. "In the devil's name—"

GWYNNE TORE off the mask he had fashioned.

"Why, Sir Charles, here's a better dramatic note than the one you've hit!" he cried. "A man trepanned and sent into far places, returned from the dead! What's more, staring into the eyes of the rascal who had him kidnaped, who proclaimed him dead-"

With one leap, Sir Charles was over the footlights and on the stage. His sword whipped out, and he paused an instant.

"You shabby rascal, you dare use such words to me?" he cried hotly.

"Nay, nay, abate your venom," said Gwynne, and laughed heartily. "I've unmasked you as liar and rogue, and I seek no more from you. You shall go your ways With Moonlight Martin, and if he doesn't lead you to the stocks and the pillory and the gallows, then—"

FURY HAD done its work, however; Hart, losing his head completely, flung himself at Gwynne, and his sword drove in. Screams of women, an unheeded shout from Spottiswood, were lost; Gwynne took the rapier through his upper arm, and grappled with Hart. At the same instant, however, the incredibly thin shape of Martin came flying from the wings, a knife in his hand.

The three men became a whirling, confused mass, struggling and writhing—Gwynne desperately trying to evade the knife that plunged at him, while he held Sir Charles in a close grip. The three of them rocked back and forth, twisting and Cursing; then they toppled and went in a headlong mass, and the stage shook to the weight of their plunging fall.

The angry voice of Spottiswood, the cries of the two Women who were rushing forward, were abruptly checked. Gwynne, With the agility of an Indian, rolled clear of the tangle and leaped to his feet, the rapier still transfixing his arm. Sir Charles remained sprawling and motionless. And Moonlight Martin came to one knee, an expression of unutterable horror stamped in his wild features—his hand still gripping the knife. The blade was fast—aimed for Gwynne, it had thrust to the heart of Sir Charles!

In that stricken silence, the boots of Martin Scraped the boards as he rose to his feet. A terrible wordless cry burst from him; with a leap, he was over the footlights and away in mad panicked flight. Spottiswood roared at the slaves to stop him. Nothing could stop him; in very sooth, he made good his boast of a heel in the moon. He was out and gone, like a fleeing shadow.

Gwynne carefully drew the sliver of steel from his arm and let it fall. He found himself face to face with Sylvia. They stood, wordless, looking into each other's eyes, until Governor Spottiswood came stamping up to them.

"Egad!" said he, a grim smile In his eyes. "Egad! Have ye both lost voice? 'Tis high time to let fall the curtain on the tragedy that's turned to a happy ending!"

But neither Gwynne nor Sylvia heard what else he said, for the curtain was indeed fallen upon all the years between.

NOT UPON THE SLEEVE

COLD WAS the night; and the beleaguered town lay hungering. Powder lacked not, but fuel was scant, and fool priced high. Howard Smith shook the snow from his coat and shivered, and tightened the muffler about his throat.

"You're a fool," said his companion roughly. "Still time to turn back; we'll get another man for the job. I never thought you'd be the one to show up."

"Turning back is bad luck," said Howard Smith in his quiet insistent way.

The other man caught his arm, with a stifled groan.

"Will ye not listen, Howard? If no one else knows you, she will: and I tell you, she's lost her head over this Captain Blount, with his noble family and all! You'll get no mercy. It's the noose or a firing-squad, of a certainty."

"If caught," amended Smith. "Yes, no struggle is so savage, so bitter, so terrible, as a civil war. And that's what this is, at bottom. But why worry, old friend? I'm safe."

"Oh, you're a fool, I say!" exclaimed the other man.... "We part here, then. Once past that door, you're on your own. Blount's the man you deal with—Burgoyne's aid and secretary. To think he's the man, of all men, with whom she's in love! A young fop, I understand."

Howard Smith looked at the lantern-lighted door beyond them, the wide, heavy door of a tavern whose frosted windows glowed with ruddy light. To the door was affixed a large printed notice.

"You know, it's nut a little thing I have to do," he said reflectively. "No other can serve as I can serve, or play the part I can play. I must do it, because that Virginia gentleman out yonder on the heights depends upon me. I didn't know Peggy was in Boston, of course, but it's too late now to back out even if I so desired. I've been passed through the lines; there'll be reports

about me and so forth. Well, go your ways! You know where to reach me, each Monday and Friday; I know where to reach you at need. Good luck."

"And the same to you." The other man pressed his hand warmly and went crunching away down the crisp-footed street.

Howard Smith turned to the door. As he inspected the placard posted there, a slight smile twisted his thin, wide lips. The lantern outlined his face: a handsome, thinly carven profile, the face of a scholar with deep, strong eyes.

The printed notice, in huge type, announced that the comedy of "The Busybody," followed by the farce "The Blockade of Boston" for the first time on any stage, would be presented at Faneuil Hall on January 8, 1776; that is to say, four days hence.

Smith opened the door and entered; he walked with a decided limp, and this limp naturally made him a marked man.

The tavern rang with voices and scraps of song. It was crowded with officers, whose scarlet coats, pipe-clayed belts and gilt epaulets made brave show. The smell of hot grog and mulled wine was in the air, countering the blue hate of tobacco from long clay pipes. A silence fell as Smith entered, raid all eyes went to him as he opened his coat and removed the heavy

muffler, to reveal snowy linen, excellently cut ferments of the latest fashion, the gold fob and seals of a dandy. He smiled at the men about the nearest table.

"Your pardon, gentlemen," he said with calm assurance. "I am in search of Captain Horatio Blount, of General Burgoyne's staff. I understand he is here?"

His Majesty's commission meant rank, birth, pride of caste, influence; rarely did it entail snobbery or gaucherie. Several officers were on their feet at once, voices cried out for Blount, and Smith was led into the adjacent room, where a group sat at a table. Blount rose. He was a young man, dark, slender, with a forceful air oddly unnatural.

Howard Smith, quietly at ease, bowed slightly, and gave his name.

"My business with you, sir, is of a private nature," he went on. "If you will have the goodness to grant me five minutes? I am the bearer of a letter from Major André, who is now in New York."

"Oh, by all means!" exclaimed Blount "And how's André, the gay dog? Damme, sir, he should have been an artist, not a soldier…. But come along, come along. You're a stranger here? I knew of no ship arriving."

"I came through the American lines," said Smith.

The other halted. "Eh? You men they allowed you to come through?"

Smith smiled. "Certainly. Why not? I made no secret of being from New York."

"Egad!" exclaimed Blount, upon the silence. "Then the Yankee peasants are getting wondrous lax of a sudden!"

"On the contrary, sir. They did not consider it worth while making war upon a crippled man. My foot was crushed in a carnage accident in Pall Mall, last year."

These words in conjunction with Smith's limp, produced an instant, awkward apology; Blount, in confusion, led the way to a private room.

Smith's letter was produced and read. Blount warmed up immediately, cordially.

"Why, you're the very man for us!" he exclaimed, shaking hands. "Stage experience; you know the theater; you've written for it…. Gad, you must meet Burgoyne at once!"

"I had the honor of knowing him two years ago in London," said Smith. "In fact, I gave him some slight assistance with the first play he wrote, one for the marriage of his brother-in-law, Lord Stanley. Garrick afterward put it on at Drury Lane, you know."

"Better and better! Have you dined?"

"Not yet. I've secured lodgings with Madam Draper."

"An excellent woman, devoted to the cause," broke in Blount, and took his arm. "Come, join us at table; famine may be upon

Boston, but we still eat. I'm to join the General in an hour. You shall accompany me."

Back to the company, with a general introduction and a more particular one to the table Blount had left. Room was made, and Howard Smith found cordiality on all sides. "Wine with you, sir-an honor!" The gentlemen, both officers and volunteers with the force, were still awkwardly conscious of that crippled foot.

Smith lost no time in establishing himself; his background was simple. Born in New York, he had gone to England three years ago. A year at Oxford, and be had abandoned college for Fleet Street; with the officers around, he soon found many mutual friends. The carriage accident had left him unable to move for long months, until at last he took ship for New York. There, after meeting André and others, he had come on to Boston.

He did not say that he had spent nearly a week in the camp of General Washington, whose half-organized army was holding the city in siege.

THE NAME of André was an open-sesame, for the young major was the most popular man in the army. Was he promoting theatricals in New York? Zounds, sir! He had put the theater upon its feel here—most delivish talent imaginable! He and Burgoyne together had done it.... And what were these rebels like? One heard there were actually some gentlemen in their rabble.

"Oh, that reminds me!" exclaimed Blount. "We must get to the General. He'll be glad of whatever information you can give about the rebel forces."

Leaving was not so easy, for the amateur theatricals held a stout place in all hearts. Many of these officers had rôles in the forthcoming production on January the 8th, with female rôles being taken by belles of the town—that is to say, of loyalist families. Boston in general considered this very improper and shocking.

"These New Englanders have demmed amusing prejudices,"

drawled someone. Did ye hear about the ranting preacher last Sunday, who proclaimed that the theater was the anteroom to hell? A fact, 'pon my honor!"

"He may be the one whose meetinghouse Howe has just pulled down to make fuel for the troops," spoke up another, and a roar of laughter and profane comments ensued.

Howard Smith, looking on and listening, gathered that Puritan Boston had sundry laws against theatrical performances, and that these officers gleefully went out of their way to offend such New England prejudices. Indeed, their playbills were ironically sent to Washington and other leaders of the rebel troops.

And this, oddly enough, had caused Howard Smith to be in Boston; those playbills had opened the way, had inspired his presence. Only a crippled man could serve in this spot; only an habitué of Fleet Street and of London theaters could have fitted into his present rôle....

The two men got away at last, bundled to the ears. Arm in arm with Captain Blount, Smith had now no fears of sentries or night-watch.

He had, further, come to a shrewd estimate of his companion. Blount, who admittedly was on his first campaign and had his commission by dint of family influence, was no soldier at heart. His forceful manner was an assumption that concealed a gentle, sensitive nature; he had arrived from England in the fall, and had scarcely heard a shot fired. He was, as he confided boyishly, a bit of a poet at times.

So they arrived at the house where Burgoyne was billeted; the sentry passed them smartly; they were with the General.

A pleasant, kindly, handsome man, Burgoyne; young and talented, he was more at home with a pen than with a sword. When the two men entered the room where he sat writing before the fire, he dropped his quill and came to his feet, hand outstretched.

"Howard Smith, upon my soul! An apparition, bred of cold

As Howard Smith inspected the placard,
a slight smile twisted his thin lips.

New England stars? Nay, solid flesh! Welcome, man; what miracle has brought you? Did you drop from the skies?"

"No. Through the rebel lines. Any friend of General Burgoyne, said they, might pass and welcome."

"The deuce you say!" Burgoyne caught Smith's whimsical twinkle, and broke into a laugh. Then, noticing the limp, he stiffened. "Hello, what's this? Hurt? A chair, man, a chair Blount, get that decanter of Madeira. This demands a toast!"

Explanations, greetings, messages from André, news from London.... Then Blount broke in with eager word.

"He's just through the lines, General Burgoyne! He can tell all we want to know!"

"A miracle, sure as my name's John Burgoyne!" The General lifted his glass. "Your health, Smith! Now for the word. What sort of army have these rebels?"

SMITH LIED judiciously.

"Poorly trained troops, if at all, but plenty of them. They seem well armed, to amend their lack of training. Their numbers astonished me. A good ten thousand men, I'd say."

"A rabble," said Burgoyne; "but they can fight."

"They've been completely reorganised, I understand," went on Smith.

"We observed some sort of celebration on the second," said Burgoyne; "no doubt in honor of His Majesty's most gracious proclamation."

"On the contrary," Smith rejoined, "I believe it was in celebration of the reorganization of their rabble army, and because of a Union Flag received from their Congress, as they call it."

"Oh, that reminds me!" broke in the General. "I must ask you about that flag; we're devilish anxious to nuke use of it in the theatricals. Blount, write down what Smith has to say, like a good chap, and get the word to General Howe. Then we can settle down and be at our ease."

Blount obeyed, and Smith spoke freely if not truthfully. He liked Blount; the young officer had solid worth and be was briskly competent. When the task was done, Blount himself took the report to headquarters.

Left alone, Burgoyne relaxed.

"Gad, Smith! The age of miracles is not passed, eh? I've had Blount scraping the town for someone to help us, and here you turn up like an angel!"

"In disguise," said Howard Smith. "How can I be of any help to you?"

"Our theater here. We've put on performances since early in the fall."

"Oh, I see! Well, General, London knows you for an amateur actor of ability. And your play?"

Burgoyne leaned forward. "Look, man! this is something more. We're showing these scurvy provincials a bit of culture, I admit; out we're hard put to it on certain technical points, in acting, in stage managing, in stage business and so forth. Your appearance is providential. I hereby appoint you manager of His Majesty's amateur playhouse. Yes or no?"

"Why, yes, if I can be of any service!"

"Good. Then that's settled. Tomorrow night's rehearsal will see you in charge. The General leaned back. "Now, have ye seen the playbills?"

"Yes."

"Then lend me your ear. I've writ a farce, 'The Blockade of Boston,' which badly needs some help from you. It's not generally known that I writ it, of course; Howe says it might be ill taken if 'twere known that an officer of general rank produced a farce; but all the same, it's mine," Burgoyne winked. "And I must not forget about the flag. I want to use it, when my *Washington* makes his entrance. What sort of flag is it? Can we get one?"

"Easily made," said Smith, "They told me it's the first flag that's been adopted for their forces. It has thirteen stripes, red and white, to signify the colonies, and in the upper left square, the English Union."

"Damned rebel effrontery!" declared the other with swift choler.

"Oh, they don't call themselves rebels," Smith put in. "There seems to be no intention of resigning allegiance to His Majesty, although there's a good deal of talk about it."

"Well, the rascals will soon have another sort of talk to busy 'em. Pity that any gentleman like this man Washington should demean himself to lead such a riffraff."

Smith shrugged. "So they said about Cromwell, a hundred and thirty years ago."

"Eh?" Burgoyne's large and intelligent eyes drove at him. "Surely you've no sympathy with these peasants in arms? You've too much sound common sense."

"Naturally. Who spoke of sympathy? He's an able man, however. By the way, I met your friend Major André, as you know; he seems an extraordinarily brilliant chap."

Burgoyne waxed ardent on the new subject, and the danger was avoided.

FURNISHED WITH a pass that safeguarded against any peril, Howard Smith went to his lodgings, later, highly satisfied with all things—except his own business here. Except from one direction, he anticipated no risk whatever. It was the rôle he played that irked him, and plagued him sorely. The business of a spy is never a pleasant one to any man of honor; it must be undertaken, as Smith had undertaken it, of necessity.

Lying awake in the cold dark night, he thought of how his old friends in New York had pleaded with him to do this work; of how he had been sent on to Washington in the camp before Boston town; of how the bleak Virginian had waxed vehement over their hot punch and persuaded him to the errand, with a fiery energy that brooked no protests.

"Think you I'm a rebel in arms against my King and brother officers, to pleasure an idle hour? Think you I take pride in being called traitor, by those whom I've honored? Think you, Mr. Smith, that I enjoy dishonor? No, but by God, my own heart and intellect tell me otherwise! I do what I can; that's the motto for a man, these days. We have the damnedest, direst need of you. If Howe attacks, we're lost; give him false information to keep him from it. He's starving; so are we. Take this position in Boston, and keep us informed; play your part.... I'd do it myself if I could—my hand on it, my word on it! All religious cant aside, I believe, sir, that the Creator has given honest men one sure guide; my appeal is made solely to your sense of duty. Integrity lies in the heart, not upon the sleeve."

True, perhaps; none the less, it irked him until he fell asleep....

Burgoyne took him next day to headquarters. He met Howe, the hard-driving, capable general in command. "Give him information to keep him from it!" Smith give the information, quietly confident; somehow, one never mistrusts a crippled man. These Britishers knew nothing of his earlier history, of bit hotheaded outbursts in New York against injustice and tyranny, of how he had been pitched neck and crop back into the heart of England by his scandalized family. Now his family themselves had

*"These New Englanders have damned
amusing prejudices, 'pon my honor!"*

become patriots, swept out of New York, gone somewhere and
scattered—he knew not whither. And he was here.

He walked about town that afternoon. He visited Madam
Draper's establishment, where her fiery loyalist news-sheet was
printed; he dropped into a shop or two; he turned with dusk
into the bookstall kept by his friend from New York. Here he
leaned over the brown calf volumes to speak a low word to the
one man who knew him.

"Send the sore report that Howe will not attack for the present."

"Thank God!" breathed the other man. "How goes it?"

"All well."

"It's important that there be no postponement of the theatricals on the 8th. We must have word of any change; something's planned for that night."

"Very well. Unless you hear from me, all goes well. Better not get in touch with me as planned; it will be safer for me to reach you."

A nod. He walked out into the street, a book under his arm, and went his way. Six o'clock was close. Six, at Faneuil Hall, for a dress-rehearsal.

THE ASSEMBLAGE was prompt. Burgoyne was here, and Captain Blount, who had a small rôle in the farce; a dozen officers besides, and half as many ladies. The flickering footlights were lit, end two huge whale-oil lamps illumined the stage, but the body of the house was gloomily dark.

Howard Smith was presented to the company, most of whom remained seated in the pit for the present, as the new stage manager; there was no chance for individual introductions, as a hot discussion instantly arose, With the performance three days away, rehearsals had been most lamentable, and Burgoyne was of the opinion that it might be well to postpone the affair for a week.

"Suppose, gentlemen," suggested Smith, "that we settle the question after this rehearsal? Postponement would be a bad thing for the morale of all concerned. Boston is very largely in sympathy with the rebel cause, I find, and we should give these good folk no handle for jeers and scoffing. Perhaps, with your coöperation, we can smooth away all difficulties and carry on."

Amid eager applause, rehearsal was called.

At once, Smith saw where the trouble lay; the lines were ill-learned, and the amateur prompter was slack, while much of the "business" was poorly done. The act finished, he tore into the players, showed them where the faults lay and how to correct them, and assumed the prompter's job himself. They went through the act again, and Burgoyne was delighted.

"Zounds! Now we have something!" he exclaimed. "On with the game, lads! No need of postponement, if the remainder goes like this!"

It went better, indeed, and with two more rehearsals "The Busybody" would be in good shape for presentation. The players stood back, removing wigs and costumes, and the members of the "Blockade of Boston" company came on the stage. And Howard Smith found himself looking into the mocking eyes of Peggy Williams.

He bowed over her fingers, touched his lips lo them, heard her low words.

"So you've changed sentiments, my dear Howard, since we last met? I wonder! Change of pace has brought change of mind, perhaps?"

They were cruel words; they stung.

"Quite true, Mistress Peggy," he said. "Men change, but women do not, it seems."

This drove deep; she bit her lip, blood rose in her cheeks, and in her eyes Smith perceived that he had made a mortal enemy. He was too angry to care.

AT THEIR last meeting, before he went to England, they had quarreled bitterly. She had no sympathy with the colonies, she was of a Tory family; more, something had come up to utterly disillusion Howard Smith. He had gone overseas heartbroken. Looking back, he could see clearly, in the focus of distance, the coldly cruel workings of her heart. No, she had not changed.

Yet she was beautiful, with an icy but stately beauty that enthralled men. He witched her now, doing a scene in the farce opposite Captain Blount, and saw again how magnificent was her loveliness and charm. Then he wakened.

"Here, here!" he broke in. "Pardon me, Blount—you're losing

"Pardon me, Blount," he broke in, "—you're losing all the effect there."

all the effect there. Let me show you the way of it, if you don't mind."

"Gladly," said Blount, stepping aside.

Smith had a fair copy of the farce in his hand. He took up the scene with Peggy, who played an American shepherdess. (No doubt Burgoyne took for granted, that there were such creatures in New England.)

"One moment, Mistress Williams," he cut in. "As I conceive

the author's meaning, those lines should be delivered with a crass and stupid air, to offset their violence. You are the tender, unsophisticated, silly little *Amaryllis*, prating of liberty; let it waken laughter in the audience."

"Hear, hear!" came from Burgoyne. "Capital, my lad, capital!"

Peggy's eyes flashed: but she curtsied and went through the lines again, to applause. Smith yielded place to Blount, and the rehearsal went on. Afterward, Smith was speaking with Blount when Peggy came up to him, smiling.

"My aunt is here, Howard; I'm stopping with her. You must come and pay your respects. She'll be delighted to see you again, especially with your present political views."

"Eh?" Captain Blount spoke up, surprised. "Then you two know each other?"

"We're old and very dear friends," said Peggy sweetly, "from New York before the war. We shall expect you, Howard! And now may I ask your escort, Captain Blount? I promised Aunt Kate I'd be back early, and you know how she worries."

Burgoyne approached, with an imperative gesture to Blount. He bowed over Peggy's hand, then turned to his aide with a low word.

Howe has agreed to a reconnaissance in force day after tomorrow; the morning of the 7th, sunrise. See to it that orders are sent the commanders whom we've discussed. Colonel Halkett in charge. If the Yankees weaken, he's to push on through."

Peggy and her escort departed, Burgoyne took Smith's arm with warm commendations of his work, and war was again forgotten in the stage. The other ladies departed with their escorts; the lights were extinguished; Howard Smith was dragged off by enthusiastic officers to the nearest tavern, there to talk late into the night over a bowl of rum punch.

Later, Smith again lay awake, staring into the darkness. Now he had a message of vital import to send, and he revolted against the doing. Back into his mind came the speech of the grave, hot-tempered Virginian. "My hand on it, my word on it; integrity lies in the heart, not upon the sleeve!" He fell asleep at last, comforted.

WITH MORNING, he visited the book-shop and delivered his message.

"Get it through at all costs!" he concluded. "If the reconnaissance breaks through, a general attack will follow. Washington must learn that it's a test of his lines!"

"It will get through," was the earnest response.

Afternoon brought Captain Blount.

"Smith, I must have at you; information has reached me," said Blount, plunging at it doggedly. "It's told that—gad, man, I blush to repeat it!—that you're here as a spy for the rebels. There it is," he hurried on. "I can't believe it, I know it's not true, that it's some mistake. Give me your word it's not so, and the matter's closed."

"I think much of my honor, Blount," replied Howard Smith gravely.

"Damme, man! Anyone can see you're a gentleman!" burst out the other. "Therefore give me your word, accept my apologies, and the matter's ended."

"That I'm no spy?" Howard Smith smiled suddenly. "No. I'll not involve my honor in any such question."

Blount eyed him hard, puzzled and miserable and dogged.

"Look ye: I'm told that you're known in New York for a rebel. That you were prisoned there for sedition and treason; that you near killed a King's officer—"

"True, quite true," said Smith coolly. "Before the war, in hot youth; errors, for which I was punished. Then I went to England. I was no spy there, I can assure you! And now I'm back here, drinking the King's health with right good will and doing my bit to encourage the morale and stage presence of His Majesty's officers. And," he added with a humorous twinkle, "a spy needs two good feet to run with. I've but one."

Blount's face cleared. He joined in Smith's laughter, but uneasily.

"Forgive me," he said with contrition. "I knew there was a mistake, but—"

"There was no mistake," said Howard Smith gently.

"Deuce take me if I can understand you!" exclaimed the other. Smith took his arm.

"Don't try; I'm easily understood. Look elsewhere, my dear chap. I know the source of this ridiculous story. Shall we discuss it?"

Blount drew back. "Zounds, no!"

"Right. You and I alike would go far to defend the good name of a woman. Here no such thing is at issue. I loved Peggy Williams, Blount, with all a boy's devotion; why, when we quarreled I came near to throwing myself into the river! When I took ship for England, my sleeve was wet with tears, the first night out."

Thawed, discomfited and disarmed by these confessions, Blount remained irresolute. Howard Smith went on with a quiet poise that made his words doubly impressive. And he said the one thing that could win this man's confidence and belief.

"In view of what's happened, Blount, I must tell you that I greatly wronged Peggy Blount. One of those things that can never be recalled. Jumping at conclusions, I thought her heartless, cruel, utterly selfish and inhuman. Yes, I confess it. I even charged her with it. When, in reality-"

"She's the finest and noblest of women!" Blount exclaimed fervently, Smith assented.

"Yes. Therefore, quite naturally, in view of my asinine conduct, she bears a grudge. Who wouldn't, under such circumstances? Poor woman, to be the victim of a boy's petulance and fiery misapprehension! What she said about my conduct in New York is more than true; when we parted, I was a reckless, silly, drunken fellow—"

"Say no more, I beg of you!" Honest Blount caught his hand

and wrung it. "My dear old chap, I understand perfectly: I've been a bit of a fool myself, you know. I cherish your friendship for this confidence—'pon my word, I do! And I shall respect it, believe me. I would that you and Peggy might be friends again."

"No, no! I've injured her too deeply for that," said Smith, shaking his head. "Let matters rest. The fault is and was my own, quite entirely. If you attempt to patch matters up, 'twill only hurt your own standing with her. So let be."

"With all my heart," replied Blount, quickly. "We shall see you tonight?"

Smith smiled. "Why not?"

"And, I implore you, forgive me for even suspecting you of such base actions."

Smith winced. "Tut, tut!" he broke in. "A great man once said

to me words which bear upon all the events of life: Integrity lies in the heart, not upon the sleeve. Worth remembering."

Captain Blount departed, much moved.

Smith lit his pipe, thoughtfully, not too happily. So, he had weathered that storm! He felt sorry for Blount, once more: a fine young fellow, blind to the truth, honest as daylight. Somewhere in the future, poor Blount had a sad disillusionment awaiting him.

The evening's rehearsal passed off without incident. Mistress Peggy, bound later to dinner and an assembly, was a marvelous creature in shimmering gown, shimmering jewels, shimmering furs; as Burgoyne commented, she was enough to turn the head of any man alive, but Howard Smith viewed her with indifferent

"I'm leaving," Smith said abruptly. "I can't go on with this."

gate. That she had eyes only for Captain Blount, and he for her, was obvious enough. Smith wondered if she were really in love. It was quite possible, he thought cynically; Blount was heir to a title and a fortune, across the water.

BOSTON WAKENED next morning to the sound of gunfire. The rattling volleys rose and died, the cannon fell into silence; back to quarters came the troops and the wagons with the wounded, and cursing officers, amid ironic cheers of patriot city folk. The reconnaissance had failed, and the snow upon the far heights lay reddened.

Smith did not stir abroad that morning. A thin snow was drifting down and the streets did not tempt him. Thus, he heard no details until he came to table at noon. Madam Draper, burning fire and fury against the rebels, had several officers among her lodgers, and she had full knowledge of the morning's repulse—though she would scarcely publish it in her Tory sheet.

"A disgrace!" she fulminated. "Who ever heard of such dishonor? That rabble actually turned cannon upon His Majesty's troops! They are blind to all sense of decency and virtue! They were planted behind barricades, instead of fighting in the open like brave men! What's the world coming to, that such dishonorable tactics are permitted?"

"To war, madam," said one of the officers, and Smith suppressed his smile.

"However," added the good lady, "a sloop-of-war arrived in harbor an hour ago from New York, with dispatches. Perhaps we shall have some better news from that quarter. I hear that two of the staff officers engaged in a brawl this morning, too; a duel may come of it."

"Did you hear their names, madam?" inquired somebody with interest.

"A captain on Burgoyne's staff—I think Blount was the name," she replied. "The other was an officer on General Howe's staff; I have not yet learned the details."

Howard Smith, warmly muffled, limped through the streets

to Burgoyne's billet. He got no news here. Burgoyne was at headquarters and Blount with him; dispatches had arrived from New York with the sloop, and others from England, and headquarters was in ferment. The orderly on duty knew nothing about any duel but "hoped to Gawd new orders would Jerk the cooped-up bloody army out of this 'ere Moody rebel town, Repulsed by them ragged peasants…. Gawd bli'me—who ever 'eard of such goings-on?"

Rehearsal at six; the final dress-rehearsal. Smith turned up early at Faneuil Hall; thus far, he had learned nothing further, but here came news thick and fast, at members of the cast drifted in. Smith listened with dull incredulity.

A brawl? Worse, far worse; during the ghastly affair of the morning, Blount had actually drawn sword on Colonel Michaelson of Howe's staff, attached to the party. Why? A mystery. Gad, what a fool! To do such a thing, in face of the enemy! After all, superior officers were superior officers. Rumor went that Blount was under arrest.

"No, he's not," spoke up someone. " 'Ware, gentlemen! Here he is now."

Here he was, escorting Peggy. Before the footlights, she dropped his arm and turned from him. Her voice struck out in cold hauteur.

"You need not trouble, Captain Blount. I shall arrange otherwise for an escort home. Our acquaintance, sir, is at an end. Whether you are cashiered or resign, 'tis all one to me."

Openly said, cruelly said… Blount bowed to her, very white. The other officers surrounded him eagerly; he shook his head. Howard Smith met his gaze, saw he was hurt to the very quick, saw the proud, bitter anguish in his eyes, and came to the rescue.

"Places, gentlemen! Captain Blount, will you have the kindness to act as prompter for the comedy and allow me to give more attention to the stage? Thank you. Orchestra, ready?"

In response, the fiddles struck up, and the comedy began.

AT THE back of his mind, Smith remained aware of Captain Blount. He was puzzled. It was worse than a mere hurt; the man seemed mortally stricken, almost in a daze. Burgoyne was not coming tonight, someone murmured significantly, was settling some affair with General Howe. Smith caught the aside. She had spoken the word cashiered-did it mean that Blount was done for, his career ended? And what had occasioned his mad action?

The comedy was finished. The actors dispersed; those for the farce took the stage. An orderly from Burgoyne arrived with a package. It was the rebel flag, just finished, to be used in the General's farce. Smith shook it out-thirteen stripes, red and white, the British Union in the corner. He tossed it to the actor who represented General Washington, uncouthty uniformed, with trailing rusty saber and comic wig, and went to where Blount stood at one side.

"Join me for supper, afterward," said Smith.

"Eh? Oh, thanks very much! Afraid I can't," Blount's frozen demeanor broke. "Sorry, old chap. I must back to the General at once."

"Well, cheer up. Don't take it so hard. After all, it's just her way."

"Her way? Oh, you mean Peggy!" Blount broke into a harsh laugh. "Upon my word, Smith, I wasn't thinking of her."

"You'll not let us down tomorrow night?"

"Trust me, old chap! I say! Shall we dine together, after the performance?" Blount spoke impulsively. "I'll be free then, you know."

"Delighted! I'll speak to Madam Draper, and we'll have a bite in my room. Now go into your part, and keep your chin up, and if you need a friend, count on me."

Blount warmed. When he stepped on the stage and bowed to Peggy Williams, his color had returned; he smiled, he was himself again, he had a new bearing.

"A toast, Blount!" Smith exclaimed. "A toast to the future!"

Afterward, he quickly disappeared. A group of others departed with Peggy.

Next day, Boston buzzed with rumors. Word had come ordering evacuation, they said, but this was impossible until more ships arrived. Evacuation! Tory citizens quailed at the thought; rebel sympathizers could be recognized by their broad grins.

In the afternoon, Smith went to the bookshop, for the last time.

"I'm leaving," he said abruptly. "I can't go on with this."

"Howard, you've done magnificent work for the cause!" came the response. "Go, if you like. We'll replace you. When?"

"Tomorrow."

"Agreed, then. Nothing will interfere with that performance tonight. I trust?"

"Nothing."

EVENING, AND a clear night in prospect, as six of the clock approached. Smith, limping along to Faneuil Hall, breathed with a new freedom; he had done his work, he had served, he was through with it all. A weight was lifted from his heart.

The hall blazed with lights and flared with color. Everywhere were uniforms; Howe was here, and his staff, the good Tory ladies of the town had turned out in their best, officers of the fleet and of the army were crowded into the hall. On either side of the stage, as was the custom, they were six deep.

Howard Smith, in the rear, saw to the costumes, put stage-fright to flight with a word and a smile, and went to the prompt-er's place. He greeted Blount with a hearty clap on the shoulder, but was shocked by the young man's haggard air. No time to talk now; he went ahead, the signal was given, the fiddles struck up, the buzzing tongues in the house fell silent.

The comedy ran through its course, and ended to a thunder-ous burst of applause from the jam-packed house. The players took their bows, and joined the throngs beside the stage. Smith, in the wings upstage, sent word to the orchestra. The fiddles struck up the prelude to the farce.

The imitation *Washington*, in full comic regalia, trailing the flag behind him, was on stage, awaiting the curtain's rise, when Smith was aware of a commotion. One officer halted another, almost beside him, with excited words.

"Have ye heard? They say the rebels are attacking in force—Charlestown—"

The curtain lifted.

Offstage, Howard Smith was aware of stamping feet, of new commotion, of startled voices; a fall figure brushed him aside and strode out on the stage—a sergeant of grenadiers.

STOPPING SHORT, the sergeant flung up his arm and shouted:

"The Yankees are attacking our works on Bunker's Hill! They've crossed the Neck and are inside our lines!"

Scattered applause broke forth; to most of the audience, this was part of the farce.

But the figure of General Howe came erect instantly. His voice burst out in a stentorian-alarm shout:

"Officers! To your posts, all officers!"

ONE STARTLED, incredulous instant-then the entire house was in frantic pandemonium.

Behind the resplendent figure of Howe, officers were bursting from all sides for the doors. Those on the stage went leaping through and over the orchestra, overturning fiddlers and drummers; actors were frenziedly getting rid of costumes and wigs. Shriek upon shriek went up. Women, taken by stark panic, screamed and fell, fainting. They were unregarded. Shouts of men drowned their cries. There was a mad crush for every exit. Scenery toppled and crashed. Seats and benches were splintered. From the streets outside came the clatter and bang of gun-carriages, horses at mad gallop.

The stage was cleared. A single figure remained, unhurried, unexcited. Howard Smith turned, and saw Blount approaching him.

"What?" he exclaimed. "Aren't you off with the rest?"

"No," said Blount. "The order was to all officers. I am no longer an officer. My resignation was handed in today and accepted."

Smith looked at him for a moment; the man was ten years older overnight.

"Good," he said cheerfully. "Come along; slip out the back way."

They passed in silence through the reverberant streets, hearing the distant rattle of volleys and boom of cannon.

Neither spoke until they were in Smith's room, where a fire burned and a cold meal was set on the table.

They threw off their cloaks and hats; then Smith filled the wine-glasses and picked up his own.

"A toast, Blount!" he exclaimed. "A toast to the future!"

The Englishman smiled mirthlessly, lifted his glass, and drained it.

"You toast what does not exist; no matter," he said.

"Sit down. Tell me about it. What's all this about a duel? Did you really fly out at Howe's staff officer?"

Blount stretched out in a chair and sighed in weary relaxation.

"Yes. The thing struck me to the heart; I lost my head, went all to pieces. I've no doubt I'd have killed Michaelson on the spot without regret, had I not been restrained. It's haunted me ever since. I dream of it."

"What on earth are you talking about?"

Blount tilted his head in surprise. "Mean to say you don't know?"

"I haven't been able to get any explanation."

"It was a rebel, wounded. He was alongside the road—a poor devil, bleeding, in rags," said Blount. "He staggered to his feet and shook a sword at us, and shouted something. 'To hell with the King!' I think it was…. Well, Michaelson rode at him and cut him down." Blount paused, then broke into a passionate cry: "Needless, useless, cold-hearted cruelty! The poor devil could have done us no hurt. He was a man, wounded. Michaelson split his head with his saber…. Oh, God! Well, there it is. War, of course; I was a fool. Yet I'd do it again."

HOWARD SMITH was silent for a moment.

"Why, Blount, I honor you!" he said then softly.

"I resigned, perforce," said Blount. "They would allow no duel."

"I see. Here, more wine; you need it. You've done the right thing. No regrets! And so this is why she threw you over so publicly, eh?"

"Lord, no! Again Blount looked up. "She said she'd give me my answer when we reached the hall; she did so. Publicly. But not because of that. And, Smith: I've come to understand what you said the other day. You generous rascal! It was not you who did her a wrong. You lied to me. You discovered what was in her, you feared to tell me the truth."

Howard Smith's lips curved in a slow smile.

"Why, what's this? You really do understand, do you? Yes, I admit it, Blount; you were in no shape to comprehend the truth. Apparently you are now. What's happened to make the difference?"

"I'll tell you," said Blount, and broke off. Then: "Gad, to think of it! This morning I had everything in the world, everything! Tonight, nothing. In one day!"

"One day is a mere speck to the gods; it can be an eternity to us," said Howard Smith. "No man may consider himself except as one point in a line that is itself in time a mere point.... Well?"

"You know there were dispatches from England this morning?" rejoined Blount. "Among them was news for me. Everything's gone crash at home. The pater died suddenly; every penny's been lost in speculation. My mother died a couple of years ago. I've nothing left—nothing! Nothing there, nothing here; everything swept away in one day! And Peggy—well, I told her about it. You heard her answer. She dropped me like a hot cake, and did it in public, so everyone would think it was on account of the other matter. Calculating, what?"

Smith whistled softly.

"So your eyes are opened to her reality! One blow upon another, each to counter-balance the one before.... Curious!"

Blount gulped down his wine. "I'm damned glad to be able to talk it out to you. What's ahead? I don't know, I must get away from everything and everyone who knows me. I must start afresh, from the bottom."

"No harm in that; may do you good." Smith leaned forward. "See here! Go with me. I'm leaving town tomorrow. There's a new horizon waiting for us—for a crippled man and a man without a future. All America's waiting, Blount! Chances, opportunities, everything. You weren't made to be a soldier. I'm unable to be one. Very well, accept the fact and let's find our own future together. Chuck the past and forget it; face forward! What d'ye say?"

BLOUNT LISTENED with eyes kindling, alight, then suddenly ablaze. Color leaped into his cheeks. He sprang to his feet, sending his chair back with a crash, and thrust out his hand to grip that of Smith.

"Done!" he said. "Done! And it fits. It fits you, it fits me, it even fits her.... Zounds, man, it fits!"

"What does?" asked Smith, smiling at the younger man's reawakening of eager interest.

"Something you uttered the other day. 'Integrity lies in the heart, not upon the sleeve!' I've remembered that speech. Great words, noble words!"

"They were said to me by a great and noble man," answered Howard Smith. And as he spoke, the roar of distant cannon shook the icy windows.

AN AMERICAN COMEDY

MRS. HENRY'S "afternoon" at the yellow brick house in Fulton Street was an event in the theatrical world—a small world, more shunned than courted in the year 1787. John Henry, whose lameness demanded a crutch close at hand, was a partner with Hallam in the management of the American Company, so called because most of the players were English.

Royall Tyler, in fine blue broadcloth with golden seals dangling from his flowered silk waistcoat, was an erect and soldierly figure, as he should be, having soldiered for the past ten years. He knew most of the players, and as he glanced about the drawing-room he caught suddenly at the arm of Tom Wignell, his particular crony, who played such juvenile leads as were no longer suited to the famous Hallam, now in his fifties.

"Tom! Look—that woman by the fireplace! Who is she?"

Wignell, who had lately got his wardrobe out of pawn by Tyler's help and was not only gayly attired but in rollicking spirits, turned, looked and grimaced.

"God preserve us! A school-teacher!" said he. "That's Mrs. Hallam's friend, Lillian somebody... I forget her name. No matter. Come along and I'll present you. She teaches in the Female Academy opposite Trinity Churchyard—a noble situation to improve the young mind! Come on!"

Tyler was dragged over to the fireplace and presented grandiloquently.

"Mistress Lillian! Allow me the honor of presenting Fortunatus, a rugged specimen of our New England manhood—my friend Royall Tyler, of Boston, late major on the staff of General Benjamin Lincoln and instrumental in putting down Shay's rebellion up north—an authentic American from Harvard College, cut out for a lawyer but turned soldier. Excellent family, never been out of New England before and now never going back, his eyes having been dazzled by the footlights of the John Street Theater."

Mistress Lillian laughed heartily. She had gorgeous red hair, twinkling eyes in a pleasant young face, and a direct, energetic manner.

"Fortunatus! A nickname of good omen, Major Tyler," she said. "Mrs. Hallam has spoken of you, I think. And I must confess that I'm surprised to find you frequenting such company."

"Your surprise is only equaled by my astonishment," retorted Tyler cheerfully, "to learn that so charming a woman teaches school, and can so far demean herself as to consort with the base personages of the stage!"

"Good land! I'd lose my position in a moment did the Academy know it!" she exclaimed, with a comical grimace. "But it's worth it. And I like people. I like these people."

"And the act of Congress is still in force," said Tyler, "by which anyone in the service of the country who attends a play shall be dismissed. However, I've resigned the service, so I'm safe."

"Whatever is Mr. Hallam so furious about?" asked the lady.

TYLER TURNED to follow her glance, knowing that there was only too much truth in what she said about losing her position. Falling into association with Wignell and others, he had himself become fascinated by the hitherto despised Thespians. A Bostonian of blue blood that held the theater in utter horror, he had now settled down in New York to enjoy himself, and he was doing it beyond measure.

Hallam, a ruddy, hearty man who for the past thirty-five years had been the central figure in the budding American stage, was talking with Wignell and was evidently in a passion.

John Henry, limping up to bow over Mistress Lillian's hand, shrugged at her query.

"It seems that Mrs. Hallam was walking in Nassau Street this morning, and a pack of urchins ran after her shouting foul names," he explained. "Lewis takes the matter ill, quite naturally. Any man who could make the theater respectable in the eyes of Americans could have fame and fortune for the taking! Tyler, there's a task befitting you."

"Not so; it's a woman's task," broke in Mistress Lillian, her eyes sparkling. "And a woman could do it. Didn't some actress marry a lord, years ago?"

"Aye," said Henry. "That was Peggy Cheer; she took Lord Rosedale to the altar. But lords are out of fashion these days, and rare to boot."

HE MOVED away. Tyler, who was fascinated by the red-haired teacher, remained. He liked her charm, her energy, her sparkle, her lack of all pretense. He saw that she, like himself, was vitally interested in the people around them, perhaps in the stage itself.

"And just how, Miss Lillian," he inquired, "would you go about making the stage respectable?"

Hallam caught the words, during a lull in the buzz of tongues, and came over to them.

"Aye, how can such a thing be done?" he demanded. "I've tried—and failed—for the past thirty years."

Mistress Lillian took up the gage instantly.

"By means of a play," said she. "You're an Englishman, Lewis; you produce English plays. Well, this is the year 1787, not 1750. Our people look on the theater as an English importation. Revolutionize their whole outlook, give them a play dealing with Americans, by an American playwright!"

"I would in a moment, but no such playwright or play exists," said Hallam. "Find me such a play, and I'll produce it gladly—good, bad or indifferent!"

Tyler looked at Miss Lillian, and deliberately winked. Then, resolutely, he carried her off to the little garden in the rear of the brick house, handed her into the rose-arbor, and seated himself opposite her.

"Madam, I have guessed your secret!" he exclaimed. "And here, in the privacy of these roses, it may safely be discussed. God help you if any other guessed it! Your shame would be recounted to children yet unborn, if you know what I mean—the disgrace would probably put the Female Academy out of business!"

She laughed lightly, but her shrewd eyes were appraising him, not unkindly. He was good to look upon, with his grave, strong features, and his dancing eyes.

*"Mistress Lillian, allow me the honor of presenting
Fortunatus—my friend Royall Tyler, of Boston."*

"My secret?" she echoed.

"Precisely. I read it in your face, in your eye, as you spoke to
Hallam. 'Thou art the woman!' And you have written, or are
writing, a play."

Color stole up her cheeks.

"Well, I—I've tried," she confessed. "At least, I'd like to write
one. I know what it should be, too, but somehow I can't make
it sound right."

"I know precisely how you feel," said Tyler. "I have the same

*"Man, it's wondrous fine!" Wignell
exclaimed. "Those two girls—perfection!"*

trouble—that is, with the female rôles. You see, I left college at
eighteen, and for the past ten years I've been tramping around
New England with the Continental Army, and I just don't know
how women talk."

Her face lighted up. "Oh! You, too! But it's the other way
around with me—I can't make my men talk as they really should,
and I don't know the New England speech very well, and my
character of Brother Jonathan is a New Englander!"

"Dear lady, Providence has directed us this day, my word
on it!" exclaimed Tyler, perhaps with more feeling than he was
aware, for she colored again. "Tom Wignell has been lending me
a hand with the work; I knew nothing about the theater until
I came to New York. But I can fill your play with round New
England oaths that will send a shudder through the quills of
the Female Academy—"

"I can put in my own oaths, thank you," she broke in. "It's
the dialect that I don't know, the ordinary way of speech. Really,
Major Tyler, it would be wonderful; but you must take all the

blame for it—for the play, I mean. For it to be written by me would be impossible. It would indeed be a disgrace; I would be a woman shunned and ostracized—and, you see, I support myself; I need to keep my position at the academy."

"Be damned to the money! I have plenty for two or a dozen—"

Tyler did not utter the impulsive words that rose to his tongue. Leaning forward, he phrased his thought in less startling language.

"We must talk about this. Would it cause any scandal if I called at the Academy to take you for a drive?"

"Heavens, yes!" she exclaimed. "That is, unless you can assure them of your deep respectability. Miss Semple is from Boston or near there."

"Then account it done; my family has a good name, at least," said he, radiant. "I'll rescue you from the Semple dragon on Sunday, Miss Lillian— Oh! That's all I know of your name!" he added, in dismayed confusion. "In fact, it's all I want to know, but since you're a rather practical young woman, and I might have to ask for you at the door."

"The name is Gentry," she said, bubbling with amusement. "But remember, you must promise to be the author of the play!"

"The promise is given," said Tyler.

SUNDAY BEHELD his carriage and spanking pair of bays throwing the Academy into a flutter by carrying Miss Lillian away; and it beheld Royall Tyler definitely in love. He even admitted the fact that same night to Wignell.

In the little tavern in Nassau Street, around the corner from Theater Alley and the John Street playhouse, the two of them sat late with pipes and a bowl of punch. Wignell read the first scene that Tyler handed him, and roared with delight.

"Man, it's wondrous fine!" he exclaimed. "Those two girls argufying over the foibles of dress—why, it's perfection! You've hit 'em off to the very life! Where'd you learn so much all of a sudden?"

Tyler beamed. "I'm in love, Tom; you may as well know it first as last. I'm the happiest man in New York this night! Though, to be honest, I doubt if she'll have me. She's so radiant—"

"Yes, I know all that by heart," broke in Wignell. "But do I know her?"

"You do not," lied Tyler. "She's a young lady of the town. Not so young, either; a woman, not a chit of a girl. A woman who's wise and lovely, a very rose in bloom!"

"Watch yourself, Fortunatus!" said the cynical Wignell. "Where's the thorns, eh?"

Where indeed? Tyler asked himself this question during the days that followed, and found no answer. There were stolen meetings with the Hallams, or at the yellow brick house in

The play was an enormous success: it was, on the instant, the talk of the town.

Fulton Street; good Mrs. Henry could keep a secret. There were furious scribblings, exchanges of thought and word and action, while the play grew marvelously under Tyler's hand; and, as he came to know Lillian Gentry better, as he came to realize that his ambition was by no means hopeless, he wondered uneasily whether the gods might not indeed become jealous.

He had everything; he had too much, and knew it well. Miss Semple's Female Academy smiled upon him, not guessing that he was a friend of actors. He had family, money, position, and to these the greatest gift of all bade fair to be added. There was nothing to prevent. Upon him grew a dread that perhaps he had too much; did any man have a right to such complete and unalloyed blessings and happiness?

As the play grew, as its scope widened, Lillian became more firm in her refusal to have any public share in it. The meretricious standards of fashion, the foibles of the day, were sketched with merciless precision, as contrasted with the artless simplicity of *Brother Jonathan*. Lillian unremittingly worked over the dialogue, ever putting in something new and apt, holding up to ridicule the smug conceits which she daily encountered, with a sparkling reality that amazed Tyler. Indeed, she confessed that she had drawn much of this from real life, as he drew *Brother Jonathan*.

"But not a word—don't breathe a word, even to Wignell or Hallam!" she pleaded, and Tyler promised anew, and kept the promise.

"The Contrast." Tom Wignell was responsible for the title, in a burst of delighted roaring mirth. It was Wignell, indeed, who thrust the play under Hallam's nose.

"Wait for the right moment, till we're rehearsing 'Romeo and Juliet,'" said he. "When Lewis is playing *Romeo,* he's in excellent good humor; he forgets his fifty years and becomes young and passionate again."

So here, rehearsal ended, he gave Hallam the completed play.

"A tasty bit for the managerial eye, worshipful sir," said he, and screwed up his face, adopting a nasal drawl. "Why, aint cards and dice the devil's devices? And the playhouse, where the devil hangs out the vanities of the world on the tenterhooks of temptation—you won't catch me at any playhouse, I warrant you! How's that, Lewis? The speech is mine, the character is mine, I speak for it this minute and must have it! But read the comedy, and rejoice."

Hallam read it. He called the company together, and in huge delight read it to them all. Tyler, who was present, was astonished by the enthusiasm evoked. But had Hallam accepted it? he asked.

"Accepted it?" roared Hallam. "Sir, the play is in production! Now let's discuss the terms."

These mattered little to Tyler. He signed what was put before him, and rushed off to tell Lillian the news. Sitting in the prim little reception parlor of the Academy, he told her, under his breath.

Her eyes widened on him—not in ecstatic joy, but in swift terror.

"Royall—I am afraid," she murmured. "Afraid! Except for your sake, I'm almost sorry that I ever put pen to paper! None of them know—upon your honor?"

"Upon my honor," said Tyler. "Not a soul suspects that I'm not the sole author. And why worry? There's nothing in the play to betray your hand. I'll sneak you in to one of the rehearsals."

"No, no! I'll have nothing to do with it!" she exclaimed. "Nothing! That's final. Not now, nor later."

In vain he attempted argument and protest; she remained adamant. And when Mistress Lillian was adamant, there was nothing more truly adamantine in this world. Tyler argued until Miss Semple, scandalized by the length of this visit, rattled the door-knob significantly; it did him no good, and he departed knowing that he, and he alone, must be known as author of "The Contrast."

He thrilled to his name on the announcements. The newspapers were full of the news; a play by an American was a huge novelty. The publicity increased, the rehearsals were on, the night of the first performance arrived.

TYLER CALLED that afternoon at the Academy, to be coldly informed that Mistress Lillian was indisposed. He was *persona non grata*, most emphatically so, now that it was known that he was actually a playwright and an associate of players. In fact, he received a note next day requesting that he would never again bring the evils of dissolute living and vice before the eyes of the innocent young ladies of the Academy by presenting himself there. He tore up Miss Semple's horrified epistle with a laugh. He might well laugh.

The play was an enormous success; it was, on the instant, the talk of the town. The sensation it created was tremendous. Its ridicule of the vices then so fashionable in England, its authentic American note, its open derision of smug hypocrisy and above all its piercing cleverness, made it a mad success overnight.

During three days, Tyler was overwhelmed by the publicity all this entailed. And during these days, he heard nothing whatever from Lillian Gentry. He wrote letters, he sent messengers; Mrs. Hallam went to the Academy and was turned away from the door. "The Contrast" played to crowded, delirious houses and all New York raved about it.

AT LENGTH Tyler, vaguely conscious of impending storm and a bit alarmed, braved the den of the lioness in person. He was resolved to see Lillian, to speak with her, at any cost. Tom Wignell, in whom he confided to a certain extent, accompanied him as far as the corner, deeming it best not to defile the Academy with his presence.

Tyler, upon mounting the steps, had just rung—when the door opened and a number of ladies came forth, Miss Semple herself bidding them adieu. Upon sight of Tyler, standing aside to give them passage, there was a flutter; he was conscious of stern looks, of chill glances. Then, as he stepped to the door, Miss Semple firmly closed it in his face—but not entirely. Tyler's foot intervened.

"Good morning, madam," he said, through the crack. "I have come to see Mistress Lillian, and I intend to see her if I must scandalize your school and the entire neighborhood. Will you have the kindness to practice the courtesy you no doubt teach your pupils?"

Thus challenged, Miss Semple flung wide the portal and planted herself in the opening, her very ringlets shaking with indignation.

"You unspeakable scoundrel," she declared, "you have been told—"

"No falsehoods, if you please," broke in Tyler. "I'm not asking your opinions. I'm here to see Miss Lillian."

"That viper whom I have sheltered in my bosom is no longer here," was the retort. "Now will you have the goodness to depart?"

"I will not," said Tyler. "Frankly, I don't believe you."

Miss Semple gasped. "Oh! This passes all bounds! We have discovered your low and vicious imposture, sir: A play-actor, a companion of players, indeed! A person who stoops to sell his very soul for filthy lucre! A—"

Tyler broke in:

"Madam, will you have the kindness to summon Mistress Lillian?"

"She is not here. She has been dismissed from her position, upon our learning the shocking fact that she, a teacher in this abode of innocence, became so contaminated by your acquaintance as to share in your disgrace."

"I don't understand, I'm afraid. To what disgrace do you allude?"

"The authorship of this shameful and vile play which has secured such deplorable notoriety, sir, that I must blush at the very mention of it! In all the years that I have conducted this Academy, its good name has never before been sullied. And to think that this calamity should have been caused by a deceitful woman who was trusted and—"

"Apparently you are laboring under a delusion," cut in Tyler coldly. "If you refer to my play 'The Contrast,' Mistress Lillian had nothing to do with it. I, and I alone, am the person responsible."

Miss Semple eyed him with venom.

"From a person of your description, this brazen effrontery might be expected. It is quite useless to descend to falsehood, sir. The ladies who were just here, and who honor this heretofore unsullied institution with their patronage, have traced the matter beyond any doubt. Miss Gentry's association with you, alas, is all too well known. The language used in the play, its opinions and speeches, are directly traced to her in three specific cases. She shall never darken these doors again; nor, I trust, will your presence contaminate this threshold."

Tyler smiled. He attempted no further argument; it was obvious that Lillian had, indeed, drawn her characters, and had used words and phrases, from the very life.

"Very well, Miss Semple. If you will tell me where to find Miss Lillian, I shall be only too happy to accede to all you desire in the matter of purity."

"I am unable to give you any information," she retorted icily.

"You had best do so, I warn you." Tyler's temper rose. "If you make it necessary I'll raise a scandal that will rock your smug select circles—if I have to obtain a search-warrant and come here with officers!"

"Indeed!" she laughed defiantly. "And upon what right do

That face, so wan—
"Lillian!" said Tyler.

you base your impu-
dent demand?"

"Upon my right
as the fiancé of Miss
Gentry."

Miss Semple
gasped again, and
drew herself up in
dignity.

"So! You would
drag down to your
own level this young
woman whose char-
acter and morals you
have so insidiously
seduced! I would have
you know, Mr. Tyler,
that she left this
place yesterday, after
having confessed her
fault with tears of
shame. Aye, sir, she
confessed! She was

very lucky to escape legal prosecution, as I told her frankly, but
for the sake of her family, whom I have advised of her disgrace,
that matter has been waived. I did not ask her destination, she
did not impart it to me, and I desire to know nothing of her
actions."

Tyler bowed and turned away, accepting defeat. But he was
now alarmed. The fact that neither he nor the Hallams had
received any news of Lillian was disturbing. That she had been
broken down and had confessed her share in the play, indicated
only too well what she must have been through.

A S H E crossed the street, Wignell joined him with a cheery
question.

"Gone," said Tyler. "Dismissed. Disgraced. Left the sacred precincts yesterday and not a word from her!"

"Ha! This demands consultation," said Wignell. "All signs point to the tavern and a touch of the proper spirit. Come along, disconsolate swain!"

"It's no light matter," said Tyler, deeply worried. "Tom, I'll have to confess the truth; don't let it go any farther, on your life." He told Wignell the facts about the play and kept nothing back.

"A bad matter made worse," said Wignell. "So that's how you got such damned fine women characters! Taken direct from the Academy! Well, it's nothing to laugh over. The first thing to do is to scour the town for Lillian. Where does she come from? What family has she?"

"A sternly puritan mother and sister in some upstate town. I forget the name, but I have it wrote down somewhere." Tyler frowned. "She was their sole support, Tom. That damned virago has advised the family of her shame—oh, devil take it all, when I think of the state Lillian must be in mentally, I could wring the neck of that blasted Semple woman!"

"You'll be in a worse state if you don't get a grip on your nerves," said Wignell truthfully. "Now, I'll keep the secret; fear not. Get a letter off to the mother, and we'll go to work frisking the town for Lillian. If she feels that she's disgraced for life, we'll get her out of that frame of mind in no time. Have you popped the question yet?"

"No," replied Tyler. "But I think we understand each other."

"A woman never understands such matters until the bargain's signed and sealed," said the cynic Wignell. "All right. Get the town's name, and write. This afternoon we'll go to work here."

Tyler complied; the town was a small one in western New York named Gibsonville, of which he could learn nothing. Then he set about the search in the city for Lillian Gentry with Tom Wignell's whole-hearted assistance.

DAY FOLLOWED day, with no result; a week passed. It seemed impossible that she could disappear without a trace, unless some foul play had occurred. Tyler's worry became alarm, and deepened into anxiety of the sharpest. No response came from Gibsonville. He wrote again and again; he sent money; but he drew completely blank. He advertised, he offered rewards, all to no avail.

Meantime, the furious success of the play continued, as it was to continue for months and years. Tyler paid no heed; he withdrew from the company of the players, he would not appear in public, he was wholly absorbed in the search that now became an obsession. Another week passed.

Suddenly, one morning, Wignell showed up at his lodgings in high excitement.

"I've found her!" he cried. "Come along, Tyler, come along! The man's downstairs who carted her things. He knows the place!"

Tyler, half shaven, rushed down and talked with the carter whom Wignell had brought. Yes, the man could give him precise information. He had called at the Academy and had taken Miss Gentry's trunk. Where? To Harlem, to the house of one Gansevoort; a mighty pretty place, said he.

Heaping money on the man, Tyler dressed and hastened forth to the livery-stable where his horses and carriage were kept. In ten minutes, with Wignell at his side, he was driving north out of the city at a mad pace. They came into Harlem with horses foam-white, found the Gansevoort house on the edge of town, found the stolid Gansevoort himself—but nothing else.

Yes, said Gansevoort, Miss Gentry had been with him—but had not given satisfaction. She had departed the last weekend, leaving her trunk here. There were eight children to be cared for, and what with the cooking and the housework, the job offered plenty to do.

"She was willing enough," said Gansevoort, "but I was afraid from the start she was too much of a fine lady, and so she was. Now we've got a black woman, and the place gets looked after. Where did she go? How do I know? She'll get no reference from me, that I can tell you! Why, I give you my word she'd be till ten o'clock at night just doing the housework, let alone the sewing and darning and keeping the bricks scrubbed!"

Tyler walked back to the carriage with set, bitter face.

"A slavey—my God, a scrub-woman!" he said. "Tom, we must search the town."

They did so, and at the post-house came reward. The tavern-keeper remembered her well. She had taken the post on the Sunday—yes, the Albany stage. A sweet creature, said he, with a big bundle and a mighty sad face: ill, she was. George, the driver, had told him she went clear to Albany; that was all he could tell of her.

Wignell, perforce, returned to New York. Tyler went on to Albany with the carriage, and was there all the week, with no result whatever.

He returned to New York by boat, his search fruitless. Wignell met him; he looked ten years older, and his eyes were like gray stone eyes in a dead face. He had hoped desperately to find some message, some letter awaiting him here; there was no word of any kind.

"I'm packing," he said. "Then to Albany again, where I have searchers at work. If I learn nothing there, I'll go on to Gibson-ville. It's somewhere in the western part of the state."

"Hallam wants to see you—"

"Hallam be damned!"

"But, man, it's about your next play!" cried Wignell. "You must do another at once!"

Tyler turned a look of torture upon him.

"There'll be no next play, Tom. I'm done with it for good and all. I never want to hear, speak or think of the theater again—never! Toss me that carpetbag, will you?"

"But won't you at least see Hallam?"

"I'll see nobody."

THREE WEEKS later, Tyler drove into Gibsonville. Since his letters had received no answer, and since his search in Albany had produced nothing, he was certain that the answer must be here.

The place was little more than a village, a cluster of farmhouses grouped about a church, a store and a post tavern. When he had put up his horses, Tyler fell into talk with the landlord and asked in regard to Lillian Gentry.

"I don't know of her, your worship," was the reply. "Seems to me I have heard some talk about a Gentry girl who left town; must ha' been afore my time. There's Miss Abigail, and her mother; that's all that's left of the family. Cap'n Gentry, he was killed in the war, fightin' under Gates. I guess he didn't leave much behind him."

"What kind of a woman is Mrs. Gentry?"

"The Widder Gentry? Well, your worship, she's a tarnal proud woman. Right proud family all around, though gosh knows they got nothing much to be proud of, far's I know! I hear tell they used to be rich folks afore the war. They got a fine house, and a farm that keeps 'em in vittles. My wife's brother runs it, and he allows the widder is terrible hard in her dealin's. Her house is the green one up the street, second one past the meeting-house. And if you're aiming to sell her something, use the contraption on the door that knocks it for you. The pull-bell don't work, and if you knock with your fist they won't never come to the door. Mighty aristocratic folks, you bet; aint fittin' to have such feelin's in this country, but I reckon they aint Tories, account him having been in the army."

Tyler walked up the street, passed the church, and turned in at the Gentry gate. Now that he was here, foreboding deepened to fear in his heart; he knew not what he would find, but had a feeling it would be nothing good....

As directed, he used the door-knocker. The house reëchoed emptily to the sound. After a moment, the door opened; he bowed to a young woman, primly attired, who looked at him with eyes of fear.

"Good day," said Tyler. "Is Mrs. Gentry at home?"

"Yes," was the response. "Will you come into the parlor?"

"My name is Tyler. I'm trying to get some information about Miss Lillian—you must be her sister?"

The young woman ushering him into the formal parlor looked at him with eyes filled with actual terror. Before she could make any response, another voice sounded.

"Abigail! Did I hear my name?"

"Yes—yes, Mother," stammered Abigail. "It's a gentleman—" She still looked at Tyler, but now with something very like horror. "It's Mr. Tyler."

"Oh!"

Mrs. Gentry swept into the room with the word. She was an angular woman, tall and severe; in her eyes Tyler read a chill that was a thousandfold more uncompromising than the angry vehemence of Miss Semple.

"May I ask what you seek in this house, Mr. Tyler?" she demanded.

"Why, of course! I'm hoping to get some information about Mistress Lillian. You see, I'm a friend of hers."

"I know all about your friendship," said Mrs. Gentry. "I know about you, Mr. Tyler. The letters which you had the presumption to address here, are awaiting you. Abigail! Get the packet of letters from my room."

"But—good Lord, Mrs. Gentry!" exclaimed Tyler. "I don't know why you should treat me as though I were some enemy! I've no intention of forcing myself upon you. I only hope to learn where your daughter is."

"I have no daughter, Mr. Tyler, except this child Abigail," said Mrs. Gentry inflexibly. She took the packet of letters that Abigail brought, and handed them to him as though the touch of them burned her. "Here are your letters, sir."

"Do you know where Lillian is?" demanded Tyler. A glance at the letters showed that none of them had been opened. "I have sent her money—"

"Your money is not desired here, Mr. Tyler, nor yourself," was the reply. "I must now ask you to leave this house."

Tyler met her gaze. "If Lillian's here, I intend to see her. I don't know why you say that you have no daughter of that name—"

"I had a child of that name who brought vile disgrace upon this house and upon my family," said Mrs. Gentry with uncompromising hauteur. "She forfeited the right to be known by my name, Mr. Tyler. I believe you're fully aware of the shame her conduct in New York has entailed."

"I'm aware that she's a woman who might well be ashamed of such a mother," lashed out Tyler. "A woman of the finest, noblest character, so far above your petty and intolerant viciousness as to put you to shame indeed! And whether you like it or not, I'm going to find her if I have to walk through this house."

Mrs. Gentry turned. "Abigail! Ring the bell for the farm-hands, and tell them to eject this obnoxious gentleman of the stage. Do you hear me?"

"Yes, Mother," piped up the frightened Abigail. Then, as she looked at Tyler, something came into her eyes—some sudden gusty courage and resolve. "Lillian's in the spring-house," she blurted out, and fled.

Tyler bowed to Mrs. Gentry and walked out of the door, white with fury.

He strode around the house. At some little distance, in the rear, he saw the small structure that must be the spring-house. The *clop-clop* of a churn came to him as he drew near it. Something moved there—someone came into the doorway—a woman, toil-weary and ragged of dress, whose drooping figure was not that of Lillian at all. But the hair falling about her ears and face—that gorgeous red hair—that face, so wan and pallid—

"Thank God!" said Tyler devoutly, as he heard her cry out.

"Lillian. Lillian—what on earth does this mean?" He hurried to her, caught her in his arms.

"I should ask what it means, Royall," she said, her breath sobbing in her throat. She regarded him with something of the same terror Abigail had evinced, a woman's terror, not of the body but of the senses. "I heard—they told me the disgrace was such that you—you were ruined, your career was ended—that I had brought it all upon you!"

Tyler burst into a wild, mirthless, incredulous laugh.

"Good God! Why, it's insanity, rank madness, all of it! They never gave you my letters? Look, here they are, unopened! We've been searching night and day to find you; why didn't you come to me, in New York?"

"I was afraid." Her eyes flickered with the memory of that fear. "For you. Miss Semple—the other women—they were going to get the law upon you, they said. Oh, it may seem strange to you: to me it was terrible, terrible! And I had confessed, had told everything; I was afraid to face you, Royall. I was ill, too; ill and bewildered.... A woman has no place to go—"

"You have now, by the Lord!" he said.

IN THE little tavern around the corner from the John Street Theater, Tom Wignell sat with Lewis Hallam over a bowl of punch; he was laboriously deciphering a letter.

"Well, speak up!" growled the veteran actor. "What does he say about another play? When is he coming back?"

"He isn't," said Wignell. "Says he's going to Boston and stay there, and be a lawyer—a canting, sniveling rantipole of a lawyer!"

"Are those his words?" demanded Hallam suspiciously.

Wignell grinned. "Well, words to that effect, anyhow, Lewis." Putting out a hand to his mug, he lifted it high. "Here's a toast to him, a toast to Fortunatus!"

Hallam clinked mugs solemnly. "To Fortunatus that was," he corrected. "And to the first play written by an American....

Damn it all, Tom, what are we going to do if he won't write another play?"

Wignell emptied his mug with a flourish and wiped his lips.

"Wait; there's a postscript to his letter that answers your question."

"Read it, then."

Wignell leaned forward, peering at the paper with an impish light in his eyes. He traced with his finger imaginary words across the blank lower part of the sheet.

"Here's what he says, Lewis: *'Happiness is where the heart is, and let the world go hang!'* And amen, say I."

THE FINGERS OF SATAN

PICCADILLY, ON a warm evening of August, and a bizarre figure striding through the throng—a figure gaunt and tall, hat jammed over eyes, collar turned up, hiding the lower part of his face as though in fear of recognition.

Street lights were dim and few, in 1833. The little that could be seen of the man's features was pallid and cadaverous; his dress, however, was eloquent of wealth and fashion, with a foreign touch of color, of glinting gold.

This man, pausing to let carriages pass, was approached by a whining beggar. He fumbled in a pocket, found nothing, uttered words of pity in Italian, whereupon the beggar heartily cursed him. With a careless wave of the hand, he strode on. Suddenly he halted!

In an alley entrance sat a blind man, squeakily playing an old fiddle. It was the theater hour and many people were passing, but none dropped coins into the beggar's hat. His music was excruciating, and but drove his listeners on still faster.

"There," muttered the gaunt man in Italian, "there were my own destiny, except God kept me from it!"

He felt again in his pocket; and again found nothing. He hesitated; then, impulsively, went to the beggar, stooped over, touched the man's arm. Gently taking the squeaky fiddle and dirty bow, he twisted the tuning pegs and then cuddled the fiddle under a strangely jutting chin. The greasy bow swept across the strings.

A gasp escaped the blind beggar. A few people paused, in astonishment; more began to gather. The fiddle no longer squeaked. Under those agile, enormous hands it became alive with exquisite voices. The gaunt man was playing a few bars from the "Magic Flute," over and over but never twice alike, ever with new variations. Now the melody was haunting, tender; now it became a fast and furious jig of mirth; now it was satiric, mocking, jeering.

The throng increased. A carriage halted at the curb, then another. The beggar sat staring upward, all agape. The player, with his foot, prodded the beggar's hat toward the circle. A sudden savage discord rang out; he kicked again at the empty hat.

The hint was taken. A few coins came tumbling down, more clattered on the stones. As though in reward, the Mozart melody swung into an almost human voice of poignant sweetness. It melted into an angelic chorus of double-stopped notes, as the hat was passed back to the carriages and returned weighted with coin.

"Lor' lumme! It's 'im!" A sharp, strident voice burst upon the hushed obscurity. "It's 'im, the devil's fiddler! There's the Old Nick standin' at 'is bloody elbow, mates—"

The player thrust fiddle and bow into the blind man's hands and turned to depart; he was too late. From the crowd erupted a burst of voices, angry, applauding, threatening. A surge forward, and hands were tearing at him. The voices became frenzied. His hat was knocked off; a new howl arose at sight of his features, framed in long black hair—cavernous, craggy features with a huge jutting nose and huge jutting chin. Applause was drowned by hysterical mob-fury. Another surge; the beggar was overturned and sent sprawling with pitiful helpless babblings.

The gutter always tries to destroy what it cannot comprehend. The gaunt man was famous; all London had been talking of him, telling fantastic and terrible things about him. Now the gutter had him, and get away he could not. Dim figures pressed in upon him, pinching and bawling, striking, shoving.

"Nicolo!" A woman's voice, almost at his side, lifted in Italian. "This way, Nicolo. Come quickly!"

A momentary opening showed. He hurled himself at it, his tall, stooping figure gaining place. A woman's hand caught his. He burst through the crowd and was guided into the alley mouth. A woman, running with him, led him along the dark, tortuous maze, and after them poured the shouting, howling throng.

"The devil's fiddler!" Yawping cries shrilled up. "Satan 'imself—fetch 'im down! Stop un, lads!"

Stones and brickbats clattered. Things had taken an ugly, vicious turn.

SPATTERED IN filth at every step, ducking alertly, the
gaunt man felt himself pulled to a halt and drawn into a doorway. He followed blindly, gasping for breath. A door slammed
behind them. The woman's hand jerked him on. Up a rickety
stairway, then into a room where a tallow candle guttered upon
a table. The door closed.

They were alone. The sounds of pursuit died away. Panting,
the man sank into a chair before the table. He stared at his
rescuer, his black eyes enormous in those pallid features.

She was not pretty. She was, indeed, of appalling ugliness;
a young woman, swarthy, ill-dressed, emaciated like himself, a
tattered shawl about her head. As she surveyed him, a smile that
was like a repulsive grimace distorted her lips, yet her dark eyes
were alight and dancing and glorious.

"Nicolo, Nicolo! The fiddler who made King William pay

double to hear him!" she exclaimed in Italian. "The man who's in league with Satan! Some of these English worship you, others try to tear you apart. You assist a blind beggar; when they recognize you, they suddenly see the devil at your elbow!"

His shaggy brows drew down and he stared at her.

"Who are you, woman?"

Her laugh broke harshly. "Oh, I've heard what they say about you! Sold yourself to the devil; murderer, criminal, imprisoned for years and only released to give a concert; an inhuman person, a corpse-body inhabited by Satan! No wonder the mob nearly murdered you after your first concert here. But I, alone in all England, know the truth. Think back across the years, Nicolo! You can't remember?"

Still breathless, he shook his head silently, intently. She smiled again.

"Think! A boy, a young man already aged, kept in a room behind the shop on the Genoa wharves; tortured, beaten, starved by his beast of a father, made to slave endlessly at music. Whipped, kept like an animal by that brute Antonio, that later he might make money for the brute. A boy, reaching through his barred window, pitifully, for the grapes and oranges, the crusts of bread, sneaked to him by the little girl next door—"

The gaunt man swept to his feet, arms flung wide.

"God in heaven!" he burst out. "The little angel, Graciella!"

He enfolded her in those long arms with sobs, with laughter, embracing her while tears coursed down his sunken cheeks. Then he held her off, staring.

"You, my little angel! Do you know that I searched Italy for you in vain, year after year? I found your people had gone to Marseille. I searched there, searched the coast, all the south of France, vainly; you could not be found. You, the one person to whom Nicolo Paganini owed a supreme debt! You, the one unselfish creature in all his wretched life! And tonight I find you—once more a rescuing angel."

He embraced her anew, in torrential emotion. She gently

drew away, forced him back into his chair, and drew up a stool for herself.

"Yes, you've found me. You, the great virtuoso, the rich and famous Paganini, the man who owns all earth and heaven— you've found your little Graciella, the daughter of the fish-merchant."

THE ACRID mockery of her voice plucked at his senses. He asked:

"Why did you never get word to me? Where have you been? How did you get to England?"

"As a dancer, my Nicolo; of all things, a dancer! Look at me, regard me well; I'm no more beautiful than yourself, and a woman. A woman, ugly as sin and damned by her ugliness. That's the end of all my dreams and ambition. Now, by working in the downstairs shop, I get this attic room and some scraps of food. I'm forced to virtue. The good God was so intent upon preserving my virtue that I was given no choice in the matter."

The bitter, fleering words drew a shiver from him.

Oddly enough he was a man of impulse, not of intelligence; in many ways he was not intelligent at all. Almost totally lacking in education, tormented over long periods by virulent illness, he knew only one thing, but that supremely—his violin. The years of suffering which had warped his body, had left his mental faculties equally warped, in a solitary magnificence of spirit. He saw nothing with the perception of other men, did nothing after their accustomed fashion.

"Ugly? Yes, yes. What of it?" he said vaguely. He leaned forward; his eyes warmed. "You weren't hard and bitter in those days, Graciella! A little child like an angel. How I used to listen for your voice! It was the one beautiful thing my accursed life knew. Do you remember what you used to call me?"

She smiled again. A smile heightens the beauty of most women; but with this woman, a smile intensified her ugliness.

"*Poveretto Nicoletto!*" she answered softly. "I felt so sorry for you, little Nicolo! Sometimes I could hear you sobbing, sobbing half the night. And sometimes when you were ill and fevered, you would babble queer things about angels. I was afraid your father would find out about how I brought things to you—"

She broke off abruptly, with a gesture of warning. A door had slammed, feet sounded on the stairs. She looked up and nodded.

"The padrone, owner of the shop below. He has been in England many years; a violent, terrible man, who has committed many murders. But he pitied me. He lives in the next room."

Her voice died. Paganini was paying no attention, had scarcely heard the words. A long breath escaped him. He leaned back and his somber features cleared.

"It's like a dream! Well, I've found you at last. I can give you all you desire; it will make me happy. Money? I have abundance."

"I care little." She shrugged. "Strange, how some of us would sell our very souls for money, like the padrone! Yet, to some of us, how little it means! Ah, Nicolo, you've come too late to help me. Once I had great ambitions, great visions; all dead now. I

hope merely to keep alive, and some day to crawl back like a dog to die in the sunlight of Italy."

He was watching her intently, plucking with his long fingers at his full widely curved underlip. He frowned, trying to comprehend her words.

"Visions? I don't know; I have none," he said. "I know only friends and enemies—many enemies. People hear things and hate me. A man in Paris tried to stab me, because Satan was in me. Bah! I'm no beauty, as you say, but I bewitch them all with my violin. Pretty women, great gentlemen, bitter enemies—I bewitch them all!" He touched the red ribbon in his lapel. "They give me medals, honors, money, love. Why? Because I scorn them, yet my music compels them! My violin is power!"

"Very true. But I have no violin; only this, as ugly as my face."

She stood up swiftly, held her shabby dress tightly about her body in scornful display. It was no more beautiful than her features; it looked ill-shaped and awkward, with powerful flanks and legs.

SUDDENLY SHE moved, turned, pirouetted, did a few steps across the room and back. The whole impression of ugliness vanished, lost in an epitome of flowing graceful motion. With a shrug that expressed much, she resumed her stool.

Not even death, it was whispered, could still those fingers which even Satan abode; and so it seemed at this moment.

"Tell me," demanded Paganini, "what one thing you most desire, Graciella."

She stared, a singular expression in her face.

"Queer you should ask that! I've heard for years of your greatness. I love music, Nicolo; with all my heart I've longed to hear you play. I could never buy a ticket for your concerts. But tonight, on the street, I gained my supreme wish. I heard you!"

"That? Nonsense!" he burst in disdainfully. "An absurdity, a scratchy caricature of music! You shall hear real music from my Stradivarius, and that's not all. Hm! Tomorrow morning I'm going with my manager Laporte, to meet Alfredo Bunn, the Englishman who manages Drury Lane Theatre. I'll make him give a concert for you. If I, Nicolo Paganini, say you're a great danseuse, all London will be at your feet."

She shook her head, with melancholy finality.

"No, my poor Nicolo. These English won't look twice at me. They won't have lessons from me; no one will. They turn their eyes away, as from some hideous animal. When I try to get chorus-work, they look at my wretched body and wave me away before I do a step. Besides, you can't affirm that I'm a good dancer. You've not seen me dance—"

"Be quiet, be quiet!" broke in Paganini, with gusty vehemence. "Could I play second fiddle in some orchestra? No. It's the same with you. I just saw you take a few steps; I know all about you. Two bars of music, two steps—I need no more to tell if genius is at work! You have the truest beauty; sureness and grace of movement. Did you ever see Taglioni without her costume and lights? *Pouf!* A peasant girl! But on the stage, divine! And, Graciella, you're like your name, the essence of grace. In many ways, you're like me. We're akin, you and I."

"Like you?" she murmured.

He leaned forward with earnest assent.

"Like me, but more fortunate. I'm a man accursed. You've mentioned the wild stories, but you don't know half the calumny and lies that surround me. Here!" He stretched out his left hand and flexed the ringers. "Look at them: set wide apart, the knuckles big and long from pulling them each day, each hour! But people say Satan gave me those fingers. They accuse me of murder; they say I spent years in prison. They cover me with lies. But what's the truth?"

He paused for breath, and touched his right side.

"I scarcely know a well day, Graciella! I have sudden seizures. Any food I take causes frightful pains; I live chiefly on liquids. Sometimes, even in concert, I am gripped by intolerable agony and can hardly stagger off the stage before I faint. I must spend weeks and months in complete rest; then new calumny overtakes me—they say I have gone back to prison!

"When I toured in Ireland last year, no one happened to see me arrive, so all Dublin believed that Satan had flown me there overnight.... Everywhere the same; calumny, hatred, scorn, envy! Worship and praise and adulation, yes; but it does not make up for the other. People turn their eyes away from me in horror, as they do from you. Therefore, I shall help you."

She started to speak. He cut her short with peremptory words.

"Keep your mouth shut! I have an idea; let me think. There's a trick to everything. I have secrets. In three days' time I can make an ordinary violinist into a virtuoso. Money? *Pouf!* As you say, that's the least of all things. I owe you a greater debt. I shall pay it. These English are queer, but they have kind hearts. They love mystery."

Enthused, his faculties wakened and animated, the whole man was transfigured. A flame leaped in the large black eyes. He was concentrated, tense, engaged in what for him was the hardest labor—thought.

Then, abruptly, Paganini flung back his head in a burst of mirth; harsh, raucous mirth, for laughter lay interred with his lost youth.

"*Corpo di Baccho!* You shall dance for me, and I shall play for you! Is it agreed? Then swear it, here and now!"

The woman assented in wondering astonishment. He rose, shaking back his hair. Then he grimaced.

"This damp English air has spoiled my coiffure; I must get it recurled tomorrow. Well, write down where to reach you—this address. Write in English. You'll hear from me in the morning, and shall leave this vile hole forever. Remember, you're sworn to do as I say! I'll provide costume, stage, everything. You shall do two dances—what music do you wish?"

Writing, she glanced up and shrugged. "Cherubini—no! Two movements from Gardel's ballet, if you like."

"Set down the titles in English. I don't know a word of the language."

She obeyed. He seized the paper, folded it, tucked it into his waistcoat pocket—and became rigid. His hand seemed glued to his side; he caught his breath sharply. Into his face there came a livid, frightful pallor, and his eyes dilated.

A choking word escaped him. He took two staggering steps, collapsed against a chair, and came to the floor with a resounding crash. He lay senseless, one hand pressed to his side, coat open; in the candlelight, the golden seals of his fob glittered.

C A M E   A   rush of hasty steps. Into the room burst the padrone, a hairy fellow reeking of garlic and cheap wine.

Graciella, kneeling in panic beside the fallen man, looked up. "Help me, Antonio!"

"So you've had luck at last—a miracle!" bawled Antonio with coarse laughter. Then he leaned forward. "Ha! Gold! Here's a bird worth plucking! Did you knife him?"

"Don't be a fool," snapped Graciella. "He's a friend of mine. Look at his face—the great Paganini! He became suddenly ill."

"Paganini? Tell that to the pigeons, you slut! Paganini? The King of England, perhaps! Gold, eh? Rings on his hand—here, get away from your fine gentleman! I'll make sure of him, then we can strip him and heave him out into the street."

His hand flicked out a stiletto, a thin and pointed Corsican blade. With a cry of protest and horror, Graciella caught his arm. At this moment the eyes of Paganini opened. He looked up, perfectly conscious yet incapable of any motion; his contorted features were bedewed by a sweat of agony.

"Stop, Antonio, stop!" cried the young woman. "He's a friend of mine, I tell you!"

With a furious blow across the face, Antonio sent her sprawling.

Out on the empty stage floated the white vision, to sink gracefully in obeisance, then lift like a soaring bird. "I knew it, I knew it!" muttered Paganini.

"Remember your place, you slut," he sneered, and dropped on one knee. A cry of rage and surprise escaped him. "Hello! The rascal's awake! Take this, you rogue, to shut your mouth for ever—"

He drove down a blow. Graciella, writhing half erect, caught the hairy arm and deflected its aim. The point of the stiletto scratched her wrist and arm; she clung on, with frantic cries. They were abruptly silenced when the free hand of Antonio struck her across the face, again and again. Still on one knee, he lashed her with his fist.

She struggled desperately. A moan of utter despair broke from her; still clinging to the black-limned arm and wrist, she sank down. Antonio struck her again, and this time knocked her clear and broke her hold. But he himself, still on one knee, lost balance, and with a torrent of hot Italian curses, toppled over and fell full length.

It so happened that he fell half across the outflung left arm of Paganini; and, instead of scrambling up again, he stayed as he was.

The guttering candle flickered upon a singularly inactive scene where nothing seemed to happen: The woman, dazed, half senseless, wiping blood and tears from her face and moaning piteously. Paganini lying asprawl, one hand still pressed to his side, but his large black eyes aflame with a wild burning light. And the bulky, hairy Antonio lying there as though held down by some invisible force; his brutal features empurpled, his breath gurgling, his eyes rolling wildly and bulging out with every instant. He made ineffectual motions as though trying to tear something from his throat, and could not.

SPASMODIC FURY shook him. He writhed and twisted half around, and shuddered. Then the light fell upon something gripped to his throat. As he came down, the left hand of Paganini had fastened there; those long, demoniac fingers, steel-thewed from constant work on the fingerboard, sank in with inexorable clutch. Not even death, it was whispered, could still those terrible fingers in which Satan abode; and so it seemed at this moment.

Presently Antonio shuddered again and beat at the air with clawing hands, and then went limp. The gripping left hand spurned him, let him go, and his body fell half under the table as it rolled aside. Paganini moved, gasped with pain, came to one knee and then rose. He went to the moaning Graciella, caught her arm and lifted her.

"Come! Wipe the blood from your face. Help me; I'll help you," he said, still agasp with the inward agony that half doubled him. "You must leave here now, instead of tomorrow."

He pressed out the candle-flame. In the darkness, their scuffling feet sounded, then the slam of the door.

NEXT MORNING, in his ornate office at the new Drury Lane Theatre, Alfred Bunn sat in a rather uncomfortable discussion. The impresario was plump and prosperous; in another three years, indeed, he was to guarantee the great danseuse Taglioni thirty thousand dollars for an engagement. Just now, however, he was dealing with someone who had an even sharper eye on the shekels.

This was Laporte, the interpreter, friend and manager of the great violinist. Laporte announced his terms, and budged not. Paganini, who did not understand a word of what was going on, sprawled in a chair in front of the empty fireplace. Mr. Bunn, who was doing his best to get better terms, shook a newspaper at the imperturbable Laporte.

"Look at this article!" he exclaimed. "Look at these calculations—three thousand guineas is what you make from a single performance, at the prices you charge! You rent the house from me for a miserable hundred, pounds, put the tickets at outrageous prices, and become rich!"

"That," said Laporte, comfortably taking a pinch of snuff, "is the whole point of our engagement, Mr. Bunn. It would be odd if we desired only to make you rich! A hundred quid is the usual price for your house; we pay it, or take Covent Garden or another."

Paganini, aware of dispute, leaned forward and spoke.

"Tell him," he snapped in Italian, "to sign this moment, or we leave. Also, I have a further piece of business to settle with him. Then I have an engagement with the Marchesa di Genova, so there's no time to waste in talking."

His burning eyes gripped the impresario. Poor Bunn emitted a gasp, received the ultimatum, and with a sigh approved the contract for the 5th. Then Paganini tapped the arm of Laporte.

"Now, tell him that I want his theater on Thursday night, the 8th."

"Eh?" Laporte gaped at him. "But, maestro, you've just decided on the 5th for the concert! People won't come again,

"Poveretto Nicoletto!" Her gasp was like a moan.

three days later. They're already saying that you've given too many concerts this season."

"Shut up, imbecile! Do as I say," snarled Paganini grimly. "This has nothing to do with you; it's my own affair. Tell him! He's to make a contract with me personally, not with you, for the use of the house on the 8th. Tell him! I'll pay the same figure; tell the shoulder of mutton quickly!"

Laporte obeyed. Mr. Bunn, happily unaware of the names Paganini applied to him, heard the good news with reviving heart. A hundred pounds was, after all, a hundred pounds, and as long as he got the artist down in black and white, he was content.

"This day week, eh? Very well." He drew up paper and dipped a quill. "But, Mr. Laporte, he must find his own performers. I cannot engage artists at the price—"

Assured no artists were to be engaged, he nodded and went

on writing. Presently Laporte picked up the agreement, sanded
it, and translated it to Paganini.

> "I agree to give One Hundred Pounds for the use of Drury
> Lane Theatre, for a concert, for One Night (Thursday, 8th
> August). Mr. Bunn to find Servants, Lights, Printing, Adver-
> tisements, and the usual Band, with all the expenses of the
> Theatre, except Performers.
> "Dated August 1, 1833."

With a nod of approval, Paganini spread out the paper, took
the proffered quill, and affixed his painful sprawling signature,
adding the date in Italian. Then he leaned back and handed a
scribbled, dirty scrap of paper to Laporte, who was obviously
mystified by the whole affair but dared not protest.

"Tell him the orchestra—or band, as he calls it; good God,
what a name for honest musicians!—is to play these two selec-
tions only. The Marchesa di Genova is to dance to the music;
when she is through dancing, the orchestra may leave. Understood?"

Not at once. This departure from program usage horrified
Mr. Bunn, who liked to do everything just as it had been done
at Drury Lane for the past century. Laporte, fingering the paper
curiously, gave it a second look and then glanced at Paganini.

"Strange, maestro!" he observed. "This paper seems to have
been smeared with blood!"

A mirthless, terrible laugh shook the violinist. He held out
his left hand and flexed it in the air.

"Why not?" he said, with a ghastly ironic smile. "Does not
Satan reside in these long fingers? I was sacrificing to the devil
last night, my dear Laporte. Have you not heard the morning's
rumors about some rascal who was found strangled to death?"

"For God's sake don't joke about such things!" exclaimed
Laporte, horrified. "If anyone understood your words, there
would be fresh calumnies in the papers."

He turned to Mr. Bunn, who wanted to know about the

Marchesa di Genova. Laporte had never heard of her. Paganini, however, enlightened them; he told much that was not true, in fact, and hinted at marvelous things, and at romance. The unknown Marchesa began to assume mystery and therefore importance, in Bunn's agile mind.

"Now," pursued Paganini cheerfully, pulling at his underlip, "tell the side of beef that no one is to be admitted to see the Marchesa dance; after her dance, I myself will play, but no tickets are to be issued, no advertisements are to be given the newspapers."

Laporte was positively horrified at this whimsy of casting good money to the winds. He protested; whereat Paganini uprose with a roar of curses that speedily set him on the right track. Bunn, who was already convinced that this gaunt violinist was a madman, shrugged and assented. Besides, Mr. Bunn was thinking about something else.

The Marchesa was a noble Italian gentlewoman in distress; she always danced masked and never showed her features, even to her pupils—ha! The press was full of stories about the gallantries and romantic escapades of Paganini, usually giving them a much coarser name, and Mr. Bunn was already licking his lips when the gaunt violinist took his departure.

Relieved of that Satanic presence, Mr. Bunn eagerly pressed queries upon Laporte, who concealed his worried ignorance with a show of very becoming reticence. The upshot was that Mr. Bunn still licked his lips, and was like to burst with secrets repressed. Not the wildest of wild horses could have kept him, and certain of his noble patrons, out of Drury Lane Theatre on the following Thursday night.

IT WAS a drizzling night, swirling with fog from the river. The front of the theater was dark, the hoardings were empty; inside, it was different. Here, all was a glow of light, upon a cavernous empty house, except for the orchestra pit, where a dozen musicians strummed and pitched into tune.

In the dressing-room of the Marchesa, a masked woman held

out her hands to the lean grasp of Nicolo Paganini. He, as usual, was in his eternal black, a high white stock contrasting with his long curled locks; but she was in a glitter of gauze, with paste gems shimmering, and about her throat a necklace of glorious blood-red coral.

"Nicolo! It is like a dream, a dream!" Her voice, from beneath the mask, was vibrant and musical, rich with tremulous emotion. "See, how cold my hands! I am afraid; I'm no longer young, Nicolo. Perhaps I've forgotten all I knew."

"Fear not," said he gravely, and bent his lips to her fingers, very courteously. "Genius like ours, little angel, has no youth or age; it is immortal."

"Are there many people in the house?" she demanded.

"Don't think of that; think only that whispers have spread all through London about the mysterious danseuse, the masked Marchesa di Genova. Come! The orchestra is ready. Allow me to escort you to the entrance."

A S H E led her to the wings, he ignored gawking servants and stagehands, made a gesture to the waiting Laporte, and the music swept up. Out on the empty stage, before the footlights and the reflectors, floated the white vision, to sink down gracefully in low obeisance and then lift like a soaring bird.

"I knew it, I knew it!" muttered Paganini, as he watched. His hand gripped the arm of Laporte. "Look at her, man! Behold true grace, the ecstasy of motion that comes only with inborn genius! Where is that side of beef, that shoulder of mutton?"

"Signor Bunn?" Laporte gestured at the yawning emptiness of the theater. "Out there, somewhere; I think some fine gentlemen were with him."

Paganini watched keenly, intently; the number was nearly over when he saw her startled realization, saw her eyes, incredulous, focus on the empty seats. To the concluding strains, she tripped into the wings and nearly fell into his arms with a swift outbreak of words.

"Nicolo! What does it mean? The house is empty, empty!"

"Little angel, it is on the contrary full to the doors!" he exclaimed with sonorous assurance. "It is full of old memories of the Genoa wharves, of whispers in the night, of a boy's sobs, of a voice saying: *'Poveretto Nicoletto!'* Listen! Do you hear them? That is the applause other ears cannot hear, for those sounds are echoes from the heart, little Graciella. Now! There is the cue. You're dancing divinely—encore!"

Her second number ran its course. When it finished, half a dozen voices burst forth from the recesses of the boxes— acclaiming and vociferous voices, ringing with enthusiastic plaudits. Graciella curtsied low, then left the stage.

Paganini was not in the wings. Instead, Laporte was waiting with a huge dark cloak; he flung it about her shoulders, uttering excited words.

"The maestro was right; you're divine, signora! These English have seen something this night! But come; he ordered me to escort you to a box."

The musicians, disgruntled and muttering, were leaving. He escorted Graciella, who was radiant but bewildered, to a box above the stage.

Into the glow of the lights came Paganini, violin in hand— suddenly, with that long gliding step which men said was borrowed from the devil. He settled the instrument between jutting chin and the apparently malformed left shoulder; and then he played.

None of his tricks here. None of his string-breaking, his fantastic striving for effect, none of his bewildering pyrotechnics; but, under those white fingers, the ruddy Stradivarius sang.

The cloaked figure in the box leaned forward, intent, absorbed. Through the hushed darkness lifted no melody, but an improvisation more wonderful than any melody, holding a multitude of things which only one listener could recognize. The choked treble sobbing of a boy, the lilting chants of fishermen about the wharves, the strident clangor of church-bells, the lift and surge of waves; the tremulous sobbing again, and upon it the soft angelic voice that recurred and recurred in golden liquid notes, until it evoked one startled gasp from the figure in the box.

"Poveretto Nicoletto!" Her gasp was like a moan.

Paganini glanced up, smiled; suddenly the music shook with life and laughter, in an ecstatic swinging dance that fairly swirled with intoxicating rhythm.

Laporte, though he had listened unmoved to concert after concert, stood in the wings, lost in utter amazement; sweat streamed on his face and he stared like a man bemused. On and on rose that swaying, rippling flood of music, ever lifting and lifting until it swung into a great triumphant pæan that swelled almost intolerably—and was ended, abruptly, upon one crashing organ-chord from all four strings. And then the strong white fingers plucked at the strings and broke them asunder, with a jarring clang. Paganini bowed to the box, and was gone.

GRACIELLA FOUND him in his dressing-room, limply sprawled in a chair, head drooping in exhaustion, while Laporte carefully wrapped the violin.

She came to Paganini with hands outstretched, with tears glittering below the edge of her mask, with voice heart-filled and unsteady.

"Nicolo, ah, Nicolo! Now I understand. It was beautiful and glorious, beyond all words! How can I ever thank you? How can I ever repay you?"

He rose and bowed above her fingers.

"By dancing for others as you danced for me; by remembering my one urgent advice—never remove your mask. By advancing the opportunities now before you. Repay me, little angel? Never! The debt was all mine."

He broke off, to look over her shoulder at the figures crowding in the passage. A laugh shook him.

"But there; leave me, Marchesa, and go to those who await you. I think the worthy Signor Bunn has offers for you. His noble patrons will be at your feet, too."

"Nicolo!" She caught at him. "Listen to me! You speak as though we weren't to meet again!"

"Dear Marchesa," he said gravely, "in half an hour I leave by the Dover coach. I must be in Paris for a concert three days from now. Farewell, and may you ever remember gently the man who is so like to you in many ways—and so far beneath you. *Addio!*"

He took the arm of Laporte and together they passed out to the street. But Laporte, as the swirls and eddies of fog closed around them, was lamenting the three thousand golden guineas lost that night. The fog swallowed them. They vanished from sight. Across the half-lit, shrouded stage echoed the ghastly croaking laugh of Paganini.... The play was over, and the curtain fell.

THE LIGHTS in the room were switched on, and Dr. Haberlin turned his smiling countenance to me.

I sighed a little, and broke from the enchantment of the past, to accept the cigar he offered.

"A good touch, that final laugh from the fog!" he exclaimed, complacently. "How did you like my sound effects and voices?"

"How the devil did you get them?" I demanded. "I've meant to ask you before this how you handled the illusion. You did it with a phonograph?"

He shook with hearty laughter, and wagged his forefinger at me.

"No, no, my boy! That's my secret, and remains my secret until it's safely patented! You can't screw that out of me. But how did you like the little drama?"

"Your notions of drama," I said tactfully, "are rarely original. Tell me one thing, Karl; was there any truth in that ghastly strangling episode?"

He pulled at his cigar, eyes a-twinkle behind his thick lenses.

"My boy, no one to this day can tell you the truth about Nicolo Paganini!" he said at length. "The man remains an enigma, a composite of legend and mystery and deep sadness; a fascinating orchestral theme, for those who desire to play upon it."

"But the Marchesa—little Graciella?" I demanded.

He reached around to a table on which were piled all manner of documents and theatrical records. From the pile, he took a strip of white satin and passed it to me, silently.

It was a playbill of 1835, printed on satin as the custom was for benefits and exceptional engagements. It announced the farewell appearance, before her departure to Italy, of the famed danseuse and teacher, Marchesa di Genova—the dancer who had never removed her mask.

HE WHO TURNED BACK

THE SNOW was crisp underfoot, the streets odorous with the pleasant smell of wood-smoke gushing from every chimney. Two people walking arm in arm came to a halt just before they arrived at the lighted windows of the Calvert Arms.

"Careful!" said the woman, who was muffled in a hooded wrap. "Remember, we must not be seen together—it is imperative!"

"Damn this deceit! Still, I suppose it's necessary," broke out the man, also heavily cloaked. "Well, Heathdown is waiting for me; and with him there waits fame, dazzling fortune, all my bad luck changed to good—if I say the word. I can't tell you a thing about it, much as I'd love to—"

She broke in swiftly: "That means you don't dare. It's something you're ashamed of. Oh, my dear, my dear!" She clutched at his arm, and her voice broke for an instant. "I don't understand you any more! I've come all the way from London, only to find you the best-hated man in America.... You, of all men!"

"I can stand it," he said. "You've come from London to act with the Court Masqueraders. It's only chance that we met here again."

"But I knew you were here," she said softly. "Listen, my dear: You're mysterious about this great good fortune. You're uncertain about it. You've not made up your mind. Well, I shall say just two words to you, and I shall pray that they give you light!

The best-hated man in America—your road to fame carved in frozen blood of hatred! That's not the man I love, nor shall love."

He was silent briefly. Then: "Perdita, you're all the world to me," he said, his voice hoarse and strained. "That's from my heart. Give me your two words; I swear to you on my honor that they shall guide me."

She laughed—not with mirth, but with almost hysterical emotion. She drew him close, and their lips met; at the same instant, she pressed a paper into his hand.

"Read them before you come to any decision, my dear," she said, and drew away. "But remember to obey them, unless you would lose me and yourself both! You've taken the wrong road since we last met; turn back, turn back! And now, good night."

He stayed her. "Wait! Shall I see you tomorrow?"

"No. Tomorrow night after the performance, yes; if the opening goes off well, if you escort me home after the celebration,

we'll not be missed. I'm going riding with Heathdown tomorrow afternoon…. Good night!"

She was gone, hurrying away.

He strode past the lighted windows. In their glow, he was revealed as a young man, his features agleam with indomitable strength and energy; power flashed from him like an actual physical force. He glanced at a playbill set up before the tavern doors. It announced that the new playhouse would be opened on the morrow, January 15, 1782, with "The Recruiting Officer," given by the company of Court Masqueraders, direct from London.

He hastened on. Baltimore was a small city, crowded with officers of His Majesty's forces awaiting transportation home— officers on parole. Yorktown had been surrendered long since, but evacuation was slow. The war was not yet over. New York was still held by the British, and Washington sat in Newburgh, waiting grimly helpless for the final curtain, his shrunken army half-starved and mutinous.

Under another lighted window, the young man paused briefly. He opened the folded paper in his hand and read the two words written there; his face changed, his lips set, a frown drew down his brows. Seen thus, he did not look so young—though under thirty, yes. He hurried on, and came to a house-door before which stood an orderly holding a horse. The orderly saluted.

"Sir Guy is expecting me?"

"Yes sir."

He turned in, knocked, and was admitted. A moment later he entered a room where two men, one in uniform, sat before a fire. Wine and glasses and pipes were on the table. He spoke abruptly, forestalling any greeting.

"Good evening, Sir Guy. General Tarleton sent his regrets, being unable to come at the moment; he has commissioned me to represent him fully in this business."

Sir Guy Heathdown stood up in obvious surprise, quickly masked. He was a handsome, rather heavily built man of thirty-odd, an aide on the staff of Lord Cornwallis, a perfect example of the opinionated, foppish, aristocratic officer of the old school.

"Yes, yes," he rejoined, shaking hands and winking covertly. "I understand. Colonel Smith, eh? Our visitor is here." He turned to the civilian in rough woolen garments. "Mr. Cochrane, this is Colonel Smith of General Tarleton's staff."

"Oh!" said Cochrane, a dark, glowering man. "My talk's for Tarleton. He's the one man for the job. If he doesn't want to put Washington in British hands, and end the war at one crack, I'll go elsewhere."

"Your pardon!" Smith broke in with a winning smile, and shook hands with him. "You don't understand. The General has bound himself to act upon my report, Mr. Cochrane. Matters of supreme import came up at the last moment, but I'm wholly in his confidence, I assure you, and Sir Guy can answer for my discretion."

Sir Guy did so, but it was not necessary. So charming was the smile and frank air of Smith, so strong was his personal magnetism, that Cochrane was mollified at once. The three men pulled their chairs to the table; glasses were filled, and pipes were lighted from the candles, and Sir Guy introduced the business in hand.

"Smith, only the three of us know of this affair. Cochrane is a loyalist, true blue; he's suffered much from the rebels. Clinton, in New York, recommends him unreservedly."

"Wait," barked Smith. "Does General Clinton know what's afoot? I wouldn't trust that incompetent fool a foot beyond my sight!"

"Clinton knows nothing of it," replied Cochrane, displaying some surprise at hearing such words.

Sir Guy broke in, with a laugh: "Colonel Smith has a rough tongue, Cochrane, and scant respect for his superiors; so much the better, perhaps. That's why Tarleton trusts him."

Cochrane nodded and tamped down his pipe.

"I live in Newburgh," he said, "close to the house occupied by Washington. I'm not known as a Tory; in fact, I'm supposed to be a rabid rebel! I've risked a good deal in coming here, and came only because Tarleton is the one man in your whole army who can carry out my scheme. His name has become famous since his Southern campaigns."

"Aye," assented Sir Guy. "By sheer brilliancy, he's won his way from volunteer to general-the only fellow in the army who's got anything out of this damned war."

Colonel Smith grunted. "What's he got? A name that's hated, they tell me, like poison itself! Bloody Tarleton, they call him. Tarleton the murderer! Because he suppressed force with force. Because he made mistakes, yes—gave no quarter in the heat of battle, if you like. No halfway measures, says he! And now he's a broken man."

"Come, come!" said Sir Guy uncomfortably. "He's not broken, merely because he lost his entire army at the Cowpens. Gad! How many armies have we lost in this cursed wilderness of a country? Well, Mr. Cochrane, let's have it."

"Tarleton's my man," said Cochrane dourly. "He's not afraid to do things, which is more than most of you Britishers can say. Here's the scheme. I'm selling my property; have sold it, in fact, but don't turn it over until next week. My family have gone to safety in Canada. I propose that Tarleton, and not more than one other officer, ride north and meet me in Trenton next Monday. I'll take 'em on with me to Newburgh, as teamsters in charge of my wagons. Wednesday night we'll be in Newburgh, and I have a boat ready on the river. On Thursday night or the next, as occasion offers, the three of us will seize Washington, put him in the boat, and deliver him in New York. I know precisely how it can be done, with a minimum of risk. Once we have him, we're all safe. The rebels won't risk our putting a pistol to his head and blowing out his brains."

Smith's eyes glowed with excited fervor as he listened. "Isn't he guarded?"

"Not too well," said Cochrane coolly. "There's a path from my grounds into those of his headquarters. We can reach the very house without a challenge. I'm well known there; no one will suspect anything. With such a man as Tarleton to help, I'll guarantee success."

He well might, for his rugged strength, his resolution, his bold spirit, were obvious.

"Gad!" exclaimed Smith eagerly. "What a game, what a prize!" He checked himself, and puffed rapidly at his pipe. "See here," he went on. "Before we get too impetuous, what's to be gained by this action?"

"The war!" said Cochrane, and Sir Guy nodded assent. "With Washington in our hands, with Simcoe coming to relieve the incompetent Clinton in New York, we win the war. It's not yet lost, I can tell you! Washington's army is a mere shadow, unpaid

"Perdita, you're all the world to me," he said. "Give me your two words; I swear on my honor that they shall guide me."

and starved, deserting in droves every day. He's the spirit of this rebellion. Vermont is at odds with the rest of New England, and has made a separate peace with Canadian commissioners. If you have the sense to see it, I'm offering you fame and glory and the end of the war at one blow!"

"You are, by the Lord Harry!" cried Smith. He leaped to his feet and began pacing up and down the room. "Eh, Heath-down?"

"Absolutely," said Sir Guy. "And I'm the man to go with you— with Tarleton, I mean."

Smith turned on him, gay, mocking, incisive.

"What, Sir Guy? You'd accompany that tradesman's son, that nobody from Liverpool who has fought his way to a general's commission? You'd lend your name and prestige and good right arm to such a man?"

Heathdown scowled. "Damme, Smith, Tarleton is the most brilliant fellow in the army today! True, he began as a volunteer and has ended as a brigade major; but I happen to know that he's not ended, that Cornwallis has recommended he be gazetted a brigadier when we get home."

Smith shrugged, and addressed the visitor:

"Mr. Cochrane, I must discuss certain aspects of this proposal with Sir Guy. Are you stopping the night? You shall have a personal response from Tarleton in the morning."

"I'll come for it tomorrow," said Cochrane, "but not in the morning; I don't want to be seen here. I'm stopping with a farmer a couple of miles outside town, a relative of mine. I'll come at eight tomorrow night—here."

"Very well."

COCHRANE DEPARTED. Sir Guy saw him out, came back, slammed the door and strode to the younger man.

"Damme, Tarleton, what's the reason of this nonsense? The man can be trusted."

"Undoubtedly." Tarleton, who had been frowning down at a paper, folded it again and tucked it into his pocket. "My dear Heathdown, you didn't get me into this affair because of personal affection. Suppose we abandon pretense. You don't fancy me any more than I like you. We've clashed ever since we came into contact."

"Granted." Sir Guy dropped into a chair and stared at him hard, accepting the direct challenge. "None the less, I give you credit for your abilities. This fellow Cochrane wanted you, as you heard."

"And you'd go so far as to work with me for the good of the cause, eh?"

"The cause be damned!" rapped out Sir Guy. "I'm thinking of ourselves; it means fame, glory, advancement, if we lay this rascal Washington by the ears!"

"I suppose so," said Tarleton reflectively. He cocked a leg over his chair-arm comfortably, puffing at the long churchwarden pipe. A thin smile touched his lips. "You know, when all of us clubbed together last year to get this playhouse built, and to bring out a company of players from London, we little dreamed that they'd get here to find that the rebels had won the war!"

"It's the devil's own luck," said Sir Guy. "Who would have imagined that the whole army at Yorktown would be surrendered tamely? Clinton's fault, of course. If he'd relieved us from New York, things would have been different."

"I wonder," said Tarleton…. "Well, the players are here; and I understand you're being monstrous attentive to Mrs. Robinson. A most charming woman, indeed."

"Oh, Perdita's not bad," said the other, not seeing the sudden hard glint in the eyes of Tarleton. "She was the mistress of the Prince of Wales, by all accounts; a flighty creature who apes the fine lady. Still, she serves to pass the time."

TARLETON FLUSHED slightly, but remained quite calm. "You've offered me a great thing tonight, Heathdown, a great thing!"

"Not for love of you," said the other flatly.

"Oh, that's understood! I'm a tradesman's son, not a grand gentleman. I've no influence at court. I've fought my way up and up, here in America; and reaching the top, I've been badly smashed. Now you afford me the chance to pick up the broken threads and go on my road once more."

"Trust you to do it!" said Sir Guy, not without a sneer. "You're thick-skinned. You have none of the sensibilities of good blood; the finer things are lost on you."

"And preëminent in you," said Tarleton softly, almost sarcastically. "If we bring Washington into New York as a prisoner, our names will ring throughout England. You'd not expect me to turn back on my road and refuse the chance, would you?"

"You're no such fool," Sir Guy rejoined easily. "And the scheme can't fail. I've gone into the details with this Cochrane. Stap me, but the man's a marvel! He has covered every possible objection, every point. It can't fail!"

With his lace handkerchief, he dusted tobacco from his tunic. Tarleton watched him with interest, and laid the pipe aside.

"Much as I dislike you, Heathdown," he said pleasantly, "you have a way of doing things that I envy—a facile grace, shall I say? A *finesse* were the better word. Oxford never taught me such things."

"It's a matter of blood and birth, not of teaching," said Sir Guy complacently.

"I'm not even a good dancer," went on Tarleton.

"But you're a devilish good cavalry leader."

"Perhaps. That doesn't help to success with the ladies,

"Here's the scheme," said Cochrane: "The three of us will seize Washington and deliver him in New York."

however; and I must confess to you that I've lost my heart to one of these players."

"Eh? Zounds!" Sir Guy gave him a quick glance. "Which one?"

"That's my secret. However, it's a serious matter; a matter for life."

"Hello! You can't do such a thing, of course." Sir Guy stiffened. "His Majesty's uniform, you know—all that sort of thing. Marriage? To an actress? Absurd."

Tarleton smiled a little, watching his host pour more wine.

The best-hated man in America—Bloody Tarleton! This was a fact, and it hurt him. During these years of fighting the rebels, he had made mistakes. He had driven relentlessly to whatever goal he aimed at; the tradesman's son was not only an officer of rank, but admittedly the one brilliant leader who had been evolved by these fiercely-fought campaigns.

Now, with every other British soldier south of New York, he was technically a prisoner of the rebels; actually, free on parole. Here, where least expected, a chance had been given him to strike one of his daring, lightning blows, to seize the arch-rebel himself; a typical Tarleton stroke! To carry it through, would be to wipe out the memory of his late reverse at the Cowpens, and to press forward on his road to glory.

If he had been cruel, it was not for love of cruelty; if he had been brutal, it was for efficiency alone. He, a tradesman's son from Liverpool, had gone his way with a hard hand and had won success; should he turn back now, because of two words written on a folded paper? Yet he had learned many a lesson during these years. The feel of that paper in his pocket rendered him thoughtful.

"Don't do anything foolish with one of those baggages," advised Sir Guy, over his wine. "They don't expect marriage, Tarleton, except with some valet or servant."

"You're an aristocrat, but I'm not," said Tarleton. "I'm talking of sincere love."

"But, damme, you're an officer!" broke in the other heatedly. "It would end your career instantly if you married an actress, man! You can't disgrace your uniform and the service—it won't be allowed! Do it, and you'll be finished for life."

THIS WAS true, but Tarleton broke into a laugh of real amusement.

"Our differing views of disgrace and dishonor! 'Pon my soul, Heathdown, you've given me good advice, and I appreciate it," he said. "Returning to the great question: I fear that, in this proposal of Cochrane's, you've forgotten one thing."

"Name it."

"Why, we're on parole, aren't we? Word of honor, you know."

Heathdown stared at him hard.

"Nonsense! A compulsory promise isn't binding. Our parole given to rebels, to scum of the earth, to *canaille*—"

"Who beat us and made us surrender?"

"Such a parole isn't binding, I say!" Sir Guy brought down his fist on the table. "And besides, we're justified in breaking it. What we do is done for His Majesty."

"Or for ourselves?" put in Tarleton slyly.

"Upon my soul, you amaze me!" exclaimed Sir Guy. "This is no enterprise of war, of arms; we're bound not to fight again, and we'll not fight."

"Oh, I see! You make it all very clear; merely depends on the point of view, eh?" With a nod, Tarleton rose. "If anything turned up to prevent my going—"

"Then, by gad, I'll see that the scheme goes through, myself!" exclaimed Sir Guy. "You and I and Cochrane know of it; not another soul. So much the better! Should you be kept from the work, I'll see that it's done."

"And you'll do it splendidly, better than I would myself," said Tarleton, smiling. "I fear that I've lost my grip, of late; success doesn't appear so necessary in life. It's even a matter of regret that these rebels should, perhaps justly, name me Bloody Tarleton!

Well, I'll see you tomorrow. The play's at five, the supper afterward at eight. I'll turn up here to meet Cochrane just before supper, then. But I'd like a word with you before the play, to settle these arrangements."

"Hm! I'm riding for an hour or so at two—back at four." Sir Guy winked jovially. "There's a tavern out on the Williamsburg road, where I'll have business with a lady. I'll be here at four, however. Will that serve?"

"Admirably," said Tarleton, and having learned what he most desired to know, took his leave, without a handshake. Neither he nor Heathdown would pretend any cordiality.

He walked thoughtfully back to the house where he was billeted.

There, by the fireplace, in his own room, he unfolded the paper, looked again at the two words written there, and fell to staring into the flickering fire. Heathdown was a nobleman by blood and training; he was not. Here, as Tarleton realized full well, was the parting of the ways for him.

He had always taken what he wanted, roughshod. He had money, which would cover a multitude of sins in London or in the army. He rather despised men who lacked his own driving energy; he had beaten them down without mercy asked or granted. So on the field of battle....

But the nickname of Bloody Tarleton was indeed an unpleasant appellation, and, so he felt, it was undeserved. And now—to go on? Here was the chance offered. The mere matter of parole caused him scant worry. If he decided to go on, that point could be evaded, as Heathdown would evade it. What did matter to him was the writing in his hand. He loved Perdita madly, with all his impetuous nature; the two words written there burned into him as he sat.

He was fully warned, and now faced decision. If he followed his own road to glory, in his own manner, he would attain it most surely, though he might lose her. But in these recent weeks he

*Mrs. Robinson
was the toast of the
hour; gayety was
her peculiar charm.*

had come to doubt the value of his own road. He had learned hard lessons.

Turn back? Then he must risk the career that meant so much to him. He must risk it for love of her; he must twice risk it, if he was to obey these two words. And if he drew back, it would do no good to anyone, for Heathdown would go ahead with the scheme and push it through.

He undressed and turned in, with a sigh; destiny hung in balance.

MORNING CAME cold and clear, sunlight glittering on snow; the day was like a keen sword, radiant in every scintillant atom. Tarleton shaved, dressed, and toward noon betook himself to the Calvert Arms. Thus far, he had reached no decision. He was preoccupied, gloomy, in a vile humor. His orderly followed, wary of the danger signals.

The tavern was in a buzz, being filled with the players of the London company and with officers of all ranks. Tarleton strode in, doffed his dragoon helmet, hitched up his saber, and greeted the ladies of the company. He was careful to address Mrs. Robinson with the same grave courtesy he showed to all; yet it was hard not to devour her with his gaze. Here, as in London, she was the toast of the hour, her wit and sparkling radiance lifting her above the others, as her warmly fresh beauty lifted her. Gayety was her peculiar charm. She was like a singing bird in her merry abandon, as though life touched her not at all. Yet he knew how deeply and bitterly life's burin had graven into her heart and soul.

Tarleton found a seat between Mr. Wall and his wife, two of the leading members of the company; Wall, indeed, was manager and leading man, and had been in America for many years past, war or no war. Amid the buzz of talk, Perdita leaned forward and spoke, with the merest flick of her eye at Tarleton to lend her words import:

"Mr. Wall! I pray you, bring to my memory those lines you

were quoting the other day at rehearsal, from some old play. You said Marlowe had used the last line in one of his plays, I think."

"Yes, in '*The Jew of Malta,*'" Wall rejoined. Actorlike, he cast a swift look around to make sure his audience was attentive, and launched forth into rolling declamation:

> *"This is the vault of high nobility,*
> *This is the flaming spire of noble hearts;*
> *That man should feel within himself divine*
> *Philanderings, and know the inmost urge*
> *Steadfast unto the heights. For honor springs*
> *Eternal from the soul; it hath no reason,*
> *No cause, no birth, no learned panoply,*
> *Nor can it purchas'd be for recompence.*
> *Thus spake the Roman sage in days of old:*
> *Honor is bought with blood, and not with gold."*

Applause rang high, thundering from all in the room; and amid the excited outburst, Tarleton once again caught that passing touch of Perdita's glance, as though to emphasize the words that had just been uttered, but there was no need.

"Honor is bought with blood, and not with gold." That final line leaped in his heart; that, and the two words on his pocketed paper. He came abruptly to his feet; he had suddenly found himself—all the curtain of indecision was rolled away; he knew what must be done and how he must do it.

Striding outside, he found his orderly and gave curt orders.

"I'll get a bite to eat. Have my horse here in ten minutes; and make sure both pistols are fresh loaded, with new flints. I'm going alone. You remain here. Take my helmet home and bring me the tricorne riding-hat instead and the big cloak."

When the orderly returned, Tarleton pulled on the hat, enveloped himself in a voluminous woolen cloak that completely hid his uniform from sight, and went riding away. He had even left his saber behind at the last moment. Only his spurred boots and the big pistols holstered at his saddle gave a hint of the military.

He took the Williamsburg road and cantered steadily along,

with set purpose. New snow lay thin upon the road, more thickly upon the fields and the blackened ruins of farmhouses as though to hide the brute scars of war. With spring, the farms would be peopled again, the ground would be tilled, the houses rebuilt; the war was as good as over now.

"We are going," he thought, with dim realization. "We, the enemy, will be far away; these people can take up their ruined lives again. We shall be soldiers in some farther country, destroying once more, killing those whom we are told to kill."

He shook off the queer fancies, laughed wonderingly at himself, and struck in his spurs. The horse quickened pace.

Four miles out of town, the inn showed at a crossroads, a rude sort of tavern with a forge at one side. Tarleton rode up, dismounted, and walked in. The landlord greeted him, and he handed over a coin.

"Does the post stop here?"

"Yes. About five o'clock, if it's not late."

"Give me writing-materials. I want you to send a letter for me."

He sat at a table near the wide, warm hearth where food was simmering, and wrote his letter in curt phrases. He signed no name; merely the words *"A Friend."* He folded and sealed the letter and applied wax, sealing it with the imprint of a golden guinea from his pocket. Then he addressed it and took it to the landlord, with another coin.

"Lor!" exclaimed the man, staring at the superscription. "To General Washington, at Newburgh, in New York.... Why, he was here once, mister! Comin' back from Yorktown, last fall. I'll get it off, you bet."

Tarleton mounted and rode back the way he had come, but slowly now, very slowly.

Halfway back to Baltimore, near a blackened stone chimney where a house had once been, he halted. He saw them coming, riding toward him, and awaited them. They drew rein, Perdita flinging out a gay greeting in laughing surprise, Sir Guy biting his lip with suppressed fury. Tarleton nodded, removed his hat, spoke gravely.

"Mrs. Robinson, your servant! I deeply regret that I must interrupt your afternoon's diversion; matters of the greatest urgency have arisen. It's imperative that I consult with Sir Guy immediately. May I ask you to have the kindness to turn and ride back to town? We'll follow and overtake you within a short time."

He met her steady, questioning gaze. His strong, hard features were unyielding; this had to be done, no power on earth could prevent—it showed in his face, in his eyes.

"Egad, Tarleton, this is insufferable!" broke out Heathdown, but Perdita turned to him and smiled.

"No, no; what is a woman, in the necessity of war?" she said lightly. "Venus yields to Mars with good grace…. It has been a pleasant ride. Don't linger too long!"

Then, turning her horse, she blew them both a kiss and sent the animal jogging back toward the little city.

Heathdown was white with anger; Tarleton was quite grave,

"I knew you'd miss. You must," said
Tarleton, and he aimed and squeezed.

unemotional, calm. He dismounted, took the reins of his horse, and gestured toward the blackened chimney.

"Come," he said briefly. "Out of the road. It's better so."

Sir Guy glanced at the lessening figure of Perdita, started to expostulate, then assented; for Tarleton, without another word, had started away through the snow. He sent his horse after, and broke silence.

"Stop me, but I think you must be mad! What's the meaning of this nonsense?"

"Meaning enough," said Tarleton—and plowed ahead.

With a bewildered, angry oath, Sir Guy followed. They came to the farmhouse ruins, and there Tarleton halted. Sir Guy swung out of the saddle.

"You've passed all limits, Tarleton," he said. "I don't know what to make of this interference. It's demmed impertinent."

Tarleton smiled slightly. "No, nothing personal at all; you misunderstand. It's about the Washington matter."

"Oh!" said Sir Guy. "Then this isn't the time or place—"

"But it is," broke in Tarleton, unmoved. "I've decided, Heath-

At the word "Five!" they stopped and faced about, less than thirty feet between them.

down, not to have any parcel in the affair, as not consistent with my honor. It's a question of parole, of my pledged faith."

"What?" Sir Guy stared. "You have the impudence to insinuate that I'm no fit judge of such a matter?"

Tarleton inclined his head slightly, and threw aside his cloak and hat.

"Your judgments as regards yourself are no affair of mine. I'm the sole judge of my own actions, Heathdown."

"You're a blasted fool!"

"Perhaps. I've decided to turn back on my road; honor is bought with blood, not with gold. This entire proposal appears to me utterly shameful and dishonorable."

"The art of war, as elucidated by Banastre Tarleton, lieutenant general!" exclaimed Sir Guy, in white heat of mockery. "Tarleton, the lion of the Carolinas! Bloody Tarleton, whose name will linger long in America!"

Tarleton whitened, but showed no other trace of passion.

"This discussion," he said calmly, "must not become personal, Heathdown. I'll not permit it. Too great issues are at stake."

"You're right." Sir Guy, who was quivering with fury, assented and controlled himself. "Then it's settled, for the moment. I'll look you up later, sir. I shall go ahead with this affair and see it through to the end."

"No," said Tarleton quietly. "I've sent an anonymous letter to General Washington, warning him of a plot to kidnap him. I'll tell Cochrane tonight that the scheme has been betrayed and he must give it up."

Sir Guy blinked at him, then erupted in a torrent of oaths.

"You damned poltroon! You downright traitor!" he stormed. "Upon my soul, I know now that you're a madman!"

"No," rejoined Tarleton. "Washington is an honorable man, a gentleman; a rebel, but a brave soldier. No man of honor could see such a man, even an enemy, exposed to such disgraceful plots. It is my place to prevent the attempt, since I know of it."

"Prevent it? You?" Sir Guy drew a deep breath. "By God, you will not! I'll have you court-martialed, arrested, the moment I'm back in Baltimore! And I'll see that this scheme goes through in spite of you, in spite of your warnings! I'm the man to do it, and I'll do it!"

"I can well believe as much," said Tarleton. "I'm sorry. You leave me no choice, for it's my earnest intention to stop this foul action here and now. I had honestly hoped to avoid personal recrimination, but—"

He moved, swiftly and sharply; his gloved hand struck Heathdown heavily across the face. He stepped back from the spluttering, infuriated man, and went to his horse.

"Damme, you'll answer for this, and now!" raged Sir Guy. "D'ye hear me? You kennel-bred cur, I'll have satisfaction!"

"You shall have it." Tarleton, who had taken the two pistols from the saddle holsters, approached him and extended the weapons. "Take your choice. Back to back; count ten paces, turn and fire."

Sir Guy seized one of the weapons.

"This is irregular, without seconds, but you've left me no choice," he cried.

Tarleton looked at him from a face of stone.

"None," he said gravely. "Such was my purpose."

"Then I'll have your life for it, you madman! Count five instead of ten."

"Agreed," said Tarleton, and turned his back. "You do the counting. Ready?"

"Aye." Heathdown backed against him. The click-click as the two pistols were cocked sounded clearly on the air. "One— two—"

They took-five paces through the snow. At the word *"Five!"* they stopped and faced about; less than thirty feet of whiteness lay between them. Heathdown's pistol exploded, gushed smoke and flame.

"I knew you'd miss. You must," said Tarleton, and he aimed, and squeezed. He was famed as a dead shot.

The rushing wind of afternoon blew the smoke away. Heathdown's knees buckled; he pitched forward on his crimsoned face, shot between the eyes. Tarleton walked to him, leaned over, and retrieved his pistol from the dead hand.

"I'm sorry," he said quietly. "After all, you didn't miss by much."

True; his tunic, between left arm and side, was badly ripped.

He shoved the pistols into the holsters, donned his enveloping cloak, and mounted. As he settled feet in stirrups, he looked at the scarlet-coated figure; a flurry of new snow was lifting on the wind, whirling over man and tracks.

The horse moved, plowed back to the lonely road, and headed toward Baltimore. From an inside pocket, Tarleton drew out a folded paper, opened it, and read the two words written there. He sighed.

"I've tried," he muttered. "I've done my best. It is true that honor is bought with blood and not with gold!"

He looked again at the two words in the woman's delicate, uncertain handwriting: *"Act nobly."*

He tore the paper into tiny fragments that wafted away on the wind and rode forward to Baltimore, to Perdita—and to the future, with its knighthood and honors.

YOUNG MAN WITH A BANJO

S PEAR, BULKING tremendous in his buffalo-robe coat, came into the room, his deeply graven features cheerful despite all.

"Come along!" he announced briskly. "Gad, it's cold in here! Come along and we'll take a look at things. If we can scare up some way of heating the house tonight, we'll post a sign and give 'em some sort of performance."

Booth stirred and stood up. He was a boy of nineteen, with wide brown eyes; his pinched features told of hunger, and he shivered in the overcoat he wore for warmth. He cast a glance at the banjo in its case, lying on the bed, and laughed bitterly.

"My father was right. All I'm good for is to strum the banjo between the acts."

"Buck up, my hearty!" exclaimed Spear. "They tell me the stage-coach will be in sometime this afternoon; the road's been opened. We may get mail, anything may happen! At the worst, I can get ten dollars for this buffalo coat, and that will buy us food."

"These people have no money themselves," said Booth, reaching for his hat. "There's an actual famine all through these mining-camps. What fools we were to come here! Well, on your way.... I'm with you."

They left the ramshackle structure of logs, boards and canvas, and started for the theater.

Nevada City, on its hill above the creek and cañon, was a

*"The maddest and
merriest you know,"
said Booth.*

dismal place although perched upon foundations of gold. This
winter of 1852 had been a severe one with rain and snow and
washed-out roads. The log cabins and makeshift houses, the
theater with its imposing front, had been redolent of activity
and wealth a few months before, beckoning the little company
of actors up from San Francisco. They had worked their way
from camp to camp, finally getting here—to a winter of disaster.

Their cash long gone, their credit exhausted, their performances too heavy with gloom to appeal to starving miners,
they were now unable to get away; starvation was facing them,
if they remained.

"Your father's in the East now?" asked Spear, as they
approached the theater.

Booth winced slightly, as he usually did at that name.

"Heaven only knows!" he said, his face clouding. That mobile, dark face had more than a boy's strength; it held the firmness that comes only from suffering and endurance. "He should have stayed in California. He played to packed houses in San Francisco."

"I was on the wharf the day you landed with him," said Spear. "I remember that way he had of looking at people—a deliberate, challenging survey. Arrogance? Yes, but a heroic arrogance! You were at his elbow."

"I was his guardian," said Booth. "I've been his guardian for years past. Once here, he got rid of me and went his way."

Spear made no reply; he had ventured upon too delicate ground. It was no secret that Booth, the great Junius Brutus Booth, a world-figure as an actor, had been checked in his mental vagaries only by the son whom he despised and yet endured as guardian. His was purest genius, so akin to madness that the line of demarcation was but feebly drawn. Glancing at the dark, strong young face beside him, Spear shook his head; what a hell life must have been for this boy!

"Spear! Look—what's that sign on the door?" exclaimed Booth. A dread premonition seized him. They stood before the theater, looked at the sign, looked at one another. It bore the one word "Closed."

A shaky, bitter laugh came from Booth. "Why, then, this is the end! Or is it the end, Spear? No food, no fuel, no way to earn any, no credit…. No, it's not quite the end. A few more things might happen to reach despair's crowning height!"

"They had threatened to close the house," rejoined Spear, the practical. "Well, it's done; now there's only one thing we can do! Get off in the morning, hoof it to Marysville, and disband there. Thank God it's all downhill road!"

His hearty, cheery laugh had no echo in young Booth's heart.

IT WAS found that the Marysville road was open and the stage would be through sooner or later, and with it mail. In vain Booth pleaded with the agent for passage out, even if only for

the three women of the company. No pay, no passage, said the
agent briskly; and no credit for actors either.

"Good-by to the buffalo coat!" said Spear, eternally cheerful.
"What say, Booth?"

"That settles it," the latter assented. "But first, the banjo!"

"Nobody wants a banjo; we've tried. The coat's in demand.
You run along, and I'll hang around here and drive a bargain.
If the stage turns up any letters, well and good; if not, I'll bring
home enough for a feed all around, and off we go in the morning for Marysville and Frisco!"

Edwin Booth wondered at the elasticity of the older man,
as he tramped back to the cheerless lodgings. Youth does not
suffer, either mentally or physically, as do elder years; yet he was
suffering frightfully from bleak despondency. He was, indeed,
at the brink of utter despair. All the blithe resilience had long
ago been beaten out of him.

ARRIVING AT his lodgings, he dropped into a chair and
huddled into it for warmth, with his soaked boots off and a
blanket wrapped about his feet.

He was alone with his memories; they were things of terror,
for they were bound up with his father's name and wild career.
The words of Spear had wakened them in his heart. He sat with
eyes closed, drifting back along the years. How often had he
witnessed from the wings the magnificence of that man whose
name he bore, the strange erratic genius whose art reached the
sublime! How often, away from the stage, had he participated in
what Spear so aptly termed the heroic arrogance of that unex-
ampled spirit!

He had suffered from it; for the elder Booth had condemned
his son to small parts, had ridiculed his heritage of genius.
"Strum the banjo between the acts!" had been his ironic and
contemptuous fleer. Such memories burn; and now, cast adrift,
young Booth eyed the banjo with grim intentness. It had helped
to get him here, at least, and it might help to get him back to
San Francisco.

Nothing beckoned there. His brother Junius had been trying vainly for some theatrical opening; the entire Booth family seemed doomed, he reflected bitterly. With the father's departure for the East, the stage had gone to pieces in Eldorado. Actors were driven to touring the mining-camps, to desperate straits in saloon and dance-halls, not infrequently to suicide. He looked at the banjo and closed his eyes again, with despair in his youthful heart.

What magnificence, despite everything, had lain in the erratic soul of that father! Even the aberrations of that clouded brain held a touch of the bizarre glory of the melancholy Dane, or of the splendid doomed Moor of Venice. Upon the lad's mind stole the strange scene in Sacramento, that city so close to the golden diggings and all their harsh reality—the scene involving Charles Fairfax.

Even now the memory appalled him, in its possibilities. He had seen Junius Brutus Booth do and say some remarkable things, but never anything like this. They had gone up the river to Sacramento for an engagement that was ill-timed, since the city was filled with sad wreckage from the mining-camps; the greatest tragedian in the world could not compete with the everyday tragedy all around.

The dwindling audiences put the elder Booth into one of his savage and terrible moods, when nothing was too extravagant to appeal to his bizarre fancy. The boy, living in acute fear of what might happen, was wakened from sleep one night by his father bursting into the room, holding a lantern high and booming at him sternly:

"Up, scion of the ill-fated house! Up and dress! It is the witching hour, and we are called to battle with the demons of this world.... Up, I say!"

Trembling, young Booth obeyed. His father was garbed as *Hamlet*. The disheveled hair, the wild and rolling eye, the contorted but masterful features, told their own story; help was needed bitterly, and there was no help. In vain the boy made use of desperate pleas... he was abruptly ordered into silence.

His father led the way through the dark hotel to the street. At the hitching-rack stood horses. He was put into one saddle, his father took the other, and they rode through the night. Whither, on what errand, the tragedian would not say.

And they were not alone. In the darkness were murmuring voices; flitting figures, afoot, on horse and mule back, joined in. Presently they were part of a hurrying procession. To young

Booth it was all bewildering and ominous. They were making for the edge of town; they were out of the city now, and flaring lights showed ahead, and trees, and a gathered crowd whose massed voice held a note of savage purpose.

Into the crowd they plunged. Booth's clarion accents cleared a way, and they rode on to the central scene as men gave them passage with mutters of amazement. Here, beneath the trees, the jetting flares lit up everything brilliantly; the noosed ropes hanging over the tree branches, the dozen masked figures with rifles and pistols, the two bound and helpless men who awaited their fate.

The meaning of it all rushed upon young Booth: this was a lynching-party; these masked men were Vigilantes who had taken the law into their own hands. California was filled with

"The end! No food, no way to earn any!"

tales of them. The appalling number of murders and killings
going on everywhere, before which the law was helpless, were
being checked by more direct methods. Indeed, one of the
masked men was reading aloud the charges of murder upon
which the two captives had been tried and condemned.

"It's a lie!" burst forth one of the two, a fine-looking man. "I
can prove where I was at the time, if you'll give me a chance!"

A chorus of yells shouted him down. Then, upon the yells,
grew another voice that hushed them. Booth, dismounted, was
striding forward, voice and air majestic.

"Vengeance! Vengeance!" Upon one and all, the words burst
with new meaning. "Vengeance is mine, saith the Lord! Upon
what warrant doth this court obtain? Under whose seal and
hand run its decrees?"

THE EFFECT of these words, sonorously declaimed
by this fantastic black-garbed figure of majesty, was beyond
description. Any interruption of the proceedings by a person of
their own world would have met instant disaster; but here was
someone distinctly not of their world.

"We don't want any interference here, whoever you may be,"
spoke up one of the leaders. "Justice is being done."

"Justice!" Booth rolled out this word with all his grandilo-
quence. "Justice! And you are men who speak of this divine
quality sacred to the gods! You draw it to yourselves, you make it
part and parcel of your own habiliments! Interference? Heaven
forbid! Sooner may this right hand decay and wither in the
sight of all, than interfere with justice! My friend, how are you
named?"

He turned to the prisoner who had spoken, and the latter
replied quietly:

"Fairfax. Charles Fairfax."

Booth started back a pace. "Fairfax! You, a baron of England,
a scion of that noble family.... Ah, my friends, listen to me!"
He turned suddenly to the masked men. "Grant me this boon,

I pray you; let me speak for these two human creatures here condemned!"

"All right, say your say," rejoined one of the hangmen.

EDWIN BOOTH had watched his father perform on every stage from end to end of the country; well he knew the incredible power which this man could exert over an audience, but never had he heard such uncanny and gripping eloquence as now broke forth from the elder Booth.

It was enhanced by mystery. No one knew or guessed who this strange black-clad man could be; "some preacher," was ventured and passed around. The magnetism of the man was not in his words, however, but in his character, his personality, his invisible ego bursting through the flesh to reach those who listened. In the ruddy flares, with passion and hot emotion leaping from every heart, with death trembling among the trees overhead, the force that he exerted was superhuman.

At first, few of the crowd understood his words or knew what he was talking about. Now he struck into a eulogy of the Fairfax family, the friends of Washington; this man before them was Lord Fairfax, and upon that name Booth strummed the whole gamut of the Revolution and the heritage of America. Was this English lord, who had come seeking his fortune like any ordinary clodhopper, to be hanged of a midnight because the court would not give him a chance to clear himself?

Let him be hanged, then! The watching Edwin, himself almost fallen under that spell of voice and personality, suddenly realized that his father was ranting very shrewdly; he was dragging in everything from *The Iron Chest* to Shakespearean scraps, and turning them to excellent account. Hanging was murder; good! And what was murder, but killing a body to let free a soul?

"I too have murdered." Low and intense were the words, yet they came like a very thunderclap upon the silence. Booth whipped out his dagger. He was acting, now, with all his usual passion; remorse, guilt, agony... at the portrayal of these emotions he excelled, and greatest was remorse. And yet, perhaps he was not acting, entirely.

"I too have murdered—" The words were dynamic. Young Edwin, and he alone, knew how *Macbeth* was talking upon the night, and how this tortured power borrowed from *Othello* and many another rôle. "Why, then, good morrow, friends! We shall be as brothers, as very brothers! Your souls harrowed to the quick like mine…. You have not murdered hitherto? Then you have missed the very essence, the marrow of real agony! Listen, good friends; here murder speaks to you, a true familiar of my haunted spirit."

Terror? A murderer spoke there, with subtle revelations of horror. The superbly cadenced tones, the balanced diction, had never rung so true; even to ears that missed the words, the meaning was clear. The man writhed before them in his access of remorse and guilt; then, suddenly, he began to pick out individuals around him—men whose pistols, rifles, bowie-knives made them conspicuous.

"And you—have you too shed men's blood? Have you drained life from some pallid corpse that once walked blithe and sprightly? Nay, nay, refuse not answer! Here we're friends together, murderers all! Or you, whose beard would shame a very Shylock, come, confess! Upon what night sped you the fatal ball, or used that noble blade to hack the life from some sweet human creature made by God? Why, here new victims wait! Well met! Well come, kind friends—kind murderers like myself—"

He shook them. His laughter was horrible to hear; far more horrible was his appeal to this man and that—his cunning, and his ghastly camaraderie. Madness? It was stark, staring madness, as young Edwin knew too well; and yet there was something about it so glorious and splendid that he listened with a catch in his throat. In this rough, turbulent crowd composed of all nationalities there must have been many a hand red with blood, for killing and banditry was a common occurrence at the mines.

Suddenly some Frenchman in the crowd broke the spell with

a fleering jest about the preacher. Other Frenchmen and Latins shouted him down, but Booth swung around and seized the stage again. In his magnificent French, which enabled him to offer Racine before audiences of that blood, he rolled out his theme anew; instantly he had captured them, and he held them still spellbound, although the greater part of the throng were ignorant of his words. This did not matter, however; his power over an audience was the same in any tongue.

ABRUPTLY HE was back to his original subject—the house of Fairfax. He pictured English lords giving up lands and titles to settle in America. He dragged in George Washington and the Revolution all over again. He pointed to the staring man close to being hanged—Lord Fairfax, Baron Fairfax—and demanded his freedom with a peroration upon justice which outdid his former efforts. As Edwin was well aware, he knew absolutely nothing about this man or the reason for the lynching except the name of Charles Fairfax, and upon that name he built, in a grotesque flight of fancy which reached the heights.

"By God, the preacher wins!" yelled somebody. "Turn em loose, boys!"

So, in the end, young Edwin found himself riding back into town with his father, with Fairfax mounted double behind him, the crowd streaming along through the night. Back to the dark, gloomy hotel and up to the elder Booth's room, with a magnificent disregard of the horses, and Fairfax must come along to have a drink.

"I owe you a great deal, sir," he said, rather awkwardly. "There was a miscomprehension in my case, though how you knew of it, I cannot say."

"I know of much that ordinary mortals ken not," said Booth darkly.

"And your name? I must have it," Fairfax exclaimed.

"The name, sir? The name?" Booth turned and jabbed his finger at young Edwin. "There is the name! The lad Edwin,

named for mine ancient friend Edwin Forrest. I am Junius Brutus Booth, my lord!"

"I might have known it!" Fairfax shook hands, with renewed thanks. Then he said: "But how, Mr. Booth, did you know so much about me?"

"About you?" The tragedian bent his brows upon the man he had rescued. "I don't know one damned thing about you, sir."

"But my name! You knew everything—my family—"

"Oh, that!" Booth snapped his fingers. "I built upon the name of Fairfax, that was all, and it took their fancy. Why the devil are you staring at me? Why does it so astonish you?"

"Why, sir?" And the other smiled. "Because I *am* Baron Fairfax. I came into the title in '46, but I didn't suppose that a soul knew of it, because I've kept it to myself. I intend to go into politics, here in California, and it might work me great harm if known."

"Interference? Heaven forbid!
Sooner may this right hand decay
and wither in the sight of all,
than interfere with justice!"

Silence descended upon the room. Booth stared at the man, and for once Edwin saw his father utterly disconcerted. He could have sworn that fear rose in those dark, glowing eyes. Here was no acting. Booth seemed to shrink, and then turned with a gesture toward his son, as though passing on all responsibility for something that affrighted him.

"If you have cause to remember this night," he said, "then remember me not, but bear the memory toward this slender son of mine, whose genius is pure and splendid as once was mine own."

It was almost the only compliment Edwin could remember from those lips.

H E C A M E back to himself with a start, and shivered as he drew the worn overcoat more closely about him. Memories fled; here was the harsh present. That sad and tragic father had

402 Young Man With a Banjo

left, solitary and wandering once more. This was Nevada City, gripped in cold and famine.

"Genius pure and splendid!" Those words drew a bitter laugh to his lips as he glanced about the rough room. *"Poor and shabby* would be more like it. And now what? Somehow, struggle back to San Francisco, where my, good brother is probably starving as well. The two Booths in starvation rôles! And always, in the background, that specter—"

Specter, indeed; that father of immortal genius, now become a mere wandering trouper, like a dread shadow ever against their backdrop of life. Was there indeed a curse that went with genius? And yet on so many occasions, as in that Sacramento episode with Fairfax, the erratic father's madness had held a queerly haunting touch of what could only be termed some deep unknown sanity....

The afternoon was over; the winter sun set early. Booth shivered again as he thought of what the morrow must bring. He had made his start in life, he had begun his career, in an ironic futility that would have drawn a grim laugh from that man of heroic arrogance, as Spear had so rightly termed him. Arrogance? Perhaps; yet to Edwin, there was something desperately lovable in that arrogance. Himself deeply affectionate by nature, he had suffered too long with that older man not to hold him in a wildly passionate love that excused all his faults. Those years had schooled him harshly, yet they had schooled him; he had served devotedly, loyally, bravely—and all for nothing. Or so it seemed to him, unconscious of the character these bitter years had evoked within his shell, and molded bit by bit.

A step shook the ramshackle place. He looked up; the step had halted at his door. The instant of waiting struck him with ominous presage. He called out sharply:

"Well, come in, come in!"

The door opened. Spear stepped into the room, and Booth nodded to him.

"Oh, it's you! Did the stage arrive? No letters, of course, except old duns; yes, I see you've one in your band." Booth checked himself as he met the gaze of Spear.

"A letter from my sister, in New Orleans." But Spear was no longer cheerful; his customary jaunty air was gone. He looked heavy and old and sadly grim. Booth, meeting those grave eyes, suddenly caught the unuttered message; he came to his feet, and a cry broke from him.

"You've had news of my father.... He's dead! Is that it, Spear?"

The other assented. "I'm bitterly sorry to be the one to break the news, Edwin. Yes. You've said it. There's another letter here for you, probably with the same word. He played in New Orleans to capacity houses; it was a tremendous success. He started upriver by boat, and was found dead—"

"He died alone," said Booth, as though stunned, and sank back into his chair. "Dead! Alone and among strangers—dead!"

OBLIVIOUS OF time, he sat alone with bitter memories of that man of sad and tragic genius, as the day sank into darkness, and with it all his life. Wanderings, failures, poverty—of these things were the bread of genius made, and of sorrows.

At such a moment, this final blow was crushing; it took the spirit out of him as no more material blow could have done. His grief was real and it was intense....

A knock, and Spear entered, bearing a lamp and a plate of food.

"Sit up, lad, and eat," he commanded. "For your body's sake, eat! God knows there's not much; but the others send you their sympathy and love to sweeten the fare."

Kindly words, these, and young Booth forced himself to obey.

"You know, I had always hoped there'd be a change of fortune—for him," he said. "That hope bore me up through everything. That some day his life would know smiles once again and tenderness, and an end to wanderings! To think that the end came to him alone—that's what hurts."

"Then you're far wrong," said Spear bluntly. "You're grieving for him as you see him, not for him as he was."

"What d'ye mean?"

"I mean that he had a glorious end!" said Spear. "You're full of sentiment; he laughed at sentiment! He's dead; well, you'll be dead some day; I'll be dead. Nothing extraordinary about his dying, except for the blaze of happiness it must have brought him. He died upon triumph, a ringing, superb triumph of his art! He lived for his art; the poor damned clay of Junius Brutus Booth was only a thing to be scorned. Would you have had him go down like the elder Kean or old Mathews—worn out and lost in the horrors of futility? Devil a bit of it! His end came as he'd have chosen himself, with his name thundering on the lips of audiences—why, I wish I were as sure of the same fate!"

"That's something to think about," said Edwin, and was comforted, for the words held a profound truth, as he could recognize.

None the less, he slept little that night.

THEY WERE out and off with the sun, after a scanty breakfast, due to what was left of the proceeds of the buffalo-robe coat. Off, luggage in hand, young Booth with the banjo slung over his shoulders; two Australians, an Englishwoman, the others Americans—off and out of town, down the snowy road for Marysville, tramping along with song and story to throw off the burden of disaster, courage to the fore and making plans already bubbling with optimism.

But Booth walked alone, except when Spear fell in beside him. In vain he tried to summon up high spirits; the weight was too crushing. The sense of failure bore him down, and for him the future was blank indeed.

The miles of snow and mountain road fell behind; they passed Grass Valley, Rough and Ready—occasional mining-camps that gave curious stares but afforded no haven. Thirty miles to Marysville, tramping grimly determined while the morning waxed to noon and the afternoon waned toward sunset. There were no other travelers on the roads except the stagecoaches that went whirling past with cheery greetings or bibulous jeers.

Long after dark the welcome yellow lights peered forth, and they came dragging themselves wearily into the growing town.

Spear asserted he had friends here, and departed in search of them; Booth went to the hotel and made a desperate plea for credit, hoping that his name might at least be known.

"Booth? Never heard of you, mister," said the proprietor. "I don't hold by no actors anyhow—wouldn't trust one of 'em acrost the street. What's that, a banjo? Say, are you the young feller with a banjo that come through here in the fall? Well, by gum! Tell you what I'll do: I'll give you and your folks supper and lodgings if you'll give us a tune in the bar."

Spear drew blank; his friends had gone. But here was warmth, food, a bed—they took turns at entertainment in the smoke-filled saloon, young Booth strumming lustily, a song here, a recitation there. It was the most successful performance the troupe had put on for many a long day.

WITH MORNING came farewells, and disbanding. The parting with Spear came hard; they shook hands and agreed to meet later, if luck came to either. Then Booth slung the banjo over his shoulders and struck off down the street. His way lay alone, to San Francisco, a hundred miles: a fine morning's walk, he told himself—and got out of the town and away from the others as swiftly as possible. Thank God the snow lay behind, now!

He tramped along, every mile taking him closer to the settled country and the fair valleys. Three days, he told himself, and he would be there. Then what? He would meet his brother Junius, get sufficient funds to reach the East—and then what? The damnable question was like iron in his soul.

Failure, utter failure, precisely as his father had predicted for him if he attempted the stage. Nothing awaited him at the end of this walk except the confession of failure; he was the only Booth who had gone down to disaster, complete and irretrievable; this realization haunted him every step of the way, and brought in its train a temptation that he pondered calmly along the weary miles.

Suicide—was not this the best way out, after all?

The thought was not repellent, here in this new country, as it would have been in an eastern city. Here suicide was a common occurrence. Men who had bartered everything except their souls, in the effort to find gold, too often let their souls go with the rest. Or those who had found gold and lost it again, or those weary of vain struggle, rid themselves of the body and thus ended it. Among the ranks of actors in this golden land, suicide was almost an epidemic.

To young Booth, it was thus nothing to shrink from, but a project to entertain with serious weight. He had nothing left to fight for or with. The thought grew with hunger and weariness and the passing day, and late in the afternoon, when he came stumbling into a little town where four roads met, he was nearly at the point of affirmative decision.

Not much of a town—log shacks, a saloon and tavern, a few stores, farming lands stretching down the sunset. Here, obviously, was the place to spend the night, and Booth headed for the saloon and tavern with intent to try to barter the banjo for a lodging. He was aware of a man sitting on a bench outside the tavern door, and the man spoke to him.

"Hi, there! Young feller, what'll you take for it?"

"Eh?" Booth halted and blinked at the man, a rough, hearty man whose right leg was a wooden peg and whose voice had a strange accent, neither English nor cockney but a touch of both. "For what?"

"For what you've got," replied the other, chuckling. "I could do with it."

BOOTH CAME to the bench and sank wearily upon it.

"You look sane, so I'm probably mad," he said. "What on earth are you talking about?"

"You, swinging along with a banjo over your shoulder and

youth in your eye! Give me youth, and I'll trade you all the world for it."

"Oh!" said Booth. "Is the world yours?"

"Used to be. Squire's the name; I'm a new chum here—came over from Australia last fall with five hundred quid in my pocket, a song-and-dance act that had top billing, a wife and two kids; and an engagement."

Booth gave his name; apparently Squire had never heard it.

"You're a lucky man," Booth said, "especially to have an engagement!"

"Oh, that went right after I landed-theater burned down," said Squire.

"Well, you've got plenty left, and you don't look old. Why wish for youth?" Booth asked.

SQUIRE CHUCKLED as he filled a clay pipe with rank tobacco, and got it alight.

"Young man with a banjo! My God, what I'd give to be in your shoes!" said he, and stretched out his wooden leg. "See that pin? Dancing days ended. Kids took smallpox and died. Wife ran off with a Chilean; I think she went a bit off her head when the kids passed away. Blood-poisoning from a cut took my leg. Jonah, reg'lar bloody Jonah, that's what! The money went over the tables, and here I am, wishing I had your luck."

"Wishing you had—" Booth lifted his head and looked at the man, and caught his breath. "My luck!"

"Two feet, youth, and a banjo.... Aye, mister, that's luck! And I've got a job here as groom and hostler; I can hustle around on this wooden pin, you bet! Give us a tune on the banjo, and I'll teach you a jig step that'll bring down the house! Just got time 'fore the up stage gets in from Vallejo.... What say to a drink of beer?"

"By all means," said Booth. The other hopped up and went into the saloon.

Booth uncased his banjo. Laughter seized him—laughter

that was only part mirth. Suicide? The temptation was banished for ever. He suddenly looked back at himself with a shudder of repulsion, and laughed the harder; why, here was a situation into which his grim father would have flung himself with gusto!

"And so, by heavens, shall I!" said Booth. He looked up to see Squire coming with a mug of beer in either hand; accepting the one offered, he bowed, clinked glasses, and drank with a heartfelt sigh of gratitude.

"Now for the banjo!" said he, and uncased the instrument. "So you were a dancer, eh?"

"None better from Melbourne to Ballarat!" exclaimed Squire, tossing off his drink at one long swig. "If I do say it as shouldn't, you'll never get a better teacher. What sort of a step will ye have me teach?"

"The maddest and merriest you know," said Booth, laughing, and swept from the banjo strings the lilting, catchy rhythm of "Garry Owen."

When the up stage from Vallejo turned in before the tavern stables, it was upon a singular and memorable sight. A number of bearded, red-shirted miners and farmers had poured from the tavern, and were delightedly watching two figures, amid roars of applause and wild shouts to "keep going it!"

One of the two was a young man with a banjo, who maintained a continual strumming while he capered back and forth. The other was a man with a wooden leg, obviously teaching him the steps. This pleasantly incongruous proceeding had fascinated the watchers, and nobody paid the least attention to the arrival of the stage in the sunset, until from one of the disembarking passengers broke a shout of recognition and amazement.

"Edwin! Edwin! For the love of God, man, have you gone stark mad?"

Young Booth clashed the strings, halted, and recognized his brother. He tendered Squire a bow, and extended the banjo and pick to him.

"Good friend, my evil destiny has caught up with me; the

lesson is finished. Take this instrument and keep it in memory of one whom you taught more than you know." He swung around and clasped hands warmly with his brother. "Junius! Well met indeed, brother; why, it's amazing! Whither bound?"

"To find you. To Marysville, Nevada City.... Why the devil haven't you answered my last two letters?"

"I've had no word from you for the past six weeks."

"I was afraid of that. They've gone astray.... I came myself to get hold of you. And to find you here, acting like a madman— well, I'm speechless." Junius Booth shrugged. "You've not heard the terrible news?" he added, lowering his voice.

"Plenty of it. I've heard the news, also, that our father is happy at last."

The elder brother stared at him. "Damned if I can understand you, Edwin! See here, I've brought news that's simply tremendous. But we can't discuss it here. I must get my bag from the luggage-box.... Go into the tavern, order dinner and a bed for us, and I'll be with you in no time."

"Dinner?" Edwin lifted his brows. "You're serious? You're able to pay for it?"

"For God's sake, get about it, will you?" snapped the other, impatiently, and turned to secure his bag before the stage departed.

THEY COULD not wait for dinner; over a drink, Junius poured out his news. Edwin listened, at first with incredulity, then with stupefied amazement. It came to him, literally, like a bolt from the blue.

"Maguire, the old impresario, has built a new theater, the San Francisco Hall," went on Junius. "I'm joint manager with him; actual manager, in point of fact. We've got a splendid company together—Robinson and the Chapmans, all the finest talent in California. There's plenty of backing. It's to be a roaring comedy house that's certain of success—"

"Wait!" intervened Edwin. "What you said about me—it doesn't make sense! I'm no comedian."

"No, but you can fill in occasionally. However, you're to be featured in all Father's great parts…. I've already announced you as appearing in all the famous rôles of the English drama. Your career is beginning, Edwin! I know well that our father's mantle has descended upon you; all his fire, all his genius, is yours and not mine."

Bewildered, young Booth pulled himself together.

"But I don't understand! How the devil did this happen?" he demanded. "How did you convince anyone that I was an actor?"

"I didn't." Junius dropped his voice. "One of the backers insisted upon it, I understand. I don't know the man at all; however, it's been put through and settled to the general satisfaction, so for the love of heaven accept the matter and don't object!"

"Object? Far be it from me to object," said young Booth. "Who is this mysterious angel in human form? What's the man's name?"

"Nobody's supposed to know, so keep it quiet," his brother replied. "I don't know him myself. Some politician, I understand. Charles Fairfax is the name. You know him?"

"No," said young Booth.

N O — F O R A moment recollection did not come to him. Then he sat stunned and silent; until suddenly he gripped the table and came to his feet.

"Hold on!" exclaimed Junius. "I have a toast to propose, before dinner comes."

"Just a moment, brother," replied Edwin. "I'll be back instantly. A duty that I should have attended to long ago."

He stepped outside the tavern. The stage had long since departed; the place was dark and empty, the stars were out. From somewhere came a feeble tinkle as Squire attempted the banjo.

Young Booth removed his hat and looked up at the stars.

"I've been remiss," he said softly. "For all that is and was, dear Father, accept my heartfelt thanks, my love, my humble gratitude. Good night."

He came back to the table and sat down. His brother surveyed him critically.

"Gad, man! You look positively sparkling!" He lifted his glass. "Well, here's the toast: to the beginning of a career at the San Francisco Hall, and may it make Edwin Booth the greatest actor in the world!"

ABOUT THE AUTHOR

H. BEDFORD-JONES is a Canadian by birth, but not by profession, having removed to the United States at the age of one year. For over twenty years he has been more or less profitably engaged in writing and traveling. As he has seldom resided in one place longer than a year or so and is a person of retiring habits, he is somewhat a man of mystery; more than once he has suffered from unscrupulous gentlemen who impersonated him—one of whom murdered a wife and was subsequently shot by the police, luckily after losing his alias.

The real Bedford-Jones is an elderly man, whose gray hair and precise attire give him rather the appearance of a retired foreign diplomat. His hobby is stamp collecting, and his collection of Japan is said to be one of the finest in existence. At present writing he is en route to Morocco, and when this appears in print he will probably be somewhere on the Mojave Desert in company with Erle Stanley Gardner.

Questioned as to the main facts in his life, he declared there was only one main fact, but it was not for publication; that his life had been uneventful except for numerous financial losses, and that his only adventures lay in evading adventurers. In his younger years he was something of an athlete, but the encroachments of age preclude any active pursuits except that of motoring. He is usually to be found poring over his stamps, working at his typewriter, or laboring in his California rose garden, which is one of the sights of Cathedral Cañon, near Palm Springs.

www.ingramcontent.com/pod-product-compliance
Lightning Source LLC
Chambersburg PA
CBHW060217030726
47499CB00004B/1092